MUD
LILIES

MUD LILIES

a novel by

INDRA RAMAYAN

Cormorant Books

We acknowledge financial support for our publishing activities: the Government
of Canada, through the Canada Book Fund and The Canada Council for the Arts;
the Government of Ontario, through the Ontario Arts Council, Ontario Creates,
and the Ontario Book Publishing Tax Credit. We acknowledge additional
funding provided by the Government of Ontario and the Ontario Arts Council
to address the adverse effects of the novel coronavirus pandemic.

LIBRARY AND ARCHIVES CANADA CATALOGUING IN PUBLICATION

Title: Mud lilies / Indra Ramayan.
Names: Ramayan, Indra, author.
Identifiers: Canadiana (print) 20210362375 | Canadiana (ebook) 20210362391 |
ISBN 9781770866409 (softcover) | ISBN 9781770866416 (HTML)
Classification: LCC PS8635.A46145 M83 2022 | DDC C813/.6—dc23

United States Library of Congress Control Number: 2022930281

Cover photo and design: Angel Guerra / Archetype
Interior text design: Tannice Goddard, tannicegdesigns.ca

The interior of this book is printed on 100% post-consumer waste recycled paper.
Printed and bound in Canada.

Manufactured by Houghton Boston in Saskatoon, Saskatchewan, Canada
in March 2022.

CORMORANT BOOKS INC.
260 SPADINA AVENUE, SUITE 502, TORONTO, ON M5T 2E4
www.cormorantbooks.com

To all my heroes.

CHAPTER ONE

BEFORE MY FIRST RAPE, I thought I was pretty. I used to play with makeup and pretend to be a supermodel getting ready for a runway show. I'd cover the lamp with a pink pashmina, tune the radio to the Chill Channel, and imitate the starry-eyed, fish-lipped expressions of magazine models in the mirror. After the rape, I found my reflection revolting. I hated my face, my future, and my fate. I hated myself so much, I put my life up for sale.

I sold the only thing I had for money.

And then I got so tangled in the weeds of my trauma, I couldn't touch my life anymore.

So I gave the rest of it away.

I didn't even try to salvage the shreds of my being as they fell away and ripped open dangerous portals to the darkest of people. People disguised as friends, mothers, and lovers. People who fit my narrative that the world was evil, and I'd never be safe. That *better* was for everyone else, and mediocre was the best I could ever hope for. That I should never want for anything more than to survive for one more day — and often, I'd wish not to.

That's how Blue got in. He breezed in through one of those portals when I was broken wide open and bleeding my desperation into a world that didn't care. He pulled me so close, I couldn't see his darkness. All I felt was the frantic neediness of a ruined teenager clinging to the last pieces of herself. I had to hold onto something, so I held onto him, and it's taken me five years to start letting go.

I used to dream of Blue almost every night. It made me feel like a puppet dancing in random sideshows for the devil. In every dream, I was leaning against the countertop, and he was kissing me. But in my dreams our brains weren't sick, and he wasn't dead yet. And every single time, I'd wake up to screams — his or mine, I still don't know.

The screams have begun to fade, but now I hear a faraway weeping, like a lost child crying in a ravine. My childhood ghost is restless beneath the surface of the shallow grave where I buried her. She wants out. And I want to dig her out, but I'm still too scared to see her.

I tell her that we're fine, that I've made real progress, and I have a future. I'm in my fourth year of my Bachelor of Arts degree and on my way to graduating with distinction. But I cannot silence that broken little girl. She says she's still in pain, and her cries have become constant. She's been crying for years, and she won't stop. She's demanding to be heard. I keep telling her that I'm not ready, that my wings are still broken, and that I am deeply flawed. But I know there is shelter, even beneath imperfect wings, where I have found much of my own healing. She is getting louder and more restless. She tells me that I can fly with broken wings. I just have to try harder.

This is my story.

I MET BLUE ON a smoky summer night. British Columbia's forests were on fire, and record-setting temperatures held people hostage inside air-conditioned malls and bars. The smoke had travelled over the Rockies and cloaked the city of Edmonton. The smog hung heavy; the city sweated ashes. The air was thick and disorienting and made me feel as though I'd been dropped onto the set of a Quentin Tarantino movie. My eyes burned; my throat ached. I was pissed off about having to go to an outdoor art show with Brenda, former hooker turned cleaning lady after what she'd called an "economic meltdown" had sent her to a mental institution for a few months. I guess that's where Jesus showed up, and she claimed to have joined hands with the Lord. It's also where Prozac, sobriety, and her new hippie Alcoholics Anonymous sponsor, Penelope, came along. I think Brenda used her cleaning job as an attempt to offer reparation to God for all the blow jobs she'd sold over the previous thirty years. I wondered if someday Jesus would come and rescue me too.

I should have known Brenda was no good when she'd "rescued" me four years earlier. What kind of person finds a teenage girl crouched down outside a truck stop in the wee hours of a cold spring morning and thinks, *Opportunity!* But I was a kid — a scared kid. I remember squinting up at her through raw, salty eyes, and despite her denim shorts, stiletto heels, and hot pink bikini top with devil's pitchforks on each of her sagging breasts, she sounded like an angel when she leaned over me and said, "Honey, I'm gonna take care of ya."

I got up from the curb and followed her into a cab. A few days before, I'd been a regular teenager: anxious, angry, and reclusive. I'd gone from hiding in my bedroom to riding in the back of a Yellow Cab with a stoned hooker and a pervy driver who stared in his rearview mirror as though we were the prelude to a porn flick. Brenda smiled at the driver. He smiled back and said, "Call me Mo!" She winked at him and lit up a joint. Mo winked back and took the joint out of her hand. He sucked it long and hard while waggling his eyebrows at me. I shook my head *no*. When we pulled up in front of an abandoned auto body shop, Brenda said, "Head on up them side stairs. I gotta pay the driver."

Them side stairs looked like they belonged to abandoned buildings I'd seen pictures of during my grade six field trip to the archives. I half-expected police tape on the door. Instead, a faded sign that read *OFFICE* greeted me just above eye level. I turned the loose doorknob, and the biting smell of *old* slapped my senses sharp. Old carpet, old furniture, dirty dishes, and cigarette butts. Pungent. Rank. My new life. Two armchairs from the seventies leaned against each other in front of a rickety coffee table littered with porn magazines, beer cans, fast-food bags, and overflowing ashtrays. A hot plate sat askew on top of an old beer fridge, like it had been tossed there in a hurry. I thought, *I should run! But where? Back to the truck stop?* Besides, running would take guts, and I'd left my guts on the basement floor with *him*.

I plopped onto a stinky armchair and squeezed my eyes closed. I knew I could never go home. There I was sitting in the middle of a trash pile, like a lone dog discarded at the dump, my future in the hands of the first taker. I'd run from one trash can to another. My childhood home, a 1950s red house shaped like a perfect box. Plain and practical. My dad had inherited it when my railroading granddaddy dropped dead on the basement floor with yellow eyes and a rock-hard liver. My grandma had died before I'd been born. My dad followed in his father's footsteps. First the railway, then the house. And then the bad energy and trauma that lingered inside the walls.

The house should have been a good thing for my dad. No mortgage and only steps away from the railyard. But he didn't like the proximity of the Dover Hotel, right down our back alley. The hotel had been built in 1912 and stood two storeys high. It proudly advertised weekly and monthly rates and off-track betting in giant red letters. On the east side of the hotel was the tavern entrance where the barflies smoked and where drunken fights were settled. The west side of the bar wasn't any better because it housed the Cold Beer Store, whose entrance was just as popular a hangout as the tavern doors. My dad had told me, "If I ever catch you anywhere near that hotel, it will be the first time I beat you."

My dad's words had worked. No matter how brutal the weather, I'd always detour a couple of blocks to stay off the bar's radar. But what I couldn't avoid were the bar buddies my mom brought home to "keep her company" while my dad was out of town working on the railway. And then there was Clayton, the bar buddy who never left. The one who'd moved in so quickly, he personally had to pack my dad's things to make room for his own.

My mom had felt differently about the house. She didn't have to work, and she could walk to the bar, where she'd made plenty of pub friends to keep her company. So I grew up with the sounds of sirens, train whistles, and traffic. Most nights, I'd hear drunken garbles, yelling, and whoops from the late-night bar stragglers. I'd awaken to the occasional drunk sleeping off too many pitchers on our lawn, and one time, I came home to a black Ford Tempo with a smashed-out windshield at the foot of our front steps.

BRENDA BREEZED THROUGH THE door about ten minutes later, her face flushed and her bikini top crooked. She grabbed a sheet from a closet, threw it on the floor, handed me a bunched-up sweater, and said, "This should do ya!" And then she went down a narrow hallway and slammed a door. I curled up on the armchair and gently rocked myself to sleep. It seemed I'd only slept an hour when Brenda woke me and said, "Git up, girl! We's goin' to meet Milos!"

Milos looked like a cross between a hunter and a hit man. A hundred pounds lighter, clean hair, and a quick shave, and maybe he could have been handsome. He wore a white dress shirt, unbuttoned and untucked, and leaned against a black Lincoln as though he were taking a smoke break after winning a bar fight. True Religion jeans and scuffed cowboy boots with steel tips on the toes made me wonder if he'd ever been in theatre. Like he'd played the role of a gay cowboy and made off with the wardrobe. When we walked toward him, he pushed himself upright, extended his giant hand toward me, and said, "Hello, buttercup."

I giggled, and my face went hot. His Serbian accent made my stomach jump, as though a mob boss had just asked me to dance. I was used to being around guys who wore ball caps, boring and ordinary. Guys who used words like *flange* and *spandrel*, often in between burps. Not some black-haired European who called me buttercup.

The clouds parted for a moment, and the sun shone on Milos's blue-black hair. He swept his hand toward the back door of the car, swung it open, and said, "We go buy pretty dress for pretty girl, no?" For a moment I felt special, like a prom queen getting into the back of a limo. But the fast-food bags on the floor and the stench of pine and vanilla air fresheners quickly pulled me back to ordinary.

Brenda hopped in the front seat. "We needs some coffee, Milos. I feel like I got boats 'n shit floatin' around in my head."

"Coffee for everyone!" Milos said and then jerked the car into drive.

The three of us spent the afternoon wandering around Northside Mall with extra-large coffees in our hands. Brenda led the way, stopping at a store crowded with a lot of neon clothing in the entry. Rap music blasted out of cheap speakers, and an even cheaper salesgirl sang along. The tops had built-in boobs, and the pants and skirts looked like shiny plastic. It reminded me of the crap my mom used to wear before she hooked up with my stepdad, Clayton.

"Whatta ya think of this little charmer?" Brenda said, holding up what looked like a neon-green tube.

"What is it?" I said.

"Whatta ya mean, 'what is it'? It's a dress, darlin'!"

"Oh!" I rubbed the fabric between my fingers. "It's pretty."

"And it's five bucks!"

"Get her other colour too," Milos said, reaching for his wallet. "I buy green one!"

Brenda and Milos bought me three spandex minidresses: hot pink, lime green, and electric yellow. Because we'd blown most of our budget, Brenda said I'd have to settle for second-hand shoes. They decided we'd check out Goodwill. Milos said, "We eat! Then shoes." He took us to Burger Baron and bought us poutine and cherry sundaes. We ate together at a picnic table tucked under a dead tree in the corner of the parking lot.

"Hey! Tell ya what, girl. I got a special pair of shoes I've kept hidden away in my closet for like — a hundred years. I made shit piles of cash wearin' them. They're like lucky charms," Brenda said, licking fake whipped cream off her fingers.

I held a french fry like a cigarette and flicked my hand back. "What do they look like?"

Brenda widened her eyes and gave her head a hard shake. "They're fuckin' gorgeous, girl! They're purple platforms, open on the toe, six-inch heel. Oh yeah, and they got a little strap around the top of your ankle, kind of like a dog collar."

"Wow, Brenda! They sound beautiful."

"They are, sunshine. I ain't worn them in about ten years. Kept them in my closet for someone special." She winked at me and shoved a handful of my fries in her mouth. "Ya know what, girl? I think yer pretty special, and I got a good feelin' about our partnership. I'm gonna give 'em to you."

I shook my head. "I can't take them. They sound like they have a lot of sentimental value."

"That's what I'm tryin' to say. They got a lot of value, and I wanna give 'em to you. Show a little gratitude!"

"Okay." I nodded and reached for the last french fry.

"And?" Brenda squinted and raised her hands up by her head.

"Um, thank you very much, Brenda."

"That's better, girl." She laughed and swiped the last fry from my fingers.

Milos sang along to Jack Johnson all the way home. He kept smiling at me. I smiled back. I closed my eyes when we drove past the truck stop where Brenda had found me weeping on the curb the night before. When we got home, we spent the rest of the day watching *Saturday Night Live* reruns. After we finished eating pizza and chicken wings, Brenda said, "Why don't ya model some of them sexy dresses for us? And them shoes I gave ya too?"

A few minutes later, I wobbled down the hall in stilettos with the neon-green dress shrink-wrapped to my body.

"Ya better learn to walk sexy in them shoes," Brenda said.

"I'm trying."

"Learn to strut that peachy little ass of yers."

"I need a bra and panties," I said, pulling the dress over my butt cheeks.

"Quit tuggin' on it! You ain't gettin' no bra and panties. We needs to show off them little teenie treasures of yers. How do ya think yer ever gonna earn yer keep if ya don't learn to market that ass?"

I didn't respond. My *little teenie treasures* still hurt from the night before.

"You better remember, sweetheart, yer lucky ole Brenda found you beggin' at the Flyin' J instead of one of them dirty truckers. We's gonna make you strong — be an entrepreneur and take charge of yer life. You won't ever be nobody's bitch but yer own. No more beggin' and cryin' outside truck stops. You be livin' in a high-rise with a view of the downtown! Are ya pickin' up what I'm puttin' down, girl?"

"Okay, Brenda."

"Not just okay! How 'bout a 'Thank you, Brenda'?"

"Thank you, Brenda."

"Now remember. You's gonna owe me for helping yer little runaway ass build a good life for yerself. Do ya understand me? This ain't no friendship shit. It's kinda like a joint venture."

I nodded and kept practising my walk in the six-inch stilettos.

For two days I staggered around Brenda's apartment in those stupid shoes. My hips ached, and my feet blistered. Brenda sat on the couch with Milos, barking orders at me: "Swivel on yer toe. Push yer butt out more. Arch yer back, girl!" On the third night, Brenda disappeared for a while and came back with a bottle of Captain Morgan and cans of root beer. I guzzled the first drink quickly. Milos gave me another. My body warmed up. A lot! I started dancing around like a pop star. I'd never had alcohol before, but I already knew I wanted it again. It made everything seem so easy, like I'd been beamed up into an alternate universe where everything felt like the height of a teenage crush.

Brenda and Milos laughed and cheered me on. They said: "She's a catch, what a face, dancer's body, sell like hotcakes." I felt *special*.

"We's gonna call ya Jade," Brenda said, "cuz of them crazy green eyes of yers."

I didn't bother to tell her my name was Chanie. Besides, she hadn't asked my name or my age. She hadn't asked me anything about where I came from or what I was doing at a truck stop at four o'clock in the morning. I didn't care. As long as the rum kept coming and they didn't make me go back to my mom and Clayton, they could call me anything they liked.

"You certainly got the looks, girl, but we's gonna have to teach you some skills to go along with them. Did ya ever do a blow job before?" Brenda slurred as she wrapped her arms around my neck.

I blushed and said, "Not really."

"Well, it's gonna be the core of yer business, girly-girl! I tell ya what. Me and Milos are gonna teach ya."

Milos belched and undid his belt buckle. I tucked my chin to my chest and shimmied closer to the wall. Brenda pointed at me and barked, "Hike up that dress, Jade! Get Milos ready for ya!"

I didn't want to. Rum or no rum. For some reason, I'd believed that my new job would happen in a dark room underneath a blanket. I'd be naked only in front of strangers, not my new pseudo parents. Brenda glared at me; Milos grinned. Fear and alcohol brought my hand to the bottom of my dress, and I tugged it up — just a bit. The booze made it seem like everything would be okay.

I did everything they told me. When I gagged and started crying, Milos pulled my hair harder and said, "Streets not so easy. You are lucky girl to have nice man like me train you." He yanked my head from his lap. "Go get on chair!" I scrunched my face and clenched my fists. It wasn't the first time I'd seen that depraved look in a man's eyes. I closed my eyes, rode it out, and prayed that it wouldn't always hurt so much.

"Gotta toughen you up, Jade!" Brenda laughed. "Can't be cryin' like that when yer at work."

Milos slapped my ass and said, "Don't cry. I take care of you on street! If man is bad, I beat him." He lowered his eyebrows, made an O shape with his mouth, and punched his fist hard into his palm. "I like to beat!"

I ran to the bathroom to wash my face, afraid of what I'd see if I looked in the mirror. But I had to make sure my mascara hadn't smeared. "We's use waterproof, girl. That way when ya cry, nobody can tell!" That's what Brenda had said when she'd done my makeup earlier that night. Claimed she was "showin' me the tricks of the trade." I squeezed my eyes tight and heard my dad's words: "Be brave, Chanie. Be brave." Brenda pounded on the door. I looked in the mirror. Be brave — *Jade.*

Under Brenda's tutelage, I blossomed into a high-value hooker, whatever that meant. Every john in the city smelled my youth, my desperation, and my self-destruction. I guess there's nothing more tempting than reckless fourteen-year-old sex for sale on the streets. I don't even know how much money I made. All I know is that my mouth hurt, and my insides burned like fire. I also know that I cried a lot, and then one day, I just stopped crying.

FOUR YEARS LATER, ON my eighteenth birthday, Brenda and I stood under the bright red service sign at the Don Wheaton Chevy dealership on Whyte Avenue eating red velvet cupcakes from Crave. The glow from the neon Chevy signage bounced off the showroom glass and spread over the sidewalk where I stood fixated on a black Camaro. I wondered how many tricks I'd have to turn to afford a car like that. Plus, where would I park it? Certainly not at my trash-can apartment building on 107 Avenue and 110 Street. I'd even had a john refuse to park there when I invited him in for a drink after we'd had an exceptionally long date at the Road Runner Motel on the south side. He looked right at me and said, "Holy fuck! Are you kidding? I'd never park my Vette here."

The fact that he'd been willing to park his *Vette* at the Road Runner Motel for three hours while being entertained by a hooker confirmed that my neighbourhood was tragically bad and probably a dangerous place to live. I got out of his car with a red face and resigned myself to a life sentence of staring wistfully out the tiny window of my second-floor bachelor suite. I smoked a joint and eased myself to sleep with the fantasy of someday living in a one-bedroom on the top floor with a balcony. That and a bus pass.

My stomach rumbled, and I snapped out of my Camaro fantasy. I wanted to go home. I looked over at Brenda, who was admiring the same car as I was. Her face looked soft under the night lights of the street. She'd been clean for three months, and it was starting to show. Her skin didn't look so tight anymore, her jaw had relaxed, and her eyes were almost alert. But she still looked tired. And she looked worn out from a lifetime of booze and hooking. Maybe a few more months of self-care would lessen the telltale signs of a life gone awry. Or maybe not. Maybe those signs were her cross to bear and would someday be mine too.

"Brenda, let's go," I said, wanting to go find some food.

"Relax! I got a big birthday surprise for you at my new building," Brenda said.

"Oh my God, not Milos!"

"Jesus, girl. No, it ain't fuckin' Milos."

"Oh my God! Promise me it's not Milos."

"For fuck sakes, girl. He's gone back to Serbia."

We walked toward the top of the south riverbank off Saskatchewan Drive. The city lights distracted me from the chilly April evening. I focused on the traffic rolling through the downtown hills, the headlights like mini shooting stars darting around in the dark valley beneath the dense downtown lights. Before my world had become so dull, the city lights had charmed me into believing that, tucked in between all the glass towers, something great awaited me. That had been when my innocence still had a voice. But that voice had faded away in the same way that long, dark winters can make you forget the hot summer sun.

I followed Brenda through a grey industrial door at the back of the high-rise where she lived and worked as a cleaning lady. The 1964 building was the freak of Saskatchewan Drive. It stood out amongst the wealthy towers like a misfit pigeon in a flock of tropical birds. According to Brenda, the owners were connected to the building as though it had been built from their own bones. It had a forever home on top of the riverbank thanks to those owners, who'd continually defied greedy land developers. It was not, and would never be, for sale. For many, the weathered tower, with its old windows and faded brick façade, was an eyesore. But for those who could otherwise never afford high-rise living in the heart of Old Strathcona, it was a gem.

Inside the back entry, an orange notice that warned residents to not smoke in the common areas of the building had been stuck to the drywall with electrical tape. Right next to it, a neon-yellow note, written with a dark-green Sharpie, warned of letting unwanted visitors into the building, which at the moment was me.

We came out a side door into the main area. The lobby had an entire wall made of glass brick, and the opposite wall had two grey industrial doors that were both labelled "Mechanical Room." The elevator had a full-length mirror on the back wall, and the buttons looked like white peppermints with faded black numbers. Brenda pressed 9, which we identified by the location on the number pad because the floor number had probably worn out sometime in the eighties.

I walked behind Brenda and tried to ease my anxious belly as she struggled with the lock on the door. What kind of surprise awaited me behind the sticky lock of Suite 902? How many men would be waiting inside for me? What kind of gross experience was I about to embark upon in the interest of *earnings*? The new Brenda was still a work in progress, and I more than half-expected Milos to be behind the door.

"Here ya is, honey!" Brenda said, jerking her thumb toward the inside of the suite, like a wayward hitchhiker losing patience.

"It's empty," I said, walking into the centre of the living room, my eyes scanning every corner, bracing for her surprise to jump out of the dark.

"It's yer new home," she said and snapped the light on.

"Don't play games, Brenda." I made a beeline for the balcony door to see the city view I'd often dreamt of.

"This ain't no game! I scored this little sweetheart for ya from my boss! And two months' free rent." She grabbed my hand and pressed the keys into my palm. "Didn't I tell ya that someday you'd be yer own woman, livin' large in a high-rise with a view of the downtown?"

I stepped onto the balcony and looked at the city's core crammed with glass towers and industrious people, the trees in the valley, the North Saskatchewan River, the High Level and Walterdale bridges, and the hills and winding roads. I couldn't wait to smell the summertime campfires that trailed up from the river valley parks and bask in the Telus Building's winter-season Christmas trees that illuminated the entire side of the tower in red, green, and yellow. My favourite sites of the city, including the majestic Hotel Macdonald, were right there in my living room. Maybe all the blow jobs had finally paid off.

THE NEW BRENDA, UNDER the wings of her sponsor, Penelope, had agreed to undertake healthy hobbies and activities as part of her recovery. I couldn't connect Brenda 2.0 to my brain. I couldn't exorcise the hooker in her and allow her to morph into the hippie cleaning lady she attempted to be. The version of her who called me her dear friend, her rock, her sister. She even called me Chanie instead of Jade for a while. My instincts knew better. Alcohol was only one of the things that made her dangerous. Art shows, yoga classes, and meditation would do nothing to dispel her dark nature. The only program or sponsor capable of neutralizing Brenda was death.

Penelope was a big fan of local farmers' markets and art shows. Brenda, in her attempt to be a team player, agreed to go to the Whyte Avenue Art Walk, but insisted on dragging me along like an old security blanket. The sun was strong, and the smoke was making me miserable, but I trudged along for two hours feigning interest in paintings I wouldn't use as a floor mat. I was grateful when it was over, and even more grateful to get away from Penelope's insistence that all my troubles would fade away if only I'd let her balance my chakras.

We took a shortcut through End of Steel Park on our way home. While we walked down the back alley of our building, I debated about whether I should have a few drinks and go make some cash or blow off work altogether and have a Netflix marathon instead. I didn't notice Blue until he piped up and yelled out to Brenda.

"What's in the bag, Brenda?" He squinted at us, cigarette dangling from his lips, the smoke blowing into his icy eyes. His face had a bit of scruff, like he hadn't shaved in a couple of days. He reminded me of those forty-something skinny guys who ride around strip mall parking lots on BMX bikes: wiry, weathered, and always smoking. Blue looked at me, leaned over, and picked up a beat-up yellow dishwasher. Effortlessly, cigarette intact, he tossed it into the box of his ratty Chevy.

"I got a nice paintin' for my wall," she said, the hooker in her taking over. She swayed her body from side to side, chin down, eyes up, chest out.

"Who's your buddy, Brenda?" Blue nodded to me. "Is she your lover?"

"I only date men!" I snapped.

"Oh, whatever." Blue broke into a wheezy smoker's laugh.

"I bet your computer has a lot of viruses, pig!"

"You bet it does. It's so slow I gotta turn it on on Tuesday if I wanna beat off on Thursday." He tossed his head back and broke into a coughing fit. "And if I can't get it going, I call up one of you bitches to come and take care of it for me." Blue grabbed his crotch and smacked me on the back of the shoulder.

"Don't touch me!" I slapped his hand and walked away. Brenda laughed and followed me through the back door. "Who the eff is that guy?"

"That's Blue." Brenda smiled. "He's an old buddy of mine. Just moved back from out East. He's one of the maintenance contractors for the building."

"He's a dick, and he looks like a ferret."

I went to my suite and made Kraft Dinner. I mixed Captain Morgan and root beer in a Big Gulp cup, stripped naked, and curled up under a blanket with my iPad. I passed out in the midst of a hair-pulling, vase-throwing fight between two big-breasted blondes on *Ex-Wives of Rock*.

When I woke up, I was still kind of drunk. The quiet made me nervous. I don't like silence much because I have what I'm told is a contemplative mind. Anxious. Depressive. Addicted. That's how a doctor at the Medicentre had defined me. He'd written the name of a shrink on his prescription pad. I said, "Don't waste your ink," and never went back.

I had been a little more tired than usual. The hours were hard, the men sometimes harder. Something dark had shifted in my mood, much darker than I'd ever known, like someone had stuffed my pockets with rocks and shoved me into a swamp. I couldn't even get out of bed some days. I'd pull the covers over me and shut my cell phone off. It was easier to be invisible because it took too much energy to witness my life. Everything felt like I was watching it on TV, like it wasn't really happening. My walls, clothes, books — even my text messages seemed surreal, like writing I'd read on a bathroom wall someplace a long time ago.

A few days later, completely out of food and money, I had to go to work. I hoped that some loser would pay me three bills for a "girlfriend experience." Even though I'd have to let him kiss me, it beat having to hustle up three or four blow jobs for the same amount of cash. It would be a quick ticket to some lasagna, instant coffee, and a few more days of refuge under the covers.

I got out of bed. My body ached as though I'd driven across the country without sleep. I flicked on the bathroom light but snapped it off again when I saw my dead eyes looking back at me. My stomach grumbled, but my cupboards were empty. A quick trick and I could at least grab a bagel. I jammed some earbuds in and rode the bus downtown to my usual spot, a section of the street the girls called *Headquarters*. By the time a green Ford pickup pulled up to the curb, I thought I'd faint from hunger. I looked down for a moment, took a deep breath, and forced a smile.

"Hey, big guy! What's your pleasure tonight?" I leaned in the window. He looked like the bull-riding type, mid-twenties maybe, cowboy hat shadowing his face.

"How much for all night?" he said, sounding like a drunk Dwight Yoakam.

"How's five hundred bucks?"

"Four-fifty and you got a deal. I got us a motel room right up the road." He spat a toothpick out the window.

"Cash up front!" I said and hopped in the truck.

I don't remember much after that except waking up on the floor of the motel. My head throbbed, and I felt sticky between my legs. My body told me everything I needed to know. I'd never been so tired of myself and my sick little life. I remembered my school counsellor telling me to think of things that bring me hope to offset thoughts of suicide, but there really isn't much hope. It's all a farce — regurgitated quotes from self-help books. I used to think of hot summer nights, but on that hot summer night, I lay on a motel floor freshly raped and robbed by some dirtbag farm kid.

I used the dresser to help pull myself up. When I saw myself, the blackened eye, the swollen lip, the whore in the mirror, I clenched my fists and swung as hard as I could. The glass exploded, even angrier than me, grateful to release years of degradation it had witnessed in that dump. I yanked a shard from the edge of the frame and dug it into my right wrist and then feebly attempted my left. I guess I must have screamed loud enough that someone called for help because sometime later, somewhere in my pain, rolling around on the floor bleeding dark pools of blood, a paramedic pinned me down.

I woke up at the hospital. Nobody called anybody for me because I didn't have anybody to call. They didn't do a rape kit because I was a whore. They held me for twelve hours and gave me some watered-down chicken noodle soup. I left the hospital with a bag of cookies and a whole lot of gauze on my wrists, wearing the same torn and bloody clothes I'd been admitted in.

I REMEMBER THE MOMENT I fell in love with him.

When I limped in from the hospital, Blue was sitting on the floor in the hallway digging through his toolbox. He glanced up at my bandaged wrists and calmly pointed at the drop sheet in front of him, as though he'd been expecting me. I dropped to my knees and let him pull me against him. We rested against the wall, and he held my head on his chest. "I'll keep you safe," he said. His words wove through me. My heart fluttered like a frantic bird battling a strong wind but slowed to the rhythm of his heartbeat, measured and strong, like a metronome. His inhales and exhales, like waves, easing me — falling away ...

The golden hue of the sky mesmerizes me. I want to stop and stare, but something tells me to keep moving and push forward up the mountain.

Almost there. So tired ... Running to something. Something that matters.

Finally, the summit. The grass cools my skin; the air is crisp and moist. A monochrome forest lies beneath the ridge. Trees with pewter branches reach toward a sepia sky as though praying to the heavens; their metallic leaves, lavish and playful, sway back and forth. They wave to me; they wave to one another. They celebrate beneath a mandarin moon as though world peace is real. A flock of copper owls gathers, their feathers luminescent, emerald eyes aglow, lighting the woods the way a vigil lights the hearts of the grieving. They tiptoe toward me and lift their wings; their wild souls infuse me — hypnotize me. I feel love. Peace. Beneath their feather dome, I rest.

CHAPTER TWO

"I WOULDN'T GET TOO close. She might wake up swingin'! I'd poke her with a broom or somethin'."

"Are you the boyfriend?"

"Nope! Just a friend."

"What's your name, sir?"

"Blue."

"Blue what?"

"Blue *fuckin' Velvet*, man. Why are you askin'?"

"Why are you being so hostile?"

"Cuz I fuckin' hate cops!"

Cops ...

Waking up felt like sliding down a hill, grasping at branches and ledges and whatever else could save me from tumbling to the ground of my shitty little life. I clung to the forest, the owls, and the stillness, but the real world slid back so fast that the copper owls and shiny trees became a blur. When my vision cleared, I saw two big cops towering over my bed. I scrunched up my face and closed my eyes as though I could will them away. But they remained, tall and stoic, like two giant skyscrapers blocking the sun.

"Wakey-wakey, princess," Blue said. "They've come to take you in."

"For what?" I blinked hard a couple of times.

The older cop raised his manicured black eyebrows and said, "Seems you trashed a motel room last night."

I rubbed my eyes. "Do you mean when I got raped and beaten and left on the floor?"

"On your feet, Ms. Nyrider. We have to take you in."

I looked at his name tag. "Is your name really Constable Law?"

"Yes, Ms. Nyrider. Now get up."

"Only if you tell me who your esthetician is."

"Up!" Constable Law said, raising his perfect eyebrows again.

"I need to get dressed." I got off the bed completely naked, any sense of shame long buried. The younger cop's cheeks turned pink, like he'd suddenly developed a fever. I didn't care. I felt like the world had already stripped me bare. Ever since I'd sold my first blow job, I'd lived in a constant state of disgrace. Nudity paled in comparison to the vacancy in my soul. Strippers had it easy, though they'd tell you different. Their customers had to be three feet from the stage, couldn't touch them, and if they did, the bar would turn their pack of steroid bouncers loose. The only bouncer I'd had was Milos, and only if I could find him when I needed him.

I scanned the floor for something to wear. I chose a skin-tight apricot tank top with a rum stain on the left breast, lime green booty shorts, and a pair of fuchsia pumps I'd drunkenly kicked off a couple of nights before. I slid my feet into the shoes and shimmied toward the door.

"Do you have a *lawyer*?" Constable Law chuckled.

I leaned against the door frame, squinted hard, and said, "Let me check my Rolodex."

He smirked and dangled handcuffs in my face. "Okay, smart-ass. Come with us."

I put my hands behind my back and dropped my head.

"Seems she knows the drill." The young cop laughed.

I turned and looked at him. "Hmm. I'm going to call you Constable Outlaw."

"Ha ha, smart mouth. I've seen a thousand of you, girl! You're as ordinary as a Tim Hortons coffee."

"I love Tim Hortons coffee," I said to Constable Law. He grinned and gently nudged me out the door.

The hallway welcomed me with its usual musty scent. It stuck to my palate every time. I never got used to the dank aroma and offensive carpet tile, more subfloor than carpet. The actual carpet — old, faded, and orange — looked sour to me, like some drunk guy had puked up the imminent cancer cells nesting in his intestines. I glanced out a window flecked with dirt, cracks, and dried spit. The outside world was perpetually gloomy through the filthy glass.

The crisp air refreshed me. Fat, smoky clouds hung low, threatening rain. My snoopy neighbours, habitually unemployed and waiting around for the mailman, watched me walk to the police car parked partly on the curb as if responding to a murder in progress instead of a medicated hooker sleeping in her bed. I kept my eyes down. Two baby-pink gerbera daisies wilted on the sidewalk, their petals limp and muddied by dusty shoeprints. They stretched toward their broken water vials, reaching as hard as they could toward their sustenance. Their faces looked determined, committed to their life purpose of being happy.

Constable *Outlaw* shoved me into the back seat of the cruiser. "Can we stop at the Hortons?" I asked and then laughed out loud as he slammed the door. The stench of regurgitated hot dogs had seeped into the upholstery and oozed into my sinuses. I leaned against the window as the cop car weaved down the winding hill of Queen Elizabeth Park Road toward the downtown valley. I gazed up at the business towers as we cruised past Telus Field, where my dad had taken me to watch an Edmonton Trappers baseball game when I was eight years old. I didn't call it Telus Field; I called it John Ducey Park because that's what my dad had called it. He said that a stadium that had been standing in the valley since 1933 had earned the right to keep its name from simpler times and not sell out to big corporations like the rest of the world *these days*.

That day should have been fun. A rare day out with my dad, just the two of us. But I couldn't focus on the game. I couldn't stop looking at my dad's long face shadowed beneath his CN Rail ball cap. He wasn't watching the players. He spent most of his time staring at his feet and picking at his nails. I wondered where he was and if I was welcome there. I wanted my dad to be happy, like the other dads cheering and waving foam fingers in the air. But he withered away beneath the black clouds, so I stared at the floor and followed him into the darkness. We sat like two faded cardboard cut-outs forgotten from the better days of 1933, displaced and soon to be discarded.

I'd been too young to understand why my dad got so mad when the game was rained out after the first inning. It's not like he'd been watching it. "There'll be other games," I'd said, hoping to cheer him so he'd spend the day with me. But he kept his eyes fixed on the road as he drove us home, where he'd go hide out in the garage, like he always did when he wasn't away working.

"No, Chanie. Today was their last game. The team's been sold to a rich guy, and it's being moved to Texas."

"Don't be sad, Dad. Maybe we can move to Texas too." I forced a smile and hoped that our house in Texas wouldn't have a garage.

I stared longingly out the back window of the cop car as we drove along Rossdale Road. When we reached the top of Grierson Hill, the stadium had faded from my vision just like my dad had faded from my life. I felt nostalgic for something that felt like home. But I could never go home. I'd never really had a home. I never really had a chance. I was a hostage in the back seat of a cop car and a hostage in a life I never chose.

I pushed my dad's sad face out of my head and tried to distract myself with the scenery. I focused on the old EPCOR Building. But it looked sad too, its weathered beige and boring concrete exterior a stark symbol of how fast our world deteriorates. I thought of how the Chateau Lacombe, a once glorious, sleek, and eye-catching building, paled in the shadows of towers like the all-glass thirty-six-storey Manulife Place. A world obsessed with bigger, better, newer. Everything else fading in the background, like the stadium. Like my dad. Like me, someday soon. My youthful body, forgiving of long nights and little sleep, would become old and outdated and be replaced by sleek young girls who, too, would inevitably lose their lustre and end up in the back seat of a cop car.

INSIDE THE POLICE STATION, a sturdy female cop gripped my arm and steered me to a shadowy room that resembled an abandoned library. A wobbly black metal bookshelf threatened to collapse in the back corner. Two burgundy armchairs that looked as though they'd been stolen from a trailer park lawn sat side by side. They'd been angled toward each other as though I'd be having a chat with a talk show host.

"Today's your lucky day," the female cop said. "Some of the bleeding hearts in the community have a program for kids like you."

Kids like me?

I looked at her name tag: Constable White. She looked like a former Roller Derby girl who'd retired her tattoos, helmet, and kneepads in exchange for a badge and a gun. Maybe she'd even changed her last name from Blanco to White so she wouldn't seem so badass.

She looked me up and down, leaned closer, and said, "I suggest you shut your smart mouth and listen to what the worker has to say when she comes in."

"I hope she suggests a lobotomy."

"What's that, smart mouth?"

"Sounds good, sir." I saluted Constable White and plopped down into a chair. I waited for her to get lost so I could rest my eyes. My temples pounded. The bruises on my body pulsed like twisted lullabies waltzing with my anxiety. I leaned back in the armchair, pulled my knees to my chest, and burrowed down the best I could. But every time I closed my eyes, I flashed back to the motel room. The broken glass. The blood. The ambulance. *Blue.*

I woke up to the scent of lilacs and the sound of rustling pages. A dark-haired woman in her mid-forties was sitting in the armchair next to me. I guessed she was French or some other exotic breed. She wore black-rimmed glasses and a leather jacket with a white blouse underneath. Her nails looked like little pink pearls had nested on her fingertips. She held a blue paperback in her hands: *The Bone Cage* by Angie Abdou.

I propped myself up and put my feet on the floor. "I'm sorry. I must have dozed off. Good book?"

"There's no need to apologize, Chay-nee?"

"It's actually pronounced Shaw-nee."

"I'm sorry, *Chanie*. Lovely name."

"Thanks." She wasn't the first to mispronounce my name, but at least she was polite.

"Anyway, I'm sure you're exhausted." She held the book up for me to see. "Yes! An amazing book! It's on the Canada Reads list!"

Canada Reads?

She marked her place with a receipt and set the book down. "My name is Rie. I'm a psychologist, and I'm in charge of a new program for young adults like you."

"Like me?"

"Young people who've had some run-ins with the law and don't have stable family supports in place."

I rolled my eyes and slumped back into the burgundy abyss of the armchair.

"Would you like to hear about it?"

"Do I have a choice?"

"We call the program Begin Again. It includes a series of counselling sessions, academic upgrading, and career planning."

All shit I didn't care to hear about. But I liked the way she talked to me. Articulate. Clear. Breaking everything into tiny sentences, digestible, like the puny pieces of cheese I fed the mice in the garbage room of my apartment building. Nonetheless, I wasn't interested. I was beyond saving, like the dead daisies on my sidewalk. I forced a smile and said, "No, thank you."

"It's in your best interest to consider this option. I've reviewed your file, and you are looking at jail time at this point. You've had several — well — six clashes with the law."

"So I get raped and beaten, and *I'm* the one going to jail?"

"It's not really like that. You've damaged property on more than one occasion. You don't pay your fines, and there are outstanding warrants for your arrest. Yes, you are a victim, but you are also accountable for your behaviour."

"I'm so sick of everybody and their fancy social worker words — victim, accountability, warrants. Why can't people leave me be?" For the moment, jail seemed okay. No rent, no phones, no blow jobs, no sweaty, emotional men. I could rest, maybe learn yoga, read books, and get free counselling.

Rie leaned forward and raised her eyebrows. "Will you please consider what we're offering you?"

"Nope."

"Let's see, Chanie. You can either go to jail or go into our program. Jail means no freedom, no takeout food, no cellphones, movies, friends, or dating."

I needed the world to shut up! I began to understand why people confessed to crimes they didn't commit. Anything to be left alone. The pain meds had worn off, and I craved the refuge of my dark apartment, where I wouldn't feel like a dissected frog at a science fair. Jail would mean constant surveillance. No more hiding out. No more Captain Morgan, weed, Tim Hortons, or lasagna from Rigoletto's Café.

"Okay, Rie! What do you need from me?"

A sharp knock on the door startled me. Constable Law walked in. "Are you hungry?"

"Always." I smiled.

"What would you like to eat?"

"A chicken bento with California rolls." I laughed. I hadn't even known what a bento was until the week before when one of my regulars took me for a guilt meal after he'd choked me too hard during his role-play fantasy.

He smiled and shook his head. "How about Tim Hortons?"

"Everybody loves Tim Hortons!" I smirked and slumped back into my chair.

CHAPTER THREE

EXTINGUISHED.

On a slab in a morgue.

If I'd dug a little deeper and gone a little further, I'd have left the motel in a body bag instead of on a stretcher. My attempt to make myself invisible had failed. Now I was too visible, sitting there with my wrists wrapped in bright white gauze with Rie sitting next to me, her head down as she scribbled away on a clipboard. Soon I'd have a student ID number. People would look for me. I'd be *accountable*.

"I'll be right back," Rie said, setting the clipboard on the table.

I held my wrists up in front of me. The bandages mocked me, reminding me that I'd tried to leave my life, but instead I'd just chopped up parts of my body. I'd made part of my outsides match the core of my insides — torn up, bloody, and gross. Where other girls would wear tennis bracelets, I'd wear the reminders of my wish to be gone.

I picked up a black Sharpie marker from the table and wrote NEXT TIME on my left bandage. My dad used to say, "No matter how dark it is, Chanie, always remember, the sun is making its way back to you."

Fuck the sun.

If things didn't look up by the time I graduated from Begin Again, I'd make it happen. Except the next time, I wouldn't mess it up.

Rie came back into the room and stood in front of me holding a new, pink clipboard to her chest. She took a deep breath and said, "Do we need to put you on suicide watch?"

I quickly covered my wrist with my right hand. "I don't think so."

She stared at me, chewed her lower lip for a few seconds, and took another deep breath.

"I'm fine!" I threw my hands up. "Plus, the shrinks at the hospital assessed me when I got bandaged up."

Rie nodded. "Here's my business card. It has my cell number on it. If you need me, call."

I'd never call. Not even if I was dying on a curb three feet away.

I nearly moonwalked out of the police station, a new wave of gratitude for my dingy apartment propelling my steps. I had to get away from cops, shrinks, and programs for *girls like me.* I needed time to regroup. The previous twenty-four hours had felt like I'd been driving down a foggy highway, making the miles, but disoriented and lost. It felt as though I'd been whisked off my bed and tossed into a ghetto version of *The Wizard of Oz,* flying through the air at the whim of some trickster entity. Except I didn't have Toto. But what I did have was my new pop-up boyfriend, Blue.

"Hey, Charie! Come sit down." Blue patted the tailgate of his Chevy as though he were camping in a rest area and not illegally parked in the loading zone of the cop shop. "I got you a Teen Burger, but I ate your fries. They were getting cold."

How long had he been waiting for me? It creeped me out that he'd been popping up in the strangest places, as though he'd been given an advance copy of the script to my ghetto *Wizard of Oz* freak show. It made me uneasy. Men were only nice when they wanted to do filthy things to me. I didn't like them. I couldn't trust them. They were tools, really, economic means of keeping me in rent, food, and booze.

I didn't like surprises, either. Surprises like Blue sitting perched on his tailgate, my recent rape rodeo, cops, counsellors, and restoration programs. Surprises came with price tags. New friends were never free. Like when Ariel, the lavender-haired, busty goddess who'd transferred to my school, had befriended me and my first-ever, grade-seven boyfriend, Ulysses. The three of us had become inseparable, so much so that Ulysses and Ariel claimed to have developed a sacred bond. Soon after, Ulysses took me aside to tell me that he and Ariel wanted to explore their sacred journey together. He took my hands, looked into my eyes, and said, "Chanie, it's like I'm a coyote and you're a bunny." Whatever the fuck that meant. And what did that make Ariel?

I squeezed my eyes tight and yanked my hands away from him. I wasn't going to let "the coyote" see me cry. I ran home, *like a bunny*, washed Ulysses off my hands, and burrowed under my bedcovers, where I cried myself to sleep. A few hours later, I woke up to my stepdad, Clayton, sitting on the edge of my bed with a bundle of pink roses wrapped in cellophane.

"What are those for?" I sat up and pulled the covers to my chin.

Clayton put his hand on my thigh and squeezed. "Your mom

sent me a text to tell me you were in bed bawlin'. I figured it had to be about a guy! Do you want me to go kick his ass?"

"Maybe," I said, trying to shuffle away from his hand.

Clayton squeezed harder. "You just gotta say the word, Chanie, and I'll lay the beats on him. Teach him not to mess with my girl! He's a loser. And he's got a stupid name. What is it again? Unit something? Uni—corn?"

"Ulysses!" I started laughing.

Clayton leaned closer to me. "You can't worry about guys like Uniquon. He's a dumb kid. Sees a pair of tits and goes into a coma. Some guys like skank, you know, porn star looking. Other guys, well, they like a different look, more natural, like you. Like that Holly Berry girl — you know the one — the one that Billy Bob nailed in that movie."

I assumed he meant Halle Berry. I'd never seen her "get nailed" by Billy Bob, but I just nodded.

"His new girlfriend's name is Ariel."

"What in sweet fuck kind of name is that? *Ariel!* That's what we call car antennas! Get up. I'll take you and your mom for pizza! We can even watch a movie tonight in the den."

"I'm not really hungry," I said, moving my leg away from his grip.

"I'm not askin'." He yanked the covers off me. "And wear that little yellow dress and pretty bracelet I brought back from Fort Mac for you."

Clayton took us to Coliseum Steak and Pizza. He and my mom polished off three pitchers of beer within two hours. I pretended to watch football on the screen above their heads. I pictured Ulysses and Ariel holding hands in the school hallway, floating away on their cosmic journey, while I stood alone, like an outlier, waiting to combust.

"You're not thinkin' of that little asshole, are you?" Clayton tossed a lemon wedge at me.

"Kind of," I said, tears welling up.

My mom wavered slightly, her top lip curling into a drunken snarl, the early warning of her loose mouth and hands soon to follow. She pushed against the table, her huge boobs resting on the tabletop, and said, "Did ya fuck 'im?"

"No!" I snapped.

"Come on, Tressa! Chanie's not that kind of girl," Clayton bellowed in his big beer voice.

"Yeah, Mom!"

Clayton smiled and leaned back in his chair, flexing his arms as he reached behind his head, his hairy belly peeking out from below his T-shirt. "Chanie's more the blow job type."

My mom laughed and leaned into Clayton. "Yeah, always wavin' that tiny ass of hers around in them tights she wears."

"I'm not like that!" I started crying. I had an idea of what a blow job was, but I'd never done it and had no plans of doing it! They laughed like howling dogs while I quivered like a *bunny* with a belly full of fleas.

"I'm not like that!" my mom mimicked, sending her and Clayton into stitches.

The waitress glanced over and walked up to the table. "Everything okay here?"

"She's fine," my mom snapped. "She just can't take a joke."

"Time to go, big guy," the waitress said, pulling the bill from her apron and setting it down hard on the table in front of Clayton.

"Drop me at the bar," my mom said on the way out of the restaurant. I assumed she had become quite a legend at the old dive bar.

BLUE SHOVED THE TEEN Burger into my hands. He lit a cigarette and blew a smoke ring. "So, what's the situation? Are you going to jail?"

I leaned against the tailgate. *It's got to be sex. What else could he want from me?* We had nothing in common. We'd never had a conversation other than a few words here and there, and before falling asleep on his chest in the hallway, he'd repulsed me. *But I'd slept so well in his tattooed arms.*

"It seems I can join a program for what they call girls like me," I rambled as though he and I were best buddies. "I have to come back at four o'clock this afternoon to sign the agreement, plus, I have to swear that I won't drink, do drugs, or engage in illegal activities."

Blue flicked his cigarette butt and squinted at the sun. "How are you supposed to make a living?"

"Apparently, welfare will kick in for a year or so." My face reddened. Somehow, accepting welfare seemed even worse than prostitution. "Then I guess I'll go on to the glamourous life of a secretary. Who knows?"

"Well, let's get you home and cleaned up."

We didn't talk much in the truck, mostly because I was nervous. *Was he planning to come upstairs?* I had nothing to offer him. I'd sucked back the last of my booze before my attack, and because I'd been raped and arrested, I didn't have the cash to go to the grocery store to restock my food supply. I wondered if there was a lone can of soup hidden behind the dishes somewhere. Or a bag of Mr. Noodles.

Blue parked the truck in the handicap spot outside the back door. He turned the ignition off and hopped out. "Come on, girl! What're ya waiting for?"

He followed me into my suite. My underarms were sticky,

and other than the half-assed sponge bath I'd received in Emergency, the rape was all over me. My skin cried out to be clean. "Get yourself a nice bath fizz. It'll help." That's what the ER nurse had said when she brought me ice chips. A bath fizz! Raped and nearly dead and she suggests a bath fizz. Two minutes later the doctor walked in, wagged his finger in my face, and said, "No baths for two weeks, young lady." He flashed an election candidate smile, plopped my chart into a plastic holder, and disappeared.

I'd wanted to tell the doctor that I never bathe; I only shower. That bathing in water polluted with the remnants of the men I'd scrubbed off would be like swimming in hazardous waste. But bandaged wrists and internal injuries had left me with one option: sponge baths. A two-week sentence to whore's baths. The irony.

Blue took my hand and walked me into the bathroom. "Let me help you get cleaned up." He twisted the creaky taps and stepped back while the water spat and sputtered out of the old faucet.

"I'm okay."

Blue held his wrist under the running water. "You are *not* okay."

I was not okay.

Blue walked over and stroked my arms and shoulders. My skin rose into goosebumps beneath his fingertips, like tiny soldiers standing at attention. I softened against him. His heartbeat stirred a wistful longing in me, like he'd opened a treasure chest full of mysteries. He gently stripped my clothes off and eased me into the tub, the shallow water drinking me in like a warm sunbeam. I wanted to sink deeper, immerse myself so he couldn't see the fingerprints of all the men I'd sold my body to.

I pressed my palms to my cheeks and slumped forward while he massaged me with a sudsy bath sponge.

Blue took a sharp breath. "Oh, Jesus Christ, Chanie."

I followed his eyes down my body. My long, dark hair clung to my scrawny collarbone in strands. Dark-purple bruises and red scratches splotched my breasts and ribs like an incomplete jigsaw puzzle — multicoloured, patchy, and ready for the trash. I pulled my knees to my chest but couldn't hide the ugliness of the beating I'd taken. I scrunched up my face because I didn't want to cry. I would rather have been sucked down the drain than cry over a rapist. I had to stay strong. There was no other option. Sitting in a tub being washed by a man I barely knew — I didn't want to fall apart, but I did.

"You're all right now, Chanie. He can't hurt you anymore." Blue draped a towel over my shoulders. "It'll get better. Right now, it's painful."

I wept as we watched the trail of water rinse the blood, sweat, and violence toward the drain. Blue dried me off and rubbed French lavender body lotion on my skin. I didn't fight him. I rested against him because I had no energy, but he had enough for both of us. He held me for a long time. When he let go, I couldn't take my eyes off him: his calloused hands, the tiny white scar on his upper lip, his blue diamond eyes.

We rushed to my four o'clock meeting with Rie so I could sign my shitty deal. She looked remarkably rested for a woman who probably didn't get a lot of sleep. I sat across from her with an extra-large coffee loaded with cream and sugar.

"Do you want to talk?" Rie leaned forward in her chair.

I shook my head.

"Why don't you want to talk?"

The corners of my lips drooped.

"Don't you want to get help? Have goals and dreams? Friends? A support network?"

I didn't know what I wanted other than to not cry in front of Rie. Seems I'd cried more in the previous few hours than I had in the last four years. Part of me knew I didn't want to feel bad anymore. I didn't want to be unpredictable and explosive. But anger kept me alive. Without it, I hid in my bed, got drunk, and silenced my mind with Netflix or any other distraction that helped me forget who I was.

"Tell me how you're feeling," Rie said.

How could I explain my insanity to a woman who seemed so normal? *I'm irrational, ruled by electric nerves, exhaustion, alcohol, and hangovers. All the prying and attention since my latest rape feels suffocating, but I feel desperate to be seen for some reason, and I want to cling to something, but I don't know what.*

"It always feels like something's wrong. My insides feel like there's bees and mosquitos buzzing around, picking apart my chest. It's never quiet. I get drunk because it makes the bees quiet down. I can pretend we're friends, and we all get along until I'm sober again."

"Do you believe you can get well?"

"I'm too much of a fuck-up to get well. You can't fix me."

"I'm not here to fix you, Chanie. I'm here to help you remove the obstacles to your own personal growth."

"What does that even mean?" I shot Rie a hard glare.

"I believe that humans are naturally wired to thrive, given the right conditions. I'm here as a partner on your healing journey. Together we can work to remove the things that harm you and find the things that heal you."

"Why would you want to do that? You don't even know me."

"I've learned as much from my clients as they have from me, if not more. I've seen extraordinary transformations in the most downtrodden people. I see something in you."

I shook my head and looked at the floor. "Like what, my lonely funeral?"

"For some reason, Chanie, you stay alive, even though suicide attempts seem to be commonplace for you. Why do you try to commit suicide?"

I closed my eyes.

Rie waited about a minute while I sat in silence. "Okay, why do you drink?"

"So I don't have to feel my life. I don't think as much when I'm drunk."

"Maybe not feeling your life is why you try to end it?"

I snapped my eyes open. "Why would I *want* to feel it? I'm a hooker with anxiety and, apparently, addiction issues, according to you and the city police."

"Do you remember a time when you enjoyed your life?"

I closed my eyes again and tried to think of something, but all I could remember was the last time I'd seen my grandmother alive. We'd spent the evening decorating her Christmas tree. She'd brought out a checkered box stuffed full of decorations: pink glitter butterflies, glossy snails, candy cane hearts, polar bears, a variety of long-tailed birds, owls, hummingbirds, and ribbons and bows. Like any five-year-old would have been, I was awestruck.

A bright blue peacock with long tail feathers fell off the top of the pile. I reached my hand toward it, but my mom yelled at me and slapped my hand. My grandma shushed her and told her to leave me to sleep overnight. When my mom had left, my grandma gently placed each and every ornament on my palm and told me fantastical stories of where they'd come from. We even named our favourites, like Magenta the Pink Peacock and Piper the Snail. She got me a stool and let me hang as many ornaments as I could. Her patience. Her tenderness. Soothing at the time, but a stabbing memory since.

I opened my eyes and looked at Rie. "No!" I snapped. My throat was thick, and I wanted to sob. I felt like I was five again, reaching into the dark for a grandmother who'd been ripped from my fingertips. Cancer had stolen her only two years after it had taken my grandpa. And then my mom threw out everything my grandparents had owned, including the ornaments and knitted blankets I had loved so much. Everything good came with a price. Booze was the only thing that kept my carousel of sad and scared horses from flying off their platform and shattering to pieces.

Rie leaned toward me. "You don't always have to feel like you do. We can work together to find things that bind you to your life. Suicide is a symptom of something else. Often, it doesn't mean that you want to die. It means that you don't want to keep feeling the way you do."

I exhaled a long, heavy sigh. "It's the only way to end the sadness. I think the world is mean. I see stray cats suffering in alleys, baby seats in back seats while I'm in the front seat giving blow jobs, cops beating up hookers and homeless guys. Men beating, raping, and exploiting me, and a crazy bitch of a mother who never bothered to look for me. I'm always bee-keeping my insides. I think the only way to kill the bees is to kill myself."

"We can help you. Are you willing to let us help you?"

"You don't get it! It's like having a psycho killer inside my brain. Unpredictable!"

"You have to commit to wellness. We can work together to get you well, but you have to commit to it. Your mental health is more likely to be fatal to you than any john you might meet on the street."

She had a point. I tossed my head back and rolled my eyes.

"Are you willing to commit to our program?"

"Okay!"

"Okay what, Chanie?"

"Okay, Rie. I'll commit to your program."

"That's wonderful, Chanie. I'll be with you every step of the way. We *will* get you healthy!"

What had I done?!

When I left the police station, I sat on a sunny bench outside and waited for Blue. I read the copy of my agreement that Rie had tucked into a pretty dark-blue journal with a salmon-coloured lotus flower in the centre:

I will not consume alcohol or drugs with the exception of prescribed medication.

I will take my prescriptions and attend three counselling sessions per week.

I will not engage in illegal activities.

I will show up Monday to Friday at the Hope for Tomorrow Centre.

I will complete all of my assignments.

I will complete my after-hours assigned volunteer service.

I will act with honesty, integrity, and respect.

Counselling helpline is available 24/7 (staffed by our dedicated practicum students).

Blue pulled up with Brenda in the truck. She leaped out and threw her arms around me. "Girl! Why didn't ya call me? Blue told me all about what happened to ya! Why should I hear this through the grapevine? You're still my baby girl. Brenda can take care of ya!"

I wanted to punch her in the throat. "Where's Penelope?"

"Penelope! She's off with all her yogi friends. I ain't got no time for that voodoo shit."

"Hop in," Blue yelled, double-parked. He flipped off a UPS driver who'd honked his horn.

Brenda squeezed in next to Blue and yanked the sheet of paper from my hands. "Now show me this nonsense ya had ta sign." She pulled out her pair of Dollarama glasses and mouthed her way through the words. "This is all bullshit, honey! You gotta be there tomorrow? You shoulda told them to go fuck themselves."

"And go to jail?" I snarled, wishing she'd shut up. Old hooker, drunk again! AA clearly out the window. And why her sudden interest in Blue?

"See, honey, ya just don't know how to play the system. That's why ya should have called me up, to represent yer interests!"

When we got home, Brenda insisted on making her famous grilled cheese: white bread, cheese slices, and a slathering of Cheez Whiz. She claimed it was a special night and made her other specialty — macaroni with a can of tomatoes. I wanted takeout, and I wanted her to get out so I could be alone with Blue.

"I guess I better get to bed early," I said, hoping she'd leave. "I have to be at school tomorrow morning to meet my worker for orientation."

"Wait a minute, my girl! I got you a surprise." Brenda jumped up and ran over to the door. She pulled a bottle of Captain Morgan out of her purse. "The Captain is here!" She jumped up and down.

"Jesus Christ, Brenda! I can't drink."

"You've had a rough couple of days," Blue said. "Maybe it'll help you sleep."

"Yeah, Chanie!" Brenda cheered. "Loosen up. One or two won't hurt. You'll sleep it off like water."

One or two wouldn't hurt ...

"Do we have any root beer?" I asked.

"Does your momma not know her girl?" Brenda pulled a bottle of Barq's out of her bag.

CHAPTER FOUR

ON MY FIRST DAY of school, I had dry toast, Advil, and the hair of the dog for breakfast. I felt like a zero. Nothing good could come from someone like me. Rie had said she believed in me, and, for a short blip in time, I'd believed in me too. Until the rum blew in my ear and said, *Follow me. Forget about the cowboy, the blood, and the glass.*

The first drink had warmed me like hot chocolate on a snowy day. The second drink stoked the heat; the third one fired up my soul. I almost didn't drink the fourth until Blue whispered, "Don't worry, babe. I'll get you a big coffee when I drive you to school in the morning."

My pop-up boyfriend had flopped. No coffee. No ride. Just a drink-stained bus ticket on the countertop. I brushed my teeth three times, but the taste of sugar, shame, and stupidity lingered on my palate. I picked clothes out of the laundry basket: a mango-coloured T-shirt, yoga pants so thin they might as well have been nylons, and a pair of dark-brown ankle boots. I pulled my hair back, moisturized my face, and spritzed myself with apple-scented body spray.

I got to school, which was not really a school but rather an old five-storey brick warehouse named the Hope for Tomorrow Centre, abbreviated HFTC. On one side stood McCaughey's Funeral Home & Crematorium and on the other side Joanna's Psychic Arts/Hair Salon. The black smoke billowing from the stacks of the funeral home was from dead people. That's what one of my clients had told me when I'd blown him in the parking lot. He'd said, "One day, you'll be nothing but a puff of smoke — cremains — probably sooner than later given your big mouth and chosen profession." He'd nicknamed me Cremains and had come to see me weekly until, one day, like a puff of smoke, he'd disappeared.

According to Rie, the city had created the HFTC to help people like me. Two hundred and ninety grand worth of renovations had salvaged the old teardown and transformed it into a learning centre and emergency refuge for the homeless. The faded words *City Furniture Co. 1941* still fought to be seen against the stone-washed bricks stripped almost white from a hundred years of sun. Pigeons soldiered on despite the huge plastic owls and pigeon spikes on the edges of the roof. Two gigantic, castle-like doors dwarfed the stragglers seated on the steps, huddled together, clinging to steaming white Styrofoam cups.

I heaved one of the castle doors open. Rie was standing at the top of the steps as though she'd been waiting for me. "Good morning, Chanie!" She smiled and put her hand on my shoulder. "I'm so pleased to see you here today."

I nodded and looked away.

"Follow me, and we'll get your intake papers taken care of."

We walked down a wide hallway. The smells of soup, sweat, and salt-and-vinegar chips permeated the air, as though taunting my hungover stomach to heave. Locker doors slammed, running shoes squeaked, laughter, chatter, and a million variations of text alerts and ringtones beeped and chimed. The noise droned like a distorted radio in my head, making me feel squirrelly, making me want to run back out the castle-like doors. The walls were plastered from floor to ceiling with electric murals and positive words drawn in fat neon letters: *Love, Hope, Faith, Believe, Jesus Loves You.*

The intake went relatively well considering I had to put my hand on a Bible to make my pledge. Thankfully, swearing on a Bible had no greater meaning to me than swearing on a copy of *Hustler*. I stood there, slightly drunk, repeating after Rie: *I will not drink. I will not do drugs. I will not engage in any illegal activities.* We smiled at each other and nodded as if we'd just agreed to meet at Tim Hortons for lunch.

I stayed close to Rie while we walked down the hall. All eyes were on me. Girls with overbleached translucent hair chewed their gum and glared through their dramatic fake eyelashes, puckering their frosty lips like anime dolls. They wore dangly earrings, and their wrists were heavily adorned with bracelets and bangles. I wore no makeup, and my wrists were wrapped with white bandages. The boys were awkward, gangly, and pimply, and stared at me too. I didn't know the likes of these young kids in the hall. They vaguely resembled the kids I'd left behind when I'd run away. Since that time, my immediate circle had consisted of Brenda, Milos, the men who paid me, and working girls like me.

I'd had only a couple of friends during my school years. I'd been a fairly normal kid, other than I liked to study and read. My fellow students were more into romance, sports, and normal teenage things like make-out parties and drinking. But I'd stayed away from parties and the "cool crowd" because the girls were mean and gossipy. There was a particularly nasty trio of bitches named Josie, Joanne, and Jackie. When they weren't busy obsessively rolling frosted-pink lip gloss on their bitchy mouths, they were spitting insults at any girl they perceived as a threat to their self-made Barbie kingdom. They only attacked when they were in a pack, which seemed to be always.

My indifference must have annoyed them because they started calling me a "fuckin' little whore." Then, when Marilyn Monroe–shaped Shanna came along, they added her to the "fuckin' little whore" list and pelted her with the same insults. So, Shanna and I bonded and became friends. Neither Shanna nor I felt like whores, or even knew what a whore actually was. I'd never have thought that the trio of bitches had fore-shadowed my future, as though anyone could have known the trajectory my life would soon take. But sometimes I feel like their negative energy helped spiral me into the streets.

It was bad enough dealing with the trio at school, and though I hated my home, it was still a place of refuge from the mean girls — except for the main mean girl, my mother. I came in late one afternoon and went upstairs to change my clothes. I pulled open my top drawer, and it was empty. I yanked the other drawers open, and the same thing. Not a stitch of my clothing to be seen. I ran down to the basement, where my mother was doing laundry.

"Where are all my clothes?" I snapped at my mom, who'd been folding laundry in the basement.

"Chanie, I'm going to take you shopping for something decent and not the spandex and tank tops you like to run around in. For God's sake, you look like a hooker!"

"You're the one who bought me those clothes!" I said, panic slowly starting to take over.

"Well," she said, pausing in mid-fold of Clayton's hoodie. "I hate to have to tell you this, but one of your classmates called to tell me that she and her friends are worried about you."

"Why?" Maybe someone had finally seen my pain, my languishing. Maybe I had an ally?

She took on her condescending bitch tone. "They're embarrassed for you. The girls at school think you dress like a slut and you're getting the wrong kind of attention."

I took a moment to absorb her comments. "Are you *fucking* kidding?"

"No! I'm not kidding! Not only are you failing your classes, you're acting like a floozy. Clayton's even noticed your *budding* sexual behaviour. Imagine how embarrassed I feel to have such a loser for a daughter!"

"Oh! *Clayton.* I see!" My ankles weakened. "I want my clothes back!"

"Too bad, you spoiled little bitch! You'll wear what I tell you."

"How can you do this?" I started crying.

"Poor little Chanie. So hard done by," she said, drooping her mouth and rubbing her eyes exaggeratedly. "If you don't fucking like it here, there's the door!"

That's when I'd realized that I had no home and I had no friends, so I'd stopped getting attached to people and places. Everything was temporary. That made it easier to ignore the looks and whispers of the other students. They'd be temporary too.

I turned my attention to Rie. "Why are there so many Jesus slogans everywhere?"

"The local churches provide a lot of support to the program. Some students find that a commitment to faith helps them make good decisions and stay straight. Pastor Josh will guide you. He teaches classes and counsels students. You'll love him!"

"Seems like unicorns and rainbows to me," I whispered, as though trying to announce to someone unseen that I was way too cool and worldly to believe that some being up in the sky was judging my every move. Even the amazing Jesus, who, according to Brenda, forgives all sins, would shake his head at some of the things I'd done for money.

"Let's get you to orientation for your assessment exam," Rie said.

Assessment exam! What kind of Hitler-style school would give a student an exam the first day? Ambush! I'd dropped out in grade eight and certainly hadn't taken up independent study as a hobby. My math skills were on the level of street math only. The only classic literature I'd read was George Orwell's *1984*, but it had freaked me out, so I hadn't bothered finishing it. Plenty of trashy romance and crime novels, though. Lots of Internet articles, blogs, and some poetry, like Danielle Steel's *Love: Poems*. If I failed, did that mean jail?

I followed Rie into an empty classroom. Two huge whiteboards stood at the front of the room. Orange and green numbers covered their surfaces; lines and arrows pointed up and down and circled around other numbers, with the final arrow twirling into a heart. Books of all shapes, colours, and sizes dominated most of the shelves. Old desks resembled cars jammed into a parking lot on Dollar Days. The walls, and parts of the small windows, were plastered with tacky murals and huge Jesus slogans. The room felt like the hobby room of a hoarder. Every corner from floor to ceiling had been used for storage, decoration, or desk space.

I sat on a wooden chair and tried to eavesdrop on Rie's

conversation with a boyish-looking man dressed in an emerald golf shirt and khaki pants. His teeth were way too white, like if they sold a toothpaste called Crazy White, he would be the guy on the box. His skin screamed green-juice vegan: clean, smooth, not a toxin in his body, his cells alive with purity. Infomercial healthy! I'd have to be rebirthed by Buddhist naturopaths to ever look that fresh.

"Hello, Chanie." The boyish man walked toward me and extended his hand. "I'm Pastor Josh."

Great! Pure Pastor Josh is here to save me.

He handed me a fat booklet and an orange pencil. "This is the assessment exam. It'll help us determine your education level. Then we can build you a proper learning plan."

Once the exam results were in, my "proper learning plan" would start at a grade-five level. Everyone would know I was a big zero. They'd have my criminal record and my assessment exam to prove it. I'd need ten years of tutoring to get up to a high school level and another ten years of counselling. I wondered if they'd give me bonus points for every rape I'd survived? Every assault? Every attempt I'd made on my own life? Surely those events deserved life experience points. Why couldn't they just give me crayons and finger paints so I could whip up another Jesus pic for the wall?

Rie seemed to sense my anxiety. "Can we get you some water or anything?"

"A muffin and a coffee would be great. I didn't get a chance to have breakfast." *Other than dry toast and rum.*

"Would you like to pray together before the exam?" Pastor Josh said, beaming his vegan light. Happy tonic seemed to fizz out of him, through his eyes, his smile, and his voice. Even his movements were light and floaty, like a mystical being. I figured that when nobody was looking, he broke into random dance moves and skipped instead of walked.

"I'd really rather eat," I said.

"Okay, Chanie. Get started, and I'll find you a snack." Rie patted my shoulder and left the room.

The exam pissed me off. It made me feel exceptionally stupid and hopeless. I couldn't remember much from my social studies classes, or any of my classes for that matter. I'd been a great student, up until grade seven. Straight As and special credit for writing a fantasy novella about a kid named Angus and his powerful unicorn. But then my dad died and Clayton moved in. I didn't mean to start failing. At first, I'd just stopped eating. Everyone said that was normal given "what I was going through." But then I stopped sleeping too. And started shaking a lot. And then my grades tanked, and the doctor gave me Ativan. My mom told me to get over myself. She and Clayton made it a game to mimic me in whiny baby voices, manipulate my words, and make up stories about my bad behaviour for their drinking buddies. I didn't bother to defend myself because they'd always revert to their canned response, "If you don't like it here, there's the door."

I chose "the door" at the end of grade eight, a week before summer break. The same weekend my mother had left town to *relax* on a yoga retreat. I'm not sure what my mother needed a retreat from. Maybe her big fake tits and horse-teeth smile had exhausted her. Always having to act like her life was so hard "bein' so beautiful 'n all."

The retreat had been my stepdad's idea. He'd even paid for it and offered to keep an eye on me. He said he'd make sure I didn't have any boys over, as though that were a regular thing. I'd had one boy over one time. I'd asked my friend's brother

Cory to come over so I could show him my floral solar lights. I had closed the door of my bedroom and snapped the lights off so he could see the flowers glow in the dark. Within seconds, Clayton exploded through the bedroom door screaming about us "gettin' up to no good in the dark." Cory took off for the front door and almost ran right into my mom, who, coming home from a hard day of shopping, flew into a rage and grounded me for six weeks for "bein' a floozy."

While my mother packed her translucent Lululemon yoga pants and neon sport bras, I begged her to let me stay at my friend Shanna's house.

"I'm nervous here alone with him!" I pleaded.

"You are ridiculous! And ungrateful. You can stay right here with Clayton and take this opportunity to get to know him better. He's been like a father to you, Chanie."

"My *father* didn't talk about blow jobs and Halle Berry 'gettin' nailed by Billy Bob'!"

"Chanie, that never happened. You are delusional."

"You were right there!" I snapped.

"Chanie, you just don't want to see me happy. You are such a selfish little ingrate."

"He *always* walks in when I'm changing. Or comes into the bathroom to pee when I'm in the shower!"

"You are a liar. That only happened once!"

More like once a week! I'd started showering at the school gym, if I could. I'd even asked Shanna if I could shower at her place while Clayton was laid off because he was *always* home. She never asked why. She just told me to bring my own towel and make sure I was gone before her parents got home.

The next night, I lay hypervigilant in bed. My ears rang, my eyes stung, and little blue floaters peppered the darkness. Every sound sent electric shocks through me. My intuition pecked at me like a poisoned bird as he came up the stairs. I held my breath as though total silence could keep him away. Clayton punched the light switch on my wall and slurred, "Ya little tart! Get yer ass downstairs right now!"

His beer breath infused my bedroom like evil incense, the scent of depravity. I imagined myself bolting out the front door, but I knew if I tried, he'd knock me senseless. He'd slapped me a few times for "bein' disrespectful." One time he'd cracked me so hard I fell into the door frame and bruised my face. My mom kept me home from school because, she said, "We don't need no teachers pokin' around in our family business."

I clutched my grandma's rosary and marched in quick, jerky steps toward the Man Cave in the basement. Don, Clayton's welder buddy, fat, bald, and covered in body hair, smiled widely, his brown teeth replicas of rotten corn. He lifted his beer off his big gut to salute me.

"Come and watch a movie with us," he said, waving the remote control in his non-beer hand.

I tried to say, "I don't want to watch a movie," but when I opened my mouth, my voice came out like a raspy meow.

"Sit your skinny ass down." Clayton shoved me down on the floor next to Don. His feet reeked and made me gag. I pulled my knees up to my chest and dug my nails into my legs. "Look at the TV," he said, nodding at Don to press play. "Here's how ya make your skinny ass useful."

I squinted at the screen, my neck rigid, shoulders shrugged up to my ears. A scrawny teenage girl sat naked on a couch with two old men, scruffy, like game hunters, one on each side of her. She resembled me, but maybe even younger. Her shiny brown hair, streaked copper from the sun, was braided into pigtails with big yellow bows. Her dull grey eyes, large and shaped like oversized almonds, brimmed with tears. She had small fuchsia lips, skin almost airbrushed, cheeks dark red. Her breasts were small, her hips and ribs prominent, and her chest heaved. They pulled her legs apart. She had no pubic hair, nothing to cover her, nothing to save her. She closed her eyes.

"Yum!" Don belched and shoved me onto my side, slapping my ass.

"Drag 'er up here," Clayton growled and patted the couch.

I curled into a ball as Don dragged me off the floor, but I wasn't strong enough. I couldn't scream. I couldn't move. My nightgown came up over my head, and the fabric of my panties cut my skin as Clayton tore them off. The girl on TV stood up. One man thrust behind her and bent her over the seated man, who grabbed her by the back of her hair. I looked at her face. My nostrils flared in rhythm to hers, our eyes glazed over like the freshly dead, and our faces shone with tears. In that moment, we became sisters. Allies. She was all I had to hold onto. If I could connect to her, I could survive, so I held her tight. I closed my eyes and pretended we were crouched down, hiding in a closet, hands tightly clasped, waiting for a hero. When I opened my eyes, the on-screen men were done with her. She was gagging, crying, and vomiting. Soon after, so was I.

My mom came home early when the yoga weekend turned out to be a dry retreat. "Who the fuck holds a retreat without any wine?" Classic drunk bitch. She must have found wine on the way home because she staggered in sometime during the night while I was lying on the floor of the Man Cave, too terrified to get up. Don and Clayton told her they'd come home from the pub and found me tag-teaming two teenage boys. My mother stood me up and slapped both sides of my face.

"Get the fuck out of my house, you nasty whore."

Those were the last words she said to me. She threw me out the door with nothing but a jacket and a bus pass in my pocket.

I was too scared to talk to anybody, but I couldn't be alone, so I rode the bus until Edmonton Transit shut down for the night. I walked thirty blocks to a twenty-four-hour truck stop where I curled up outside the restaurant doors, exhausted and hysterical. That's where Brenda found me.

After I finished my exam, Pastor Josh said, "Things may get hard, but just know that's normal. When you get closer to your goals, the enemy gets stronger." I shook my head and went to the cafeteria for my free lunch — the best part of the day. After lunch, I attended a group lecture with twelve other new Begin Again students. Rie told us to think about how we would like to introduce ourselves and what our personal goals for the program were. I pictured myself standing up and saying, *My goals are to not get caught drinking and working as a prostitute while I'm in this program.*

Later on, Pastor Josh came to give us a sermon of sorts and told us we could be anything we wanted to be. Something about how our dreams may not look like they can come to pass in the natural world, but we serve a supernatural God. More fat letters for the walls, if you could find a space that wasn't already plastered with some stupid saying. I could never be a virgin again, supernatural God or not. I would never have parents who loved me, a safe home, a mind clear of the violence and immorality I'd seen. God was not the answer. You can praise Jesus all day long, but street whores are perpetually haunted.

At the end of the day, grateful to be free again, I burst through the gigantic wooden doors onto the pigeon-shit steps with a new energy. It almost felt like Pastor Josh had rubbed off on me. It was 3:50 p.m. Blue's shift ended at 4:30. The thought of riding the bus with the musty people made me queasy. Their crinkly chip bags, noisy zippers, and shoddy headphones made me want to blow out of my skin. But I'd endure them if it meant seeing Blue.

Like kismet, Blue walked out the front door of my building just as I walked up the driveway. How convenient. Not the least bit staged. A reward after my shitty day. A little smirk tickled his mouth, and his eyes were alert and playful like he'd slept a solid eight hours and hadn't stayed up half the night drinking with two burnt-out hookers.

"How's our future lawyer?" Blue laughed.

I shrugged my shoulders. "Where was that big coffee you promised me?" I giggled and gave him a playful shove.

"I get paid next week. Until then, you'll have to suffer." He slow-motion-punched my shoulder.

"Well, I gotta run," I said, as though I were busy.

"I'll stop by later."

I smiled.

CHAPTER FIVE

SINCE I'D BECOME A hooker, my reflection disturbed me. I applied makeup mechanically and let my dark hair droop over my shoulders. No posing, no play. Just work. My teenage fascination with clothes, makeup, and models had long disappeared with my cotton-candy dreams of a first kiss, graduation, and wedding gowns. But something about Blue had resurrected a playful curiosity. And for the first time in years, I turned on the Chill Channel and took my time getting ready.

When I was done with my makeup, I stepped onto the balcony to get some air. I looked across the valley and noticed that the Hotel Macdonald had lit up its south walls with magenta spotlights. I'd always been fascinated by the Mac, a seven-storey castle built on top of the riverbank in 1915. One of my regular clients told me that it had been shut down in 1983 due to "a state of disrepair," and the only reason it wasn't demolished was because the City of Edmonton had declared it a Municipal Historic Resource in 1985. Three years later, Canadian Pacific Hotels bought it and spent millions of dollars restoring it to its original beauty.

Begin Again was like my Historical Resources Act, like the

City's way of saving "girls like me" from our own personal demolition of tricks and addiction. The school counsellors were tasked with buffing the shards of Jade into the smooth edges of Chanie. My history as Jade would not clean up like a majestic castle. It would never shine like the French-Renaissance beauty with its turreted towers, bold archways, and majestic entryway pilasters with concrete gargoyles perched on each corner. There were no craftsmen who could polish me back to a tabula rasa. There were no protective gargoyles guarding the entryways to my life. But at least, now, there was Blue.

I brewed coffee and fidgeted on the edge of the bed. I tried Netflix. A bunch of football players on *Friday Night Lights* were pulverizing a truck with baseball bats. I didn't care. My ears were wired to the sound of the elevator doors opening and closing in the hallway. Every creak, squeak, and bang rippled through me.

The apartment felt cold, like something was missing. It hadn't felt that way before Blue. Before Blue, I didn't wait for boys to show up at my door — I hid behind it. My life had switched from street whore to schoolgirl as though I'd been handed a new script. Raped on Saturday night, arrested on Sunday, enrolled in school by Monday. Blue playing the role of the knight in shining armour. And the new me, like a dog, waiting by the door.

Blue showed up around nine o'clock. It wasn't hard to act surprised because I'd resigned myself to the idea of him being a no-show. I opened the door to find what looked like a weathered James Dean leaning on a rail waiting for a bus. The scent of patchouli fought to overpower the smells of cigarette smoke and leather. He handed me a brown paper bag with a big smiley face drawn on it in black marker and said, "Brought you some

Captain Morgan." Then he walked in, kicked his shoes off, and reclined on the bed.

I took the bag into the kitchen and looked for clean glasses. "Thanks, Blue. Maybe I should be buying *you* drinks for all the favours you've done."

"Don't worry about it, girl. One day, I'll need something from you."

I turned off the coffee pot. There wasn't enough ice in the freezer for two drinks, so I mixed a big one for us to share. Pastor Josh would say the inconvenience was God trying to tell me not to drink. P.J. had his ideas, and I had mine.

I carried the drink over to the bed. "I don't know anything about you."

"Not much to know."

"Are you from here?"

"I'm from out East. Came here because my mom got sick. Says she has fibromyalgia."

"I see," I said with a slow nod, like I knew all about it. I made a mental note to google it — if I could spell it.

"She's slowed down quite a bit. Old party girl, that one! Mind you, she still drinks a little, but thank God she hung up the miniskirts and thigh-high boots. She stays home and sits on the porch my asshole dad didn't finish building in that flea-bitten trailer park she calls home." Blue rolled his eyes and chewed one side of his bottom lip.

"Does your dad live there too?"

"Nope! Dead at forty-two. Lung cancer."

"That's terrible." My eyes trailed to his top pocket, where a pack of du Maurier cigarettes peeked out.

"Does your mom smoke too?"

"Yeah! Why?"

"No reason." I figured if I had to explain the logic, it had already escaped him and his mom. "Do you want to listen to music?"

"Sure. I'll plug in my iPhone, and we can listen to my playlists."

I took a quick trip to the bathroom. By the time I'd returned, Blue had dimmed the lights and refilled our drink. April Wine filled the air with playful lyrics and promises of love. I'd heard "Tonite Is a Wonderful Time to Fall in Love" in a trick's car about two weeks before. He'd insisted on singing along while I blew him, which made me break into fits of laughter. He told me if I couldn't take him seriously, he'd kick me out of the car. I said, "I take you very seriously, American Idol." And then I walked home.

We sat in silence for a while. I didn't know if that was normal because I'd never been on a date, so I tried to act natural, like my skin wasn't tingling and my cheeks weren't burning up. I matched my breathing to his and challenged myself to sit still. When he leaned close and whispered, "I've been dying to kiss you since the first time I saw you," a cyclone swirled in the bottom of my belly as though he'd turned back time and made me thirteen again. Clumsy. Awkward. Innocent.

That was the night I lost my *true* virginity. Blue made me feel connected, like I was no longer alone in the world. We blended like a striped lollipop, each layer something better than the last. Sweet and sour, creamy and warm, like raspberries and hot fudge on vanilla soft serve. I relaxed into the sheets, my muscles melting like whipped cream. I breathed deep, full breaths, each inhalation taking me to the top of a mountain, each exhalation to the bottom of the sea, before finally drifting away into a snowy dream.

Majestic pines a thousand feet tall circled a pond set aglow by the moon. Snowflakes waltzed languidly down from the navy-blue sky, dusting the trees and the ground with a shimmer. Blue and I skated on the icy pond, our faces pink from the winter air, smiles white like falling snow. We raised our palms to the sky and lifted our faces to the moon, our chests open and expanding as we glided backwards across the multicoloured ice illuminated by Christmas lights. We waved at happy bystanders, smiling and laughing, but a big bang startled me. I shook it off, returning to the winter night, skating and waving, but the banging got louder, more frantic, and my dream pulled away.

"Chanie, open the fuckin' door! I know you're in there, probably feelin' sorry for yerself. Get yer tight ass out of bed and open the door," Brenda hollered.

Blue jumped up and yanked the door open.

"Jesus H, Chanie!" Brenda rushed in and leaned over me, her spit flecking my cheek. "Tanji's been callin' all night. Where the fuck is yer phone, ya little idiot? He called me sayin' he can't get through to ya!"

I pointed to my phone on the milk crate next to my bed. I'd turned the ringer off when Blue had arrived to keep Brenda from trying to join the party. She swiped at my phone and knocked it to the floor.

"Pick it up!" she barked.

"You dropped it!" I snapped. Blue picked it up and handed it to Brenda.

She squinted and held the phone up to her face. "Ya got thirteen messages, girl! Did ya think for a minute that I might need ya?"

"Jesus Christ, Brenda! I don't work for you anymore. What business is it of yours what I do?"

"You little bitch!" she shrieked. "You'll be done workin' for me when I say yer done. Tanji wants to see ya, so clean Blue up from between yer legs and get goin'!"

I'd served Mr. Tanji and his buddies for four years. His real name was Hazrat Ali Abdullah. I'd met him when I was fourteen, shivering outside in the deep freeze of winter, when he pulled up in a shiny black car he called his 435. He had greyish-green eyes and wore a gold turban that made him look like a king. His black moustache was so precisely striped with silver streaks, it looked as though it had been hand-painted. He had two Starbucks cups in his cup holders, as if we were old carpooling buddies and he'd picked up a coffee for me on his way to work. He said, "Hop into my car, you poor thing. I won't hurt you. I just want to take a look at you." I jumped in and wrapped my frozen hands around the hot cup. "It's a chai latte. Spicy like me!" he said, winking as he hit the accelerator.

I wrapped the sheet around me and stood up, eager to get Brenda out of my apartment. I wanted her to stop humiliating me in front of Blue.

"I need you to leave, Brenda. You're not my pimp!"

"Ya need to go serve yer client. And things gonna be changin' around here, Jade!"

Jade! Like she would always own me.

"You better go to work," Blue said.

Brenda smirked and crossed her arms. "You heard him, Jade! Get goin'!"

I looked at Blue, but he just nodded at me like an unfamiliar neighbour greeting me in the hall. I reasoned that he wanted me to go to work because he didn't want me to get in trouble. *The only reason.* If Brenda hadn't shown up, we'd still be in bed figure skating under the winter sky.

"I better not hear from Tanji again tonight, Jade!" Brenda yelled and clapped her hands.

An hour later, I jumped into Mr. Tanji's 435. He handed me a chai latte, and we drove in silence. I was grateful to be with him and not some other client. He paid well and didn't make me kiss him or do nasty things. Most often, he liked for me to strip naked and lie on the bed tied up for him and his friends to "experiment with." He had his own collection of toys to use on me, but he respected my limits. Tanji liked the show. He wasn't there for sex.

When we got to the motel, Mr. Tanji handed me the room key. "Here you go, Jade. I'm going to pick up the boys."

The motel room felt like the last day of fall: lonely, chilly, and sad. The beds were lumpy and dishevelled, as though someone had hurriedly pulled the covers over the dirty sheets. I turned on the TV to break the silence. Britney Spears gyrated on the hood of a red sports car, her sad face singing about some guy who'd left her. I'd left my energy at home with Blue but brought Jade, the shell of Chanie, to get the job done. I hated Jade, but I needed her. And when Mr. Tanji walked in with two young East Indian men, one in a purple turban, the other in yellow, Jade tousled her hair and smiled.

"Meet Amal and Amal," Mr. Tanji said.

"Hello, boys," I said as I stepped out of my dress and positioned myself on the bed.

The men were relatively gentle, except one of the Amals insisted on having sex with me again after the others were done. I told him not to kiss me, but he kept trying, which seemed to amuse Mr. Tanji and the other Amal.

"Come on, Mr. Tanji!" I pleaded. "You know the rules."

"It won't hurt you, Jade. I'll throw in another hundred."

"It's not about the money," I whimpered.

"Oh yes, Jade. Of course it is. What else could it possibly be about?"

After we finished, Mr. Tanji offered to drive me home. "Come on, sweet girl. I'll buy you another chai latte."

I shook my head and looked away. "I need some air."

He nodded and said he'd see me soon. The 435's engine roared, and he left me alone in the alley behind the motel.

A cool breeze stroked my face, reminding me of Blue's kisses. How would I act the next time I saw him? I'd never really had a boyfriend before, only tricks who paid for my time. I didn't think any man could want me because Brenda always said, "You're used goods, Chanie. Nobody wants a used-up girl."

A light sweat broke out on my face, and I felt like I'd caught a flu bug. My bladder throbbed, but I'd peed right before leaving the motel. The Westin Hotel clock showed 12:23 a.m. I picked up my pace. Figured I'd cut through the alley behind Donicello's Eatery to save time. I'd need a ton of caffeine to fake my way through school the next morning, especially if I'd picked up a flu. My symptoms worsened, and my legs weakened, but I pushed forward past the gates where the working girls hung out.

Red and blue lights lit up the backstreet. Three cop cars, an ambulance, and two fire trucks blocked the alley. The lights made it hard to see, but a silhouette ran toward me yelling, "Dead! Dead! Dead!" I recognized the straggly teddy bear swinging frantically from his left hand — Schizophrenic Al, our local homeless guy. Al had named the teddy bear Dingo. I'd learned that about a year before, when Al had been beat up trying to save Dingo from a bunch of drunken douchebags out celebrating their grad.

Brenda and I had seen the guys run away that night. We'd found Al clinging to Dingo by the garbage bin, so we called an ambulance. Al screamed and swung at the paramedics, spitting at them every time they got too close. A couple of cops showed up and started roughing him up. That's the night I began truly hating cops. Al kept swiping at the ground and saying Dingo's name. I saw the little bear a few feet away, so I picked it up and handed it to the burly female paramedic. And just like that, Al took Dingo in his arms, climbed into the ambulance, and gave the cops the finger.

"She's dead, dead, dead!" Al screamed in my face.

"Whatever, Al!" I said, certain he was having one of his fits.

"Perry, Perry, Perry!" He jumped up and down, Dingo swinging from his hand.

"What do you mean Perry's dead?"

"Perry's dead, dead, dead!"

I ran down the alley toward a group of sobbing hookers, scanning the crowd to make sure I didn't run into the arms of my enemies. Girls had never liked me. When I'd first come out on the street, the veteran hookers preyed on me, particularly a big blonde named Samantha. She called herself Bunny Hollywood. I called her Samazon. One night, Samazon and her massive tits had jumped in front of me. "You think you're pretty special, eh? I'm gonna kick your ass!"

I took a deep breath and closed my eyes, certain her huge fist would split my head open. I waited to hear the crack of my skull on the pavement, but out of nowhere, like a superhero, came black-haired Nikki-Lynn. She said, "Back the fuck off or I'll cut you!" Nikki-Lynn, Wonder Woman. She even looked like Wonder Woman with her black hair, dark eyes, and super-hero body. She'd bought a Wonder Woman costume and wore it the whole Halloween week. She said, "I can't believe how much these morons will pay to fuck a superhero."

Nobody knew where she'd come from. She just showed up one night. Nothing scared her, not even death. She said she believed in other lives — reincarnation. Claimed it was her only hope to be reborn without the memories of her cursed lifetime. Brenda once tried to tell her she couldn't work the corner we'd *earned the rights ta!* Nikki-Lynn said, "Brenda! Do the right thing. Retire and get a job at a hot dog stand so you can continue your life's work with wieners."

A few months later, Bunny Hollywood was found wrapped in plastic and stuffed under a bedframe at the Travelodge. Perry and I cried. Nikki-Lynn said we had to be strong. She barked at me and said, "Put them shoulders back, little one. You're a target for the murderers and freaks out here. They drive by every night and look at us like we're steaks in a fucking cooler. And they pick the weakest one."

"What do we do?" Perry shrugged.

"Walk like you got a gun on ya!" Nikki-Lynn made trigger fingers.

"How do you walk like you have a gun?" Perry laughed.

"Like everyone can go fuck themselves! You walk real fast. Stick yer chest out like a schoolyard bully, keep your head up high, and glance around a lot — like yer the one lookin' to fuck someone up. Makes 'em think twice about picking you!"

Shortly after, Nikki-Lynn went missing. Wonder Woman who taught us to walk like we had a gun was gone.

And now Perry was gone too. I started running toward the pack of people gathered by the garbage bin. The red and blue lights made it hard for me to see clearly, so I slowed myself and edged close to the building wall.

"Oh my God, Jade!" Jenna, an old veteran hooker known for her discount blow jobs, sobbed. She threw her arms around my neck, almost toppling me to the ground. "Perry's dead. They found her strangled by the garbage bin. Fucking strangled!"

I gagged a couple of times and leaned against the wall. My legs buckled, and I kneeled down on the pavement. Perry had worked for Brenda and Milos too. They didn't like us hanging out. They said it distracted us from our jobs, as if we needed great focus to be hookers. We had eerily similar stories, both raped and tossed out of our childhood homes and discovered by Brenda. On the streets at fourteen, Perry dead at seventeen.

Perry had broken free of Brenda and Milos when she'd hooked up with an ex-boxer. Once upon a time he'd been a *champion*. He *knew people*. He promised to save her. Then he started using her as his punching bag. Messed her up so bad she'd show up at my place begging me to hide her. He found her and threatened to kill me if I didn't "mind my own fucking business!" It hurt when she chose him over me. I judged her for letting a man come between us, and I thought I'd never understand why she stayed with a guy who beat her.

I stood up and tried to walk away. The voices and chatter pierced my ears like bottle shards. I wanted to throw rocks at all the people gawking at her, snapping pictures with their cell phones. Perry had been my friend. Just a kid. Not a sideshow for Facebook freaks. A white truck slowed down and honked. A ball-cap-wearing redneck leaned out the passenger window and hollered, "Just a dead whore, folks! Nothin' to see here!"

The crowd shifted. My vision tunnelled, and I could see her body. At first glance, Perry looked perfect: blond hair, rosebud lips, long, bronzed legs in white go-go boots. I blinked hard, and my vision sharpened. A yellow tarp floated down over her body as though in slow motion, the very last seconds I'd see her on Earth. Her purple face, blackened neck, eyes wide open. The terror of her death very much alive and crawling all over me.

I flagged a taxi and checked my phone. Seventeen text messages from Brenda.

> Perry's dead you stupid bitch! Get yer ass home now!!!!!!

> Where the fuck are ya? Blue and me been drivin' all over lookin' for your sorry ass!!!!

"Can you turn up the radio?" I asked the cabbie. He nodded and cranked it up. I turned off my phone and sobbed all the way home.

When I got to my apartment building, Blue was sitting in my living room, compliments of Brenda's master key. "Why are you here?" I asked, noticing the empty bottle of Captain Morgan on the bed.

"I heard about your friend. Thought you could use a little support."

I collapsed on the bed next to him. "Please keep Brenda away tonight."

"I'll tell her you're home, and I'm taking care of you."

"Thank you, Blue."

He reached for my purse. "No problem. I'll just run her Tanji cut upstairs."

CHAPTER SIX

I TASTED MY DEATH.

It tasted bitter, like a young life lost to a murder should.

I saw my body on the ground next to a trash bin. I wore white go-go boots, blue lips, and a blackened neck.

The yellow tarp coming down on me.

I'm dead. But I'm sweaty. The dead don't sweat.

I jerked awake, my body charged as though wrapped in electric fence. Fear paralyzed me. I didn't want to move because moving would make Perry's death real. My impending murder — real. Bunny Hollywood, Nikki-Lynn. There were other dead girls too. Some jobs got downsized. Hookers got murdered.

My bladder throbbed. I curled onto my side and pulled my knees up. Blue hogged the duvet, so I wrapped the top sheet around me. So much sweat, my body purging the virus I called my life. Rape, attempted suicide, Amal and Amal, and Perry.

Perry ...

I bit my lower lip and muffled a sob. My teeth chattered, and nausea forced me to sit up. Second day of school and I was dry heaving and dizzy. But it was school or the streets. I would go to school; Perry would get an autopsy.

Something was wrong. I felt infected. The hot-cold, dizzy, bladder-burning type of ill that made my ankles weak and my vision blur.

"Blue." I rubbed his shoulder, trying to keep calm before my panic attack spun out of control. "Blue, please wake up."

Blue wrenched his shoulder away and buried his face in the pillow. The silent *fuck you*, a game my mom used to play to torment me. I'd almost rather he'd slapped me. He'd left me alone the night before and said he'd only be a minute when he took my Tanji money to Brenda. A minute had turned into two hours, and he'd returned drunk, bitchy, and distracted. We didn't talk about Perry. He just ignored me and jumped into bed. He was snoring before I'd even turned out the light.

When I was twelve, my mother ignored me for three whole weeks. She said she didn't want to waste her breath on such a stupid child. I stopped eating and started shaking all the time. I spent my nights pacing in my bedroom trying to come up with ways to make her want me again. It would have been easier if she'd just dug my heart out with an ice pick. I began to think I had died and was a ghost trapped in between worlds, and she couldn't see me. But my dad had talked to me, and so had my teachers, so I thought maybe my mom was right when she told me I was dead to her.

By the end of the third week, I still couldn't adjust to being invisible. I skipped school to buy my mom flowers and a card. If she knew I still loved her, maybe she would resurrect me and stop treating me like a ghost. I brought the flowers home and stood in the kitchen doorway extending the bouquet in front of me. She walked right up to me and paused, like she was going to say something. My heart swelled with hope. Then she backhanded the bouquet out of my hands.

I swear that the spirit of my dad's heart leaped through the air to try and save the flowers. But it spattered on the floor along with the daisies and the roses, as sad as the flowers splayed all over the hardwood. His face reddened, and he slammed his fists down on the table. I ran out the front door. They scared me when they fought. And they fought a lot. Later that day, when I'd snuck back into the house, the remnants of the flowers poked out of a beer glass on the table. They looked timid and embarrassed, like they'd been shamed and were yearning to go back into the earth.

I needed Blue's attention. The room started spinning, and my stomach flipped. Sweat beaded on my brow and the back of my neck. I tried to breathe away the dizziness. How would I get through a year of school when I'd crippled myself with a bladder infection and no sleep on only the second day? I couldn't lift my head, my bladder burned like an inferno, and I needed medication.

"Blue! There's something wrong," I whimpered.

Blue groaned and rolled over, the stench of his hangover making me queasy. "What's the problem, Chanie?"

"I can't miss school, and I'm really sick."

"Stay calm, Chanie. I'll drive you. Just get there so they don't put you in jail, and then if you have to faint or whatever, do it there. Just show up."

I peeled myself off the sheets and sat on the edge of the bed. Blue sat up and took my hands. He helped me stand, held me against him, and then walked me to the bathroom.

The bathroom was like a torture chamber. I sat down to pee, squeezed my eyes shut, and clenched my fists. I let the first stream of urine flow and pursed my lips tight to stifle a sob. It burned as though steel wool dipped in acid was dragging through my insides. When the flow stopped, it felt like an evil creature was dangling from my bladder and was trying to rip it right out of my body. The toilet water looked like cranberry juice. Sweat dripped down my face, and I panted a few times to ease the pain. I wrapped my hands around my shoulders and began to shiver.

"What's going on in there, Chanie?"

I started crying. Blue came in and helped me gather myself. Pride escaped me. It seemed that no matter how many men had beaten, raped, or violated me, my need to be rescued allowed a small space of vulnerability to exist. I let him take my hands, take control, and followed his lead.

When we got to school, Blue leaned over and opened the truck door for me. "Just take a deep breath and get in the door. Then sit or lie down, whatever you need to do."

"Thanks, Blue."

I aimed for the doors as though navigating through a narrow tunnel. My legs weakened, so I grabbed the handrail to help get me up the stairs. I teetered on my feet and put my back against the wall. It felt like a plague had overtaken me and poisoned my blood. I slid down the wall and pulled my knees against my chest. My bladder pulsated in rhythm to my heartbeat. Every time I tried to stand up, my dizziness forced me to slither back down. I would simply die if I peed myself in front of the entire school.

"Ya can't come to school high, whore!" a pock-faced kid barked as he ran toward me pretending to line me up for a kick.

"Shut the hell up! Can't you see she's sick?" A girl with bright orange hair kneeled in front of me, her backpack falling to the side. "My name's Ginger. Are you okay?"

"I'm not okay. Please get Rie for me."

I woke up in a Medicentre with my feet in stirrups. A plump nurse was gripping my hand tightly. She gave me a sympathetic smile, as though trying to tell me it wasn't her idea to let the doctor perform a pelvic exam while I was out cold. The white-haired doctor slid his stool out from under him as he stood. "You have a severe bladder infection. It wouldn't surprise me if this has spread to your kidneys. We'll need to put you on an IV drip to start the antibiotics. I also tested you for sexually trans-mitted diseases." He rolled his eyes at the nurse, turned his back, and slammed the door on his way out.

A few hours later, Blue showed up with Brenda to take me home.

"Ya better rest, ya little slut. God knows what ya were up to last night to make ya so sick! Ya don't have the luxury of havin' womanly problems, if ya know what I mean," Brenda said, shaking her finger in my face. "My back's been buggin' me more than usual. Might be time to cash in on all the favours you owe me, so ya better take care of that precious ass of yers."

"I can't really worry about that right now, Brenda!" I rolled my eyes and pressed my forehead against the passenger window of the truck.

"Whatta ya mean, Chanie! You's gonna have to do what a strong woman would do. Man up and do right by me. You'd be nothin' without me. I gave ya the apartment ya live in and taught ya how to be a strong woman. Not some whiney book-worm lookin' to join the herds of sheep wastin' away in office jobs every day makin' barely enough to pay the rent. Havin' to ask for a piss break, clockin' in on someone else's schedule. Ya gotta fight for freedom, girl!"

"Just like you're so free now," I said. "Relying on a hooker and a vacuum cleaner to pay your rent."

"Well, I tell ya one thing! I'd never waste my life on books 'n shit when I made the wages of a CEO when I was out there workin'. Yer the one who said, 'I wanna be strong and free. Wanna be my own woman.' You said those things, and I made them happen for ya!"

"Oh my God, Blue!" I pleaded, hoping he'd shut her up.

"Yeah, Brenda, ease the fuck up. Chanie's sick," Blue said.

"Blue, the world ain't easy, and this little princess better remember that nothin' is free."

"Brenda, shut the fuck up or your long walk home won't be easy," Blue said as he reached over Brenda and squeezed my hand.

I squeezed his hand back and pretended to pass out.

Rie left me a voice message to give me permission to stay home for the rest of the week. In the meantime, she arranged for Pastor Josh to drop off my schoolbooks so I could get a head start on things. I must have told her about Perry when she'd driven me to the Medicentre because she said to let her or Pastor Josh know if I needed someone to talk to about the "loss of my friend." Nice euphemism for *some psycho strangled her*. I couldn't be around anyone except Blue. When Pastor Josh arrived with my books, I sent Blue down to the lobby. I couldn't stomach P.J.'s gleaming teeth and fizzy prayers.

Blue plopped my books down next to the bed. "Holy fuck! That guy's way too happy."

"Yeah. He's a ray of sunshine."

"Oh yeah! He told me to tell you that he personally blessed these books for you."

"Lucky me."

"Yeah. Stupid Bible thumper."

"Hey, Blue." I chewed my fingernail. "I'm scared to go back

to work. I think I could end up dead, like Perry and Bunny Hollywood."

"You probably will if you keep hooking." Blue looked out the window and smirked. "I used to visit this one girl a few years back. Workin' girl like you. Big titties, nice ass. Anyways, she ended up in the ravine chopped up and stuffed in a suitcase. Real shame. She gave a good blow job and didn't rip me off like a lot of the other bitches."

"Oh my God, Blue!"

"What? Do you think you have someone watching over you? There ain't no God for the whores on this planet."

"What am I going to do?" I started crying. "I'm supposed to clean up my life, but I can't live on welfare pay. Now I can't even pee properly or get out of bed."

"Calm down. You're just messed up from all the drugs they gave you. You'll get back in your high heels again." Blue laughed and smacked me on the shoulder. "Cheer up. I'm going out to get us some food. We can talk when I get back."

I didn't respond. Maybe my bitchy silence would teach Blue a lesson for not taking me seriously. Nobody ever listened to me. I think my dad had wanted to, but his endless battles with my mother had left him worn out and tired. He didn't even leave a suicide note. The only thing he left was a bloody corpse in a Cromdale Hotel bathtub and a shotgun that the police confiscated. I think in his heart he wanted me to be great, but he just didn't know how to make that happen because nobody in his life had ever wanted him to be anything but gone. I'm still pissed at him for leaving the Earth. If he hadn't left me, Clayton wouldn't have raped me.

I couldn't sleep, despite the medication. The coloured bindings of my schoolbooks lit up like street signs as the sun beamed in through the windows. My eyes were drawn to the titles: *McGraw-Hill Education: Preparation for the GED Test*; *Life Skills for Adult Children*; *An Adult Child's Guide to What's Normal*; *Basic Meals and Home Skills*; and yet another book with pink lotuses floating on a murky grey background, *The Lotus Still Blooms: Sacred Buddhist Teachings for the Western Mind*.

I got up and brought the books to bed with me. At the bottom of the pile, there was a binder with a sheet of paper slipped into the clear casing on the front. At the top of the page, the words *Begin Again Program Manual* popped out in big fat lime-green letters. A black silhouette of a lotus flower was centred on the page. I opened the binder to the first page.

Welcome to Begin Again. If you commit to this program, the sky's the limit! This is an opportunity to build a healthy and productive life with the support of your teachers and peers. Your program includes the following components:

- GED (General Equivalency Diploma) Preparation
- Life Skills
- Home Economics
- Basic Money Management
- Addictions Counselling: Individual & Group Sessions (24/7 access to counsellors through our helpline)
- Career Counselling and Guidance
- Job Support and Community Service

In addition to the core program, we offer the following to qualified candidates:

- College/University Preparation (additional up-grading to assist students to gain entry to a post-secondary program)
- Assistance with Student Loan Applications, Bursaries, and Scholarships

*ALL STUDENTS are required to participate in the daily prayer/meditation sessions and are required to keep a personal journal.

I arranged the mass of pillows behind me, propped myself up, and began to leaf through the binder. I liked some of the content, like learning how to cook and plan meals. I loved food but didn't care much for prayer and meditation. Money management intrigued me because no matter how much cash I brought home, I never had any when I needed it.

Blue didn't come back until after dark. It seemed like a long time to pick up takeout. By the time he came in, I'd read the entire binder and had skimmed the contents of the GED guide.

"What are you reading?" Blue asked, his words slightly slurred.

"Just some school stuff."

"Learn anything?"

"That what I think is normal is not and that I have to be reprogrammed."

"We're normal, Chanie. It's the rest of the world that isn't."

"Where's the food?" My stomach growled.

"Oh yeah! The food. I got sidetracked. Had to go to a jobsite to help someone out."

"No worries. Let's order pizza."

"Sure. But I want to talk to you about something first."

My stomach turned, and I felt hot. *He's leaving me.* I took a deep breath. "What is it, Blue?"

"You know how you're scared to go back to work?"

"Mmm," I mumbled.

"And now you got school and stuff."

"Yeah, but I can manage —"

"Anyways, I got an idea that might help you out."

"What kind of idea?"

Blue leaned toward me and raised his eyebrows. "I was thinkin' I should move in here with you. Help you out with the bills."

I sat very still, unsure I'd heard him right. We didn't know each other very well, but nobody had ever showed up for me like he had: after the rape, at the police station, making sure I got to school. Maybe this was what all the girls meant when they made comments like, "When you're not lookin', that's when you'll meet *the one.*" Maybe Blue was *the one* who could save me from an inevitable death on the streets. We'd be part-ners, and I'd do well at school. I'd be able to find another way to live my life before it was too late.

"Where do you live now?"

"With my mother. Just helpin' the old bird out, with her being sick and all." Blue smiled and pulled me against him, his hands rubbing my back. I melted into him, like I could feel him inside me again, his lips on my neck, his hands on my body.

"And with all the money I'll be savin' on blow jobs, we can get takeout more often." Blue laughed and jerked away from our embrace. "Let's get some food, girl!"

Two days later, I stood in the lobby holding the door for Blue as he brought in a bunch of boxes. He didn't waste any time moving in. He said, "Let's get 'er done while you're on a week off so I'm all settled in when you go back to school next week."

"What the hell do ya think yer doin'?" Brenda's voice echoed through the lobby.

"Blue's moving in with me." I felt triumphant, like I'd won a prize that she couldn't take away. Blue came in with another load of boxes.

"Ya know, ya can't just move on in, Blue. Ya's gotta be approved and added to the lease."

"Fuck off, Brenda," Blue said as he walked out to get another load.

"Ya know what, Chanie! Ya can't just do whatever the hell ya like. There's rules ya gotta follow!"

Blue came back and dropped more boxes next to the elevator door. "Stop bustin' my balls, Brenda! I only got one day off, so I need to get this shit done."

"Do ya got an elevator key, Blue? Oh yeah, I suppose ya do because ya work here a lot. But ya didn't get Old Merv's permission, did ya?"

"Are we really gonna do this?" Blue raised his hands.

"The two of ya is so dumb! I'm just fuckin' with ya. Good news! Old Merv has gone to be with his family. He got too sick, so I'm takin' over! Say hello to yer new landlord."

"Yeah, Merv must have been pretty sick if he hired you," Blue said.

"Tell ya what, Jade," Brenda said. "I'll do ya a solid and add old Blue here to the lease. I'll make some shit up and say I talked to his references, blah, blah, blah."

"Thanks, Brenda," I said.

"No problem. But now ya's owe me even more. Remember that!"

"Yeah, Brenda. We get it." Blue said, pushing the up button on the elevator.

Maybe Blue's presence would neutralize Brenda and she'd stop showing up at my door demanding favours and "borrowing" food, clothes, and alcohol. I planned on asking her to give me back my spare set of keys. I'd tell her that Blue needed them. I'd get him to ask because I knew that if I did, she'd freak out and make a big deal out of it. *After all she's done for me …*

Blue's mom showed up as he was unloading the last of his boxes. She looked like the stereotypical mom: grey hair, plump middle, a flowered blouse, and black slacks. But up close, the lines around her eyes hinted at a once-upon-a-time young beauty who'd danced at every party and wore thigh-high boots for almost any occasion.

"Hey, Clarence!" Blue yelled to his mom.

"Is your name Clarence?" I asked.

"Oh no, honey. It's Donna. Blue, come on over here and tell the story of my nickname."

Blue walked up and balanced a box on one knee. "One night, my mom had a big house party, and some guy kept calling and asking for Clarence. The idiot who answered the phone called my mom and told her it was for her. She talked to the guy for like an hour. Her friends have called her Clarence ever since. I call her Donna or Clarence. I don't call her Mom."

"Fun!" I said, amused by their weird bond.

"Here's some sandwiches and ambrosia salad," Donna said as she handed me a bright yellow Superstore bag. "The salad tastes like Creamsicles and coconuts."

"Oh wow!" I said, opening the top of the bag. "Nobody ever brings me home-cooked food!"

Donna smiled and squeezed my arm. "Oh, honey, it's the least I can do for the girl who tamed my wild Blue."

"Stay and eat with us," I said, hoping she'd join us and keep Brenda away.

"Sorry, hon. But I gotta get going." She pulled me close and hugged me really tight, as though she was already saying goodbye forever. "I'm so glad Blue finally has a little friend."

When she let go, I squeezed her hands and said, "He's very sweet."

She frowned and said, "Oh no! He's a nasty thing, but I'm glad you see something good in him."

BLUE'S QUIRKY NATURE BROUGHT light into my dark little bachelor suite. He made me laugh and feel like I mattered. I felt like he was saving me from ending up dead on the street like Perry. Because of his help, I'd be able to focus on school and not have to worry about hooking anymore. Together, we'd find another way.

Blue reached into his pocket. "Here's five bucks. Would you mind running to the Mac's to get us a couple of root beer slushes?"

"Yum! Of course."

I walked to the door and slid into my sandals.

"Hey, Chanie. Look what I got." Blue pulled his hand out from behind his back and waved a forty-ounce bottle of Captain Morgan. "Happy housewarming!"

On my way out, the elevator clunked to a stop on the sixth floor. It always bounced around a bit before coming to a complete halt. It reminded me of Bunny Hollywood's huge boobs. She used to jump up and down and shake her breasts on slow nights when competition was hot. She named them *the bitches*. If *the bitches* had been human, they would have been showgirls. They were guerilla marketers and bounced and jiggled no matter what the rest of Bunny's body was doing. Sometimes, she would pull her shoulder blades way back to make them blow up like giant birthday balloons.

"Well, looky here!" Brenda sauntered into the elevator. "Where ya off to, Chanie?"

"Slushes for me and Blue."

"Pick one up fer me."

"Sorry, Brenda. Blue and I are having kind of a private night."

"Oh no you ain't, honey. I'm comin' to see ya both and have a little talk about the house rules."

"That's really not necessary. Now that Blue's living with me, I think we should just have planned visits. No more surprises, please."

"Fuck you. The only reason he's there is cuz his momma kicked his ass out. Sick of his dealers comin' around."

Brenda's chest puffed out as mine deflated. "Oh, come on, girl. You didn't think you were special, now did ya?"

I closed my eyes until the elevator door opened.

"See ya later, sunshine. Make sure to get Brenda a nice big slush and put some of that soft ice cream in it."

CHAPTER SEVEN

I ALMOST PUKED WHEN I stepped outside and saw Milos's black Lincoln parked in the turnaround. He'd been gone for months. Back to Serbia so Brenda could "focus on her recovery." Brenda's new focus was Blue and putting me back out on the streets. All the Jesus sayings, organic markets, Penelope the Sponsor — gone! I felt like a full moon had parked itself in my belly. The threats, beatings, and blow jobs were stitched into my DNA the way Christmas traditions were etched into the lives of the normal. I knew things were different; I wasn't alone anymore. But death vibes and visions of yellow tarps oozed through me and sent my heart into high speed.

I cut across the Strathcona Community League playground, where a group of preschool kids played in the spray park. I envied them, in their oblivious hysteria, innocent and unchanged by the world. Their moms, a few feet away, with homemade lunches and fluffy towels to warm and dry their little ones. My mom had never done that. But the Milos-free Brenda had given me glimpses of what a mom might have felt like when she'd started acting more like my buddy than my boss. She'd taken me shopping at Walmart for bedding and dishes, hung Christmas lights on my balcony, and stolen magazines from her doctor's office to cut out pictures of beautiful clothes, homes, and pets so she could plaster them all over my apartment walls. She'd even made some bad attempts to meal plan and cook for us. It wasn't perfect, but it was better. She still clung to her "rights ta my money," which sucked, but it was miles better than Milos's business model of blow jobs and beatings. And without Milos, she was cheaper to feed.

I sat on the bench in front of the Mac's on Whyte Avenue. I stared across the street, my eyes trailing along the curved edges of the two-storey Roots On Whyte Community Building. I'd been there once, when Penelope and Brenda had dragged me to a restorative yoga class at the Sattva School of Yoga. The memory stung. It had been a good day with the good version of Brenda. It had been the same day she'd taken me shopping to decorate my place. After a long day of shopping, the yoga class was a perfect ending.

The class had been weird, a lot of chanting and heavy breathing. But despite the weirdness, I'd succumbed to a deep state of relaxation. I lay in between Brenda and Penelope, our legs up the wall, our eyes covered with lavender-scented beanbags. The instructor chanted and played a musical bowl at the front of the room, the scent of incense floated over us, helping me relax even deeper. Brenda reached for my hand at the same time Penelope did. For a moment, I felt like we were so synced that if we turned our palms upward and took a big breath, we'd levitate all the way up to the sky. But even then I knew that feeling was fleeting, just like Brenda's kindness, a welcome chinook in the dead of winter. Soothing, welcoming, unusual. And short-lived. And I was right. She'd gone from reaching for my hand back to reaching for my wallet. And now Milos was back.

The loud jangle of bottles and cans on the pavement woke me back to the moment. A homeless man with piercing blue eyes and wispy white hair plopped down next to me.

"It's a hot one," he said, smiling up at the sun. "Praise Jesus!"

I smiled and said, "Do you like root beer?"

"Haven't had root beer for a while. I kinda dig it. Prefer Pepsi, though. Praise Jesus!"

I bought three slushes, but when I came out *Praise Jesus* was gone. I tossed the Pepsi slush into the garbage can. Brenda could drag her lazy ass to the Mac's if she wanted one. She'd probably threaten me, but she was a feeble drunk, easily winded even when she vacuumed the hall, which was rare. Nonetheless, she had her meathead bouncer Milos back in town and had a way of getting what she wanted. When I'd first started working for her, she had coerced some hookers into beating the hell out of me to teach me a lesson in gratitude. She called it my "Thanksgivin' day lesson" and never let me forget that she could have me beaten again.

I took the long way home past Ritchie Mill and Waters Edge before I decided to sneak through the alley. I avoided the elevator and ran up nine flights of stairs to my suite.

"Why are you so sweaty?" Blue said.

"I ran into Brenda on my way to the store." I panted. "I used the stairs coming back so she wouldn't accost me."

Blue rolled his eyes and grabbed a cigarette from his pack. "We might need to move out."

The thought of leaving Brenda and Milos behind made me feel like an eagle in flight. For four years, my life had felt like a suspended casket waiting to be lowered into the ground by Brenda's next whim. She'd told me the only way I would ever be free of my debt to her would be when one or both of us dropped dead. Before Blue came along, I didn't care which one of us went first.

"Can I ask you something, Blue?"

"Anything you like."

"Brenda told me your mom kicked you out because of drugs."

"What? That bitch is delusional. I don't do drugs anymore."

"So — you did before?"

"Do I judge you for being a whore? No, I don't."

"Jesus, Blue. I'm not judging you. I just asked a question."

"Well, it wasn't easy. I even ended up homeless for some time. Had to eat at a soup kitchen with a bunch of addicts and bums."

"I'm so sorry you went through that."

"Don't talk about things you don't get, Chanie."

I did get it, but I didn't want to start crying and ruin the mood. His tone was sharp, mean really. I figured he was exhausted from moving, so I decided to let it go. I slipped off to the bathroom to gather myself. I eased myself to the floor and rested my back against the tub and closed my eyes.

Three sharp raps on the suite door sent my heart speeding again. Blue swore a couple of times but didn't answer. Brenda yelled, "Where's that little tart, Blue? She's supposed to grab me a slush. Ole Brenda here's pretty warm from the hard work I gotta do all day long."

"Fuck off, Brenda!" Blue snapped.

"Are ya in there havin' sex?"

I got up and opened the bathroom door. Blue came over and held his finger up to my mouth to keep me quiet.

"You's both gonna be in some trouble here. I told ya's we was havin' a business meetin' about the house rules. I'm warnin' ya! Strike one!"

Blue held his middle finger up to the door and mouthed,

"Strike one!" I grabbed a towel to muffle my laughter, but he yanked it away and kissed me. He peeled my T-shirt off and lifted my skirt. For a while, Brenda didn't matter anymore. All that mattered was that Blue was with me, and I was no longer alone.

Brenda returned an hour later while Blue was standing on the balcony smoking a joint. I waved frantically at him and pointed at the door. He shook his head, cocked his hand like a gun, stepped back, and pretended to shoot. I wished the gun were real.

"The old bird came back, eh?" Blue said, stepping inside the patio door.

"Like a cockroach."

"Man, she's a pain in my ass. Let's finish up our drinks and clean up. I'll take you for pizza. We can relax and not worry about them *house rules* showing up while we're tryin' to eat."

"That sounds great!" I kissed him on the cheek.

My first real date! I wanted to look sexy and lure Blue into an evening of drinks and sex. I wore a pale pink miniskirt with a skin-tight fuchsia tank top, no bra, no panties, and five-inch black platform pumps. I sprayed bronze body shimmer all over my legs, arms, and chest. I spritzed myself with apple-blossom body spray and strolled past him, dragging my fingertips over the back of his shoulders, tossing my hair to hide my smile when he smacked my ass and whistled.

"How did I get so lucky?"

"I feel the same way, Blue."

Blue came into the kitchen and took me in his arms. "Beast of Burden" by the Rolling Stones played quietly on the radio. I let myself drift away, my head on his chest, his heartbeat whispering promises of a better life, new traditions, and freedom from Brenda and Milos. Until Blue jerked away and yelled, "Nobody ordered a clown here!"

Brenda stood in the doorway, her giant ring of master keys hanging from the lock. She laughed and leaned against the wall as though she were Olivia Newton-John in *Grease II* waiting to show off her dance moves. "Always the clown yerself, you old bad boy." She giggled and flipped her frayed yellow hair and flashed a sly smile at Blue.

She smirked at me, her dark-purple lipstick making her teeth look almost orange. Big gobs of blue mascara clung to her sparse eyelashes and had already begun to run from the corners of her eyes. A botched liquid liner job made her look like she had pink eye, and her eyebrows looked like black caterpillars that had lost some of their fur to mange. I almost felt sorry for her, standing there wearing maroon booty shorts, a neon-pink crop top, and purple thigh-high boots. But I couldn't.

I shook my head and said, "Heading back to the streets?"

Brenda dug around in her oversized bag and pulled out a mini of vodka. "Ha ha! Fuck you, Jade."

I pointed at the worn-out leather bag slung over her shoulder. "What's the big purse for? Shoplifting spree? Or smuggling a new teenage hooker to fund your RRSP?"

She used to call me her RRSP. She'd said, "That's why I get you bitches so young, so I get lots of workin' years out of ya — like long-term investments."

"Oh, come on, Chanie. What's really the matter with ya? Scared I might be temptin' old Blue here? Maybe he needs an older woman to give him what he really needs."

Blue rolled his eyes and pretended to puke. "What the fuck are you doing here, Brenda?"

"I'm comin' with you guys now that I see ya are all slutted up. Where we off to?"

"*We* are going to dinner," Blue said.

"Where's we all goin'?"

"Jesus," I said. "Go find something else to do. What ever happened to your friend Penelope?"

"Oh, that bitch gone thinkin' she's better than everybody. Can't stand her preachin' about bein' sober all the time and reaching for the Lord instead of a vodka. Shut up already."

"Jesus Christ, Brenda. Get out!" I pointed out the door.

"I ain't goin' nowhere," Brenda said, dropping her bag and folding her arms tight.

Blue grabbed her purse from the floor, walked over to the door, and tossed it down the hall. "Toodle-oo, you old skank!" He swept his hand toward the hallway.

"Who's old?" Brenda curled her upper lip. "How old are you now, Blue? Forty-two, ain't that right? That's what your momma told me when I seen 'er. She said she couldn't believe that her son at the age of forty-two had to sponge off her old sick ass."

Blue grabbed her arm and helped her out the door.

"Are you really forty-two?" I wrapped myself around him, hoping to revive our frisky mood.

"Yeah, but I sure look good, don't I?"

"I like the way you look. You're very sexy."

"I like the way you look too." Blue kissed my cheek. "I guess we have to order in now, or risk that old whore grabbing us on our way out."

"I guess so." I put my purse down and grabbed the iPad. We'd have a first date some other time.

A COUPLE DAYS LATER, I slouched in a chair at the school office waiting for my assessment exam results. It didn't matter so much anymore. All I wanted to do was go home and hide out with Blue. I loved our nightly dinners and *Forensic Files* marathons. And the sex. *The sex ...*

"Hello, Chanie," Rie said, smiling as she sat down.

"Hello."

"Did you get a chance to review some of the books I sent you last week?"

"I did. I'm looking forward to learning how to cook and manage my money better."

Rie glowed like a proud mother. "That's great! You'll learn so many good things in the program."

The sun beamed through the window, and a golden hue poured over the room as Pastor Josh walked in. He flashed his electric white teeth and said, "Rie and I reviewed your results, and you should be very pleased."

I sat up straight, a little surprised.

"You tested at a grade-ten level, which means you shouldn't have any problem completing our program in one year *if* you apply yourself and complete all of your volunteer hours."

"Volunteer hours?" *Doesn't the whole school thing count as volunteer hours?*

"All students are required to log a minimum of ten hours a month working downstairs at the shelter. You can cook, clean, read to clients, pray with people, do yoga — whatever you feel you can bring to those less fortunate than you."

"How am I going to do that with all my studies?"

Pastor Josh motioned his hand to the door. "Why don't we walk to class together, young lady?"

"Sure." *What choice did I have?*

The classroom reminded me of a cat kennel. Kids weaved around the room; some sat cross-legged on desks, some on the floor. Others leaned on the edges of shelves, and a couple of them sat backwards on top of desks with their feet on the chairs. I spotted the pock-faced wanna-be-football-star leaning on a desk next to Ginger. I shimmied against the back wall, trying to be invisible as I made my way to an empty seat, but his face lit up, and he yelled, "Feelin' any better, whore?"

"Jeremy! You big dink!" Ginger punched him in the shoulder.

"That's what I got, not what I am, biotch! Besides, I know she's a working girl. I've seen her downtown with all the other whores."

I put my books down and barked, "And you're only here because your thriving law career got thwarted?"

"Okay, okay." Pastor Josh clapped his hands and addressed the class. "This is Chanie."

"Ain't that a guy's name?" Jeremy said.

"It's a nice name, asshat!" Ginger snapped.

"I'd love to wear your ass as a hat." Jeremy winked and blew an exaggerated kiss to Ginger.

Pastor Josh kneeled before the class. A few kids lowered their chins and held their hands in prayer position at their chest. I closed my eyes and listened, but I couldn't concentrate on the prayer because of Jeremy. Ginger tapped my shoulder and handed me a copy of "A Prayer for Peace" by St. Francis of Assisi.

> Lord, make me an
> instrument of your peace.

Where there is hatred,
let me sow love.
Where there is injury, pardon.
Where there is doubt, faith.
Where there is despair, hope.
Where there is darkness, light.
Where there is sadness, joy.

I silently recited the prayer while I wondered if the class had noticed my almost-week-long absence. Did they think I was just another lazy, addicted whore who couldn't make it to class three days in a row? If they did, I blamed Jeremy. I hated him for drawing so much attention to me with his big mouth and nasty spirit. Maybe he was mean because he felt ugly. Maybe his strategy was to make me stand out to take attention away from himself. Either way, I hated him.

Pastor Josh stood at the front of the room waiting for us to take the hint and shut up. Slowly the noise and chatter dwindled. "Every Sunday morning, I lead a prayer for my congregation, and we pray for those who don't know Jesus and who suffer and mourn outside our churches. We pray for everyone. Have you ever thought that the prayers of all those who worship have saved you from a worse fate? That their love for Jesus protected you from evil and brought you here today?"

I looked at the bandages on my wrists. Maybe the prayers of all the God-worshipping people had brought the paramedics to my motel room that night. Or more likely, my screaming and wailing forced the front desk clerk to call 911 so they wouldn't have to haul another body out of that dump.

Pastor Josh continued. "Do any of you recall a time when the Lord came into your lives? Anybody?"

The room was like a tomb.

He exhaled loudly. "Ah! Silence. We must be silent to hear the voice of God. My favourite scripture reminds us of this. Psalms 46:10 says, 'Be still and know that I am God.'"

"Be still and know that I am bored," Jeremy hollered. I laughed along with the class, but when Pastor Josh looked right at me, I closed my mouth and tried to look serious.

"Okay, Jeremy, please simmer down."

Jeremy surveyed the room to measure his audience.

"Jeremy!" Pastor Josh said firmly. "Are you with us?"

"Okay! I speaketh not!"

I looked away from Pastor Josh and giggled.

"You can all rest in Jesus if you open your hearts and minds. Wouldn't it feel amazing to let go of all your worries and let the Lord take them? His will be done, not yours. How would you feel if you could allow yourselves to be saved by Jesus Christ?"

I thought a good place for me to start would be that my will be done, not Brenda's. Jesus hadn't lasted long in her life, so my confidence in Him was low. I needed to be rescued from myself, but Blue filled that role in my life. Blue lived and breathed on this planet. I could touch him and talk to him. I connected with him on a human level. Jesus existed in a faraway daydream that used language such as saith, doeth, and speaketh. I couldn't connect to Jesus's words even if I wanted to.

"Chanie," Pastor Josh called.

"What?"

"Don't you want to be saved?"

"I think I'm beyond that, Pastor Josh."

"Why do you think that?"

"I'd rather not say."

"Okay, I won't force you to talk in class, but my office is open to you every day if you need."

I wanted to say "amen" but figured P.J. had endured enough abuse for one day, so I chose to give him a nod instead.

Later that day, I met Mr. Lavoy, my English teacher. He reminded me of a tall, lanky tree. He had no hair on his head except two tiny blond eyebrows and white eyelashes that resembled spun sugar. His eyes were a dull grey, like all the hours he'd spent reading had sucked the pigment from them. He wore a big cross around his neck and a gold bracelet on his right wrist, like he might be a part-time biker when nobody was looking. I wanted to know his first name. I figured it'd be something cool like Damon or Dimitri. He stood like a majestic bird at the front of the class, his crucifix gleaming in the sunlight from the window.

"If no one loved, the sun would go out," Mr. Lavoy said very slowly, squinting and scanning our faces, as though trying to read our hearts. His words pierced the air, like we were in a church with thirty-foot ceilings. I took a deep breath, and my mouth fell slightly open just as his glance rested on my face. He smiled gently. I blushed and turned away.

I waited for Jeremy's smart mouth to pipe up, but everybody stayed calm and quiet. There must have been magic in Mr. Lavoy's crucifix. It shone like a crystal, its beams hypnotizing us into silence. My breathing deepened, and I felt my heart open up. I replayed the words in my head. *If no one loved, the sun would go out.* I wanted to kiss the air and drink the prose into my blood. The sun so sad, lovelorn, dying without love. Bittersweet, tragic, and familiar. The words of my lost childhood; the sound of my soul finding shelter from the rain and seeing the sun for the very first time.

"Does anybody know who wrote that?" Mr. Lavoy looked at me. "How about you, young lady? Would you like to venture a guess?"

I thought it had to be Jesus or some other famous philosopher. Who else could write like that?

"Jesus?" I stuttered.

Mr. Lavoy smiled kindly. "I'm sure the author would be very flattered at that guess. Do you want to guess again?"

I wanted to know so I could impress him. I envied his brain brimming with beautiful words, phrases, stories, and poetry. His sky-grey eyes and easygoing smile made me believe that literature could right all the wrongs in the world and inspire intelligence in even the most inarticulate beings.

"Did you write it, Mr. Lavoy?"

Mr. Lavoy laughed. "While I'm very flattered by your guess, I must admit that I did not. Those words were written by Victor Hugo, someone whom many of you will become familiar with. Today I will assign your annual reading. To successfully complete the program, you will have to write an exam and a book report. Don't think that reading the CliffsNotes version the night before will suffice."

"Those books are huge!" Ginger said, pointing at the massive stack of books on the floor.

"Yes. They are huge, Ginger," Mr. Lavoy replied. "The reason I assign big books is because they build big confidence. And they don't break your heart and leave you lonely as quickly as a novella or short story does. They give you something to think about — to wake up your minds. You'll learn to love and hate the characters — cry with them, laugh with them, bleed with them, and parts of you will die with them. They will make you happy, sad, scared, and excited. They may even show you new ways of looking at the world."

Mr. Lavoy began handing out books. I stared at the coral spine with big white letters: Victor Hugo, *Les Misérables*. He had two others in his hands: *The Count of Monte Cristo* and *Don Quixote*. I closed my eyes as he got closer to my desk, as though willing him to give me what I wanted. When he set the book down, I kept my eyes closed, took it in my hands, and pressed it against my heart as though I could infuse Victor Hugo's words into my being. I ran my fingertips along the spine and opened my eyes to a crisp new copy of *Les Misérables*. I smiled at Mr. Lavoy. He nodded and smiled back.

"Holy eff! This book is ten million pages long!" Jeremy said, speaking my thoughts. "What is this, anyways? Looks stupid." He picked up his copy of *Les Misérables* like it was a dead rat and dropped it on his desk.

Mr. Lavoy repositioned the book in front of him. "It's not ten million pages long. It's twelve hundred pages. You are in the program for ten months, so that works out to about four pages a day. Do you think you can handle that?"

Simple, attainable terms. Only four pages a day. If Victor Hugo could intrigue me with a few simple words, I figured I'd find treasures in those pages. Maybe I would try for five or maybe even ten pages a day.

"Lezz Mizz-er-ables," Jeremy said dragging out the z's. "My guess is that this book is about unhappy lesbians, like Chanie and Ginger, who crave dick but are trapped in a loveless same-sex marriage."

"Shut up, fag!" Ginger yelled.

"Enough, you two," Mr. Lavoy said calmly.

"This shit is gay — like Chanie and Ginger."

"Jesus, Jeremy! Does anything nice ever come out of your mouth?" I said.

"You're the last girl who should talk about anything nice coming out of her mouth," Jeremy said as he high-fived the air.

"Shut up, pig!" Ginger shouted. "You're a douchebag, Jeremy."

"And you're a pair of sluts!"

Mr. Lavoy raised his voice slightly and motioned Jeremy to stand. "Jeremy, get out of my classroom. Clean up your mouth or don't come back."

Ginger looked at me, but I looked at the floor. I waited until Jeremy left the room and then looked back up at Ginger. She smiled at me and held up her book.

"I got *Don — Coyote*? Which book did you get?"

I held up my copy of *Les Misérables*.

"Nice!" Ginger said.

When we left class that day, Ginger handed me a note.

Don't let your sun go out ...
Your friend, Ginger

CHAPTER EIGHT

"THE CHURCH IS ON fire!" Ginger shrieked and jumped out of her seat. Pastor Josh yelped as if the fire had slapped him in the face and summoned him for emergency prayers. He paced back and forth, muttered something about Jesus, grabbed his jacket, and ran out the door.

The old brick church had stood behind the school building for ninety-six years. And in moments, it would be in ruins. I'd gone there once as a kid for a funeral. I didn't know the dead guy, but my mom had insisted we show up "as a family" to support the survivors. "Funerals are for the living, not the dead," she'd barked at my dad as he turned the car radio loud. She'd strutted into the church ahead of us and wailed like a soap opera star. The widow spun around and glared so hard I dug my nails into my dad's forearm. He shook his head, took my hand, and led me out of the church.

I went outside to join my classmates, most of them treating the fire as a smoke break. Ginger had taken her jacket off and let her hair down. She smiled and waved at the firefighters as if she were a rodeo queen. Jeremy stared at Ginger, seemingly blind to the blaze blasting out of the church windows. Ginger's hair matched the colour of the flames, Jeremy's gaze the intensity. They looked like the cover of a romance novel — the wild girl waving at the heroes, the woeful boy aching for the wild girl. Black plumes of smoke streaked the violet sky, and the fire sizzled as it licked the edges of the windows and grappled toward the steeple. The old priest moaned and paced while Pastor Josh prayed loudly by his side. The fire looked down on them and gave a loud crackle, toppling the steeple to the ground at the exact moment the old priest collapsed to his knees in prayer.

"Back inside, everybody." Pastor Josh clapped his hands.

Jeremy gave Ginger a gentle shove. "Shouldn't we stay here and pray for the firemen to save the day?"

Pastor Josh pointed toward the doors. "Good one, Jeremy. Get inside."

Ginger walked with me. "Are you nervous about the grammar test results?"

"I'd prefer to watch the firemen all day."

"I know!" She giggled. "I love men in uniform, unless they're arresting me. But seriously, do you think you passed?"

"I don't know. But if I failed, my destiny will be that of a hooker."

"Oh my God, Chanie! You're so dramatic."

"Rie calls it black-and-white thinking. She told me I'm my own worst enemy when it comes to my thoughts. Too extreme."

"Our lives *are* extreme. See you in class." Ginger jogged ahead to catch up with Jeremy.

About a week before the exam, I'd made an appointment to discuss my concerns with Rie. I told her I'd been having anxiety because of the upcoming grammar and reading comprehension exam. It would be our first graded activity. Grades meant evidence. Proof of my deficiencies. I'd done well in grade school. The teachers were nice, and it had meant escape from my mom and dad and their endless shit. My grades had been solid up until grade seven, my first year of junior high. That's when everything went wrong. When I'd begun feeling sick a lot, had no appetite, and shook all the time. I had googled my symptoms and self-diagnosed as mentally ill. Rie said it sounded like the extreme stress in my home had been causing my anxiety. It was totally normal given my home life, especially after my dad shot himself.

I used to think that I saw my dad everywhere, especially in the first few weeks after he died. I felt like the gunshot that had killed him had blown away my insides and left his angry winds gusting through me. I'd become ethereal and detached, like he'd taken part of me with him, and I hadn't yet arrived in either world. My life had become a constant search for him. And my husk of a heart found him one morning pulling into Starbucks in a silver car. He was wearing a floppy beige fisherman's hat and had a long, birdlike nose. His lanky body, easily six feet tall, mimicked my dad's silhouette. I stood at the coffee shop door, fixated on him, not realizing I was blocking him from going inside.

"Is everything okay, young lady?"

My voice was thick. "Sorry — you look a lot like my dad."

"Well, he must be a *very* handsome man," Dad's doppelganger said with a Pastor Josh–like smile.

The laugh lines around his eyes showed radiance and good mental health. His happy life stuck like a poker in my gut. My dad had never looked sun-kissed and happy. And Starbucks dad certainly wouldn't pick up a shotgun and end his life in a slum hotel bathtub. I instantly hated him. I stepped out of his way and hissed, "He *was* handsome until he blew his brains out!"

Rie told me that seeing my dad in others was a normal grief response. Extreme trauma. Humans process tragedies in unusual ways. I didn't tell her I'd become obsessed with seeing him walk into the bathroom with a shotgun in his hand. Or that I wondered what he'd been wearing when he sat down in the bathtub and pulled the shower curtain closed. That the saddest thing I'd ever seen was the overflowing wastebasket of his tear-filled Kleenex in the garage the night before he died. He didn't go easily. It hurt him to die.

While I'd initially requested my appointment to discuss my exam anxiety, we'd spent a lot of time focusing on my general anxiety. Rie gently prodded me with questions about my dad, but I shut down and steered us back to my initial concerns about the exam.

"I'm going to fail my exam," I grumbled.

Rie handed me a peppermint tea. "Instead of expecting the worst, why don't you consider a new approach?"

I rolled my eyes. "Like what?"

"An approach leaning more toward creating favourable results rather than trying to control the outcome or your reaction to the outcome."

"But what if things go badly?"

"What if things go well?"

I considered it for a moment. "What's your suggestion?"

"Do you think you can commit an extra hour each day until the exam?"

I shrugged. "I suppose I can make time."

"Why don't you commit to one solid hour of study each night for the grammar and comprehension exam and then see how it goes?"

I counted the days on my fingers. Eight days away. Eight solid hours of preparation.

"Do you have your textbooks with you?"

I dug through my bag and handed the text to Rie. Multi-coloured sticky notes peppered the pages, and fields of neon yellow dominated the text, as though a painter had used a roller to cover the words.

"Hmm," Rie mumbled. "Do you want to learn how to save money on highlighters?"

Rie had spent the next hour showing me study secrets. I learned to read the chapter objectives and rephrase them as questions instead of statements. At the top of a blank page, I wrote each chapter objective as a question and tackled only one at a time until I'd mastered the content. I used my highlighter sparingly. Then I quizzed my memory and wrote the answers beneath each of the objectives. I used my self-study pages like flash cards. I wrapped up each of my study sessions by completing chapter quizzes, even though by the third day, I'd pretty much memorized all the answers.

But on the morning of the exam, everything I'd studied seemed to disintegrate. I'd sat at my desk feeling sick and nervous. I'd squinted and massaged my temples, shoved my pencil eraser into my lips, and chewed my lower lip raw. A tight band had squeezed my head, and my neck had turned to concrete. I'd convinced myself I had a flu, but the symptoms miraculously disappeared when I put my pencil down and headed out for lunch.

The church fire had added to our chaotic energy. It seemed like everyone was buzzing with anxiety about their test results, so it took the class a little longer to settle down. At first, nobody even noticed the new guy standing at the front of the room with

Mr. Lavoy. He could have been a painting: exotic and refined, skin like dark-roast coffee with two creams and one sugar, black licorice eyelashes, almond eyes, and lips the colour of cherry jawbreakers after you'd licked the first candy layer. His pupils shimmered like hematite stones, as if they could light a forest pathway on a moonless night. A black braid, thick like a horse's tail, hung between his powerful shoulder blades. He stood strong, like a bull bossing its herd, as though nothing could take him down.

"It's Pocahontas!" Jeremy laughed out loud.

The new guy glared and flashed his teeth at Jeremy. Mr. Lavoy put his hand on the back of his shoulder. "Meet Tuffy Stonefeathers. He's your fellow student, so let's welcome and respect him. Treat him the way you would like to be treated." Mr. Lavoy nodded at us and gestured Tuffy to have a seat.

I watched Tuffy as though he were walking toward me in a tunnel. The rest of the world faded away, and I couldn't take my eyes off him. My mouth moistened, and my eyes got heavy. He reminded me of a black stallion I'd watched playing in the ocean on YouTube, majestic and powerful, perfect and natural. I couldn't get enough of that horse. I'd watched the video over and over again. His strong neck was arched and elegant, and he had a shiny coat that shimmered like the body of a seal. That horse had been all I wanted to see; that horse was something I wanted to be. That's how I felt when Tuffy Stonefeathers walked toward me. But when he caught my stare, I flipped my hair and turned away.

Mr. Lavoy turned his back to write on the chalkboard: 97, 78, 75, 68, 63, 52, 50, 46, 41. When he wrote the final number, he turned to us and said, "These are the grades from the exam."

I squinted at the board and hoped to God he wouldn't

put our names next to our grades. I pictured my name in all capital letters next to the forty-one. I imagined my new nickname being *Chanie 41*. Mr. Lavoy walked around the room and placed the exams face down on our desks. He saved mine for last and took a long pause before placing it before me. I couldn't look at him.

"I got a sixty-eight!" Ginger yelled, smiling as though she'd won a beauty pageant.

"Who's the poindexter that got a ninety-seven?" Jeremy questioned, craning his neck, smirking at everybody in the room. "Has to be a super geek or someone who gives a good blow job."

"Jeremy!" Mr. Lavoy said. "What have I told you about your foul mouth?"

I lifted the edge of my paper slowly, as though a sudden movement might disturb the grade on the page. But before I had a chance to see it, Jeremy swiped it from my desk.

"I knew it had to be somebody who gives a good blow job! Chanie, our resident pro, got ninety-seven percent!" Jeremy stuck his tongue in his cheek and jerked his hand in the air.

Heat rose in my belly, and a hot red butterfly splayed over my face. My jaw clamped tight, and saliva rushed into my mouth. I wanted to spit on Jeremy, but when I looked over and saw Tuffy's perfect face scrunched up at me, I bowed my head and said nothing. Mr. Lavoy looked at Jeremy and pointed toward the door. Jeremy jumped up, kicked his desk, and spun around to flip me off before slamming the door on his way out.

Later that night, I stared at the ceiling, unable to fall asleep. The burning steeple glowed in my mind. The old priest on his knees begging God to spare his church. *Ninety-seven percent!* Jeremy's wicked mouth. *Sweet Tuffy Stonefeathers ...*

A while later, I heard Blue shushing Brenda at the door. I strained to hear what they were saying, but their language was polluted and clumsy, like they'd been drinking.

"Why are you up?" Blue snapped.

"Because you're loud! Why is she with you?"

"Oh shit, Chanie. Where the hell do ya think he's been gettin' his dinners?" Brenda slurred. "We don't get the luxury of goin' to bed early like you, schoolgirl."

"Really, Brenda? All those late nights drinking and getting high getting you down?"

"Who the fuck ya think's been gettin' yer clients looked after?" She raised her arms in the air, looking around the room. "Blue?"

"Go home, Brenda. I need to sleep," Blue said.

"Oh! Party's over now because yer little princess is awake. No problem, dickhead. Go mooch from someone else when ya come home at night." Brenda slammed the door behind her.

"Don't look at me like that, Chanie. I don't need your shit after I've worked a twelve-hour day."

"Well, what *are* you doing hanging out with her?"

"I don't have to explain shit to you, honey!" Blue threw his jacket on the bed. He clenched his jaw and sat cross-legged on the floor, bouncing his knees up and down. His breath wheezed in and out in rapid gasps. He pounded his fists on the floor and pawed at his jacket like a disoriented animal. "Fuck, fuck, fuck!"

I jumped off the bed. "Jesus Christ! What the hell is wrong with you?"

Blue's eyes darted around. "I can't find my smokes! It's too fuckin' bright in here. I can't find my smokes. Too much light! Too much light!"

I dimmed the lights and kneeled in front of him. "Let me look for your cigarettes."

"Okay," he said, still bouncing his knees up and down.

I lit a cigarette for him and brought him a glass of water. He rocked and bounced and scratched his head and chanted, "Please don't go, Chanie. Please don't go."

"I'm not going anywhere."

"I wouldn't blame you if you did. I'm no good. You're so good. So perfect."

"You are good, Blue."

"Even my mom says I'm no good."

"Well, that doesn't count. My mom would say the same about me, and she's a twat. Besides, you two seem so close."

"She was never a mom to me. Never protected me. She just wanted to party."

"I wonder if her and my mom would have been friends," I joked. "Two dive bar party stars."

"Maybe. Two shit mothers who don't give a fuck about their kids."

I sat next to him, holding his hand. We began to sway slowly, in rhythm, like a moving meditation. His breathing slowed, and his energy eased.

"You know, one time she took me down to the river." Blue squeezed my hand really hard. "Big biker party — everyone piss-drunk in the middle of the afternoon. My stupid uncle grabbed my arms and started swinging me in a circle. We were close to the edge of the riverbank, and I was screaming. Screaming for my mom. And the stupid bitch just laughed. When I finally hit the ground, I puked all over myself."

"Jesus, Blue. I'm sorry," I said, knowing how sickening it felt to have your mother betray you. "We have each other now."

Blue pulled me close and said, "We can protect each other.

I'll fuckin' kill your stepdad if he ever comes near you. I'll kill him, I swear."

I'd watched girls I used to work with have bad trips. I knew the signs and had learned to stay still and quiet while the chemicals slowly eased out of their cells. It always looked painful and strenuous, like torture. Blue looked crumpled, like a fast-food bag tossed from a car window. He collapsed on his side, clamped his knees together, and jerked them up to his chest. He shuffled around on the floor, his jaw rigid, teeth chattering so hard I thought they would turn to dust.

Blue fell asleep around half-past six. I covered him with a blanket and showered for school before rummaging through his hoodie for coffee money. I scrawled *I love you* on a pink sticky note and stuck it to the door before running to meet Ginger at the Mac's.

Ginger lit up when she saw me. "Hey, Honour Student Extraordinaire. Extra-large today? Did you and Blue stay up late celebrating your awesome grade?"

I hesitated. I liked Ginger, and we'd been getting closer over the last couple of months. She had always believed we were destined to be sister soulmates. I'd only known her for a few days when she'd stayed after class to wait for me outside. She'd run up to me and said, "I had a dream about us."

"What?"

"Yeah, I know. It's weird. I'm not a lesbian or anything. Don't get all fucked up about it. It's not like it was some porn dream, weirdo."

"What was it about?"

"We looked really old. I knew it was you even though you didn't look anything like you. The two of us were gardening together. We wore bohemian sundresses and big, floppy sun hats. And we had matching lotus flower tattoos on our arms. And you know, it seemed like we'd known and loved each other for our whole lives, Chanie. We are fated to be the best of friends. In life and death."

"In life and death, Ginger?"

"Yeah, weirdo. So get used to me!"

Would Ginger still want to garden with me if I stayed with Blue? I remembered how I'd judged Perry when she'd lived with her junkie boyfriend. I was pretty sure he was the one who'd killed her, but Blue wasn't like Perry's loser man. Blue was different. He just needed someone to give him a chance.

"I didn't tell him about the grade."

"What?" Ginger handed me a stir stick. "I celebrated my shit grade. I'd be drunk for a solid week if I'd gotten your score."

"Can you keep a secret?"

"Oh my God! Of course. I'm your best friend." She set her coffee down and leaned into me.

"Blue came home high last night. He's been working really hard, and I think he had to let loose a bit."

"What do you mean, high? Like weed, coke, meth?"

"Some kind of chemical high. I'm no expert, but it wasn't weed."

"Chanie, that shit is dangerous. He could go crazy and hurt you."

"Come on. You don't really know him. He's been through hard times in his life. He's beaten his addictions before."

"Rie told me that when you're an addict, there's no such thing as casual use."

"Yeah. Well, Rie doesn't know Blue."

"Okay, Chanie. I'll trust your judgment. But you gotta let me come over and meet this Blue."

I'd thought about having Ginger over many times, especially lately with Blue being gone so much. Maybe once Blue and I moved away from Brenda, Ginger could visit. I didn't know how he'd feel about my friends coming over. He didn't talk to me much about school, other than always telling me to keep my legs closed around all *them young guys.*

"Okay, I'll talk to Blue."

Ginger tousled her hair and smiled. "Let's get to school so we can make fun of Jeremy. He got forty-one percent on his exam. I can't wait to shove it down his throat."

By three o'clock in the afternoon, I felt like I'd been wrung out in the sun. I chose to ride the bus rather than walk home. Blue's truck was in the parking lot even though he should have been at work. I came into the lobby and saw Brenda talking to an old guy wearing a sweater that made him look like an alpaca.

"Hold it right there, princess," she barked, pointing at me.

"I have to see Blue before he leaves for work." I frantically pounded on the elevator button. Brenda grabbed my wrist and tried to twist it. I shook her hand loose and stepped back.

"Ya see, Chanie, we need to have a conversation about work. Mr. James here is all done with me, so he can take this elevator on up while we chat." Brenda nodded sharply at the old alpaca man.

"What now?" I wanted to see Blue. I'd been texting him all day but hadn't heard back.

"I don't know what makes ya think ya don't have to work anymore, Jade, but here's how it's gonna go down. Yer goin' to work this weekend, and I'm gonna make sure we get ya booked out again. Lots of yer old regulars are askin' about ya. Don't like them junkies they've been dealin' with."

"Too bad, Brenda. I'm not allowed to do anything illegal

while I'm in the program, and besides, I'm with Blue now."

"Yeah, speakin' of junkies, yer with Blue now."

The elevator door opened, revealing a blond woman in her sixties wearing a tattered paisley bathrobe.

"You the building manager?" she asked me. I pointed at Brenda.

"Whatta ya need?" Brenda said.

"A plumber. Like ASAP! There's shit — literally shit — floatin' around on the floor in my can."

I took advantage of the open elevator and stepped inside. I squeezed my eyes shut so I wouldn't cry, but I found myself blubbering as I opened the door to my suite.

Blue called out from the kitchen, "Are you hungry, girl?"

I dropped my bag on the floor, stood still, and started crying.

Blue rushed over and grabbed my hands. "I'm sorry, babe. I just had a slip is all. My boss is a real shit. I needed a release."

"It's not that."

"Then what is it?"

"That bitch never stops. I'm not her whore!" I sank to the floor, pulled my knees to my chest, and lowered my head.

"Brenda's a crazy bitch," Blue said. "It's like she watches out the window until I come into the parking lot at night. Then *just happens* to be in the lobby when I come in."

"You're not going over there to hang out?"

"Nope. I had a couple meals there because I didn't want to wake you up, coming home late and all."

"You can always wake me up. I miss having you around at night."

He handed me a cup of coffee that smelled like caramel. "Sometimes, I think you're too busy with your friends and your schoolbooks to worry about me."

"You're the reason I try so hard. I want us to have a good life."

He kissed my neck and whispered, "We could move away."

"Really?"

"Yeah, really. How are we supposed to start a life with that stupid vulture hanging over us?"

"I didn't know you wanted to make a life together, Blue."

He walked over and sat down, pulling me into his chest just like when I'd come home from the hospital. "I've never felt this way about anybody, Chanie. I feel like you're my soulmate. Since the first time I saw you, I couldn't stop thinking about you."

I rested against him and felt safer than I ever had. Like I had a hero. And I'd finally be safe.

"Have you ever thought about getting married?" Blue whispered.

"Married!"

"Yeah, married. You act like it's such a crazy thing."

"I just never thought it would be an option," I admitted. "I feel like since my stepdad messed me up, I was just damaged goods."

"Baby, you're my goods, and I love you."

"I love you too, Blue. Can we really move away? Start fresh?"

He stood up and grabbed the iPad. I hoped he was ordering food. Sometimes, Blue would look up animal memes or stupid videos to make me laugh, but he was solemn, as though reading disturbing financial news.

He handed me the iPad. "Have a look at this."

I looked at the screen and thought it was a picture of a Christmas card. Nestled in a valley at the bottom of a mountain, historic hotels, office buildings, and shops glowed orange beneath a cobalt sky. Above the golden light of the town, proud mansions sat along the mountainside. Gigantic evergreens with snowy branches hovered over yards and streets, and a purple glow emerged from the gaps between the trees. White porch lights peeked out of the darkness, warm and welcoming, like each home had chocolate chip cookies baking in the oven. It looked like a place where my ears would stop ringing and my past would evaporate into the cold mountain air.

"Oh my God, Blue! Is this place real?"

"Yup! It's Nelson, B.C. It's an old hippie town in the mountains. My party mom took me there a lot when I was a kid."

"Does it really look like this?"

"More or less. They have street markets in the summer and sell all kinds of food and those hippie-type clothes Brenda's friend — what's her name — Penelope, wears."

I leaned over and kissed him. "We're going there, baby. I'm going to work in a coffee shop, and you can be a maintenance guy at the old hotel. We can spend lots of time outside and do things like hike and kayak. I bet you it always smells like campfires in the summer."

Blue laughed. "And weed."

"How much money do you think we need to get out of here?"

"Oh, man, like twenty grand. At least."

"So, if we each save around eight hundred a month, we can go in a year or so?"

"Sounds about right. But you need to get a job so we can do this."

"I know," I said, not letting the money dilemma dampen my spirit. I'd have to come up with a way to get some cash, but I'd think about that in a day or two. For the time being, I wanted to pretend I was skiing in the purple-treed mountains, dreaming of hot chocolate and cookies.

"Should we open a special bank account?" I said.

"Oh no, baby. I don't trust banks. We can save it here."

"Brenda, the snoopy bitch, might steal it." I pictured Brenda's huge batch of master keys hanging from my doorknob.

"She won't. I'll break her slutty arms. Besides, we'll hide it from her."

"Like under the mattress?"

"Fuck, no. Give me a minute." Blue jumped into his shoes and left the apartment.

I felt light and energized, like all my stress had melted away as soon as I knew Blue really wanted better lives for us. The idea of our future gave me a reason to work hard, to look forward, and to get good grades. I would finally escape the clutches of Brenda and Milos.

"Check this out." Blue popped in the door holding up a Maxwell House can. "This can holds our future. I threw in a toonie to start."

"And at school tomorrow, I'm going to print the picture of the town off the Internet and tape it to the can." I clapped my hands together and giggled.

Blue grabbed his wallet off the counter. "Let's get some rum and celebrate."

"Yes!" I said, hoping for an opportunity to tell him about my grade. "Maybe my friend Ginger can come over tonight?"

"No, Chanie. I don't think so. I don't really want any of your little friends coming around here. I'm kind of a private person."

My light dimmed a little. "Okay, Blue."

CHAPTER NINE

JEREMY LEAPED DOWN THE school stairs, almost slipping on the ice, and ran toward us. "Hey, bitches! Wanna have a special winter celebration?"

"Fuck off, Jeremy. You scare me." Ginger smiled and flicked him away with her hand.

"Come on, Ginger. You know you want me."

"Uh — like, no!" She smiled and snuggled under his arm.

"Let's get some vodka and bust into the church tonight," Jeremy said.

"The fire site?" I looked at Tuffy.

Tuffy nodded. "Yup. The fire site."

Later that morning, Mr. Lavoy drew a chart on the whiteboard showing the differences between expository, contemplative, and persuasive essays. I tried to listen, but my focus trailed to Tuffy's neck, his cocoa skin contrasted by the pale-blue T-shirt hugging the curve of his lower back. My eyes rested softly, like Annie Pema told us to do in meditation practice. "Soften your gaze, breathe deeply, let the body breathe itself."

"I saw you eye-humping Tuffy," Ginger said after class.

"As if!"

"Oh my God! You so were, Chanie!"

I set my copy of *Les Misérables* on the desk. It looked like a used bookstore survivor, like it had endured years of being bought, sold, traded, and stuffed into boxes. I'd bent it, rustled the pages, shoved it in and out of my bag, and almost rubbed the letters off the binding.

"What the eff happened to your book, Chanie?"

I smiled at the curly edges on the cover. "I carry it everywhere I go."

Ginger raised her perfectly pencilled eyebrows. "As a weapon?"

"I just feel better with Jean Valjean in my pocket."

"Probably feel even better with him in your pants!"

"Probably!" I laughed.

Ginger had joined me in reading *Les Misérables*. She had gone to Mr. Lavoy and said, "Take back this *Don Coyote* book and give me the same one as Chanie, *La Miseries*, or whatever the hell it's called." He'd laughed and handed her a crisp new copy of *Les Misérables*. She'd declared us official reading partners and committed our lunch breaks to the fantasy life of Victor Hugo.

Sometimes, Ginger struggled to pronounce common words and inserted her own versions, so *Les Misérables* came with its own unique challenges. She called nylons *nylongs*, Cosette *Corsette*, Jean Valjean *Jon Valjon*. Mr. Lavoy shook his head and said, "Take these dictionaries and spare Mr. Hugo's words any more abuse." He'd told us to circle words we didn't understand and underline passages that inspired us. Our pages became multicoloured legends of words we loved, hated, or didn't know what to do with.

We struggled with the names of people and places, like

Fauchelevent and *Hougoumont*, so Mr. Lavoy referred us to howtopronounce.com. Surprisingly, we learned to articulate difficult words and even entertained the thought of studying French. Mr. Lavoy also gave us copies of the SparkNotes study guide and encouraged us to try the online quizzes. I personally challenged myself to ace every quiz before moving on to the next chapter, but often found myself bingeing on Jean Valjean, Cosette, and Marius. I stayed firm in my commitment and made sure to do all the quizzes when I found time, usually while Ginger rambled about Jeremy over our lunch breaks.

Ginger rummaged through her purse for a Xanax. "I'm not ready for this fucking geometry test."

I pointed at the pill bottle. "Do you think you could focus a bit more on your studies if you didn't take those?"

"Oh my God, no! I'm like a nervous chihuahua at the best of times. Maybe one day when a modern-day Jean Valjean marries me, and I don't have to worry about my next meal, I will wean myself off them. But the way I see it, it's no different than people taking blood pressure meds. I can't help it if I got bad wiring."

"Fair enough." I nodded and returned to my quiz.

We left school after our math exam and went to the mall to admire the Christmas trees and decorations. We stopped to smell candles at Bath & Body Works. Ginger sniffed and sprayed samples of body spray all over us. We smelled like pine needles, peppermint, hot chocolate, marshmallows, and cinnamon.

"When I'm rich, I'll buy candles for every season. In the fall, my house will smell like pumpkin spice and apple pie. Winter will smell like marijuana marshmallow." Ginger twirled like a princess, lifted the lid off a dark-brown candle, and swept it under my nose. "When can I come over to meet Fifty Shades of Blue?"

I raised my face and sniffed the air. "Mmm, that smells like hot chocolate powder. If I burned that in my apartment, I'd want to eat the air."

"Don't dodge the question, Chanie."

"Why do you want to meet him so bad?"

"Because you're my friend. I want to know more about your life and be able to hang out at your place so I can keep my pants on."

"What?"

"Oh yeah! My fucking roommate's an old perv. Says I can stay there for $500 a month, but only if I walk around the house without panties on."

"Holy Jesus, Ginger! Does he touch you?"

"Oh no! I quote, 'I ain't no diddler — just like *lookin'*.'"

"Oh my God! He sounds like a guy who hired me to wear pigtails and sit naked on a stool in front of him during the play-offs. Whenever his team scored, he'd jump up, grab his dick, hump the air, and yell, 'Booyah!'"

"What a freak!"

"Your roommate's a freak. He *ain't no diddler*, my ass. He can't get his dirty dick up, or he'd rape you every night."

"I know. I hate him. But he's a trucker, so he's away a lot. I can wear pants about sixty percent of the time. Plus, he doesn't rape me. And he pays for most of the food. Worst thing he's done is make me let him go down on me. I just pretended he was Jeremy!"

"Oh!" I slapped her shoulder. "Why Jeremy? I thought you hated him."

"I do, but my body doesn't. I like his sexy teeth. And he's funny."

"Ginger, what are we going to do with you?"

"You're going to let me come over and meet Blue."

"Only if I can meet Ain't No Diddler."

"Okay, but you'll have to take your pants off."

"Then he better have his wallet."

We went to the church after the mall closed. Tuffy and Jeremy were slouched on the steps smoking long brown cigarettes. They looked like dirty rich kids after a long day of laying sod at a golf course.

"Did you get the booze?" Ginger snatched Jeremy's cigarette and took a long drag. Tuffy flashed a crooked smile and held up a crinkly brown bag.

We used our iPhones' flashlights to find our way inside the church. Tuffy stayed close to me, his hand on the small of my back, guiding me up the stairs. His hand felt good, innocent, and simple — no expectations, simply a courtesy to ensure my safety. I turned my head slightly to look back at him and lost my footing, falling into him, feeling him against me. I breathed him in and, for a moment, let myself float into his heartbeat, his breath, his chest. But Blue — I had to remember Blue.

I'd expected the church to be destroyed, but it wasn't. It looked like the fire had swirled through the doors, licked the walls and ceiling, and then vanished as though something had scared it away. The centre of the room had stayed intact, as though a group of angels had been sitting in a protective prayer circle. Parts of the hardwood floor had remained immaculate, and a stack of old Bibles sat unscathed a few feet from the entrance.

"I am fucking terrified," Ginger said. "It's so creepy in here.

If these alpha boys weren't with us, I'd run out of here screaming and go home safe to the diddler."

"I'd go with you." I pointed my light at the walls.

Ginger's eyes widened when she noticed a charred wall, completely black except for a huge imprint of a cross. Small streaks spattered the bottom of it, as if it had cried during the fire. A chill snaked down my shoulders, and I shifted closer to Tuffy.

"We need Pastor Josh," Ginger whispered.

Jeremy barked at us, "Turn your lights off, you twits. Don't get us arrested!"

"There's only two paper cups here," Tuffy said. "I'll share mine with Chanie."

"Of course you will." Ginger winked at me.

I took the cup from Tuffy and waited until he looked away. I ran the tip of my tongue over the brim where his lips had been, took a big drink, closed my eyes, and smiled at the feeling of vodka warming my veins. Our fingers touched with every pass of the cup. I watched his chest and synced my breathing with his. I tried to reconnect to Blue in my mind, but I was glued to the present moment, to Tuffy's voice, Jeremy's banter, and Ginger's giggling.

"How did we all end up here?" Ginger said, glowing like a firefly.

"I came to this school because my probation officer figured I deserved another chance." Jeremy slapped his knee and laughed.

Ginger grabbed Jeremy's hand. "My mom overdosed when I was like three, and my ass of a father — well, nobody knows who he is!"

"And thanks to Jeremy's big mouth, we all know I'm a hooker," I said, taking a long swig from the cup.

"I applaud your honesty," Jeremy said in an English accent.

"Well, Tuffy. What's your deal?"

"I come from Thunder Bay. Do any of you know where that is?"

Ginger piped up. "Oh yeah! When I worked at the strip club, they sent a lot of girls there. I guess they can freelance as table dancers or something."

"Yeah! 'Or something' sounds more likely," Jeremy said. "Come on, Tuffy. What heinous crime brought you here to us?"

Tuffy looked at the floor and clenched his jaw.

I put my hand on Tuffy's chest. "Are you okay?"

"Cops!" Jeremy jumped up.

I stood up to run, looked from side to side, panicked, and froze. Tuffy grabbed my hand and yanked me toward the door. I stumbled down the stairs and pulled away from him. He dodged toward the trees, but I ran into the open field behind the school. The police car's alley lights lit up the ground like a football stadium. I weaved toward the back corner of the school but lost my footing and skidded to the ground. My chest heaved, and my lungs burned. I held my breath and strained to hear footsteps. I heard a jingling sound. Dogs! I covered my face.

"Chanie, what are you doing here?"

I uncovered my face and smiled. "Who's this handsome fella?" I asked, reaching for the white bulldog standing over me.

Mr. Lavoy shook his head. "He's Dorito. Now, what the hell are you doing? You better stand up. There's a cop walking toward us."

"I'm sorry, Mr. Lavoy."

He reached for my hand and pulled me up. I'd rather have stayed face down on the ground than face him. I put my hands over my face and turned away.

"Chanie, get it together. Now's not the time —"

"Please identify yourself," the cop yelled, his flashlight pausing on Dorito.

"Hey, Mitch. It's me, Warren."

Dorito wagged his whole body and leaned on the cop's leg. "Lavoy! What are you up to?"

There it was. Mr. Lavoy's first name. Warren. Not Damien or Dimitri, or something exotic like Laszlo or Lazarus, just Warren.

"This is my student, Chanie. She's helping me walk Dorito tonight so we can discuss her paper."

"Dorito's a good boy!" Constable Mitch bent down and scratched Dorito's chin. "There's been a report about some kids hanging out in the church. Did you see anything?"

"Nope. Just a couple of rabbits for Dorito to chase."

The two men exchanged a look.

"Okay, Warren. Call it in if you do. See you at hockey practice next week. Gonna kick your ass! Nice to meet you, Chanie."

I swallowed hard and tried to look Mr. Lavoy in the eye, but disgrace made me drop my chin to my chest. I tapped my heart and tried to say thank you, but my voice thickened, so I put my hands to my chest in prayer and bowed slightly toward him.

"Chanie, what the heck were you thinking?"

"I ... I was ... I'm ... I'm an idiot. I broke into the church to get drunk. There was this burnt-up wall with a big white cross, and I just knew — I knew it was a sign from Jesus, like a warning or something! I should have listened."

"Chanie, you're drunk. And I'm not Pastor Josh, so save it. Jesus had nothing to do with your stupidity tonight. It was all you."

"I know." I wiped my nose on my sleeve.

"So, you broke into the church all by yourself to get drunk?"

I shrugged at Dorito.

Mr. Lavoy turned and began walking toward the school. He waved his hand and said, "Come with me. Let's see what we can do to make this right."

The obligatory blow job! No favour comes for free. We walked toward the school, and while he fumbled in his pocket for a key, I considered running. But I was too drunk, and besides, he'd just saved my ass from getting tossed in jail. My phone chirped, and my heart leaped. *Perfect! I'll tell him I have to go home. There are people worried about me.*

Mr. Lavoy stopped fumbling with his key and looked straight at me. "Tell your friends you're fine and your battery's almost dead. Then shut it off."

I followed him down the dark hallway, Dorito toddling along contentedly, grunting with each step. If I blew him in the class-room, I'd never be able to focus in that room again and would throw away *Les Misérables*. I also didn't want to blow him with his dog staring at us, snorting away like a little pig. But it beat jail. Or did it?

I sat at the first desk in the row right in front of Mr. Lavoy. I didn't want to move. If I stayed still, the moment wouldn't happen. He wouldn't blow up my faith in him. I could hold on to the belief that my life might be more than a merry-go-round of alcohol and blow jobs. My stomach rumbled, and my temples throbbed. My pleasant buzz was long gone; only nausea, dread, and a dull headache remained — the usual leftovers of my life choices.

"Stay right where you are, Chanie. I'll only be gone for a few minutes, so keep an eye on Dorito."

I looked at Dorito, all white except for a pale caramel splotch over his left eye and a couple of chocolate brown patches on his back. He took a long, deep sigh, snorted, stuck his bottom teeth over his top lip, and flopped onto his side before rolling onto his back, where he broke into deep, breathy snores.

I pictured Mr. Lavoy calling Rie, shaking his head while he told her he'd found me drunk and face down in the dirt, running from the police. The two of them sighing loudly and agreeing that the school was wasting their time trying to save me. That they should kick me out and open a vacancy for a more deserving student, not an ingrate like me.

I rubbed my temples and shook my head. My knees stung as though bitchy little bees had nested inside them. It reminded me of the time my mom had dragged me to her Jazzercise teacher's house and made me play hopscotch with her daughters. They'd jumped through the chalk squares with their blond pigtails, silk bows, and checkered skirts bouncing like happy cat toys. *You can only put one foot down!* I'd sprung through the air, but my feet bound together, like I'd been lassoed by a cowboy. And then my knees were on fire, and I cried out loud for my mom. She dragged me to the car hissing about what a fucking embarrassment I was and then grounded me for three weeks.

Then came the token guilt gifts strategically placed on my bed while I was at school. Some Dollarama jewellery, cheap chocolates, Skittles, or some pink piece of clothing. Sometimes, she'd get creative and buy me hair elastics or arrange fake flowers in a plastic vase on my dresser. The gifts were never gifts, they were weapons for when she wanted to prove me to be an ingrate, ammunition to prove I was spoiled. They became objects of guilt and fear. They never brought me pleasure or made me feel loved. I think she thought that two-dollar trinkets erased the colossal blunders she and Clayton made every day with their loose lips and slap-happy hands.

I'd managed to blow any chance of a respectful relationship with Mr. Lavoy to pieces. I thought Blue might even leave me because I was too immature for him. Breaking and entering a fire site, getting drunk, and running around like a grade-nine delinquent. How could he trust me to build a new life in Nelson if he couldn't even trust me to go to school? He could never find out. I'd tell him I tripped running for the bus. That seemed believable.

Mr. Lavoy came into the room and set a food tray on my desk. "How about we have some food and coffee and then talk about a proper punishment for what happened tonight?"

"Okay." What else could I say? He'd rescued me from another arrest, and, so far, my punishment was a warm meal in a safe place. Maybe my luck would change? I remembered back to when I'd gone three full days without food, except coffee and water from a gas station bathroom tap. When I was a rookie, I'd trusted that everyone would pay me. After my three-day fast at the Esso station in some weird little town, I got angry and learned to get paid before my pants came off.

The toughest clients had been the handicapped guys. Sirus, a violinist, touched me the most. The only time I believed in angels was when he played "Ave Maria." I met him when his DATS driver brought him downtown and called me over to the window. I thought they needed directions, so I walked over.

"You look like a nice girl," said the driver.

I snapped a bubble with my tasteless gum. "That's the look I was going for."

"My pal here, Sirus," he pointed at a skinny white guy with a huge bald head, "needs a friend, ya see."

"Take him to a community centre. I have to work." I swiv-elled on one heel and started to walk away.

"I'll give you a grand for the night," the driver yelled.

I walked back to the van and high-fived the driver. "Sold!"

I spent the evening getting to know Sirus and his calico cat, Beyoncé. Beyoncé glared at me all night from an end table in the corner, like she knew I was a whore. The driver, Tony, hosted the party and kept my glass full of red wine. Sirus played his violin and began to weep. The harder he cried, the more power-ful the melody. The notes chilled me, like electric currents up and down my back. I wept along with him, like a lone coyote baying for its lost mate. I apologized for getting too drunk and offered Sirus half the money back. I couldn't explain my emotional meltdown, to him or myself. Sirus squeezed the money in my palm and said, "It's okay, sweet pea. It's just the angels making you cry. Come over again sometime." He nod-ded to his driver and told him to get me home safely.

I'd made a lot of money off Sirus over the years. He told me he'd sued a mega oil company for gross negligence when he'd fallen through a scaffold floor. He didn't mourn the loss of using his legs. Instead, he learned to play the violin, tipped his driver lavishly, and drank the finest wine with hookers of his liking. All in all, life was good until the wine wore off, and he'd weep for hours while I sat with him and Beyoncé, drunk and naked, pretending we were normal.

Mr. Lavoy looked at me. I smiled at him, like we were at a summer picnic, totally normal, totally fun. I wanted him to like me again — to respect me. I took a deep breath and spoke softly. "What can I do to make it right?"

"A couple of things."

"What are they?"

Mr. Lavoy stared at the floor for what seemed like forever.

"Can I pet Dorito?" I asked, desperate to end the silence and get closer to him. The alcohol was wearing off, and my emotions were bubbling up.

"No, Chanie. You cannot pet the dog."

His coolness stung, but I understood. I'd disgraced myself and chosen stupidity at a great cost for no other reason than to get drunk.

"How do you feel you can make this up to me?" Mr. Lavoy asked.

Please not a blow job! I stared at him. He didn't feel dirty to me. He felt decent. My years of whoring had sharpened my radar in weird ways. I wielded a sixth sense when it came to men going bad — if I was sober. But so many times I'd drunk myself into a stupor at the cost of all sense and street smarts. My intuition was worth about a dime most times, and my drunkenness had resulted in rape, robbery, assault, and abandonment on the highway in minus-thirty winters.

"I don't know what to say." I closed my eyes to try and lessen the ache of my disgrace. Would he write me off and call the cops? Call his buddy Mitch and tell him to lock me up where I couldn't self-destruct?

"Chanie, you need to give me an answer. Give me something."

I sat quietly for a long time.

"I could write lines."

"Now you're getting somewhere. What kind of lines do you have in mind?"

I shrugged. "I will not get drunk and run wild?"

Mr. Lavoy laughed.

"I wasn't trying to be funny, Mr. Lavoy."

"Okay, Chanie. I'm sorry for laughing. Why don't you write something meaningful?"

"Like what?"

"Is there something or someone who moves you?"

Captain Morgan moved me, but I figured I couldn't get away with that. I hated Brenda and Milos and could write a lot of bad words about them. The only thing I loved was Blue.

"My boyfriend."

"How does he move you?"

I squinted and tried to think of something.

"Does he make you smile?"

"Yes. He does."

"How does that smile feel?"

"Hmm … warm, I guess?"

"Come up here, Chanie."

I walked to his desk. He tapped on his keyboard and opened a blank Word document.

"I'm going to show you a little trick. Have you heard of a thesaurus before?"

"Yes, I have."

"Okay. Well, watch this." He typed the word *smitten*. "I'll slide the cursor over the word and right-click." A list of words came up: *besotted, enamoured, infatuated, taken, hooked.*

"That's amazing, Mr. Lavoy."

"How about we agree that you write me three hundred and fifty words about how you feel when your boyfriend smiles at you? Would you like to try a couple of synonyms?"

I sat down and tried to come up with a word. Dorito snored at my feet, like he was sleeping in front of a fireplace on Christmas Eve. I typed *faith*, and the words *confidence, trust, reliance, conviction,* and *belief* popped up. I glanced up at

Mr. Lavoy. He smiled and patted my shoulder. "I have faith in you, Chanie."

I had faith in him too. More than he would ever know.

"Have it ready for me by Friday next week."

"Thank you, Mr. Lavoy." I bowed my head.

"Oh, right! And when you see Tuffy, tell him to tuck in his braid next time he's trying to run from a crime scene. You'll both be doing an extra twelve hours in the kitchen downstairs this month. Nobody but me will know that it's penance."

I typed *penance* and right clicked on it.

CHAPTER TEN

I CAME HOME TO find Brenda drunk and sitting cross-legged on my floor. Her faded tank top straps hung off her scrawny shoulders, and she wore a pair of fuzzy purple pajama shorts with a Hello Kitty face print. Nobody bothered to ask me where I'd been or if I was okay, and Brenda scowled at me as though I'd walked into *her* living room and not my own.

"What the hell are you doing here at three in the morning, Brenda?" I looked at Blue lying shirtless on our bed casually blowing smoke rings from his mouth.

"That ain't no way to greet me. Sometimes yer such a bitch. Did ya ever think somethin's wrong, and I might need a friend to lean on?"

"Oh, please, what could be wrong, Brenda? Did one of your little RRSPs go back home to her parents? Or did one of them die again, like Perry? Like you give a rat's ass what happens to any of us."

"Do ya hear the mouth on this one, Blue?" Brenda nodded at Blue, too high and zoned out on the iPad to care. "C'mon, Blue. Yer supposed to support me on this."

"Whatever, Brenda. Just tell her."

"Tell me what?"

"Ole Brenda here's been injured," Brenda said, pointing to her chest.

"Sounds tragic," I said. "What are you watching, Blue?"

Brenda threw an empty beer can at me. "Don't brush me off, ya little tart!"

I swatted the beer can away. "What do you want, Brenda? I'm tired. I've had a long day and need a shower."

She belched and pointed at my knees. "I can see your knees are raw, ya little slut. Suckin' off those boys at school? Whatta ya think we're runnin' here? A frickin' charity?"

"Get lost! Just because you can't walk three feet without the thought of dick or how you can extort money out of someone through their dick doesn't mean we're all like you."

"I'm gonna call Milos to fix yer bitchy yap! Blue, how can you let her talk to me like that?"

Blue stood up, walked into the kitchen, and came back with a glass of water. "Just say what you gotta say and then go home."

"Goddammit! I hurt my back, Chanie, so I can't do my cleanin' job no more. So do ya know what that means?"

I raised my eyebrows. "That we will finally hire cleaners who actually clean the building?"

"Ain't you a fuckin' comedian! It means I'm gonna have to stop bein' so nice to ya, and yer gonna be gettin' back on the streets for work. I've tolerated this school shit for too long."

"Get out of my house! I'm not hooking because you're too lazy and underqualified to find a job."

"Well, aren't you all high and mighty now that ya think yer educated. What do ya think yer qualified for? Yer nothin' but a street whore, and an emotional one at that. Ya won't be talking back after Milos knocks those little white teeth of yers out, so watch yer step. I gave ya an inch and ya took a mile — no, more like a thousand miles."

"Get out! I need to talk to Blue."

"Blue ain't gonna save ya. It's his idea."

I yanked the door open and swept my hand toward the hallway.

Blue nodded to Brenda. "You better go so I can talk to Chanie."

"Ya better make her understand, or I'll get Milos to do it!"

"I'll fuckin' talk to her, Brenda. Go home!"

Brenda walked up to me and pretended to swipe my face like a cat. I slammed the door behind her.

"What the hell, Blue?"

"Hang on, baby. I got something to show you." Blue scurried into the kitchen and came back with the Nelson can. He reached into the can and waved a wad of bills in my face.

"Holy eff! Where did that cash come from?"

"What do you mean, where did it come from? Where do you think?"

I turned my head sideways and squinted. "Did you rob someone?"

"Hey! Fuck you. I worked hard for this money. I thought you'd be happy."

"I am, baby. I'm just tired."

"That's not all, babe. Close your eyes and reach into the can."

I stuck my hand in the can and pulled out a rose gold charm bracelet. "Oh my God, Blue. It's so beautiful."

"Just like you," Blue said. "I worked overtime hours just for us, babe. I wanted to give you something that represented our love. Our bond. And to show you that I can't wait for us to move to Nelson and put all this shit behind us."

I stared at the bracelet, its sweet charms glimmering under the dim light. A tiny heart, a panda with blue rhinestone eyes, a hot pink daisy, and an assortment of rhinestone balls and speckled flowers.

Blue grabbed it from my hands and held up a dangling silver charm that said *YOU MELT MY HEART*. "This is the one that sold me on it, Chanie. I will always treat you like the goddess you are. My princess."

I held the charm between my fingertips and thought about how I'd rested too long when I'd fallen into Tuffy on the stairs. Self-sabotage. That was all I could come up with. Here I had a chance with a man who was out buying me a beautiful bracelet while I was out getting drunk and falling all over another guy in a burnt-up church.

I threw my arms around him. "Thank you, Blue. I love it. I love you! I cannot wait to enjoy our own backyard nestled away beneath the mountains!"

Blue set the can on the floor. "Yeah, baby. We gotta focus. We gotta find a way for you to get some cash too so we can blow this popsicle stand."

I looked at the floor. I hadn't given much thought to how I'd contribute to the coffee can. I needed to talk with Rie. I figured we could explore some options, like maybe I could get a waitressing gig at the Flying J as long as I maintained a high GPA. "I need to talk with my counsellor."

"See. The thing is, we got a problem."

"What problem?"

"Brenda and Milos. That stupid bitch has got it in her head that you owe her. And I guess in some ways you do. But anyways, she fucked up her back and can't do the cleaning here anymore, so her wages dropped. And nobody wants to pay for sex with the old whore, so she can't hook anymore."

"How is that my problem, Blue? She's still the building manager, so she's not homeless or anything like that."

"See, babe — that's what I told her, but she won't hear it. And then that Serbian monster, Milos, came over earlier to 'help her explain the message' to me. He'll beat the shit out of us if we don't play the game."

I clenched my teeth and said, "I can't work or I'll end up in jail. Then nobody, including Brenda and Milos, will get any cash from me."

"Chanie, you need to trust me. You're my girl, and I told Brenda that. I told her you can't get caught. So I kind of worked something out so you can stay in school, shut her up, and make us some escape money."

"Really? Sounds too good to be true."

"I told her she has to screen any clients past me before I'll let you service them. And they need to phone in or order you online because we can't risk one of your teachers seeing you out on the street. Plus, there's some psycho out there killing girls like Perry."

"How does that help?" A chill seeped into my marrow. *Perry's purple lips, her battered neck, the yellow tarp floating over her body on the pavement.*

"Two ways, baby face. First of all, I get to make sure the guy callin' for you ain't some piece of shit that's gonna mess you up or kill you, and secondly, we get escape money to put in the can. The more you earn, the sooner we can run away together."

Blue made it sound so simple, like a game show. It made sense, I guess. Safe tricks who call in or use a secret Facebook page to order me through Messenger. I wouldn't have to stand out on the street and risk getting caught. I hated being a whore, but it was the fastest way to buy us a new life. Waitressing would have been nice, but it was unlikely that the school would approve of me getting a job. Plus, I'd known many waitresses turned working girl because they couldn't pay their rent. Perry had been one of them. She'd told me that she made more money in her first four hours as a hooker than she'd ever made in two full weeks working at Shando's Pub.

I touched Blue's arm. "What about us?"

"What do you mean, baby? This is all about us. We make the money to get away and have a good life together. It's all for us, or I wouldn't let this happen to you."

"I mean — about our relationship — like us having sex?"

"Baby, I'm not one of those insecure boys you go to school with. I'm a man. I get that life's a bitch, and we gotta make sacrifices to get the things we want. I know when you're with those guys, it means nothing. It's just work, like me installing a floor. Means nothing at all."

"But I hate giving money to that bitch."

"I know. But it's kind of like we're pullin' one over on her. She thinks you're working because you owe her, but you're actually working to pay for us to run away to Nelson. Every dollar is one step closer to getting away from her. It's the fastest way. We could never get out of here if you had a minimum-wage job."

I knew I didn't have a choice. I'd never escape without having money to run. I had to do it. At least Blue would be there to look out for me. I looked at the bracelet on my wrist. "Okay, Blue. You're right. But I need to eat and get some sleep. Can we talk more tomorrow?"

"Of course, love. It will all work out. You'll see."

I turned the lights off but couldn't fall asleep. My emotions rustled about like cockroaches chewing at my brain: guilt, fear, shame. Had Mr. Lavoy sensed my suspicions of him? Did he know how far I'd have gone to stay out of jail? I knew only one currency, but he hadn't cashed it in. Instead, he'd helped me.

BLUE LEFT EARLY SATURDAY morning and came back with a TV. I didn't ask him where it came from because I didn't want to know. It was a welcome distraction. I'd never bothered with a television, even though cable came with the rent. We got caught up in a marathon of *CSI: Miami* that enthralled us into the wee hours of Sunday morning. I liked being absent from my mind. It kept the black clouds of my upcoming return to work at bay.

I spent the rest of the weekend getting drunk and watching football with Blue. Somehow, I became a Giants fan and found myself yelling at random football players. I decided that David Wilson should have signed with a better team, Eli Manning was the king, Victor Cruz could float, and Tom Brady was a douche-bag who reminded me of Jeremy, except Brady was rich, healthy, and had great skin.

Blue cooked up almost every treat the commercials taunted us with. He baked jalapeño poppers, stuffed potatoes slathered in sour cream, Tostitos with cheese, mini pizzas, Pillsbury cinnamon buns, and chocolate chip cookies. I went out to get chai lattes, coffee-flavoured Häagen-Dazs, and more bags of chips and Doritos. We were like two old fat guys who'd been hanging out for years. We didn't even blink when our phones beeped and buzzed, and when Brenda yelled outside our door, we didn't budge. Pure bliss! Food, sex, weed, and football all day long. I slept soundly and dreamt of Eli Manning playing ball with Dorito in the schoolyard.

Monday morning came too soon. The magic of the weekend became only a memory. The reality of whoring again unravelled me. I wanted to run away, but no money meant no escape. Plus, I could never leave Blue behind. I'd make it work for us. I'd work harder than ever before and follow a strict budget. No more fast food and takeout. I could get us out of the city if I stayed strong and focused. I'd save money, get good grades, and find a solid job in Nelson.

I met Ginger at the Mac's for coffee. She looked like a weekend rainstorm, grey and cold. She squinted through the dirty window and flipped her middle finger up, laughed, and then waved me to come into the store.

"Hi, bud," I said, quickly nodding at her and grabbing a cup.

"What the hell do you mean, 'Hi, bud'? I've been worried sick about you."

"I let you know I was okay."

"Yeah. And then you went fucking missing, Chanie. Eighteen text messages! Ignored! Like I'd sent them into the abyss. Makes me worry, you know, with Blue being the way he is."

"What's that supposed to mean?"

"Well, you know ... He comes home high sometimes. I'm just worried he's not stable. I've known a lot of good guys who do bad shit when they're on drugs."

"It's not like that."

"Then what's it like?"

"Let's meet for lunch and I'll tell you what's going on."

"Okay, Chanie. But it better be good."

We headed to school.

Mr. Lavoy walked toward me in the hall. I pretended to be texting and scurried into a classroom.

"Chanie!"

"Oh, hey, Mr. Lavoy. How's Dorito?"

"Dorito won't be doing overtime on writing assignments this week, so he's probably better than you."

I shrugged and nodded.

"I booked the computer lab for you today, so you can start your writing assignment right after your last class."

"I'll be there."

"So will I. And tell Tuffy to come and see me."

"As soon as I see him, Mr. Lavoy. See you in English."

I went down to the gym for our mandatory meditation practice. Someone handed me a glossy postcard with a picture of a pink lotus flower floating on black water with a couple of bright green leaves. It said, *May I live like the lotus, at ease in the muddy water.* I sat down, crossed my legs, and nodded at Annie Pema, the Buddhist nun. She came from the Shambhala Centre, which I thought sounded like a place where people danced in grass skirts on golden shag carpet until three in the morning. But as it turned out, it was just a big room in the basement of a clothing store on Jasper Avenue with a four-foot bronze Buddha statue at the front of the room and a bunch of cushions for people to sit on. No shag carpet, grass skirts, or dancing. A similar area had been set up in the gym for us and we just sat breathing in and breathing out with our eyes half closed and focused six feet in front of us.

Meditation drove me nuts for the first while. Having to sit for so long made my back hurt, and I always had to pee. The phrase *ants in your pants* likely came from somebody who was learning to meditate. Annie Pema told us that the way we react in our meditation practice is the same way we react to our lives and circumstances. The truth in that piece of wisdom pissed me off.

I STRUGGLED WITH THE different ideologies that were presented to us. Buddhists don't believe in God and say the Buddha exists within each of us. We're supposed to find the Buddha inside ourselves through the four noble truths, the eightfold path, renunciation, and meditation. This puzzled me, but I fully understood the first noble truth: Life is suffering.

Then there was Pastor Josh and the whole Jesus eye-in-the-sky thing. I figured I'd have to consider some other religions because, otherwise, I'd have to choose between a fat guy sitting under a tree or a bearded guy who looked like a pot-smoking landscaper. I liked them both but couldn't feel either one of them inside me.

Annie Pema made me squirm. She always smiled at me with knowing eyes, like she could see beneath my skin where all the men had been. At the end of our meditation practice, she always whispered, "Now just sit in your place of peace for a few minutes and then take that peace into your every moment today." Then she'd smile like she'd just smoked a pile of weed, stand up, and leave the room.

"Hey, Chanie," Jeremy said. "Do you wanna hear me read out the four noble truths?"

I glared at Jeremy. "If only you *could* read!"

"Okay, here it goes." Jeremy wiggled his eyebrows up and down. "Number one, life sucks dick, like Chanie. Two, Chanie sucks dick because she wants stuff, and three, if you want Chanie to stop sucking dick, she needs to stop wanting stuff. And lastly, there is *nothing* that can stop her from sucking dick."

Ginger leaned over and punched him in the shoulder. "Grow up, asshat! You're just pissed off because your grades suck and you're a dirty puke!"

"Hey, Chanie," Jeremy said. "Tell me the secret of your high grades."

I looked up at the ceiling. "I guess you have two options. If you ever want to graduate, learn to study or learn how to give a good blow job."

Ginger laughed. Jeremy laughed too but told me to go fuck myself and left the room with Tuffy.

Ginger looked at me, dreamy-eyed from meditation and Xanax. "Tell me why you love Blue so much."

I paused and looked at the floor. "I don't know how to explain it. Mr. Lavoy assigned me a piece of writing about how Blue makes me feel. Maybe you can read it when it's finished."

"Ooh, like *Fifty Shades of Blue*."

I shook my head. Ginger loved romance novels and often quoted lines from *Fifty Shades of Grey*, substituting Jeremy's name in convenient passages. She saved *Les Misérables* for our daily reading. She said, "That's assigned reading. When I'm sitting around at home with my dickhead landlord staring at me, I need to be beamed up to another place. *Fifty Shades* takes me there."

"Nothing like mommy porn to take you higher, Gin Gin. I'm supposed to write about how Blue moves me and makes me feel."

"Yeah! Up and down and side to side, doggy style. There it is! Your assignment in" — she counted on her fingers — "ten words."

"I'm sure Lavoy would love that."

Ginger got serious. "So, really. What *is* going on with him?"

"Nothing bad. He needs a fresh start too. He's had a hard life. We have a plan to save money and move to Nelson, B.C.

Get away from Brenda and Milos and leave my hooking career behind."

"And where the fuck am I gonna go? You can't just throw me away. I'm coming with you."

"That would be amazing, Gin Gin! You should come."

"Sign me up, Chanie!"

"We have to save money. Can you go back to the club you told me about, with the French pervert who made you lap dance when you were fifteen?"

"Oh, Vince!" Ginger pushed her boobs up. "I can talk to that ass and see if he'll let me come back. I'll definitely need *way* more Xanax. What if we get caught?"

"I haven't thought that far in advance. You just became a part of the plan about five seconds ago."

"Hmm. Maybe he can sell me as a private special and hide me in the back room until someone buys me?"

"Maybe."

"How are you going to earn your savings, Chanie? Maybe Vince will hire both of us? We can dye your hair red and pretend to be twins."

"Sure, except my boobs are three sizes smaller than yours."

Our escape plan seemed ludicrous yet possible. I felt alive, like hope was beginning to fill up my abandoned reserves. And while we stood together on the street puffing up our chests and cupping our boobs, I realized I could never leave town without her.

CHAPTER ELEVEN

IN EARLY SPRING, TUFFY sat cross-legged with an orange HB pencil angled in the centre of a blank page, like a fancy sports car taking up two parking spaces at the mall. He stared at the page, his eyebrows slightly raised, a smirk on the right side of his mouth.

I smiled, hoping to ease any anger he might feel toward me. "Hi, Tuffy. What are you working on?"

"I have to write an essay on what I'm doing here and what I hope to accomplish." He yawned and stretched hard, his arms behind his head, his T-shirt lifting slightly.

"That sounds terribly boring." I smiled and pretended to yawn.

"What are you writing about?"

"I'm writing about how my boyfriend makes me feel."

Tuffy uncrossed his legs and sat up straight. "Sounds lame to me. Happy writing."

Whenever I looked at Tuffy, things tangled up inside me like I was doing something wrong. It was all sweet and baby pink if I kept Blue locked out of my thoughts. But he always crashed through and made me feel like I wasn't worthy of love. If I were a decent, committed person, Tuffy wouldn't make random appearances in my daydreams. But he did. And I hated myself for it.

I struggled for five minutes trying to find the Microsoft Word icon. No way would I ask Tuffy for help. *Sounds lame to me.* His perfect face and bitchy tone. Maybe I should have told him I was sorry he got caught running from the church. That Lavoy had seen him, and that I didn't rat him out. Maybe as a peace offering, I could write his essay for him. I wished I didn't care whether he was mad at me or not. I didn't understand why I did.

I googled *how to find the Word icon* and spent fifteen minutes digging through opinions and commentary on Word until I found instructions to guide me. I typed *WORD* in the search bar, and a bright white page popped up, ready for my musings.

And then I just sat there.

At 4:30 p.m., Mr. Lavoy breezed into the room wearing gym shorts and a sweaty grey T-shirt. "Almost forgot about you two. How are you coming along with your projects?"

Tuffy ignored him and returned to what looked like doodling on his page.

"I have writer's block," I said.

"Oh my!" Mr. Lavoy raised his eyebrows. "That must be very challenging."

"It is. I can't think of anything to write."

"Maybe because the subject is unworthy," Tuffy mumbled.

"What do *you* know about Blue, Tuffy?"

"All I need to know."

Mr. Lavoy spoke over us. "Chanie, do you have your copy of *Les Misérables* with you?"

"I do." I pulled my tattered book from my bag.

"Read over some of the passages you've highlighted. The ones that inspire you. And then try again."

"And what if there's still nothing?"

"Then write the first sentence. And then the next sentence. And the next."

I nodded and opened *Les Misérables*.

Tuffy put his pencil down and looked at Mr. Lavoy. "Why does she get to write about her boyfriend, and I have to write about my goals?"

"I didn't tell her to write about her boyfriend. I told her to write about what moves her. For Chanie, it's her boyfriend."

"So, if there's something that moves me, can I write about that instead?"

"Absolutely, Tuffy. Let's go over to the room next door so I can show you the tricks I shared with Chanie. We can leave her in peace to work through her writer's block." Mr. Lavoy winked at me.

After they left the room, I sat quietly and closed my eyes, hoping for an opening line. I flipped through *Les Misérables* but couldn't draw a parallel between any of the highlights and Blue. I assumed the personal strain and torture of trying to be brilliant explained why writers and artists were chronically withdrawn and bitchy. I figured Victor Hugo had to have been a huge Grinch. I looked at the clock. I only had twenty minutes left to produce some words. *How does Blue make me feel?*

I thought about how he'd held me against him in the hallway when I'd come home from the hospital, beaten, bloody, and bandaged. I remembered falling asleep in his arms and dreaming of copper owls and monochrome trees. How he'd helped me bathe and picked me up from the police station. The way he'd arranged stolen garden flowers in a Big Gulp cup and left them at my bedside. His Gordon Ramsay imitations when he baked frozen foods. The night he threw Brenda's purse down the hall and then imitated her to make me laugh. My beautiful bracelet and our future in the mountains.

I typed the first words: *When I think of you ...*

I sent Ginger a text on my way home.

> Hey, Ginger. What the eff did you tell Tuffy about Blue?

Hey, bud!

> ?????????

I just told them what they should know.

> Them?

Chanie – don't be mad. Calling you now ...

I silenced my ringer. It always hurt so much more when women betrayed me. I'd worked with so many "best friends" who'd turned into instant enemies when it came down to the two of us and a dollar. Alliances didn't exist on the street when eight girls competed on a weekday winter night for the infrequent die-hard customer. Maybe it wasn't much different in the real world. We just competed for something else.

My phone vibrated again and again, buzzing like a bee in a Pepsi can.

"Jesus, Ginger!" I snapped.

"Chanie, don't be pissed. It's not like we were gossiping about you. We just got to talking the night we ran away from the church. We were all worried about where you'd gone, and the subject just kind of, well —"

"Who's *we*? You, Tuffy, and Jeremy?"

"Yes."

"What did you tell them?"

"I just told them what they needed to know."

"Needed to know?"

"Yeah! They *need to know* that you're living with an unpredictable meth head who's in bed with that crazy bitch pimp of yours."

"That's not true! He hates Brenda as much as I do. And he's only come home high a couple of times. We're working on it."

"Be that as it may, the only reason I told the guys about it is because we need to build a little army for you, because, one day, we'll have to come and save you."

"Save me? From what?"

"Come on, Chanie. There's never a positive ending when it comes to meth heads and pimps."

"I can't talk right now. I'm hanging up."

When I got home and opened my apartment door, something grey ran across the suite and tucked all but its skinny, ringed tail behind the dresser. I let out a quick scream. I looked at the door to make sure I had the right suite and hadn't opened the wrong door, like I had after a few too many housewarming drinks the night I'd moved in. It couldn't be a rat, but what else could it be? The building was a dump, but rats? I pushed the door open slightly with my phone's flashlight ready to capture a glimpse of the rodent. No movement, but a squeaky meow rang out. I laughed so hard he sucked the rest of his scruffy tail behind the dresser.

I walked over and kneeled close by. "What are you doing in here, little guy?" I took a picture of him and texted it to Ginger.

> Hey, Gin Gin ... I'm not mad at you. Look what was waiting for me when I got home!

> OMG!!! I'm so glad you aren't mad at me. I've been sick ever since we got off the phone. Had to eat two Xanax. I LOVE THE KITTY!!

I heard Blue trying to put his key in the door, but I rushed over to open it for him.

"Who's our new friend?" I said, beaming.

"I found him behind my construction site, baby. He's so tiny and helpless. I brought him home for you to love."

"Oh my God! I love him already."

The kitten crept out slowly. I leaned down and picked him up. His little ribs stuck out under dusty grey fur. A big white teardrop dripped down from the top of his nose and branched out into a blob-like moustache over his tiny cheeks. White whiskers splashed outward from his face. He grunted as though he were a fat gerbil while he waddled around the apartment. I think my heart grew three times bigger watching him try to get up on the bed.

"What should we name him?" Blue said.

"Hmm ... Nelson? For Nelson, B.C.?"

"Nah. Too big a name for a little shrimp."

I held the kitten up in front of me. His tiny body hung long and limp, like a sock. A white stripe streaked down his belly and expanded down his legs, pouring over his feet like bobby socks.

"His front legs look like those old-timey baseball socks," Blue said.

"Oh yeah!" I laughed. "Why don't we name him Socks? But let's spell it S-O-X."

"Sox it is, Chanie. He's your cat, so call him whatever you like."

"Does he have food and cat stuff?"

Blue shook his head. "Let's head out to the pet store."

"I'm short on cash."

"No worries, baby. I can pick up the tab for my girl and her kitty."

"Thanks, baby!" I set Sox on the floor and wrapped my arms around Blue. "I love you. Thank you so much."

We got to Dollarama ten minutes before it closed. We bought cat food, litter, dishes, and a bunch of toys. The cashier rolled her eyes when she saw the full basket. Blue drove us home singing along to Redlight King's remix of "Old Man." I looked forward to a great night at home with Blue and my new kitten. My text tone rang out, and the phone vibrated on the dash.

Blue stopped singing. "Who's texting you?"

"Ginger."

"What does she want? Does she need help with her homework?"

"No. She wants to meet Sox."

"Not tonight."

"You're tired from work?"

"Yeah, I'm tired from work and rescuing kittens."

We drove the rest of the way home in silence, my mind on the fuzzy little creature waiting at home.

When we got home, Blue lit candles in lanterns and made us Kraft Dinner Deluxe. I fed Sox and showed him his litter pan. He scratched around in the sand and peed. I kissed his tiny head and told him he was a good boy. I gave him a couple of toys, ate my dinner, and the three of us snuggled up under the blankets to watch *CSI*. Sox wriggled his way onto my chest and purred himself to sleep.

MY HEAD WAS STILL at home with Sox while I walked to school the next morning. Tuffy stood on the school stairs with Jeremy and Ginger, waiting for me to show up. Jeremy pointed at me and yelled, "Hey, Chanie. Why do you look so tired? Big dick night at your apartment again?"

"Yes, Jeremy! Notice how you weren't invited?"

"Didn't notice 'cuz I don't care, hooker. I don't have to pay for it."

"For a guy with a tiny dick and an empty wallet, you sure have a big mouth."

Jeremy smirked and flipped me the finger.

Tuffy walked along with me. "Are you doing detention today?"

"Sadly, yes. How's your essay coming along?"

"Better than your Harlequin romance."

"Whatever, Tuffy." I rolled my eyes. "See you later."

I enjoyed morning meditation class. Annie Pema started the class with a reading from *The Book of Awakening* by Mark

Nepo. It was a tall, narrow book with pastel colours and a pink lotus flower on the cover. I'd bought myself a used copy online because the cover was so pretty, and many of the messages resonated with me. Sometimes, I would contemplate Nepo's daily devotion during my practice, but more often, I'd use the time to think about other things, like Blue and now Sox.

Annie Pema came in and took her place at the front of the room. I closed my eyes and counted backwards from fifty, counting only on the exhales. I got to twenty-six and slipped away ... *I'm standing in a doorway at a roadside motel. The parking lot is bare. A shadow walks out of the sunset. I feel him before I can see him, and I can tell he's beautiful. My silky pink nightie falls to my feet, and he pulls me against him. I greet him with my mouth, his lips cold and fresh, like raspberries in the rain. His skin is like cinnamon, his hair black like coal. We are making love. Pale pink feathers fall from the periwinkle sky, and I am his. But suddenly, there's Blue! His eyes are red, and he's standing over us. He tosses a match and begins dancing in the flames.*

"Wakey-wakey," Ginger whispered, nudging my shoulder. I shook my head a couple of times. Tuffy looked over, but I looked away.

Annie Pema's gentle voice brought me into the moment. "Today, we are going to name our breath and use something I learned from Thich Nhat Hanh. Take a deep breath in and then name your breaths as follows: calming, smiling, present moment, perfect moment." She waved her hand back and forth like a maestro.

I followed along for about two breaths, but my brain veered off to the image of Blue dancing in the fire, as though warning me to keep a faithful mind. *Calming, smiling, present moment*

... I'd work even harder on my piece of writing for Blue to prove that my silly fantasies meant nothing. Motels and feathers falling from the sky. Really, it all seemed so crazy.

Later in the day, I asked Rie, "What does it mean when a person fantasizes about, say ... another life in their dreams?"

"What kind of life?"

"Maybe not so much a different life, more like being with a different person."

"Hmm. It could be a number of things, like abandonment issues, or the feeling that there's something missing in your current relationship."

"So, yeah, like abandonment issues. So the fantasy person could just be a symbol of my abandonment issues?"

"Yes. Or it could be —"

"That makes sense then!" I smiled. "Let's move on."

At lunchtime, Ginger and I sat at a picnic table sharing poutine, salad, and chocolate cake. I held *Les Misérables* in one hand and a forkful of fries in the other.

Ginger licked chocolate icing from her fingers. "Which of these dickheads would be Jean Valjean?" She scanned her finger over the crowd of students.

I laughed. "Mr. Lavoy."

"Not a teacher. A student. Maybe Jeremy?"

"Oh no! Definitely not. It'd be Tuffy. He's got a big chest and sturdy shoulders. He walks strong, like a soldier."

Ginger nodded. "What about Bishop Myriel?"

"Pastor Josh is the best candidate."

"Given the slim pickings here, you're probably right."

I took a piece of cake and shoved it into my mouth. "Back to the actual book, though, I think Fantine sounds beautiful."

Ginger popped a Xanax. "Yes, she does. Even her name —

Fantine. It's like a whisper. Like a Chanel commercial with some woman wearing golden sparkles and wings for a dress flying through the galaxy to meet her date. Some dark, sexy guy like Tuffy in a tux!"

"Wow, Gin Gin. Someday you'll write for the big screen."

"I'm not just looks, baby."

"Fantine seemed so innocent. Listen to this: 'But Fantine was a good girl … We'll only say that Fantine's was a first love, a unique love, a faithful love.'"

"Holy fuck, Chanie. That's deep. Doesn't it also say somewhere she was 'ravishing, perfumed and sparkling'?"

"Yeah, something like that. She sounds so flawless and innocent — in love with a total douchebag who messed her over. What a puke! Hugo said he wasn't even hot, just charismatic. Poor Fantine. She had bad taste in men. That's why she ended up being a hooker."

"See! You and Fantine have more than one thing in common."

I rolled my eyes and said, "I think I convinced Blue to let you come over next week sometime."

"Oh my God! I'd love that. I can't wait to meet Sox!"

"Sox is the best thing in the world," I said, scrunching up my nose. The thought of his cute face and rumble purrs always made me giggle.

At the end of the day, I rushed to the computer lab to finish my letter for Blue. I needed my writing to convince Blue of my truth, my commitment to us and our dreams of Nelson. That the fantasies that trespassed in my head meant nothing. I read it over and over, using the Word synonym finder to sweeten the message, to make it more evocative, like through my words I could touch his heart and change his life.

Tuffy came over to my desk just as I'd printed my letter. His eyes looked sad. Not high-school-drama sad, but forlorn, like he'd walked a million miles in a war only to find his family gone.

"Is it all finished, Chanie?"

"Yes. Are you coming over here to make fun of me again?"

"Nope. Just want to say good luck with the final product. Ginger showed me your kitten. He's cute."

"Thanks! Good luck to you too." I walked to the printer at the front of the room to get my paper for Blue. When I came back, Tuffy was gone.

On my way down the school stairs, Jeremy yelled out, "Hey, Chanie. Did ya hear? There's another dead whore. Strangled and dumped by a garbage bin. Maybe ya wanna rethink that career of yours, eh?"

I scowled at him but kept walking. I redirected my thoughts and pictured Blue reading my letter. I envisioned tears in his eyes, him gripping my hand, and then gently folding the page and tucking it away in his pocket before giving me a tender kiss.

Blue looked sombre when I came in. The Nelson can was on the floor, empty. Sox stalked the can and leaped in and out of it a couple of times.

"Hi, Blue. What are you guys up to?" Sox came over and rubbed against my leg. I bent down to pick him up. I hoped Blue would explain the empty can so I wouldn't have to ask.

Blue pointed to Sox. "Hangin' with the cat."

"I couldn't wait to get home to you guys tonight. I have a surprise for you. I've been working on something for you."

"That's nice. But we need to chat about a couple of things."

My heart dropped to the floor, and I slumped down cross-legged.

"What is it?"

"We got to figure out how you plan to match me dollar for dollar in this coffee can. I can't be the only one contributing."

I glanced at the can. *So, zero for zero?* "I know that, Blue. I thought we could figure some stuff out."

"We already did! We got a couple of problems here."

My heart fluttered. "What do you mean a couple of problems?"

"We got Brenda and Milos breathing down our necks here, and —"

"And what, Blue?"

"An empty fucking coffee can, Chanie!"

"Well, what do you suppose I do about that right now?" *And how did the can end up empty?*

"You're gonna have to work tonight."

"No. I have school tomorrow."

"Chanie, I took an extra job laying a floor this weekend even though I won't get a day off. My knees are sore, and my back hurts. But you know why I'm gonna do that?"

I raised my eyebrows. "Money?"

"Not just the money. I'm doing it for us. For you. The woman I love. So you gotta work hard to — to support me."

"I can't get kicked out of school, and there's only so many hours in the day, Blue."

"I get that. But you have to work too. Go get ready. I'll make you a hot dog for supper, and you can get out to work nice 'n early."

"A hot dog! Is *that* supposed to inspire me to go out and suck dick for cash?"

Blue laughed. "It's kind of symbolic, don't you think?"

I grabbed my bag and went into the bathroom. Sox followed me, so I made him a cat bed with the bath towel. I ran the shower and sat down with my back against the door. The evening should have been special. I'd had plans. Ideas that didn't include selling my ass on the street. I pulled out the note and blinked the tears out of my eyes.

My dearest Blue,

When I think of you, I get this smile. It's your smile because it only shows up like this when it's for you. Sure, I smile at birds and pets, friends, grey-haired couples walking hand in hand, but when it's for you it's all of me, not just a physical action but a spiritual and chemical move that makes me take a deeper breath and open my mouth very slightly, as if I were lightly moaning. My shoulders move up like a shy teenage girl who has been asked to dance for the very first time. It's more than sexual. It's God moving through me because nothing else ever feels this sweet — surreal, because in the real world, nothing moves through me like this feeling. Nothing moves me quite like you.

I love you, Blue.
Xoxo

I let out a couple of sobs before I tore the page to shreds and flushed it down the toilet. I held my head up and stepped into the shower. The old, familiar version of me gnawed at my stomach, not a welcome version of me but the hooker who'd lived the last few years either drunk or sleeping. Part of me had thought I would magically find a way out, like Julia Roberts did in *Pretty Woman*. Alcohol, Netflix, and avoidance had kept that illusion alive. Mr. Tanji did too, because sometimes he'd do date-like things with me.

I thought back to a particularly cold night in the winter when he'd picked me up and paid me just to hang out. He'd bought us large chai lattes and then took me to watch the airplanes land as giant snowflakes filled the sky and covered the car.

"Jade, what is your name?" Mr. Tanji had asked me.

"It's Jade." I giggled.

"Don't give me that nonsense. What is your actual name?"

"My name is Chanie."

"What a beautiful name, young lady."

My cheeks warmed, and I looked away. "Thank you, Mr. Tanji. Now what's your name?"

"Okay, Chanie. Hazrat Ali Abdullah, but you already know that because, apparently, you watch the news."

"I just like to hear you say it with your accent. You know, Mr. Tanji, I've never told anybody about us — I mean, that you're on city council."

"I believe you, sweet girl."

Sometimes, I wanted to have sex with him but without the money exchange. Just the two of us at a fancy hotel. I'd wear a silky white dress, and Mr. Tanji would wear a black tux. We'd slow dance on the Hotel Macdonald patio underneath a stormy sky, and when the first drop of rain fell, he'd sweep me upstairs to a majestic suite and make love to me in a sudsy hot tub with pink rose petals floating atop the bubbles. We'd drink champagne and talk about things that mattered.

But our reality didn't include champagne or ballgowns. He only bought me to strip for him or mess around with his friends. Other than the odd lap dance, we'd had no physical interaction.

"Chanie, what do you plan to do with your life one day?" Mr. Tanji asked, taking my hand and squeezing it gently.

"What do you mean?"

"Do you have any goals? Dreams? Did you ever dream of becoming something when you were a little girl?"

I'd turned away because I couldn't answer him. But I knew for certain, I'd never dreamt of becoming a hooker.

Blue pounded on the bathroom door.

"I need a few more minutes, Blue."

"Get out here and eat your wiener. I gotta be somewhere."

Blue always acted like he was on a time clock. Brenda too. They thought their time was precious, as though they were in a hurry to make a Doctors Without Borders flight. And yet I was the only one with schedules and deadlines. I wondered what kind of client had placed an order for me through Brenda's secret Facebook page. I hoped for Mr. Tanji. We could park at the airport and sip lattes. I could tell him about my Hotel Macdonald fantasy, and we'd laugh like old friends. When I came out of the bathroom, ready to go, Blue told me to leave my phone and head down to the truck.

"What do you want with my phone?" I asked, hoping it was all a trick, just a ruse to make me dress up so he could surprise me with a night of dinner and drinks. Then I'd feel awful about tearing up my love note. I'd have to ask him to stop at the school so I could print another copy.

"Because Brenda doesn't want you takin' calls from your old regulars behind her back. We gotta change your number."

"I need a phone. Especially at work!"

"Good point. But we gotta change the number tomorrow. Now let's go. I'm dropping you off downtown."

We didn't say much to each other during the drive. Blue

wore his dirty work clothes, but it wouldn't be the first time he'd underdressed for dinner. I held on to the hope he wouldn't make me go to work.

He pulled over underneath the China Gates. The working girls referred to the Harbin Gate as the China Gates. It was built in 1987 to symbolize the relationship between Edmonton and Harbin. It stood slightly east of 97th Street on 102nd Avenue, surrounded by government buildings, one of which was Canada Place, a pink glass building with a step-style build. One of the hookers told me it was designed to mimic the shape of a Canadian maple leaf. To the north of the gates were City Hall, the Court of Queen's Bench, the Remand Centre, and the downtown police station. And only slightly to the west, the arts district with the Winspear Centre, Citadel Theatre, and the Royal Alberta Museum. Underneath the gate were the hookers.

The elaborate Harbin Gate had been painted in traditional Chinese red with a customary pagoda rooftop adorned with handcrafted, yellow-glazed tiles. It had been a gift from Harbin, a sister city to Edmonton. It was meant to symbolize friendship and welcoming. On each side sat wide-chested, six-foot concrete lions, gazing down from a pedestal, one giant paw resting on a ball with their mouths wide open. I'd read in the paper that the lions were there to protect and bring good fortune, which, ironically, they must have done for me and many of the other working girls. It was rumoured that if you touched the tongue of the lion, it would bring you bravery and good luck. If you were in on this, it made total sense to see the odd hooker climbing up to stick her hands in the mouth of the lion.

Some of the girls weaved toward the truck like a bunch of slinky cats, but they turned away when they saw me.

"What are we doing here?" I said.

"What do you think? You're going to work, Jade."

Jade!

"This isn't the deal we had! It was supposed to be online only. I can't risk getting caught out here."

"By who? Your teachers? Or the guy who's killing hookers? He just knocked one off last night, so it's safe to be out tonight. There's no way he'll kill two nights in a row."

I almost puked. *Did ya hear? There's another dead whore. Maybe ya wanna rethink that career of yours, eh?* I reached for Blue's hand, pleading with him. "Please don't make me go out there."

Blue shook my hand away. "Chanie, this isn't easy for me either. It's better for both of us if you just get out of my truck and bring back some cash. Like around $250 to put in our can after Brenda's cut."

I got out and slammed the door. I walked over and leaned up against the building, legs nice and long, one foot against the wall. "Stand sexy-like," Brenda used to say. "Keep them shoulders back and push them little titties out." I pushed my chest out and arched my back. I reached into my bag to pull out my phone. My fingertips bumped the spine of *Les Misérables*. I pulled it out and held it to my chest.

"Cops!" A shrill voice rang out, echoing off the buildings.

I snapped to attention and lurched off the wall. Five girls scattered in different directions.

"Easy, ladies," the cop yelled. "Nobody's getting arrested. Just want to chat."

I'd seen that cop before. His army-short hair and massive NFL spiderweb-tattooed arms were hard to forget, especially when they'd been the ones that had unfolded the tarp over Perry's dead body. My heart pounded in my ears, and I couldn't swallow. I pictured myself in a cell with my hair chopped off and big black rings under my eyes. I wondered if Ginger would visit me. I considered running, but my instincts kept me still. I looked up at the stars and gently stroked the binding of *Les Misérables*.

"Listen up, ladies," the cop announced. "As you know, there are three working girls who've been murdered in the last few months. If you insist on being out here, be vigilant. My advice to you is to go home."

"Oh yeah! Good idea! I got some bakin' to catch up on for my big dinner party," said a blond girl with a huge ass. Some of the girls laughed.

"Very funny. This is serious. Every single guy who drives by is a suspect. You girls have been out here long enough to know that he's looked at each and every one of you. This sick fuck is probably already hunting one of you as his next prize. Don't be the next victim. Go home!" He handed each of us a card. "This is my personal cell number. Call me if you need to."

"Maybe you and them big spidey arms can come on over and keep me safe," the big-assed blonde said.

"Get some bear spray, sweetheart," he replied, nodding to all of us.

I knew a lot of dead girls. That was the cost of my profession. I'd tried to convince myself that Perry's boyfriend had killed her. It was easier to accept that than it was to believe that there was a psycho actively hunting us. I could put her death in a container and go about my business without fearing every man who approached me. It helped to ease the feeling in my gut that I was always just a second away from being strangled and left by a garbage bin.

I'd met the first of the three dead girls a few days before her murder. A trick had just dropped me off in an alley where she was screaming at a guy in an old Malibu. Turns out, he was her scrawny pimp harassing her for cash. Her real name was Jamie, but I named her You Do the Math.

"I don't know why it's so hard to make any cash tonight! *Look around!*" she'd screamed as she spun around a couple of times with her palms to the sky. "Hmm, ten girls, one car! You do the math!"

For the few hours I'd known her, we'd leaned on the wall under the China Gates and laughed at everything. Fun girl, sharp mind. It was a slow night, so we decided to tag-team a rig pig and split the earnings. We used our profits to order a pizza and ate it on the tailgate of a blue Chevy truck that was parked on the street. While we'd been waiting for a john that night, she told me she'd read somewhere that there's a piece of DNA left inside you from every man you've ever been with. Essentially, they transfer their energy into you. That made sense to me. If I'd been absorbing their depraved DNA, part of me was becoming like them. That must have been how it got easier for me to let men brutalize me for money. Four days later, Jamie was found dead on the opposite side of the same garbage bin as Perry.

"Hey, pumpkin pie. Ya need a ride?" a skinny old guy yelled, startling me. He looked like a professor or something.

"Sure, sexy."

"What's your name, sweet thing?"

I squeezed the book one more time before putting it back into my bag.

"You can call me Fantine."

CHAPTER TWELVE

EVERY CAR MIGHT BE the last car a hooker ever gets into, but BMWs, Audis, and Infinitis felt safer than beat-up pickup trucks and unmarked vans. Especially the vans with no back windows. The skinny old guy drove a light blue BMW coupe and looked feeble to me.

"What's on your menu, darling?" He winked and gripped my knee. "And just so you know, I'm a judge!"

"And just so *you know*, I'm a hooker."

"Ha ha! And a comedian."

"Where are we going?" I hated chit-chat. Men didn't hire my mouth for words.

"I got us a room at the East Glen Motel. Somewhere I can keep an eye on my car while we do business."

"What do you want?"

"That's not very good customer service, Phantom. Maybe I want a little sweet-talking."

"My name is Fantine. And talking costs more than other things, Your Honour."

"You're funny, so I won't kick you out. I just want a quick

blow job to get me hard, and then I'm going to fuck you doggy style."

I rolled my eyes. "Sounds delightful."

"Oh yeah! You have to call me Your Honour while I give it to you."

"Tell you what, big guy! I'll throw that in for free."

The motel room felt icy, probably a lot like His Honour's wife. I fidgeted with the thermostat. The judge cracked the curtains and positioned himself on the edge of the bed. He grabbed the TV remote and tuned it to what looked like a disco show from the seventies.

"That should work," he said, glancing at his car. "I can see my baby while you pleasure *my honour*." He grabbed his crotch, chuckled, and tossed a wad of bills on the floor.

I ignored him and kept working on the heat.

"Now strip those clothes off and spin around a bit so I can see what I paid for," he barked, as if delivering a verdict. I pictured him banging a gavel on the half-assed nightstand by the bed.

I stripped naked but kept my shoes on. The floor was gritty, and high heels made my ass look better anyway. His eyes got that overdrive glaze, and he pulled his limp dick from his dress pants. I tried to get him hard with my hands so it would be easier to slip a condom on him. I stroked and stroked, but my arm got sore, and I felt like punching him. I closed my eyes and called him *Your Honour, the Honourable Bad Boy, Biggy King, Biggy G,* and whatever other monikers he demanded. When he finally got hard enough, I slid the condom on, leaned over him, and opened my mouth.

I paused and closed my eyes. *I'm sorry, Blue. I love you, Blue.* I put my mouth on him, replaying those words as I moved up and down. *I'm sorry, Blue. I love you, Blue*, like a mantra naming the strokes instead of my breaths. I kept telling myself that I was doing the right thing. It was the only way to fast-track us to our new lives in Nelson. It wasn't Blue's fault I'd made bad life choices. I was grateful he'd seen anything in me at all.

When I turned around and raised my ass in the air for the Honourable Douchebag, I bit my lower lip so I wouldn't scream. He shouldn't be in my body. Only Blue should be. I loved Blue. I hated the Honourable Jerk Off, sweating and singing along to the Bee Gees, trying to keep himself hard enough to finish the job. I bowed my head. *I love you, Blue. I'm sorry, Blue.* Maybe Blue and I could agree I would only give blow jobs, but no penetration. That way *our* sex could remain sacred.

"Say it, bitch. *Say it!*" The judge slapped my ass.

"Jesus Christ!" I shrieked and jumped off the bed. "I can't keep babysitting that limp dick of yours from behind. It's too easy for the condom to slip!"

"Too bad, slut. What are you saying? I'm diseased?"

"I should have charged you more. I'm a hooker, not a sex therapist!"

He grabbed the lube and sprayed it all over me. "Then get on your back and spread your legs."

I closed my eyes, repulsed by his sweat dripping on my face and chest. When he finally blew his load, I wanted to high-five His Honour and punch him in the throat. I hopped off the bed and ran into the bathroom for a quick rinse, grabbing the cash from the floor on the way. The judge opened the bathroom door and told me to get the fuck out of his room.

"Can you drop me off downtown?" I hoped he'd agree so I wouldn't have to spend any of my earnings on a cab.

"If you weren't such a harsh little bitch, I might have considered it. Maybe next time, you'll show a little more respect."

"Maybe if your dick was as big as your ego, I would!"

I slammed the motel door and spat on his windshield. I could get a trick on 118th Avenue, but it was a rough strip, and the regular girls would beat me half to death if they caught me on their turf. I'd been ripped off and beaten in that neighbourhood when I was a rookie. I'd learned my lesson. I flagged a cab, which meant I'd have to work longer unless I could blow the cabbie in exchange for the fare. I chose to pay him.

I made $400 by midnight. The judge had paid me $200, and then I screwed a realtor who insisted on wearing a tacky mustard blazer that reeked of curry. He gave me $200 and got me drunk on a bottle of Baileys that "just happened" to be on the floor of his car.

I got to keep sixty percent of my earnings. The other forty went to Brenda and Milos. If I didn't know what to charge, I'd call or text Brenda, and she'd make a "business decision" on my behalf. She charged an extra $25 for "business consultin'." I had the option of not using condoms for blow jobs and penetration. I could charge a premium for "bareback," but as suicidal as I often felt, I didn't want to die of a sexually transmitted disease. On occasion, when I was forced, tricked, or raped, I'd been penetrated without protection. I usually went to the clinic to get tested every three or four months — if I remembered.

Milos circled around the Harbin Gate like a piranha. He shook his finger when he saw me texting. I quickly slipped my phone in my bag so he wouldn't snatch it from me. He circled around a few more times before he pulled over.

"How much are you at, Jade?"

"My gross earnings are $400, so my net will be $240." I smirked, not mentioning the shortage for cab fare.

"Very funny, smart-ass. Shut the fuck up and give me $200."

"You only get $160 right now. Your share isn't at $200 yet, Milos."

"Get the fuck in car and suck my dick. You owe me. Remember nice man who trained you?"

"Don't remind me! Go pay someone for your blow job. The only dick I suck for free is Blue's."

A black Camaro pulled up behind Milos.

"Gotta go!" I winked and walked to the car.

"Where we off to?" I asked the driver, a twenty-something surfer-looking guy.

"I wanna get a slush first," he said, punching the accelerator.

"Okay. Is this your first time?"

"Yep!" He yanked the wheel hard, almost missing the turn into the Mac's.

"Okay, get me a slush too. And when you come out, I'll explain your options for spending time with me."

He nodded and pulled the keys from the ignition.

I thought I'd puke if I had to stick anything else in my mouth, but I managed to give him a blow job before he kicked me out of the car. He paid $120 but told me he would only pay if I let him finger me too. I needed sleep and had a case study due in the morning, so I closed my eyes and spread my legs.

It was close to 2:00 a.m. by the time I had $500 cash on me. I sat on the curb waiting for Blue to pick me up. I'd get him to give Milos and Brenda their cut. For a moment, I considered telling them I'd made $400 — pocket a quick dollar to expedite my escape plan — but Milos made us believe he possessed

supernatural accounting powers that he called "accounter powers." He'd say things like, "I have nose of bloodhound — smell
scams — slap it out of you."

Three years back, I'd worked with a girl named Misha. She'd
said, "There's no fuckin' way that fat moron knows what I
make," and tucked some bills in her bra. A few days later, Milos
beat her up on the street in front of six other working girls.
We never saw her again.

I went to sit below a streetlight and pulled out *Les Misérables*. I figured reconnecting with Jean Valjean and Cosette might
erase some of the sludge from the men I'd been with. I flipped
it open, and a folded piece of paper fell out. I opened the page
and squinted to read the words under the dim light.

> Chanie,
>
> I shouldn't like the smell of forest fires because they
> are deadly and destructive, but it seems to me that I
> like dangerous things. It's like the smoke wakes me
> up, makes me appreciate clear skies and the rain a
> little bit more. It reminds me that when we think
> we've hit our lowest low, we can go much lower.
> Fires bring horrific destruction, but they also bring
> renewal and transformation. Because, either way,
> things will never be like they were before. And that,
> sometimes, is a blessing. Maybe that's what we
> need — total destruction, because without it we
> would never renew ourselves. And only after all the
> pain and devastation, beauty somehow arises and
> new life blooms. Chanie, you need a forest fire ...
>
> Tuffy

I read it three times. It didn't resonate with me the first two times because I thought I might have been hallucinating, or that Tuffy and Jeremy were playing a joke on me. But the message seeped into my chest, and for some reason, I started weeping. I kissed the note and tucked it tightly between the pages where Jean Valjean would keep it safe. I stood up when Blue's truck rolled into the far end of the parking lot. I waved to him, grateful to finally go home. He punched the accelerator and sped toward me. I jumped out of the way. He laughed. I didn't.

"Hi, Blue." I leaned toward him.

"Get your filthy mouth away from me, girl. You need to clean up as soon as we get home. Don't touch anything — not even that shitty kitten."

"Nice greeting." I felt like he'd punched me in the chest.

"Come on! Would you want to kiss me if I'd been out licking strange pussy all night?"

"I wouldn't force you to go out and do that. This was your idea."

"You better control your little cocksucking mouth, Chanie. This is *our* idea. I'm the one helpin' you get away from Brenda and Milos, not the other way around."

I wiped away a tear and nodded.

"Well?"

"Well what, Blue?"

"You want to run away, don't you? Put this shit behind us?"

"Of course I do. Do you think I like it out here?"

"Sometimes I wonder."

I bit my bottom lip to keep my mouth shut. I didn't want to fight.

Blue reached over and grabbed my arm. "Where the fuck is your bracelet?"

"Blue! You're hurting me. Let go!" I yanked my arm away. "It's in my purse. I didn't want to lose it."

Blue let go of my arm and shook his head. "Babe, I'm so sorry. I don't know why I flipped out. I think I'm just having such a hard time with you being out here with these guys touchin' my girl! Makes me stupid!"

"It's hard, Blue. Maybe we can find another way."

"God, I wish we could, babe. But you know we need this, Chanie. *You* need this!"

"You know what I need, Blue?"

"What?"

"I need a forest fire."

Blue squinted. "What the fuck is that supposed to mean?"

"Nothing."

"Nothing is right! Sounds like crazy talk!" Blue shook his head and put out his hand. "Where's the cash?"

I handed him all my earnings and reached back into my purse. I stroked the cover of *Les Misérables* and traced my finger over the edge of Tuffy's note.

Blue dropped me off in the turnaround in front of our building and sped off, claiming he had to go meet an old buddy of his. I went upstairs and scrubbed my body with raspy bath gloves and brushed my teeth until my gums bled. I rinsed and gargled five times with Scope, but the feel and taste of those nasty tricks lingered. Blue was right. I shouldn't have tried to touch him after a night of whoring. But I'd missed him. I'd needed to touch him to bring us back to each other, to reconnect. Being with other men made me sick, but I'd had an auto-pilot switch built into me long ago. I could leave my mind and body, detach from reality, and go through the motions. Some guys sensed my absence and roughed me up to get their desired response. Most of the time I didn't care, as long as they didn't try to kill me.

The next morning, I was late to meet Ginger at the Mac's.

"What the fuck happened to you, Chanie? I need a couple bucks so we can share a muffin. I'm starving."

"I have no cash today."

"Did you get all your homework done?"

My guts twisted. "Nope."

"What do you mean?"

"I didn't get it done. I only got three hours of sleep."

"Did that fuckface come home high again? He can't keep doing this to you or you'll flunk out!"

"What the hell do you think I was doing all night? I had to go out to work. I have to earn dollar for dollar to make our plan happen."

"Oh my God." Ginger rolled her eyes. "You don't buy into that shit, do you?"

"It's not shit! Where's my share of the money supposed to come from? Jesus?"

"He's taking advantage of you. If he loved you, he wouldn't dare let another man touch you. He should be a man and save up the money for both of you while you get through this program. If you fuck up, you go to jail."

"I know that! They promised me it would be online clients only, but he made me go out last night because he said they were having issues setting up the online page."

"How do you believe this crap? There's some fucking psycho out there strangling hookers, and that *fuck* is sending you out to work!"

"Please stop bitching at me. I'm not happy about it either, but what the hell am I supposed to do?"

"We need to find you a modern-day Jean Valjean! Save you from the gutters."

"Speaking of modern-day Jean Valjean, Tuffy wrote me a letter."

Ginger nodded. "Yeah, I know. He asked me to read it over the night before he gave it to you."

"You knew?

"Yeah. And I agree with him."

"What does it all mean?"

"What do *you* think it means?"

I FORGOT ABOUT MY appointment with Rie later that day, but she tracked me down in Mr. Lavoy's room.

"Did you forget about our meeting today, Chanie?"

"The one about my dad's suicide?"

"Yes, honey. Come with me."

We always began our sessions with meaningless chit-chat, but I liked that she showed interest in my life. I loved those moments. They felt as though I were hanging out in the living room of a good mom. Like the kind of place you'd come home to over the holidays to rest and eat all of your favourite home-cooked meals.

"How's things, Chanie?"

"Things are good," I said. "I'm still reading *Les Misérables*."

"I loved that book." Rie clapped her hands together.

"I love Jean Valjean. He's my dream man. He could be my dad, or" — I raised my eyebrows — "in a different fantasy, my boyfriend."

Rie laughed. "He's a fine man, indeed."

We smiled and nodded at each other.

"Speaking of dads … I'd like to talk about your dad. We've

been putting it off for a while now, and I think it's integral to your healing."

I thought about saying I had somewhere to be, but Rie could outmanoeuvre my bullshit like a slalom skier. I took a long pause and chewed my lower lip.

"Sometimes …"

Rie waited for what seemed like forever. "Sometimes what, Chanie?" she said in a gentle voice, her expertise finely tuned to the rumbling tsunami inside me.

"Sometimes, I think it's better to let sleeping dogs lie." I tried not to cry, but tears welled up in my eyes.

"Of course it's hard to talk about, Chanie. Your father's death is very tragic, and you weren't supported through your grief."

"Oh my God, not at all! My mother didn't even feel sad. She said we were better off without that loser and to pull up my socks and move on."

"That's awful. You and your father deserved more respect. Was there a funeral service for your dad?"

"Yes." I lowered my head. Rie handed me a box of Kleenex.

"Were you able to honour him at the service?"

"What do you mean?"

"Do you feel your father had a proper tribute? A nice eulogy, perhaps?"

"Nope! No eulogy. My mom didn't arrange for one. The pastor gave a generic speech about life and death. Some of his friends got up and told drinking stories."

"That's too bad. Is there a burial site where you can go?"

"My mom cremated him and told me she tossed his ashes out on the highway."

"Oh my God! By any chance was that your father's request?"

"What do you think?"

We took a break and carried our silence downstairs to the basement kitchen. Rie made a peppermint tea for me and chatted briefly with the cook. We walked back upstairs to her office, hot mugs in our hands, morbid silence still hanging over us.

"I totally understand if you want to leave our session here for today, Chanie. But I think we should talk about some ways we can help you process your grief."

"How?"

"The first thing we have to remember when someone takes their life is that they are suffering. The person is sick, and nobody is to blame. Do you understand that your dad was unwell?"

I knew my dad had suffered. His brother Danny had committed suicide two years before my dad shot himself. Danny had driven his van to a provincial park, cut the seatbelt out, and hung himself from a tree. The park warden found him a day later. My dad never got over it. He said he couldn't believe how desperate his bastard brother was to die. That if he would have been as determined to make a life for himself as he was to kill himself, he could have been anything he wanted to be. Then he made a weird comment about whether the seatbelt needed replacing before they could sell the van.

At first, I'd assumed that Danny had died in a car crash because my parents wouldn't tell me how he'd died. I didn't really understand my dad's comment about the van and the seatbelt until the neighbour kids, who'd overheard my drunk dad crying to their mom in their garage, filled me in on the gross details. I remember I'd called them a bunch of sicko liars and then ran as hard as I could all the way home because I had to ask my dad if it was true. But when I walked into the house, my dad was staring out the window as though looking for his brother on the other side of the veil. I never spoke of it again.

"Chanie?" Rie steered my thoughts back to the moment.

"Yes, I know he suffered. His brother also killed himself."

"Oh, dear. Your poor dad. That probably made things much harder for him."

"For sure it did. And that bitch mother of mine just made it worse. She always yelled at him. Told him he was just as big of a loser as his brother. She didn't care about anybody but herself. She'd been too busy fussing over her new breast implants to notice him fading away right before her eyes."

"Your mom sounds like she has her own issues."

"To say the least. She made my dad take out a mortgage on the house so she could get her tits done and buy a new wardrobe. She could hardly wait for the bandages to come off before heading to the bar to show off her new boobs in her skanky clothes."

"How do you feel about your father?"

"Sometimes ..." I didn't want to say it, even though I'd thought it many times. I closed my eyes, took a deep breath, and tried to determine if I really felt it.

"Take your time, Chanie."

I opened my eyes. "Sometimes, I hate him!"

"Do you hate him because he left you?"

"I hate him because he left me to Clayton."

"Clayton is your mom's boyfriend, right?"

"Yes! And he's the reason I'm a whore."

"Chanie, you are not a whore. You have a past, but more importantly, a future. You are a student working toward your future."

"Oh my God, Rie! I can't be fixed. I'm too far gone."

Rie pressed her lips together. "It may seem that way. But we'll start small."

"What do you mean, small?"

"We find things for you to hold onto. Simple things, like the smell of rain. The sun setting over a canola field."

"That sounds like a dating site ad."

Rie laughed. "Maybe. But the simplest things in life are pure and consistent. Like the sun, the rain, winter, spring. These are things you can enjoy and you can count on. Nobody can take those things away, and nobody can control them. They can help you build a library of safe places and favourite things to fall back on."

"So you're saying we can build a list of things to keep me from falling through the huge cracks my shit life has caused?"

"Yes. When someone has suffered loss and trauma, small but steady things help to build a foundation, get their feet back underneath them. We support them through acceptance, opportunities, and support. And these good things will begin to grow bigger than the bad things. And you will be able to stand on your own."

"That's how I got into hooking. I was told I'd be a strong, independent woman."

"You are, Chanie. But you need some self-love and self-confidence to make healthier choices."

"Simple things, you say?"

"Yes. Can you think of something you like?"

I chewed my bottom lip and looked out the window. "I like cats, but I think I need to stop for today."

I started crying when I realized I hadn't felt the sun or smelled the rain in years, though it had always been there. I cried for my dad, my grandma, for a mom I wished I'd had. My dad's suicide, my rapes, Brenda, Blue, and all the unruly ghosts prattling in my head. I didn't want to face those ghosts, but I knew they'd eventually confront me. I wanted to be free of all my memories. I wanted to run away to where those ghouls could never find me. A change of surroundings, a new life, new goals. A new beginning where I would no longer see the ghosts of dead hookers waving to me from lonely booths in all-night diners.

"Okay. Let's just finish our tea for now and talk about what you're going to do tonight when you get home. Let's make sure we see each other tomorrow afternoon. But if things get bad through the night, call the crisis line, but tell them to page me. This is very traumatic for you, and we're here to get you to the other side."

I nodded but couldn't speak over the lump in my throat.

"Chanie, I'll say it again. We are here for you, and you're not going to have to work through this alone."

I nodded again.

"Tell me you understand, Chanie."

"I won't have to work through this alone."

"And?"

"And I'll text or call you or Pastor Josh if I have a meltdown tonight."

"We are here for you, Chanie."

If they knew I whored myself out at night, would they still be there for me?

I left Rie's office and sat outside on the steps. I was so tired, the type of tired triggered only by traumatic death and complicated grief. I called it the *death clutch*. I'd felt that death clutch on the night of my dad's funeral. It had felt like concrete in my torso and chains around my wrists. I guess our bodies never forget pain like that. It's like it engraves itself into our sinew and bone marrow and digs trenches of sorrow into the soft spots of our bodies.

I gathered myself and walked over to the Mac's to meet Ginger. We'd made plans to hang out after school. I had no idea what we were doing, but as long as it didn't involve Blue, Brenda, Milos, or blow jobs, I was in.

"Hey, Sister Act," Ginger said. "Let's load up on some caffeine before we start this adventure."

"Definitely!"

"You look like shit. Do you want to talk about it?"

"No. Tough chat with Rie today. My dad came up."

"Oh, that's shitty." Ginger wrapped her arm around my shoulder. "Change of plans! Let's go get some hair colour and dye your hair red! We'll do it at my place."

"Do I have to take off my pants?" I laughed.

"Not tonight, Chanie."

CHAPTER THIRTEEN

GINGER SHRIEKED AND DROPPED the blow-dryer. It clipped me above the ear as it fell to the floor. I screamed too, though I wasn't sure why. But then I saw him! Pete the Diddler skulking in the hallway, his chest heaving from too many years of beer and pizza. He looked like he smelled: fat, swollen, and sweaty. Big salty circles glowed beneath the underarms of his faded black T-shirt. His teeth looked like rotten macaroni, and his bloodshot eyes were deep-set beneath his long forehead. Purple blotches dappled his puffy cheeks, and he kind of panted while he stared at us.

"Holy eff, Pete! You scared me. I thought you wouldn't be home for a few more days," Ginger said.

"It's my fuckin' house, girl. Who's yer little friend?"

"This is Chanie."

"Well, you girls know the rules around here."

I laughed at him. "What rules are those?"

"No panties, girl! Drop your pants. Let's see what ya got under there." He pointed at my crotch.

I laughed harder. Ginger began undoing the button on her jeans.

"Ginger, what the hell are you doing?"

"Well, it's kind of our agreement." She looked away.

"You heard her! Get them pants down." He clapped his hands and pointed at my crotch again.

I smiled wide and said, "You can't afford me, buddy."

"I don't have to afford ya! Yer in my house!"

I started gathering my things. "Listen up, Petey. Maybe your cheap ass would be better off investing in a laptop. Plenty of free porn on the Internet."

"Get out of my house, ya little bitch!" Petey pointed in Ginger's face. "And you! Get in the bedroom."

I grabbed Ginger's arm. "Ginger, come with me."

She gently pulled away. "Yeah. Just wait a couple minutes. I need to talk to Pete for a second."

I pointed at Petey the same way he'd stuck his finger in Ginger's face. "Petey! You better take some deep breaths. Your face is purple. Lucky for your heart we didn't take off our pants. You'd be dead on a stretcher by now." I slapped my knee, threw my head back, and laughed.

I went into the bathroom to check out my new hair. I squeezed my eyes shut, snapped on the light, and eased my eyes open to check out my new look. Bright copper streaks gleamed like sunflowers flashing their faces to the sun. I heard Ginger saying, "Yes, Pete. No, Pete. Okay, Pete." She came out of the bedroom and joined me at the mirror.

I ran my fingers through my hair, holding up coppery strands beneath the light. "I love it! It's amazing. I don't even look like me anymore."

She nodded. "That's the point. A new look for a new life! Maybe you won't mind looking at the new version of yourself in the mirror."

"Good plan, Gin Gin. Every time I see it, it'll remind me that this is all temporary. You, me, Sox, and Blue are getting out of here."

"Get out!" Pete yelled from the kitchen.

Ginger grabbed my hand. "Let's get the fuck out of here."

"Nice to meet you, Petey!" I slapped him on the shoulder on my way to the door.

"Fuck off, you grinchy slut. You ain't welcome here no more."

"Hmm, I bet if I take off my pants, you'd roll out the red carpet for me, perv, I mean, Pete."

Ginger slammed the door and pointed me toward the elevator.

"What a pig," I said. "I thought my job sucked but walking around showing Petey-D my pink parts isn't up my alley either."

"Oh, he's so gross. But he doesn't beat me up, and he doesn't make me give him blow jobs or have sex."

"Oh, right! Cuz Petey-D's a limp-dicked gentleman. What were you doing in the bedroom? I hope you didn't apologize for me."

"Nope. Just promised to be more grateful in the future."

"I'm so sorry." My eyes stung with tears.

Ginger brushed a strand of hair off my face. "Why are you sorry, Chanie?"

"I'm sorry we were born as women in a world full of Petey-Ds."

We decided to ride around on the bus for a while to kill time. We were unusually quiet. I thought about my dad; Ginger stared out the window. Her phone rang four times in a row. She reached into her purse, pulled out a pill bottle, ate two Xanax, and returned her gaze to the window. Her phone chimed a few more times.

"Oh, right!" Ginger laughed. "I meant to check my phone."

"Oh my God, Ginger! How many Xanax have you eaten today?"

"I think three ... or six. I don't know." She winked at me, read her messages, and rolled her eyes.

"What's up, Ginger?"

"I need a miracle."

"Did Petey-D kick you out?"

"No. But Vince, the dick, told me if I can't work the floor like the rest of the girls, he has no place for me at the strip club."

I put my arm around her. "Don't worry, buddy. We'll figure something out. I won't leave you here." I stared at my bronze hair in the reflection of the bus window. "Maybe I can find a way to save enough money for both of us."

Ginger forced a meek smile. "Yeah, smarty-pants? With my boobs and your brains, we can take over the world."

"*And* keep our pants on."

"Maybe not yet!" Ginger smiled, but her face fell as soon as she looked away.

I got home just after eleven. Blue was outside smoking on the balcony. Sox was playing with spots of dirt on the patio door. I waved hello and went into the kitchen. A pot of leftover Kraft Dinner sat on the stove, still warm.

"Where the fuck have you been?" Blue said, slamming his pack of cigarettes on the counter. "And what did you do to your hair?"

"I texted you like ten times, Blue."

"Well, I didn't get any messages." He rolled his eyes. "You know what, Chanie, I feel like I'm the only adult in this relationship."

I picked Sox off the floor and kissed his face. "What's that supposed to mean?"

"It means, I can't be the only one going to work around here."

"I already worked and matched your contribution. Plus, I had to lie about why my homework wasn't finished."

"I don't care about your homework. What I *do* care about is the cash we need to get out of here."

"Rie showed us a budgeting template we can use to help us —"

"I — we — don't need a budget, Chanie! We *need* money."

I sat on the bed with Sox. He purred and rubbed his face against my hand. I smiled and wrapped my hand around his skinny torso. He jumped into my backpack when I took my books out. If Blue would go out, Sox and I could have some study time. I'd go to bed by one and still get six hours of sleep.

"What do you think you're doing?" Blue said, pointing at my books.

"I need to get my homework done, and it's close to midnight."

Brenda pounded on the door.

I raised my hands in the air. "I can't deal with Brenda tonight. Please don't answer the door."

Blue ignored me and opened the door to Brenda and Milos. The rancid smell of alcohol wafted in. They looked and smelled like too much rum. Brenda's dried-up skin, dark rouge, and cracked lips screamed *old hooker!* Milos giggled like a ten-year-old who'd raided his dad's liquor cabinet. His rosebud cheeks and starry eyes were deceiving. Behind that fat, boyish face lived a monster waiting for a reason to hurt me.

"Well, looky here. If it ain't Good Will Huntin'," Brenda slurred, slapping me on the arm, swinging a knock-off black patent leather Dolce & Gabbana bag for me to see.

I knew I'd paid for that bag but wouldn't give her the satisfaction of commenting. I looked down at my books.

"Guess who called tonight, Jade?" Brenda plopped down next to me.

"Get lost, Brenda."

"Get up and get dressed fancy, girl," Milos said. "You go to work."

I fantasized about getting the cops to throw Brenda and Milos out of my apartment. They didn't have the right to be there. Pastor Josh had told me so in Life Skills. He'd said, "If you are the leaseholder, you have the legal right to remove unwanted guests from the premises. But the key is to be firm and polite. Repeat the message if you must, but don't lose control, no matter what you do. You will lose credibility. Just be strong and look them in the eye."

"Please leave," I said, keeping my eyes on my books. Sox tucked himself behind the dresser, the tip of his tail the only evidence of his presence.

"Milos, did you hear somethin'?" Brenda said, cupping her ear and looking confused. She slowly dragged her fingers down a long, dangly golden earring, something else I was sure I'd paid for.

"All I hear was whining. Like a baby," Milos replied.

Just be strong and look them in the eye. I took a deep breath and looked at Brenda. "Please leave."

"What did ya say to me?" she snarled. "Did ya hear her, Milos? You'd be fuckin' homeless if it weren't for me, girl. Dead in a ditch somewhere a long time ago!"

Don't lose control, no matter what …

I inhaled, looked her in the eye, and repeated myself. "Please leave."

I hit the floor face first. Milos's meaty hand clamped the back of my neck. *Don't move. Don't cry.* I'd experienced the perverse pleasure Milos got when girls fought back and Brenda's vicious mouth the second she saw tears. I wouldn't give it to them. I'd be still. I waited until he released me and then, as calmly as I could fake, I stood up and picked up my books and pencils. I tried to stifle my tears, but I couldn't. I hurt inside and out.

Milos laughed. "See, I told you I heard a baby."

Brenda leaned toward me and squeezed the back of my neck. "You'll be goin' to see some clients tonight, ya little whore. Fuck your books 'n pencils 'n shit." She kicked *Les Misérables* across the floor. Tuffy's note peeked out at me from between the flared pages.

Blue stood by the door, calm like a bouncer at a bar. I looked to see if he'd spotted the note, but all he did was look at Brenda and smirk.

"What are you smiling about, Blue?" I snapped, trying to divert everyone's attention from the splayed book on the floor. What had happened to his promise to always protect me?

"I'm smiling at you, Chanie." He winked at Brenda.

You're living with an unpredictable meth head who's in bed with that crazy bitch pimp of yours ...

Milos pointed to the bathroom. "Get makeup on and we get going. Blue's taking us for dinner, but you work."

Brenda stuck her fingers in my hair. "I see ya dyed yer hair to look a little more like ole Brenda here. Nice try!"

"In what world would I want to try to imitate a piss stain like you?" The words blew from my mouth like a tornado. Milos's slap stung like a lightning strike, and I tumbled to the floor. I jumped back to my feet, walked over, and picked up my battered copy of *Les Misérables*. I closed Tuffy's note inside, held the book to my chest, and carried it into the bathroom. I left Sox behind the dresser because if I showed my fear for him, I knew they'd hurt him. Sox had to go. He'd never be safe in my home.

I made $360 that night and gave Blue $215, one dollar short of my sixty-percent cut of $216. Milos picked me up around three. He drove me out of the city to a dirt road with nothing but a deserted pumpjack. When he unzipped his pants and shoved my head into his lap, I took his half-hard dick in my mouth so he wouldn't beat me half to death and abandon me on a lease road. I don't know who I hated more, Milos or myself.

I rode up the elevator holding *Les Misérables* against my heart. My apartment reeked of cigarettes and old beer. Blue wasn't home. I didn't care. I coaxed Sox out from behind the dresser and sat next to him while he ate. He followed me into the living room, and we curled up on the floor next to my textbooks. Sox rumbled in the crook of my arm while I considered killing myself. All the hope and promise tucked between the pages of my textbooks couldn't help me. Not if I continued spending my nights in motel rooms and the back seats of cars.

"WAKEY, WAKEY, DOLL. CAN'T miss school or you'll go to jail," Blue said, hyperalert from all the blow he'd snorted with Brenda and Milos. "I'll drive you this morning."

"Hey, Blue," I whispered, my throat tight and sore.

"What do you need?"

I need you to honour the deal we made! I need you to protect me!

"What is it, Chanie?"

"Why did you just stand there while Milos slapped me around? You're supposed to protect me."

"Baby, I know. It was so hard for me to just stand there, but what could I do?"

"You could have stopped him!"

'If I would have jumped in, he would have got even crazier. I stayed calm to keep things under control."

"How did that help me?"

"If I'd have tried to stop him, he would have beat the hell out of you just to prove his point. You know that!"

"Well, can you at least tell him no more free blow jobs?"

"Yeah. I'm gonna go start the truck."

Two hours later, I struggled to come up with more lies for Rie and Pastor Josh. Maybe they'd believe a stomach bug had kept me up all night? Or a panic attack woke me at two in the morning and I couldn't get back to sleep? I could blame my anxiety for all my recent failings. It would provide a perfect mask.

"This is the second time you haven't done your homework this week, Chanie. And you don't look well." Pastor Josh leaned toward me, his brows creased as though trying to look deep into my brain.

"I've been struggling more than usual," I said.

"You've shown a lot of promise in a short time. You're about halfway through the program. Your grades are high, and Mr. Lavoy tells us that you have a gift for creative writing."

"Good to know." I glanced out the window.

"How are you doing, Chanie?" Rie said.

"What do you mean, Rie?" *Other than getting slapped out by a big Serb and having multiple dicks shoved in my mouth over the last few days, I'm doing great.*

"Is your anxiety acting up?"

"Yes, a lot of anxiety. And it's causing insomnia. It's bad lately. I can't study." I realized I was rambling, so I closed my mouth.

"Have you given much thought to prayer?" P.J. asked.

I shook my head no.

"What's coming up for you?" Rie said.

"I don't really know. I can't sleep, and I know I can't drink any-more to take the edge off, so I try to meditate and read, but it's not the same."

"Do you miss drinking?"

"Yes," I replied, shocked at my honesty.

"Do you think it would be a good idea to drink again?"

"I want to, but I know the answer is supposed to be no."

"What do you feel is at the core of your anxiety issues?"

I was too tired to play word games. My senses were numb, and I couldn't fake what they wanted to see and hear. I wanted to go home and have dinner with Blue so we could feel normal again, like a couple. If we could connect, everything would be okay. We could talk about our future in Nelson. He could reinforce my belief that I was working to free us, that all the suffering would be worth it. I just had to push a little while longer.

"Chanie, do you feel like it may be time to deal with some of the trauma you experienced in your home? Like the abuse you suffered when you lived with your mom?"

No! I did not.

I fidgeted in my seat. "How could revisiting my past help me?"

"Often when someone confronts their abuser, it disempow-ers the abuser and empowers the victim — I'm sorry, let me rephrase — the survivor of the abuse."

"But how does he have any power over me? I don't even talk to him."

"Do you mean your stepdad?"

"Yeah, him. And my bitch mother."

"Can you see how deep the anger toward your mom goes? You can't even say her name without calling her a bitch. The emotional charge is so powerful, I can feel it from over here. If you are that mad at your mother, can you imagine how enraged you are with your stepdad? Maybe your anger scares you?"

I shoved my hands under my thighs to restrain the urge to smash the windows out. Of course I hated them. Sometimes I also hated my dad, but it hurt too much to hate him, so I tried not to. After all, he was dead. According to Pastor Josh, Jesus would work with him to overcome his sins, and hopefully my father would choose the way of light and live his afterlife with more grace than he'd lived with on Earth. I figured if my mother wasn't there to rip him up anymore, maybe he'd have a chance at happiness.

"I hate them, Rie. I can't think about them because when I do, I want to rip this room apart and get drunk and smash everything into pieces!"

My anger didn't scare her. She calmly said, "It's okay. Anger gives us the energy to keep moving forward. It gives us the strength to stand up again and again. But it's also destructive when it's turned inward. It can make you very sick, physically and mentally. We can work on redirecting your anger to more fulfilling endeavours in your life."

"Like what?"

"Like your education and your future. Your many gifts and talents. You don't always have to feel like this. It's not a life sentence."

I wasn't sure what gifts and talents she meant. My street skills? How I could totally detach from myself when giving blow jobs to men I'd rather shoot in the balls than look at? How I could stand out in the cold with bare legs and a tank top in below-zero weather? I didn't have anything else to offer. I couldn't sing, dance, draw, or paint. I stood a couple of inches higher than five feet. My breasts were small, and I had no acting or modelling ability. I didn't subscribe to Pastor Josh's sermons about how God had anointed us with talents and gifts and how we all had a purpose on the planet. I believed that something random had brought us into the world. That we existed as depraved, self-indulgent creatures with no other purpose than self-gratification.

"What's this all about, Rie? Forgiveness for my abusers? Forgiveness sets us free? I don't believe that. I'd need a team of fifty-seven therapists to make that happen."

"Nobody's asking or expecting you to like them. Or to forgive them. Working through this can free you. Being angry all the time is exhausting. Don't you hate spending all your energy on anger?"

"I hate everything about myself." I dropped my head to my knees and cupped my hands over the back of my neck, still tender from Milos's beastly grip.

"Let's just agree to begin somewhere, Chanie. I'm going to keep reminding you that you don't always have to feel like this. Life can and will feel better."

"How?"

"We can start by looking at ways to confront your abuser."

"Like what? Going to the house and beating him up?" I sat up and laughed.

"Well, there's a couple of things we can do. We can explore charging him through the courts, or —"

"Oh my God! Are you kidding?"

"*Or* we can start by having you write a letter to him and your mother.

"A letter?"

"Sometimes, taking a step back and putting it on paper helps to reframe your perspective. It can validate your experience and help you to organize and reflect on what happened in a safe place. It may help you to put closure on the situation and give you permission to move forward on your healing journey."

"Permission! Really?"

"I know it sounds weird, but yes. Often survivors experience guilt, shame, and self-blame and don't even realize it. Survivors often blame themselves because it brings the trauma within their own locus of control, like they can prevent it from happening again in the future if they just avoid certain things."

I wasn't sure if I blamed myself. Sometimes, I'd laughed at Clayton's jokes, worn the clothes and jewellery he'd bought me, and occasionally watched TV in the basement with him. Sometimes, he'd seemed to defend me from my mom, usually when she got too crazy and there was a risk of the neighbours overhearing her. But ultimately, I'd avoided him because I'd never felt comfortable around him. I'd always felt weird and tense, but maybe he'd misread my nerves as a teenage crush.

Rie broke the silence. "You don't have to send the letter, but maybe you can finally say the things you need to say. Then maybe you can rest easier."

"How the fuck will I ever rest? He made me into *this*!"

"He doesn't have that kind of power, Chanie."

"But I will always feel like filth. Like trash — like a receptacle for depravity."

"You are none of those things. You did not deserve what happened to you. You were a kid. He was wrong, not you. Chanie, say it out loud."

"What? That he was wrong?"

"He groomed you. He was in a position of power. He

created an environment where your boundaries were not clear. He pitted your own mother against you so he could take what he wanted."

"Yeah!" I snapped. "He was the one who took it, but then I was the one who sold it for years after."

I sighed and stretched out in the chair. My life churned like a whirlwind all the time. School, hooking, Ginger, Tuffy, Blue and Brenda, Milos — and now having to face my demons head-on. The only innocent thing in my life was Sox, but it hurt so bad to think of him because I knew he had to go to a better person in a safer home.

I'd never rest easier. I never rested at all. Not even when I closed my eyes at night because almost every time I fell asleep, I saw a yellow tarp floating down over my broken body.

CHAPTER FOURTEEN

RAPE NEVER LEAVES YOU. It's not like a hard workout where you grit your teeth while it's happening, take a shower, and move on. It's like a tsunami rips you out of a deep sleep and churns your insides like a blender. And all you're left with is the slush of who you once were and, if you're lucky, a faint memory of who you could have become.

We can start by having you write a letter to him and your mother ...

"You are not a rape *victim*; you are a rape *survivor*," Rie had said.

I was also a suicide survivor. My father's. My attempts. Victims and survivors know the first noble truth: Life is suffering. Survivors wield pain like a sword; victims turn the sword inward. Being a survivor sucked because survivors have big holes in their hearts. They have great big gaps where the ghosts of mental illness chant songs audible only to the ears of the sufferer.

Rie said, "Promise me you'll call if stirring up these memories gets to be too much." *Too much* had happened a long time ago. *Too late* seemed more appropriate. I let her hug me before

I slammed her office door and made a beeline for the exit. I walked quickly, as though trying to outpace the responsibility to heal my life after Clayton and his buddy had pulverized it in the basement of my childhood home.

"Hey, Chanie!" Ginger yelled.

"Hey, Ginger. I have to get home. I'm behind on my homework and in a piss mood," I said, not breaking my pace.

"What made you go from zero to piss in all of two seconds? Come say hi to Tuffy."

I stopped and crossed my arms. "Hi, Tuffy."

"Did you read my note?" Tuffy said.

"I did, thank you." I looked at the ground.

"How did your love letter turn out? Did you give it to your boyfriend?" He licked his lower lip, squinted slightly, and smiled.

"I did not."

"Yeah, 'cuz Blue's a dink!" Ginger giggled and shrugged.

"Why not?" Tuffy asked.

"I guess I haven't found the right moment."

"Don't you two live together?"

"Maybe I'm waiting for a fire!" I turned and walked away.

Ginger jogged alongside me. "What's with you, Chanie? Got a little Tuffy under your skin?"

"You know I'm with Blue."

"*For now*, Chanie. Things change."

I came home to a coffee-stained note from Blue telling me he was back on night shift. I was glad. As long as I could avoid Brenda and Milos, I could finally get caught up on my homework. I drew the blinds and chained the door.

Sox attacked his toy mice and ran around the apartment. I scooped him off the floor and rubbed his tiny face against my cheek. I had to study, but my whole body lagged. Lack of sleep and the stress of lying was wearing me down. Rie and P.J. had said a shrink could prescribe something to make it easier. Drugs could help the right chemicals fire so I could focus better. I'd been down that road a couple of years before with Wellbutrin and Clonazepam. I'd gotten really skinny, chewed my lip a lot, and every time I looked from side to side, my brain made a whooshing sound that someone in an Internet chat room referred to as "beanbag eyes."

I needed some time off. Away from Blue, Brenda, and Milos. I wanted to sample *normal*. I wanted to get a latte and go out for a walk with Ginger instead of putting on stilettos and staying up all night risking my life. I called Ginger, but she didn't answer. I sent a text and waited. When I didn't hear back from her, I called her again.

"Hey, Chanie. What's up?"

"Do you want to come over and hang out with me and Sox?"

"Oh my God, yes! I've waited months for this momentous occasion. What's the celebration? Did Blue and Brenda finally do a bad batch of fentanyl? Like a modern-day, crack-whore version of Romeo and Juliet?"

"Very funny. Blue's working tonight, and I don't know where Brenda is. How about you hop on the bus, and I'll meet you at Chapters? We can grab coffee and walk back here together. Bring your books, and we'll get some work done."

"Yeah, sounds good. Petey-D's home watching the game, and his team's on fire. I'm glad you called. I don't feel like sitting here with his dirty eyes on me."

"Perfect! See you soon."

The hum from Whyte Avenue buzzed in the air. My heart

lifted, and my mind cleared. I smiled, raised my palms to the sky, and danced in the grass at the edge of an alley. I smiled at everyone who passed me. Some of them smiled back, and not just men, but women too. I felt safe, like I blended in with something bigger. Yoga pants and running shoes gave me freedom in a world that booty shorts and high heels never could. I felt like I was thirteen again — before Clayton happened.

I waited outside, blending in with the bustling people. The inside of the bookstore glowed a gentle orange, like the patio lights in my go-to picture of Nelson, B.C. The scent of roasted coffee beans infused the air, reminding me of nights at the airport with Mr. Tanji. Just inside the window, a woman with copper hair and muscular arms sat cross-legged with a Boston Terrier nestled between her knees. She had rested a copy of *The Essential Rumi* on his back. An older woman with long blue-grey hair in a messy bun picked through leather journals, her long fingers tracing the edges of the covers before taking one in her hands. Her teal shawl flared like butterfly wings whenever she raised her arms. She moved like a ballerina, slinky and graceful, like life itself was a dance recital.

I recognized my neighbour from the building next door. I'd only ever seen him in his silver Audi S5, but even then I could see that he was tall and fit. His grey hair didn't suit his young skin. A midnight-blue turtleneck hung loosely over his torso. He looked right at me, his eyes as blue as a Yukon lake. I'd been smiling at people all night, so I took a chance and lit up a big smile for him too. He paused, but then gave me a quick nod. I felt like dancing right there on the street.

"Creeper," Ginger said.

"Holy eff, Ginger!" I jumped back.

"What are you looking at? Oh my God! That little dog is *so* cute!" Ginger waved at the Boston Terrier through the window.

"That dog is cute, but that's not what I'm looking at. See that tall, sexy guy wearing the blue turtleneck?"

"Yeah, he looks smart and like he has a stick up his ass. Let me guess! He's your biggest client, and he's a weirdo. Like his fantasy is making you have sex with bananas while he talks to his mom on Skype?"

"Jesus, Ginger. You have a dirty mind."

"So I've been told. Let's go before he buys you and steals my chance of meeting Sox."

"He's not the hooker-buying type. He's my hot neighbour from the high-rise next door to mine. He drives a silver Audi."

"Oh my, nice neighbour! He's yummy, in a Mr. Lavoy kind of way. Maybe I can trade out Petey-D and go live with him instead."

"Then we'd be neighbours. How about a chai latte?"

"Sure thing, Mr. Tanji." Ginger winked.

The avenue danced like a movie set. Majestic trees with cobalt lights wrapped around their giant trunks hovered above the sidewalk. Neon pinks, greens, blues, and golds shone from shop signage, beckoning us to come in and buy their treasures. Guys driving glossy cars and riding flashy motorcycles cruised up and down the street, revving their engines at the sight of anything female. We stopped to pet a fat Siamese cat at the used bookstore and played with four happy dogs tied to a bike rack. I inhaled the moment, the sights, the sounds, the smell of spun sugar sweetening the air. I remembered Mr. Tanji saying, "There's magic everywhere, as long as you can get out of your own way long enough to see it."

"What pissed you off at school today?" Ginger said, tossing her cup on top of an overflowing garbage can.

"Rie wants me to write a letter to my douchebag stepdad."

"About what?"

"I don't know. What he did to me and how it affected me."

"Oh no! That sounds terrible. We might have to get drunk to write it."

"I don't think it's supposed to be a group project."

"Well fuck, Chanie. How are you supposed to write it on your own? You need support. How old were you when it happened?"

"Fourteen."

"You were a baby! Was he nice to you before?"

"Before?"

"Let's call your childhood Thirteen B.C., like thirteen years old before Clayton fucked you up. Kind of like Pastor Josh always talks about before Christ, after Christ — who can keep up with all this B.C., A.D. stuff? Let's refer to your era of innocence as Thirteen B.C."

"That's very creative, Gin Gin."

"Do you think writing it out will help?"

"I don't really know how writing a soliloquy to my rapist will help me feel better. I wonder if it'll end there or if I'll have to write a letter to every dick who's ever paid me for sex?"

"If that's the case, you'll have to take out a full-page ad in the paper!" Ginger skipped ahead of me and stopped abruptly. "Hey, I have an idea. Fuck this letter and let's go to your place and look at pictures of Nelson. We need inspiration."

"Good plan. Maybe we'll sit on the balcony."

We walked off Whyte Avenue and headed down a residential street, the darkness stark and scary compared to the blue trees and lights on the avenue. My neighbour in the silver Audi S5 drove past. I wondered if he was curious about me, if he'd ever even noticed me. Part of me wanted him to stop so

I could meet him, hear his voice, smell his cologne. But if he ever did stop, he couldn't be my knight in shining armour anymore. He'd be like everybody else, and I needed the fantasy more than I needed the man.

"There's the silver Audi." I pointed to the car.

"It looks like a car with lights," Ginger said.

"It's a nice car."

"With a nice driver. What's your deal with him, anyways? You're always like, 'I don't like Tuffy, I'm with Blue. I'm with Blue. Ginger! I'm with Blue.' And now you're into uptight old guys in grey cars."

"He's like a celebrity crush. Someone you know you could never have."

"Unless he opens his wallet — and dirty mind — and not in that particular order." Ginger giggled and punched my arm.

When we got closer to my building, I reached for Ginger's hand and squeezed it.

"Why are you so snuggly, Chanie?"

"Just thinking about when you told me about your dream where we were gardening in bohemian dresses and sun hats."

"Oh, right! Back when you thought I had a crush on you."

"Had?"

We snuck through the alley to see if Blue had come home or if Milos was hanging out at Brenda's.

"Hide!" I yanked Ginger behind a beat-up black Chevy with two lawnmowers in the box. It had *Lawn Order* spray-painted on the door in crooked white stencils. Brenda leaned near the entry door, trying to look sexy while fat Milos went to get the car.

Ginger gripped my hand. "Holy fuck! What a skank!"

"That's her, living and breathing."

"Barely. That old whore looks like a zombie. Too many dicks and not enough fruit and veggies in her diet. Maybe the old slut will kick it from scurvy. Tuffy told me about a hamster he'd had at his elementary school. It got all these weird lumps on its body. His mom, convinced the poor thing had scurvy, told Tuffy to feed it oranges. But the same day he showed up with the oranges, the hamster died!"

"Maybe that's why he's so mopey. He's pining for his lost rodent."

"No." Ginger sighed. "That's not why."

We snuck through the back door and rode the elevator up to my suite. Sox bolted into the hallway. Ginger squealed and ran after him. He somersaulted and flipped on his back, all four paws splayed, hissing and ready to kill us. I let him clutch my wrist and picked him up. He started purring, spread his toes, and began licking his feet.

"This pad ain't so bad," Ginger said. "The view is stunning. How did this dump manage to survive on Saskatchewan Drive? All your snotty neighbours must hate this eyesore."

"Brenda told me this building has belonged to a rich family for generations. The current owners don't care about it because they own, like, thirty-five other mortgage-free buildings. So they basically get high and drunk their whole lives and collect the rents every month."

"They *must* be high and drunk. Look who they hired as their building manager!"

"She worked her way up from the cleaning job. She's a high achiever."

"What do you want to bet your prince next door has a ballin' place with hardwood floors and counters made of expensive stone? He probably has paintings from Europe that cost ten million dollars. Like Vincent van Damme, or whoever that guy who chopped his ear off was."

"Vincent van Gogh."

"Yeah. Whatever. He's Vincent van Gone now."

I grabbed the iPad, and we settled on the bed. Sox curled up in a loud, rumbly ball while we googled Nelson, B.C.

"Do they have apartments there?" Ginger said, rubbing Sox's tummy with the back of her hand.

"I'm sure they do," I said, scrolling through the properties. "But they're so expensive."

"You know what would be perfect?" Ginger kissed Sox's chest. "If you and Blue lived in the upstairs of a house and I rented the basement. But not like a shit basement with tiny *Criminal Minds* windows, but a nice walkout basement like that hot NFL guy with the dreadlocks has."

"Who?"

"Some Larry Fitzroger or Fitzpatrick. I don't know. I saw his house on TV the other night when me and Petey-D watched an NFL special. His house is almost as nice as his ass!"

We giggled and googled Larry Fitz, and Larry Fitzgerald came up. I lifted the iPad and kissed the screen. "Holy mother of God. He's stupendous."

Sox leaped from the bed and ran behind the dresser. I turned to see Blue standing in the doorway, his keys dangling from the lock.

Ginger smiled and sat up straight. "Hi, I'm Ginger."

"Chanie, you need to come out here *now*!" Blue turned and slammed the door.

"Oh no!" Ginger said, fumbling in her purse for a Xanax.

"It's okay. He probably just wants to tell me something. Stay here with Sox. I'll be right back."

I went out in the hallway. Blue and Brenda were leaning against the wall, whispering with their heads down. Brenda was wearing a new windbreaker and looked like she'd had her hair coloured and blown out at a salon.

"What's going on?" I said.

"What the fuck is your little friend doin' here?" Brenda clucked her tongue. "I told ya, Blue. Ya can't count on 'er. She's a flake."

"It's not your business, Brenda," I said.

Blue took a stride toward me. "Yeah. It is, Chanie."

I jumped back. "It is *what*, Blue?"

"It is her business! I get a call from Brenda about you and your little friend making too much noise, so I gotta leave work! It's like having a fuckin' kid, Chanie. A fuckin' kid!" He threw his hands in the air.

"We weren't being ... Really?"

Blue raised his hand. "Shut the fuck up! Now that you've blown my wages for the night, you're going to work to make it up to us. Go on inside and tell your little friend you gotta go somewhere else."

"No, I'm not working tonight."

"What did she say?" Brenda said. "Do I need to go get Milos to help motivate our little *loser*?"

"Oh my God, you two make me sick." I turned to go back in, but Blue grabbed my wrist and squeezed it tightly. I yelled out in pain, but he covered my mouth with his hand.

Blue clenched his teeth and leaned into me. "You're gonna go and tell your little friend you got somewhere to be." He shook his hand loose. "And by the way, what did I tell you about your little friends coming over here?"

Ginger peeked out the door. I nodded to her and waved her back inside.

"Fine," I said. "I need to get ready. Please don't embarrass me in front of Ginger."

"We's comin' in with ya to make sure ya don't cry to yer little friend," Brenda said, nodding to Blue as if giving him the okay to let me back into my own apartment.

I went to get ready. I heard Brenda tell Ginger I'd forgotten an appointment with some friends of our "little family," but she'd get her buddy Milos to drive her home. I swung the bathroom door open and said, "Ginger will ride home with Blue and me. No need to bother Milos tonight."

"Oh well, looky here. Seems we got a little jealousy goin' on. Lil' Chanie don't want to share her friend with us."

"I'll ride with Chanie and Blue," Ginger said matter-of-factly. "It'll give me the opportunity to get to know Blue a bit better."

"Why would ya wanna do that?" Brenda snarled.

Ginger's face darkened, but she tried to smile. I knew she'd taken Xanax, but her cheeks glowed and her eyes looked wet. I couldn't have her melt down in front of them. I'd sworn to Blue that I'd kept our lives private and that Ginger and the school knew nothing of my work arrangement.

"Hey, Gin Gin. Can you do up my necklace?"

Ginger struggled with the clasp. "You look pretty, Chanie."

Blue came over and yanked me against him. "Isn't she gorgeous, this one?" He leaned closer and whispered in my ear, "How can I count on you when I can't even trust you to respect our home?"

"Thanks, Ginger. I have to meet some old friends tonight. I can't believe I forgot," I said loudly, breaking away from Blue.

"Let's go!" I grabbed my bag, realizing how stupid and selfish it had been to bring her into my world. It wouldn't be safe for her until we moved to Nelson.

Sox was tucked behind the dresser. I wanted to stuff Ginger back there too. Nothing was safe in my life. I'd have to get Sox out soon. I didn't trust Brenda and Milos, and Sox didn't like Blue when he was stressed out or high, which was all the time lately. I walked out of the building holding Ginger's hand. I pictured us jumping into Blue's truck with Sox and a bunch of luggage, disappearing from Brenda and Milos forever. I had to work harder to get us out faster.

We'd almost made it to the truck when Brenda yelled, "Hey, Ginger! We's gonna make a point of you meetin' Milos soon."

I ran back toward the building. Brenda tried to pull the door closed, but I yanked it so hard I almost pulled her outside. "You listen to me, bitch! What we got going on is between us. Don't threaten my friend. Her brother's a cop, so keep it up and you'll ruin the cash flow for all of us."

"Calm down, Jade. Ya need to show a little respect. Or —"

I pointed in her face. "Don't threaten me. Or I'll kill myself, and all three of you will have to get jobs to take care of your so-called retirement fund."

"Blue!" Brenda shrieked. "Come and get this little slut before I kill her!"

"Go inside and get drunk, you washed-up whore." I slammed the door and walked back to the truck. Ginger clenched my hand and pressed against me. She pushed herself away from Blue, as though if she leaned far enough into me, we'd fuse into one being and escape to our world of sun hats and gardens.

"Where do you live?" Blue said to Ginger.

"She lives close to Bonnie Doon Mall," I lied. "You can drop her at the Safeway. She needs apples and soup."

We drove in silence. Coldplay's "Paradise" played on the radio. We looked so normal, three people riding in a truck listening to music. My boyfriend getting my best friend home safe and sound after a night of visiting and playing with our kitten. I closed my eyes and breathed deeply, returning to my earlier vision of the three of us and Sox stealing away in the night to go live our lives in the mountains. I squeezed Ginger's hand; she squeezed mine back and smiled sweetly. I knew she was picturing us with grey hair and wrinkled skin, laughing in a sunny garden together. It was up to me to make sure we made it there.

CHAPTER FIFTEEN

"GET IN THE GODDAMN truck!" Blue punched on the horn. A nearby couple, who looked like a his-and-hers accounting team, scowled at him. He shook his fist and spat a string of obscenities. Wide-eyed and pissed off, they quickened their pace and jumped into a white Mazda3, almost T-boning a black Land Rover in their rush to get out of the parking lot.

"Ginger, you have to let go," I said, rubbing her back. She clung tighter.

"I hate them!" she sobbed. "They're gonna get you killed."

I shouldn't have brought her into my home. The filth. The depravity. Blue's aggression, vivid and open, his twitching lips, bloodshot eyes, and taut neck muscles. His volatility. His filthy mouth. And my unwillingness to label him an embarrassment because what would that say about me? How could I comfort her?

I slipped a twenty into her pocket for cab fare and disentangled from our embrace. "Get home safe. Watch out for a black Lincoln. If you see it, don't let him see where you live, okay?"

"Fuck all of them! I don't think Blue should move away with us. He's even worse than Brenda." Ginger sniffled and wiped her nose.

Blue revved the engine and started bouncing the truck.

"I have to go, Gin Gin. But text me when you're home, please."

Ginger pulled me close and said, "I'll pray for you."

I smiled. "Okay, Pastor Gin Gin."

"What the hell, Blue?" I snapped, trying to get into the truck. "Can you wait a half-second for me to get in? Jesus Christ!" I felt a pang of guilt for using Jesus' name, given that Ginger was probably begging Him to protect me at that very moment.

"What did I tell you about having friends over?" Blue stuttered, coming down from whatever chemicals he'd been into.

"I needed her to help me study."

"I don't give a fuck if you needed her because you had a stroke."

"That's real nice, Blue. Who cares if she was there anyway?"

"I do! Brenda does!"

"Like I care what Brenda wants. And why do you care so much? Aren't we trying to get away from her?"

"That's my point, Chanie. We can't have people interfering in our business. You gotta stay focused. What if she tells one of your teachers what you're doing? Then we're all fucked. You go to jail, and we go nowhere."

"She's not going to tell anyone. She wants to come with us."

"What do you mean 'come with us'? Where?"

"To Nelson."

The front end of the truck dropped and veered sideways, bounced off the curb, and slammed to a halt. An elderly couple walking a tall, skinny dog stopped and mouthed, "Are you okay?" I nodded and pretended to laugh. They shook their heads and yanked the dog close as they scurried away.

"What the fuck did you tell her about Nelson for? Are you fucking crazy?" Blue slammed his fists against the dash. "You're so fucking selfish, putting our future on the line so you can tell your stupid little friend about our plan!"

"Calm down. She's okay with it. She's going to try and save money too. She wants the same things we do."

"You're so fuckin' dumb, Chanie! Nobody wants the same things that we do. You can't trust her or anybody else. Do you understand me?"

"Blue —"

He lunged across the truck and screamed in my face, "Do you understand me?"

"Okay!" I said, wiping spit off my cheek. "I won't talk to her about it anymore. I'll tell her I made it all up."

"Yeah, make sure you do. Because if you fuck this up for us, I don't know what else we can do."

"Just take me to work, Blue."

"I'll drop you off downtown."

"What the hell? I'm supposed to get work online only. I can't keep standing outside. I'll get caught."

"Just be smart. We're all working on the website plan."

"How hard is it? It's a Facebook page or a fucking Craigslist ad!"

"Shut the fuck up, Chanie."

I stopped talking because something inside me felt like fire, and if I let it loose, I'd incinerate the truck. I tried to breathe deeply, but my ribs pulled inward, making my breaths shallow and short. I had to stay focused. I'd count the cash in the coffee can in the morning and create our savings plan using the budget template from Life Skills. I'd make it work. I'd get us out.

The truck jerked to a stop. I popped out the door and walked to the wall underneath the China Gates. Blue leaned over, rolled the window down, and yelled, "No goodnight kiss?" He laughed and drove away. When the truck disappeared around the corner, I flipped him the finger.

I texted Ginger. If she was home safe, it would be one less thing to worry about. I could focus on making my cash and going home.

> Hey, Ginger. Did you get home okay?

> Yup, sittin' here with no pants on.

> I never thought I'd say this, Ginger, but I'm glad Petey-D's home tonight.

> Me too. I'm worried for you though. Ate 3 Xanax already.

> I'm okay. See you at the Mac's tomorrow morning. XOXO

> Sun hats and gardens, my friend.

> Sun hats and gardens, Chanie.

I reached into my purse and rubbed the spine of *Les Misérables*. Tuffy's note tickled my fingertips. I stroked the edge of the page, remembering his words, his face. *"Did you read my note?"* I replayed the scene in my mind, but this time, I said, *"Yes, I read your note. And it made me feel as though I were tucked beneath your wings, ready to fly away. Let's start a fire, Tuffy." He traces my lips with his fingertips and tells me that I'm beautiful. My tongue touches his fingers, and I lean back. My heart is open, and I'm ready for him …*

I clapped my hands to snap out of it. I didn't want to be like the men who paid for me, cheaters who were never satisfied, always fantasizing about someone else. I needed to believe in Blue — our love, commitment, and connection — or none of it would make sense. I belonged to Blue. I had to be the kind of woman he could count on. We'd be okay when I got us to Nelson.

I traced the edges of *Les Misérables* and eased Tuffy's note into my hands. It glowed beneath the streetlights as though lit up from within. I'd throw it away so he wouldn't haunt my headspace anymore. As long as I carried it, I'd carry Tuffy. He'd seep into my mind and tempt me. But when I leaned toward the garbage can, my heart seized up, and I couldn't let go. I pressed my lips against the paper and let Tuffy's image float before me: his crooked smile, his brooding face. *My Jean Valjean.*

"Hey, hot stuff. What's your plan for tonight?" Words from the window of a white BMW.

"Just taking a break from my thesis," I said.

"Ha ha! You're funny. Hop in!"

The smell of Drakkar Noir mixed with vanilla air freshener made me queasy. He looked like a typical rich kid: orange skin from tanning beds, teeth bleached almost transparent, brown hair with white-blond highlights. If I'd seen him in a café, I'd have bet he was gay.

"Are you into role-playing?" he asked.

"Depends on what you're looking for."

"I'm gonna take you to my office and fuck you up the ass while you bend over my bitch boss's desk."

"A couple of things, Don Juan," I replied. "I'm not a huge fan of sodomy, so there's an extra cost."

"Don't call it sodomy!"

"What would you like me to call it? *Making love?*"

"Tell you what, smart-ass. How's $500 for the rest of the night?"

"It's not a free-for-all flat rate, buddy. There's got to be some boundaries."

"You're a whore. Don't make me laugh." He flipped his head back and laughed with his mouth wide open. "Boundaries!"

"And you're a guy who just picked up a whore."

"Fair enough. What are your boundaries?"

"If I say stop, you have to stop. And guarantee me that if anyone walks in, I'm your girlfriend and not someone you paid for."

"Why? Because you have boundaries and feel shame about your job?"

"No, Sigmund Freud. Because I don't want to get arrested, and neither do you."

"Good point, girl." He held his hand in the air for a high-five.

I declined the high-five and said, "Give me the cash before we go in."

He told me to call him Derek. That seemed appropriate because he looked like a douchebag, and Derek was a good douche name. He swiped his entry card as though granting me access to a kingdom rather than a run-of-the-mill law firm. The view was nice, but the office bar stole the show. I'd been with a lot of lawyers, and they all loved to drink. Scotch seemed to be a favourite, so when Derek asked me what I'd like, I said, "Scotch on the rocks, big guy!" and gave him the wink and the gun.

I drank three scotch whiskies and two fruity coolers while Derek bragged about his legal prowess. *I won this case and that case, and this judge was an idiot, but that judge knew his shit and knew he couldn't pull one over on me!* And oh my God, shut the fuck up! But he rambled on for another two drinks before he led me into a sparsely furnished office with a white leather chaise and a red nest chair. A plaid dog bed rested by the chaise. A tiny yellow tennis ball was tucked under the corner of the bed as though the dog didn't trust the cleaning staff. It's like it had a sixth sense about the after-hours shenanigans that happened at its owner's desk.

A dark mahogany desk with brushed nickel drawer handles sat in front of matching bookshelves filled with legal books. The desk chair looked like something out of a Crate & Barrel flyer. I propped myself up on "the bitch's" desk and noticed a picture of a strawberry-blond woman standing in front of a lake holding a Yorkshire Terrier against her chest. Her face looked warm from the sun, and she smiled brightly, her white teeth evidence of good health and a dental plan. She looked happy. She also looked fit and like she cared about her life. In an alternate universe, I could be like her. But in my universe, I hiked up my cheap skirt and handed Derek a bottle of lube so he could sodomize me while he yelled at her picture.

"What's her name?" I asked. She looked like a Victoria or a Kaleigh.

"Who cares!" Derek panted. "She's a cunt."

I mouthed a silent apology to her while he hammered me from behind. I wished she'd walk in and catch him, put an end to his career and his big mouth. When he finished, he said, "Wipe yourself off and let's get the hell out of here."

Derek insisted on buying me a latte. Told me he felt bad for being so hasty. He drove me all the way to my front door and tipped me another hundred bucks. He said he didn't mean to push my boundaries, but I think his guilt had more to do with the wedding ring in the console and the fact that I knew where he worked.

I walked around the back of the building and noticed Blue's truck wasn't there. I opened the back door and did a quick inspection to make sure Brenda and Milos weren't lurking in the lobby. When I walked into my suite, Sox peeked his head out from behind the dresser and meowed. I lifted him up and rubbed his silky body against my cheek. We snuggled on the bed with my books. The latte gave me just enough pep to finish most of my homework before I passed out and dreamt of kissing Tuffy.

Blue didn't come home at all that night. I texted him when I woke up, but he didn't text me back. I tried calling him but didn't get an answer. The fire in my stomach flared, like it had the night before, but I breathed it away and chalked it up to exhaustion.

Mr. Lavoy was the first person I saw when I got to school in the morning. He gave me a great big wave and smiled widely. I nodded to him and lowered my gaze to the floor. I didn't like looking at my teachers because I believed they could see through me, like they could feel my filth. I'd fallen asleep without showering and settled for a whore's bath before school because I'd slept late. I'd used Blue's face cloth, wrung it out, and hung it back on the bathroom hook. I'd learned enough in counselling to know that my act was passive-aggressive behaviour. I just never realized how gratifying it could be.

"Today you start your added community service, Chanie. Report to Bruce downstairs at the shelter after school." Mr. Lavoy patted my shoulder and smiled.

"Of course, Mr. Lavoy." My eyes and my body felt wrung out. I needed rest, study time, good food, and hydration. I was running on youth, caffeine, and adrenaline, but my reserves were quickly depleting. I'd talk to Blue when I got home and insist on a new strategy. I'd appeal to the money aspect. That *always* worked. I'd tell him that our earnings would suffer if I didn't take better care of myself. That if I had a breakdown, we'd have nothing.

"How's everyone feeling today?" Mr. Lavoy asked the class.

"Like Batman on cocaine!" Jeremy burst out loud.

"Like a dog in a sunbeam." Ginger laughed.

"As you all know, next week is your mid-program testing and interviews. How do you feel about that?" Mr. Lavoy smiled at me, prompting me for an answer. I'd become a bit of a teacher's pet over the last few months. The study methods Rie had taught me had resulted in consistently high grades, often making me the go-to tutor for struggling classmates and the model student for the teachers. I looked at the floor as though I was too busy to be a part of the class that day. *Too busy being a hooker and a liar.*

The mid-program review concerned me. Overall, I'd done well, but I'd missed some assignments recently. Rie and P.J. were generous with their grace because they believed my bullshit anxiety stories. But I'd been slipping. My assignments and quizzes baffled me and left me feeling hopeless. I rarely prepared for class, and it was beginning to show in my grades. Blue would have to help me. He'd have to understand.

My mandatory volunteer service had been changed from kitchen duty to client engagement. I preferred the silence and nonjudgment of dirty dishes. My initial reaction to dish duty had been disgust and dislike, but I'd grown accustomed to it and enjoyed the sense of accomplishment I felt when the wash racks were empty and the kitchen shone for the morning chef. Washing dishes had become a personal meditation for me. I'd listen to the radio, sometimes eighties music, but more often talk radio. I learned a lot about city politics and occasionally got to hear interviews and debates that included Mr. Tanji.

I multitasked quiz questions with dish duties. I wrote study questions on recipe cards and leaned them on the rack above the sink. I'd created a routine: rinse and fill the sink with hot soapy water and sort the dishes into pots, pans, and cutlery. Soak the worst offenders on the bottom with the cutlery, then pile in plates, bowls, and cups. I'd wash from the top of the stack, rinse under scalding water, and then place them on the drying rack. My efficiency paid off and usually bought me an extra hour of study time while waiting for my shift to end.

Nobody talked to me while I worked unless they needed me to fill in for someone else's shift. It also gave me a peaceful place to study. The work was honest, and I didn't have to take off my clothes or put anything in my mouth. I also didn't have to worry about some psycho strangling me and leaving me in front of a city dumpster. Other than dry hands and broken nails, the hazards were minimal.

I went downstairs to find Bruce, the program director, so he could assign me my new tasks. I had all kinds of anxiety about having to work with people because I preferred to work alone.

But I'd been pushing the limits at school for a while, so I figured I'd better make my best effort to keep the spotlight off me.

"Hi, Bruce. I'm Chanie. Mr. Lavoy told me to see you."

"Ah, yes, Chanie." Bruce smiled at me. He looked more like an aging car salesman than the director of a homeless shelter. He had a healthy belly on him and light green eyes. His hair was the colour of light sand and looked tousled and greasy, like he'd been running his hands through it all day. He was warm and easy to talk to, and I could see why the residents found him so welcoming.

"How did you like dish duty?" Bruce said.

"I didn't mind it. Gave me a lot of time to think."

"That's a positive attitude, young lady. This new gig won't be as hard physically. Maybe you can even grow your nails out now." Bruce glanced at my hands.

I curled my hands into fists to hide my ratty fingertips. Bits of pink polish flecked my nails, greatly in need of a repaint. The edges were jagged from my teeth, and my cuticles glowed red.

"Yeah, maybe," I said. "But I don't really know what my new job is."

"Basically, you're kind of like a house friend. We'll assign you various activities depending on what we're doing. For example, during the holidays you can help the clients work on murals or handmade Christmas ornaments. At other times, we lead prayers, read stories, or engage with clients while they sit and warm up. Once you have a little more experience, we can look at what other roles you may be suited to."

"Like?"

"Like helping people with forms they need to fill out for social workers, medical appointments, whatever comes up. But for today, we'll have you read a short story."

"I haven't read aloud much," I said, nervous I would mess it up.

"They're a pretty forgiving audience." Bruce gave me a reassuring smile and a nod.

"What would you like me to read?"

Bruce handed me *The Making of a Story: A Norton Guide to Creative Writing* by Anne LaPlante. "Anything you pick in this book should be fine. You'll have an hour with them. They should be here fairly soon."

The thick yellow book felt majestic, like a bible of sorts. Its cover showed the wear from a thousand curious fingertips. I flipped through the book, scanning the chapters on writing: "Avoiding the Writerly Voice: Why You Need to Show *and* Tell", "Who's Telling This Story Anyway?" Maybe Mr. Lavoy would help me write a short story for extra credit. I'd write about my future life in Nelson. I closed my eyes and pictured Blue and Ginger sitting on a patio laughing, Sox curled up on a chair, and glasses of pink lemonade with blue straws poking out. I saw myself laughing too, but when I looked at Blue, he wasn't there, and it was Tuffy looking back at me.

I shook my head and redirected my focus to finding a story. I felt like tiny weights had lined the rims of my eyelids, and my body felt flu-like. The skin on my face felt tight and dry from the makeup of the night before. I forced my eyes wide open and leafed through the stories. "Welcome to Cancerland." Too sad. I pictured my audience booing and throwing cookies at me. I flipped back to the table of contents and saw "Where Are You Going, Where Have You Been?" by Joyce Carol Oates. I'd read that story in English class just before I ran away. Our teacher, Mr. Thorne, had played a short film adaptation where we watched a creep named Arnold Friend intimidate and seduce fifteen-year-old Connie to walk out the door of her home and get into the back seat of his car. Mr. Thorne told us that the story had been inspired by the Tucson, Arizona, murders committed by serial killer Charles Schmid, also known as the Pied Piper of Tucson. When Mr. Thorne showed us a picture of him, I felt a chill like I'd never felt before.

Bruce wandered over as my audience gathered. "Be sure to introduce yourself and give them a little background info. You know what I mean."

I didn't know what he meant, but I nodded anyway.

I liked the way the crowd gathered, like avid book club members taking their favourite seat. A spectrum of ages, appearances, personalities, and challenges sat before me, ready to float away from their lives to a storyland far away, even if only for an hour. My stomach turned. What if they hated the story I'd chosen? What if they hated me? I sat on a stool at the front of the room, but I kept my eyes down because I was too scared to make eye contact. I worried that they might be staring at me with expectant eyes, and I'd have nothing to give.

But when I looked up, a room full of kind eyes greeted me. Warm smiles, hot chocolate salutes with Styrofoam cups, hands folded respectfully on laps. A smile bloomed from my heart. Bruce went around with a tray of steaming cups and bulky brown cookies. The room smelled like coffee, chocolate, and water heaters working hard. I noticed Mr. Lavoy leaning against the back wall holding a Starbucks cup. Maybe he was on standby in case I messed things up. He flashed his usual warm smile and raised his cup to me.

"Hello, everyone," Bruce said, standing behind me. "This is Chanie. She's our new storyteller."

"Hi, Chanie," the entire group responded, reminding me of AA meetings I'd seen on TV.

"I'll let Chanie take it from here," Bruce said, giving me a pat on my shoulder before he walked away.

I attempted a smile, but my breath caught in my chest. I couldn't say a word. I tried to calm my anxiety, but it felt like someone had stuffed a sock down my throat. A big hand waved to me from the back of the room. I squinted and saw Al holding Dingo on his lap. I hadn't seen Al since the night that Perry had died when he was running toward me yelling, "Perry's dead, dead, dead!" I nodded to him, and he pursed his lips and smiled the kind of smile a father would give his baby girl at her first dance recital. He gave me a nod, my breath released, and I began to speak.

I read past my allotted hour, but nobody moved. It was as though we had lifted off the planet and dwelled in a secret cave, like a group of children in a fairy tale. I sat quietly and didn't move when the story ended. People came up and shook my hand. Many said, "God bless you." Others chatted excitedly about the story. Al lingered, swinging Dingo back and forth. When everyone else had gone, he walked over.

"Chawnie," he stuttered.

"Hello, Al. And hello, Dingo," I said to the beat-up teddy bear.

"Chawnie. Why did Connie open the door to Arnold Friend? He's a bad, bad man."

"I know, Al. Arnold Friend is a bad man."

"Why did she get in his car? Do you think Connie died?" Al asked me, his eyes sad and wide.

"I think Connie's okay, Al."

"Chawnie …"

"Yes, Al."

"Promise me you'll never open your door to Arnold Friend. And *never, ever* get in his car. He's not your friend, but I am."

"Yes, Al. You're my friend." I smiled and nodded, hoping to ease him.

"I only let my friends pet Dingo. I want you to pet him." Al shoved Dingo toward me, battered from the streets but holding on like a stitched-up war vet. "Promise me, Chawnie!" He stomped his feet.

"I promise you that I will never open my door to Arnold Friend."

But I knew that I already had.

CHAPTER SIXTEEN

I UNDERSTOOD PAIN AND abuse. Those emotions felt like home. But kindness tore me up like nothing I'd ever known. Sweet smiles, cozy handshakes, and hearty expressions of gratitude softened me up just enough to contrast how shitty I'd felt my entire life. And to realize that, maybe, my life didn't have to suck after all.

"Thank you very much, Chanie. Well done." Bruce patted my shoulder, his hand big and calloused, like my dad's. "I hope to see you the same time next week."

I inhaled deeply to try to drown out a sob rising in my throat. *Please, Bruce, don't ask me what's wrong.* I didn't know what was wrong, just that *I* was wrong. My very existence was wrong. I walked away with my head down and hid at the back of the gym, where I eased myself to the floor and cried. I didn't want to feel my life. It was easier to be angry, to feel hated and unwanted. Feeling good had risks. Wanting something better for myself had even bigger risks.

I rode the bus home and snuck into the elevator. Luck was on my side: Friday night, no Blue, no Brenda, no creepy black Lincoln. Just Sox standing next to his empty dishes with a dazed look, like he had doubts about whether I'd feed him. *My life.* A dark apartment and a pissed-off kitten. I tuned the iPad to the Chill Channel and hopped into the shower, where I stayed for a long time. So long that the water turned cold. I cranked the creaky taps off and lay down in the tub, my mind immediately flashing to the image of my dad's lanky body, his long legs tucked up, shotgun between his knees. Every bathtub was haunted by his suicide and lit up the darkest parts of my brain.

The iPad sketched in and out playing blips of music. The intermittent music picked at my nerves like nasty insects nipping at my skin. I whipped the shampoo bottle across the room and knocked the iPad to the floor. It kept trying to catch a signal and finally tuned perfectly to a preacher channel hosted by Pastor Terence Travino. His Texas accent filled the room: *God wants us to explore what it means to be alive. Do you ask yourself, "Who am I and what kind of person do I want to be? Do the people I spend time with inspire me, or are they beating me down? Am I getting better each day, or am I languishing?" We have a limited time on Earth. Do you want to wake up feeling joy? Or do you wake up with a belly full of dread? Picture yourself sitting on the edge of your grave and ask yourself, "What did I do with my time on the Earth?"*

I listened for a long time. The air dried my skin, and Sox slept soundly on a bath towel. Pastor Josh often quoted Terence Travino. I usually blew it off. But that night, not only did I hear the message, I felt it. And it sent a chill through me.

I dried myself off and went into the kitchen to check the Nelson can. I needed an opening balance for my budget. I knew I'd contributed exactly $1,864. If Blue had matched my contribution, we'd be close to twenty percent of our overall goal. I reached behind the cleaning supplies and felt for the can. We kept the money in a freezer bag just in case of a water leak. Sox sat on the kitchen floor next to me, like my partner in crime. I felt the rim of the can, pulled it out, and placed it in front of me. I closed my eyes and took a breath. Nothing! Not even an I.O.U. or a shred of paper. Even the freezer bag was gone.

It had to have been Brenda! Or maybe Blue had hidden it in a safer place. He couldn't possibly have taken the cash and left? His clothes and tools were all over the apartment, so I assumed he hadn't run off. I yanked every single item out of the cabinet and scanned the empty space with my iPhone's flashlight. Still nothing! I called Blue, but he didn't answer. I punched out a text message: *Seems we're out of coffee! Any idea where it is?*

I sat on the floor and let Sox play hide-and-seek with the empty can. I didn't feel tired anymore, just deflated. Blue had ignored my message, so I sent him a few more: *Do the people I spend time with inspire me, or are they beating me down?* I paced around the suite like a stressed animal. I was spinning out on every attempt to find a solution to the money situation. I had to focus on what I could control. Rie and Pastor Josh told us every day, "Focus on what you can control, not what you can't." In that moment, I realized that I couldn't control Blue, but I could choose to study for my midterm exams because I had to stay on track. If I ever wanted to get out from under all the chaos, I'd have to be stronger than my circumstances.

I managed to get some work done before passing out with the lights on and books all over the bed. Blue came home around three in the morning. I sat up and rubbed my eyes. Sox leaped off the bed and ran behind the dresser.

"Where have you been?" I asked.

"None of your fucking business, Chanie."

"Really. How is that possible, Blue?"

"I don't answer to you."

"I see. So, I just go out and suck dick to buy our way out of this shit life we've created, and you get to do whatever you like?"

"Pretty much."

"No, Blue."

"No, what!"

"No to *pretty much!* This is a relationship. We're accountable to each other."

"I just said I don't answer to you. I'm not your partner. I'm what you'd call your stakeholder. It's like me, Brenda, and Milos got shares in your peachy little ass."

"Then who do you answer to?"

"I answer to God."

"Get serious, Blue. Where's the cash from the Nelson can?"

"Let's just say we had to cash in on some dividends."

"You're high again."

"So, what of it, *Jade.*" Blue laughed and slapped his thigh.

"Don't call me Jade."

"Or what?"

Or what? He was right. He was just one more thing in my life that I couldn't control.

"Or what ..." Blue slurred.

"Go to sleep."

"That's right, girl. Sleep!"

He tossed all my books off the bed, crawled under the covers, and turned his back to me. I did the same. He slept. I didn't.

I woke up to Blue slamming cupboard doors.

"Don't we have any fucking coffee, Chanie?"

I wanted to say *No! It appears all our coffee cans are empty.*

"No, Blue. I can run out and get you some, but then I really have to study."

"Nah, get up and I'll drive us to Tim Hortons."

We walked out to the truck, acting natural, like we'd just finished watching a movie and had a hankering for some caffeine. I wondered if people could sense our dysfunction. His drug habits. My life of lies. We looked like a scruffy couple just going for a ride. Two people out for a treat, like dogs riding to an off-leash park.

Blue drove toward the downtown location instead of to the closer Strathcona one. It felt like he wanted to waste my time and take me away from my studies, but I didn't say anything because he was twitchy and had already lost his shit on a guy turning left in front of him. I had to get focused and get good grades. I couldn't resign myself to a fate like Brenda's and become an old, worn-out whore who lived on cheap booze and poutine. That image drove me to keep trying. And the image of Perry, dead under the yellow tarp, drove me even more.

We drove through the tunnel beneath the Legislature. Blue took the corner too fast, but I kept quiet and stared out the window at the Legislature Grounds. I made a mental note to ask Ginger and the guys if they'd like to go there sometime. Maybe we could go when the Christmas lights were up or, if not, when the wading pool was open in the summer.

I'd only been to the Legislature one time. I'd been having a killer night. I could barely catch a breath between tricks. I jumped out of a burgundy minivan, and before he could even pull away, a blue Toyota Tacoma pulled up with the passenger window down. The driver, a thirtyish welder-looking guy, leaned over and yelled, "Hey! Wanna play Purple City with me?"

I wondered what kind of freak show I might be getting into

and which one of us would have to dress up as Prince? Which shitty song would I have to hear on repeat for six hours while he worshipped some unknown deity or cried on my belly? I pegged him for a closeted "When Doves Cry" kind of emo guy, or maybe worse, "Purple Rain."

I'd made enough cash for the night, so I said, "Sorry, man. I don't have a Prince costume."

The welder-guy threw his head back and laughed. "What the fuck? Do I look like the kind of guy who listens to Prince?"

I took a closer look. "I suppose not. More of a Mötley Crüe kind of look."

"That's better." He patted the passenger seat. "Hop in! Are you hungry?"

"Always," I said, and climbed into the truck.

We drove down Jasper Avenue. The trees were wrapped in vibrant blue lights, like the trees on Whyte Avenue. The City must have secured a deal on the lights, considering they'd wrapped over twenty city blocks of tree trunks and hung coloured balls all over the ancient trees in Old Glenora. I liked the lights. They gave me the feel of a fantastical world, especially when I was drunk.

"My name is Sloan," my trick said.

"And mine is Jade," I said, as he turned south on 107 Street.

"I know you probably don't care, but I lost my wife two years ago today," Sloan said, looking over his shoulder to pull a U-turn.

I'd heard that a lot. I don't know if guys thought we had a special dead-wives rate. Or if we even cared. The fact that he actually had someone to grieve over was more than most of us girls could even hope for. I never asked questions, though, for two reasons: I didn't care, and I found it hard to fake my concern.

We drove slowly along the east side of the Legislature Building, another majestic building like the Hotel Macdonald. The Leg sat on top of the riverbank, west of the Hotel Mac, right overtop of River Valley Road, adjacent to the High Level Bridge. It had been constructed around the same time as the Mac, stood five storeys high, and boasted grand entrances, spectacular stonework with magnificent carvings, and dramatically arched windows and doors. The top of the structure was a regal dome that looked as though it housed the queen and all her jewels. It was surrounded by spectacular grounds decorated with fountains, trees, and statues. In the Christmas season, the grounds lit up like a magical snow globe, and I'd heard there was a skating rink on the south end of the property.

I'd never walked onto the property because the building scared me. It was so regal and government-y, I was sure I'd be tackled by a dozen sheriffs. It housed the people who met in fancy meeting rooms wearing their suits and ties. The kind of people who were working hard to rid the world of girls like me. People who used my downfall as part of their campaign platforms, vowing to either "save" or "solve" the issues of prostitution. I wondered who'd fought for my Begin Again program. I'd ask Mr. Tanji if he knew.

"What are you doing?" I asked Sloan as he parked the truck.

"We're going to do Purple City!" He laughed and reached behind him for a thermos.

"We can't be here!"

"What do you mean, Jade?"

"It's government property."

Sloan leaned his head back and laughed another wide-mouthed laugh. "No! It's public property." He pushed the thermos toward me. "Take a swig!"

I took a swig, delighted to find a strong mix of Baileys and coffee.

"Hey! Easy." Sloan smiled and took the thermos back. "How have you never been here before?"

"I was supposed to come here for a grade-seven field trip," I said, reaching for the thermos. "But I had a flu that day." The truth was that I'd gotten my first period that morning before leaving for school. I lied and told my mom that I had thrown up and must have had a flu. I didn't tell her the truth because I couldn't stand the thought of her and Clayton having any kind of discussion that centred on my vaginal region.

"Well, let's tour it now!" Sloan said, tucking the thermos behind the seat.

Purple City, as it turned out, was an Edmonton tradition. I followed Sloan to the back of the Legislature, where we stared into the floodlights for about a minute. When I looked up, everything was purple. The building, the grounds, the valley, and the bridge. Everywhere I looked had a purple hue that made me feel as though I'd fallen into a psychedelic drug scene in a movie. I stared at the purple trees and a purple Sloan, standing next to me crying over his dead wife. It freaked me out, but I stayed calm and waited for the colour to fade, because colour always fades.

After an hour of Blue's random driving, I had to pee and had had enough of the city tour. I leaned over and touched his arm. "Hey, babe. Where are we headed to?"

"Tim Hortons. Where the fuck do you think?"

Where the fuck did I think? His hostility exhausted me. It was always a lose-lose when Blue was coming down from whatever he'd been into. He thought my education was a total waste of time. He'd not said those exact words, but one night when we were counting my earnings, he said, "Imagine how much cash we could make if you worked full-time and quit wasting your time at school." I wouldn't allow myself to consider that might have been his plan for me all along. *Could I possibly be that stupid?*

"Hey, Chanie," Blue whispered. "Look at me when I'm talking to you!"

"Okay." I twisted sideways to shut him up.

It came out of nowhere. A deep wail churned up from my stomach, drowning out the radio. My upper lip burned, like fireworks had exploded beneath my skin, blood rushing and pushing outward from the shock of Blue's knuckles slamming into my face. The bitter taste of blood flooded into my mouth, and my nose stung like I'd inhaled saltwater. The back of my head had smashed into the side window, and it felt like my brains were pouring down my back. I brought my hands up to my face, wet with tears or blood, I wasn't sure.

"Get your fuckin' hands off your face, Chanie," Blue snapped.

I tried to lower my hands, but my body was curled up so tight, I couldn't. My feet lifted from the floor as I tucked myself into a seated fetal position.

"Jesus Christ, Chanie! If you don't sit up straight and look normal, I swear to God I will knock every one of your teeth down your throat."

I took a deep breath and forced my body upright. I saw a police car right behind us. I thought they were pulling us over, but realized we were stopped at a red light. The cops were fixated on their computer screen, oblivious to the violence happening right in front of their car. Nothing felt real. In broad daylight on a Saturday afternoon, I'd been assaulted at a red light in my boyfriend's truck with a police car right behind us. And nobody knew except me and Blue.

I could jump out!

"Don't even think about it, Chanie. I will break every puny rib in Sox's body, one at a time."

The light turned green, and Blue gently accelerated. He handed me some dirty McDonalds napkins from the console. "Wipe your face. Your nose is bleeding."

I obeyed so he wouldn't hit me again. My chest burned as though my heart had ripped out and squeezed its way out the window. *Please don't let me bruise.* What would I tell Ginger? Rie and Pastor Josh? I couldn't explain away black eyes and swollen lips. He'd never hit me before. He'd just had a *moment.*

We pulled into the drive-through, and Blue ordered me an extra-large triple-triple.

"You're gonna need all that caffeine to get caught up on your homework. I'll get you home so you can get busy. You're gonna have a very busy weekend with work 'n all."

I'd been raped, beaten, and left on motel floors. I'd watched police cover up my strangled friend with a tarp. I'd accepted money to let men rough me up while they sodomized me. But nothing, *nothing* had felt so utterly grotesque as Blue's fist in my face. I wanted to hate him, but I needed him to love me more in that moment than I ever had. I wished he would reach over and stroke my face and tell me he hadn't meant it. That seeing the pain and damage he'd done to me would shake him into reality and make him realize he needed to get well. I needed him to want to be a better man, apologize, and promise he would never hurt me again. But he just handed me the coffee and drove us home in silence.

He parked in front of the building to let me out.

"You got about three hours to do some homework. Then I gotta take you to work for a bit. Brenda got you a new client. Said he'd pay well."

I looked at him and nodded. Tears rolled down my face. I bit my lip. *It's not safe to cry.*

"Come on, baby face. I love you. You know that. We just got all this stress going on all the fuckin' time. Brenda and Milos, your teachers sniffin' around. Man oh man! We're trying to get a fresh start here, and all this shit is in our faces. Like all the time! Makes a guy crazy."

He stared at me as though waiting for a reply. Like my acknowledgement of his stress would absolve him of what he'd done and erase that split second from my memory. I tried to pretend I understood. I nodded and said, "Pastor Josh says that when you're getting closer to your goals, the enemy gets stronger."

Blue leaned toward me, and I jerked up against the door.

"There's no need to get so sketchy, girl. You better relax those nerves so people don't start thinking you got an addiction problem."

I nodded.

"Baby, you know it's the stress, right? I didn't mean to punch you. I just lost my shit for a second. I told you before, it's just you bein' with those other guys! Makes me nuts. Let's just put it behind us."

"Yes, Blue. I want to do that." *I think …*

"You still love me, *right*?"

"Always, Blue. Love of my life," I said, again robotically.

"You too, baby." He leaned over me and opened the truck

door. "Remember, we're all we got, Chanie. You and me against the world!"

I stepped out of the truck and sat on the edge of a planter in front of the building. The air thickened with moisture. The clouds seemed to rush in to block out the sun as though they were trying to protect my face from the light. I didn't care if my face was bloody. I raised it up to the sky and waited for the rain to wash away the bruises, the truth, and the future that I feared.

The silver Audi slowly rolled past, my grey-haired prince looking intense and intelligent, probably thinking about things that mattered. He waited for cars to pass so he could turn into his parkade. A break in traffic gave him the gap he needed, but he glanced over and hesitated. His mouth opened slightly, and he creased his brows. I creased mine too and quickly looked away.

Brenda was sitting on the couch in the lobby, as though she'd been waiting to greet me. She came up to me and pointed her fingers in my face.

"Well, looky there! Looks like you had a bit of an accident, Jade. Sure wouldn't want to see that money-makin' face get too fucked up, would we?"

"No, we wouldn't, Brenda. Then you'd have to sell that dried-up snatch of yours for Canadian Tire money. Get the hell out of my way."

"Keep it up, darlin'! Maybe Milos can come and give ya an attitude adjustment."

"Not if I blow him, he won't!"

WHEN I'D STARTED HOOKING, my weathered reflection sad-dened me. I didn't think there could be anything worse until I looked in the mirror on Monday morning. My eyes had black-ened over the weekend, and despite the bags of frozen peas I'd pressed into my lips, they still throbbed and pounded as though trying to break free of my skin. If I hadn't given count-less blow jobs, the swelling might not have been so bad. I'd worked more hours than I'd slept. I'd pushed even harder to study while Blue was out getting high because my books were my lifeline. They were the bridge to my life of sun hats and gardens.

I made my way to the Mac's to meet Ginger. She looked out the window and ran outside. She wrapped her arms around me, and we crumpled to the ground and cried. Ginger cried even harder than I did. Maybe she cried harder because she knew she couldn't make me leave him. My pain hurt her. She was my karmic sister, like the girl on the TV the night Clayton and his buddy had raped me. One conscience, two lives.

"Chanie, we're gonna find you a way out. I promise you," Ginger said, pressing our foreheads together, her hands cupping my head.

"I don't know what to do. I can't just leave him."

"Fuck him! We gotta think about you. You need to get to school so you don't get kicked out. I'll grab coffee. Just get going, and I'll see you there. We'll come up with something believable."

"Blue said to tell everyone I went to help him rip up a carpet at work. That I was standing behind him, and he accidentally hit me."

"I hate him!" Ginger shrieked.

I rehearsed my story over and over in my head as I speed-walked to school. I had it memorized and ready. Everyone would believe me if I laughed it off and didn't make it into a big deal. I'd have to be consistent and not show a lot of emotion. I'd exit conversations quickly. I figured I could handle it — until I saw Tuffy and Jeremy standing outside. The look on their faces stung even worse than Blue's fist.

CHAPTER SEVENTEEN

KEEP MY HEAD UP. Look strong. Nobody would notice. Just a normal day: go to class, go home. Everybody else would study, then sleep. But I'd go to work, try to study, and hope that I didn't get beaten or killed. Jeremy's face made it hard for me to fake *okay*. I almost turned around and ran home. But Tuffy — he knew what to do. He took my hand, gave it a reassuring squeeze, and walked me to class.

I kept my head down all morning. When the lunch bell rang, I rushed to meet Ginger in the bathroom. "We'll hide what that bastard did," she said, smearing concealer on my face. "Thank God he didn't scar you *this time*!" She styled a long bang over my right eye, stroked my cheek gently, and took a step back to examine her work. "Hmm ... pucker your lips." She took a wand and softly blotted gloss on my bottom lip. "Now your lips look pouty instead of like they had a bad date with boxer."

"Do I look normal?"

"You look a tad slutty. Like you put your makeup on in the dark or something."

I looked in the mirror. "Holy eff! Where did you get that concealer?"

"At the strip club. We used it to cover up tattoos and bruises. A lot of girls had tattoos *and* bruises."

"It's like a group of chemists invented it for wife beaters."

"If you plan on staying with Blue, you should order a couple of cases. Make sure to gift the leftovers to the women's shelter so it doesn't go to waste when he finally kills you."

When he finally kills you.

The closing lines of my life. The epilogue. The end.

MIDTERM WEEK WAS OPEN house at the HFTC. It kicked off with a potluck meal and an afternoon of motivational speakers. Church ladies, board members, and community followers brought their best meals forward as though competing in a cook-off. Makeshift tables lined the edges of the gym and were covered with pies, cakes, casseroles, salads, scones, tarts, and three different flavours of cheesecakes. There were fruit platters, cheese platters, and more cookies than I'd ever seen. It looked like a wedding buffet for a princess.

Our first speaker looked familiar, like she might have worked the streets at one time. She looked like a young Brenda, bleach-blond hair frayed and eaten by drugstore bleach kits, reddish-purple lipstick, thick bands of blue eyeliner curled upward at the outer corners of her eyes. But most notably, the unmistakable street scowl that said *working girl*. A scowl that other hookers translated like secret code, invisible bands bonding them together in a world full of *others*.

"The name's Tamison. Graduated three years back." Her tone was strong and masculine, as though she was warning us that she'd kick every last one of our asses if we made fun of her. Her hot-pink bra glowed beneath a white tank top emblazoned with *Mike's Donair! Open Late Late Late!!* A Middle Eastern cartoon character punched a fat donair through the letters, and sauce spatter exploded decoratively up to the collar.

"Butch!" Jeremy said.

"Voice like a man, hair like a Muppet." Ginger giggled.

Tamison pulled a ragged piece of loose-leaf paper from her pocket. She cleared her throat and began reading the longest run-on sentence I'd ever heard. She soldiered through her speech with long pauses, a red face, and a few gasps for air when she ran out of breath. The gist was something about having worked her way up from Sandwich Artist at Subway to becoming the night manager of a donair joint on Jasper Avenue. "That's my story," she said, ending with a quick glare and a weird half curtsy before vacating the podium to stuff her pockets with food from the side tables.

Next, a tall, thin man with hair like Danny DeVito's introduced himself as the pastor and executive director of a Christian counselling centre. He was a much more dynamic speaker than poor Tamison, who, relieved to be finished, took off through the side door probably never to be seen at the Hope for Tomorrow Centre again.

"Faith and healing can be expressed through art and creativity," he preached, pacing back and forth, waving his hands like a Sunday morning TV evangelist. Pastor Josh delighted in his every word and lit up the gym with his snow-white smile. Clean-cut missionary kids wearing pink ties walked around handing out bags with adult colouring books and gel pens. "God bless," they said a thousand times. "Jesus is waiting for your creation!" They looked like boys from an Irish Spring commercial, fresh faced and scrubbed clean, ready for a personal dinner with the Lord Himself.

"Looks like someone painted their creation on your face,

Chanie!" Jeremy laughed and pretended to draw on Tuffy's face with a gel pen. Tuffy slapped his hand away.

"Fuck off, Jeremy! Don't draw attention to her." Ginger smacked the pen out of his hand.

"Oh, come on. She looks like she's at work. And you kinda look like that too, Ginger. Makin' me kinda hard!"

"Knock it off!" Tuffy snapped.

"Chanie," Ginger said, "we need to save you from that son of a bitch."

I rolled my eyes. "I can't talk about Blue right now."

"Quiet!" Tuffy pointed at Mr. Lavoy standing at the podium, about to speak.

Mr. Lavoy smiled. He looked well rested. Happy. He surveyed his audience and waited for us to settle down. Pastor Josh stood next to him and raised his arms like a maestro hushing his orchestra. The two men nodded to each other, and Mr. Lavoy began speaking in a tone more like a preacher than an English teacher.

"In every tragedy, there is opportunity. Opportunity to be generous, helpful, or simply grateful for the million little miracles we live each day. One such tragedy I've been asked to share with you today is that of Terek Sanders, a young man of nineteen who lost his life to a silly mistake."

A few *oohs* and *ahhs* broke out. And then silence.

Mr. Lavoy continued, "He trusted a fellow student to give him a painkiller because he'd injured his back during football practice. He didn't want to get cut from the upcoming game because he knew his team relied on him. But now he won't ever play again." He took a long pause and looked up at all of us. "Because that fellow student gave him fentanyl. Young Terek died only two hours later.

"As a result of this tragedy, Terek's father has created a one-time award. The contest is open to the inner-city high schools in Edmonton, and the winner will receive a twenty-five-thousand-dollar scholarship to any four-year program at a Canadian university. And the school wins fifty thousand dollars!" Mr. Lavoy smiled and clasped his hands to his chest, like a young girl accepting a marriage proposal. He gazed at the crowd, his energy radiant, excited, as though all the kids would be saved by fifty grand.

When the applause subsided, he bellowed, "Who wants to know the details?" He was beaming like Oprah Winfrey yelling out prizes to her audience. The crowd fed off his energy, cheering and hollering like it was the fourth quarter of the Super Bowl with Larry Fitzgerald running toward the end zone for the winning touchdown. Mr. Lavoy was stoked. He took a big breath and blurted out, "This is an essay contest!"

The cheering stopped. A couple of boos echoed through the gym. "Seems I lost my cheer squad," Mr. Lavoy joked, looking at the other teachers, who were giving him sympathetic looks as though witnessing a rabbit trying to cross a freeway. "Anyway, like I said, this is an essay contest. The top five will read their essays at City Hall, at which time the winner will be announced."

He read the remaining details in a tone resembling the side-effects portion of a pharmaceutical commercial. "In order to qualify, students must have a minimum of seventy-five percent in English 30 and references from two teachers. The essays will be judged by a panel of ten professionals from various fields." Mr. Lavoy paused, as though hoping his cheer squad might resurrect itself. "Please see me if you are interested in attempting this worthy feat." He nodded and walked away, briefly rushing back to the mic. "Oh yeah! The theme is *Believe!*"

Ginger shrugged her shoulders. "I can't even use the right words when I'm trying to order a meal combo, let alone write an award-winning essay. Mr. Lavoy talked to me about my grades and suggested that I work harder on my vocabulary."

"I can help you with that, Ginger," Jeremy said. "I can tell you ten different ways to suck my dick."

"Actually, you can't, Jeremy. You're not smart enough." Ginger winked and wrapped her arms around him. "Hey, Chanie. What's the word on Brenda these days? Is that old whore on life support yet?"

"Nope. The dirty skank is still lingering around, but I'm either at school or out working, so I don't see her much."

"As long as Blue gives her all your money, then I guess all is well for her." Ginger rolled her eyes.

"You are so dumb, Chanie," Jeremy said. "You don't have to give her shit!"

"Blue and I are saving money to start over," I replied, as though that made everything okay. Like hooking and getting beat up made total sense because it was all for the greater good.

"Blue blows your money on crack and meth, and he's gonna end up killing you," Tuffy said, as he slung his backpack over his shoulder and started walking away.

"What the eff is his deal?" Ginger said to Jeremy.

"Guess he doesn't like whores." Jeremy shrugged and raised his eyebrows.

"Or *maybe*, Jeremy, he loves Chanie, and it hurts him when you talk shit like you do."

"Yeah. Must be love," Jeremy said, wide eyed.

"Anyways, Chanie. Lavoy told me to use a thesaurus if I want to expand my vocabulary."

"I use a thesaurus when I write my papers," I said with a smile.

"Of course you do, you fucking poindexter." Jeremy punched my arm.

"Let's create a game called Synonyms for Brenda," Ginger said.

"Those words won't be in a dictionary or thesaurus," I replied. "Maybe the Urban Dictionary online."

"True. How about we call it Synonyms for Brenda That You Can Say in Front of Pastor Josh?" Ginger chuckled as Jeremy pulled her close to him.

"Rie asked to see me, so I have to run. Chat later, friends."

"I ain't your friend, Chanie." Jeremy winked and waved me away with his hand.

"We need to talk about your escape plan, girl!" Ginger yelled.

Rie, Mr. Lavoy, and Pastor Josh greeted me in Rie's office. My throat tightened. Perhaps the time had come for Mr. Lavoy to tell the truth about the night I broke into the church. Why else would they all be there with sympathetic smiles pasted on their faces? I scrunched up my nose as though it would help me devise a heartfelt promise, a commitment they couldn't refuse. Jail would put a period to my progress. End of story. No more edits or revisions. Temporary student, lifelong hooker.

"Mr. Lavoy asked us to meet as a group." Rie smiled and motioned me to sit down.

"Okay." I sat down and clasped my hands on my lap.

"Yes, Chanie," Mr. Lavoy said. "Rie and Pastor Josh agreed to have me here because I want to talk to you about the essay contest. You heard me speak today about the memorial fund award?"

"Yes, Mr. Lavoy."

"And what are your thoughts?"

"I think it's very touching — what his dad is doing in his memory."

"And?" Pastor Josh said.

"And — it's very generous?" I said, confused about what they wanted to hear from me.

Mr. Lavoy intervened. "How do you feel you can contribute to this cause?"

"What do you mean? I have no money," I said.

The three of them laughed, like I was being set up for a big joke.

Mr. Lavoy got serious. "We've reviewed your work, including your personal reflection essay. We agree that you are a talented writer and feel that you're a good candidate to enter the essay contest."

"Oh my God!" My stomach bounced off the floor. "I don't think I can pull that off."

"With some extra work and commitment, we believe you can," Rie said. "We thought maybe you could take a break from Friday story nights at the shelter and dedicate that time to writing the essay. We'll still credit you volunteer hours for your time."

"But the clients like story night." I didn't want to give up those evenings. That night was the only time I'd liked myself and believed that there was something good in me. I'd been looking forward to the next night. I'd even googled popular short stories to see if I could find something in advance.

"They do. But we asked Tuffy Stonefeathers to step in and help. He was very accommodating." Mr. Lavoy winked at me.

Maybe he should have tucked in his braid.

"You should be proud, young lady!" Pastor Josh came over and patted my shoulder. "We've seen your progress and commitment.

We support you and know how talented you are. We believe in you. Jesus believes in you. Let's all pray together."

Pastor Josh prayed. The guilt in my heart felt like a broiler. My face flushed, and my eyes watered from the sting of the toxic wasteland of lies I'd created. I wanted to jump up and say, *I'm a fraud! I'm a liar. I should be kicked out because I'm drinking and whoring and lying to you every single day.*

I lifted my chin and looked up. My mouth opened, but nothing came out.

Mr. Lavoy leaned toward me. "Is there something you'd like to say, Chanie?"

That I'm trash …

After a short pause, I whispered, "Thank you."

The three of them stepped out and huddled into a hushed conversation. Was it about my tardiness? Incomplete assignments? Maybe my face? Too much makeup — clearly hiding something. I breathed in and prepared myself to deter any suspicions with more lies. If I worked hard, I'd finish the program in a few months and be free to leave the city with Blue. I'd leave all the lies behind. But if I failed, two options remained: jail or suicide.

Rie came back into the room and sat across from me. She tilted her head sideways. *Here it comes.* My eyelids hung heavy, like wet snow on thin branches. I ached to tell the truth and beg for help. I wanted to lift the lies off my back once and for all, shake my wings and fly away.

"Is there anything going on at home, Chanie?"

"No! There isn't." My eyes fluttered, and the room seemed to shift.

"We can help you." Rie reached for my hand, her face soft, eyes tender.

I pulled my hand away. "I'm okay. Let's do our session."

Rie nodded. "Okay. Let's see where we're at for our goals so far." She read through my file and looked up at me. "How do you feel about your progress to date?"

"I don't know. I think I'm doing okay."

"You're doing well academically, but recently we've been working on your anxiety. Have you thought much about writing those letters to your mom and stepdad?"

"I've thought about it, and I'm not ready."

"I think we should try. There's a lot of relief that can come from getting it out of your head and onto the page."

"Okay! Fine." I decided I'd write up a quick hate letter so Rie would let it go. Then I could return to my basic survival mode and plow through the next few months until I graduated.

"Also, we should consider if you'd like to move on to post-secondary studies."

"What do you mean?"

"Like college or university. Your grades are high enough that you can do something more with your life."

"Better than managing a donair shop downtown?"

"Yes, Chanie. Much better than that."

Rie's blunt response surprised me. It made me sit up a bit taller.

"Really? Even if that were true, how would I pay for it?"

"Two ways. Student loans and a part-time legitimate job."

"I don't even know what I'd like to do." I closed my eyes for a second and tried to picture myself in five years, but all I saw was the yellow tarp floating down over my body. I snapped my eyes open and gasped.

"Are you okay, Chanie? Are you having a panic attack?"

I took a few deep breaths to calm myself, a new skill unintentionally derived from paying attention during meditation class. It had just happened one day. After twenty minutes of breathing deeply and repeating the mantra — *calming, smiling, present moment, perfect moment* — peace flowed through me. It felt weird. Like instantaneous healing. My ears stopped ringing, my vision cleared, and I experienced a few minutes of clarity. "I'm good," I said.

"Good for you, Chanie. You should be proud of how you just handled that. Maybe let's explore the anxiety trigger. Is it because you feel overwhelmed by the possibility of going to university?"

"I don't know what I'd study." I didn't want to end up in an office, like that poor lawyer whose desk I'd been sodomized on. She looked happy in her picture, all sun-kissed and holding her cute little terrier, but the office had a stale energy, like an old medical clinic. I couldn't fathom sitting at the same desk in the same office every day of my life with guys like Derek secretly wanting to hate-rape me.

"We know that you like books and have a gift for writing. Is there anything you might like to explore there?"

I thought about it for a second. "I don't really know."

"Can you think of a moment when you've felt really happy — alive — when your heart sang, and you felt like you were on top of the world?"

"I felt amazing when I read the story at the shelter, like I was doing something good for the people who needed it most."

"That's wonderful! Do you realize that your whole face just lit up? You could study social work or community studies? Maybe counselling?"

"Those are some pretty impressive goals." I let myself feel the possibility for about ten seconds. Then I kicked it away. I had way too many triggers to think of a career in counselling.

"Think about your goals, Chanie. And then ask yourself, what will the world always need? And further to that, what will you need for a safe and stable life?"

"A government job," I said, thinking of Mr. Tanji's gorgeous 435 and his love of six-dollar lattes.

"Not a bad idea! Let's work on some career investigation next week and start looking at programs and loan applications. Look forward, Chanie. You have a bright future."

"Thanks for your encouragement." I picked up my bag. I'd had enough for one day.

"I want you to think hard about that letter to your parents. It's heavy stuff weighing you down. If we can help you let go, it can clear the path for your future. It's like wearing shackles. You can't run with shackles on."

"Thanks, Rie. I need to get going."

"By the way, Chanie. I believe you can kick ass in the essay contest! Come to me for anything you need." She stood up and gave me the kind of hug that made me believe that we could be friends someday.

I arrived home to a happy kitten. Sox had flecks of catnip in his fur and new toys all over the floor. Fresh flowers beamed at me from the table. Speckles of baby's breath and greens floated in fresh cat puke by the door. A bottle of Captain Morgan sat on the counter next to a note from Blue. *Root beer and ice in the fridge. Out getting supper.*

I considered having a shower, but without makeup it was harder to forget that Blue had hit me. The cakey concealer covered the truth on my face and in my mind. It saved me from

flashbacks every time I looked in the mirror. "Here's the concealer," Ginger had said, shoving it into my hand before we
parted ways after school. "Hey! Just so you know, it won't mend
broken bones!"

Broken bones.

"Hi, baby! I'm home," Blue sang from the door. Sox stopped playing and ran behind the dresser.

"Hi, Blue."

"I picked up lasagna from Rigoletto's for us. It's your
favourite!"

"What's with all the special treatment?"

"I wanted to do something nice for my girl. Is that okay?"

Sure?

"I know I lost my temper, babe, but it's so fuckin' hard for me.
Not only are you out screwin' everybody for money, but you're
running around at school with all those young guys. I know
what guys want. I don't like them lookin' at you that way!"

"I'm only out there working to get us out of this shitty life.
It was your idea."

"*Our* idea, Chanie."

"Whatever! I'm doing it so we can have a future together,
away from Brenda and Milos. But you've got to stop taking
money from the can."

Blue scratched his head. "I know. I'm a piece of shit. But I
get so fuckin' tied up over those guys at your school and shit!
I gotta get high, or I'll go out of my mind!"

"The guys at school are just guys at school. They're no threat
to you." A wave of guilt blew through me like a rush of winter
wind. *Tuffy's hand on mine ...*

"Oh yeah? What about work guys? Big-money guys like Tanji.
What if you fall in love with one of them and fuckin' leave me?"

"Oh my God, Blue, I'm with you. Plus, I could never fall in love with someone who pays for sex. Jesus, do you think I have no standards?"

"Sometimes I don't know, Chanie."

His words stung. Did I have a distorted view of myself? Some working girls did anything and everything, but I had limits. Boundaries. Did that count for decency? Or had I created an illusion of myself that I could live with?

The Packers game provided dinnertime entertainment and spared me from having to make conversation. I didn't know what to talk about. Bringing up the essay contest would provoke hostility, as would any discussion about my need for more rest and study time. Moving to Nelson seemed like another trigger. He didn't talk to me about his job, and I certainly didn't want to share the details of my work nights. My heart felt sad, like it knew it was in the wrong place but didn't know where else to go.

"Are you happy, Blue?"

Blue squinted and blinked hard. "What does that even mean?"

"Is there something you need from me to make things better for us?"

"You know what, babe? Sometimes, I do need a little bit more from you."

"Like what?"

"Well, you never want to have sex anymore."

I nodded and forced a tiny smile. I went into the kitchen and filled my glass half full of rum, guzzled it, then poured another. Captain Morgan could make me love him, even if only for a few minutes. That was all Blue usually needed. A few minutes.

CHAPTER EIGHTEEN

THE NEXT THREE WEEKS passed without a lot of drama. Mostly because I shut my mouth, went to work, and handed over my earnings. I faked my life. I pretended that the Nelson can didn't even exist. That way, it didn't hurt so much. Besides, I'd found a new way to get through the days: caffeine, Tylenol 3, Valium, and alcohol.

The drugs had bought me a few extra miles. I completed some papers and even got a couple of As. But my body had other ideas. I fainted in Mr. Lavoy's class and woke up with my head on Tuffy's lap. I kept my eyes closed as he stroked my hair, his big hands easing me like ocean waves gently lapping up against a sandy shore. And then a smell like cat piss, violent nausea, and a bitchy nurse waving smelling salts under my nose.

The next thing I knew, Allister, the social worker intern, was driving me to the emergency room. He flashed me a lot of dad-like smiles, but before we got out of his truck at the hospital he stopped smiling and said, "Chanie, I'm a recovering addict, and I can see right through you and your little games."

"You don't know me!" I said, rolling my eyes. Recovering addicts pissed me off, acting all high and mighty, like they'd discovered the secret of life while puking in a dirty toilet at a roadside bar for the hundred-and-eightieth time.

"Maybe not. But what I do know is that you're blowing an opportunity to do something great with your life."

"What do you know?!"

"I know that you're the star contestant for the essay contest. Don't fuck it up. I wasted the first forty-three years of my life. Finally cleaned it up and went to school. Don't wait like I did. That's all I'm saying."

"You can leave me here, Allister. My boyfriend and his mom are on their way," I lied. My phone had been dead since early that morning, and the last thing I'd ever do was reach out to Blue and Brenda.

"I'm staying with you until the doctor comes."

"Whatever floats your boat, *All Star.*"

I fell asleep on Allister's shoulder in the waiting room. I even drooled a bit on his sweater. When the nurse called my name, I jerked myself upright and gave Allister a dirty look as though he'd tricked me into falling asleep on him. The doctor appeared almost as soon as I'd changed into the gown.

"What's going on with you today, young miss?"

Young miss! I smiled and told him I was fine, that I just hadn't eaten all day. I said that I was too busy working on a big essay for a school contest and that I'd get a scholarship if I won. And my school would win money too. It was a life-changing opportunity!

"That sounds like a lot of pressure, young lady." The doctor's smile reminded me of Mr. Lavoy's. "What's the essay about?"

Good question.

I smiled at him and took a long pause, then slowly said, "Trying harder. It's about trying harder."

"Well, that sounds like a topic everyone could benefit from. Let's get some bloodwork done and make sure you're in good shape to finish that essay."

"That's not necessary, Doctor. I promise to take better care of myself."

"It won't hurt to run some blood tests while you're here. Sit tight."

He squinted as though shielding his eyes from the sun and then disappeared behind the curtain. I ditched the gown, got dressed, and headed for the exit. There was no way I was going to let them draw my codeine-tainted blood.

I missed the bus. I saw its taillights from half a block away but didn't have enough energy to chase it. I didn't mind waiting. It'd buy me some time to figure out a lie for Blue. He didn't like me drawing attention to us. He said it *threatened our dreams*. My fainting at school would be a problem for him. *Wouldn't want anyone asking too many questions ...*

On the ride home, I tore the hospital I.D. bracelet off and stuffed it between the seats, like if I hid it then the day had never really happened. But it had happened. And the one thing I couldn't shake was how good it had felt when I'd told the doctor about the essay contest. I'd lied about working hard on the essay, but I wanted to make that lie into my truth. *It's about trying harder.*

Blue was still in bed when I got home, the apartment completely dark.

"Hello, Blue."

He sat up. "Why are you so late?"

"It's only seven. I had a counselling appointment after school."

"Holy fuck! I slept late. I gotta get up." He jumped off the bed and went into the kitchen. I heard him pull the decanter out of the coffee machine.

"Hey, Blue. I'd like to talk about school with you."

"Oh, what is it now?" Blue rolled his eyes.

"The teachers announced an essay contest that could win the school some cash. The winner reads their speech at City Hall —"

"And?"

"*And* they said they'd like me to enter the contest."

"For real." He shook his head and laughed.

"Yes, for real." I felt a surge of excitement.

"What's in it for you?"

"A twenty-five-thousand-dollar scholarship to a Canadian college or university."

"Oh, holy fuck, girl!" He clapped his hands together.

My heart jumped, and I smiled. "I know! I'm so excited!"

"Oh my God, Chanie! You are *so* dumb."

"What?" It felt like the room had fallen out from under me.

"You actually believe this shit?"

"It's not shit, Blue, it's —"

"Go colour in your little colouring book, Chanie. That's about as far as your academic career is going."

"What's that supposed to mean?"

"It means they're using you to get what they need. Those kinds of people are all the same. They'll blow smoke up your ass because there's a buck in it for them."

"That's not true. They're good —"

"What are you going to say in your speech?" Blue raised his voice and pretended to hold a mic. "Hello, my name is Chanie Nyrider. Maybe I've sucked your dick a time or two, or better yet, let you fuck me in the ass. But look at me now! Here's my shitty little words about my shitty little life so you'll all feel sorry for me and spend your tax dollars on this shitty little school."

I cupped my face in my hands. "My teachers like me. They believe in me."

"Your teachers don't like you. They don't believe in you. They have to act that way and say those things to you. It's their job! They just feel sorry for you. Nobody actually likes you or takes you seriously. That bald fuck of a teacher of yours just wants to fuck you. Your little Indian princess with the braid wants the same thing. Ginger's fuckin' brain-dead. The only things she's got goin' for her are them nice titties! Wake up, Chanie!"

"Why would they pick me then, Blue? Why?"

"Because you're the sorriest-looking one of them all. The best poster child for that pathetic school so they can keep their funding and those losers don't lose their teaching jobs." Blue wrapped his arm around me. "Come on, baby. Nobody cares about hookers. People feel like they deserve the bad things that happen to them. They think you bitches are homewreckers out spreading disease and ruining communities. Those teachers don't understand people like us."

Maybe Blue was right. People like Rie and Mr. Lavoy didn't understand my type. They told me what they were paid to tell me. It was no different than me telling the men who paid me what they wanted to hear. All about the dollar! The smartest thing I could do was get us out of Edmonton and into Nelson. I'd waitress at a pub or work as a chambermaid. Not much point in trying harder. Girls like me usually left the streets in a body bag, not a graduation gown.

"Baby, we got a plan. You can't forget the plan." Blue squeezed me tight.

"I haven't forgotten."

"I put a few hundred bucks in the Nelson can. Thought it'd make up for the loan I took out of there."

Sox shoved his way onto my lap and curled up.

"I better start driving you to school these days, Chanie. Make sure everybody knows that you got people looking out for you. Maybe they'll think twice about putting all this shit into your head."

I stared at the floor and stroked Sox.

"Get ready for work, babe. Maybe use a bit more makeup and try pigtails tonight. I hear them young girls out there have been givin' you a run for your money."

THE NEXT MORNING, BLUE caught me on my way out the door. "I'm driving you today," he said.

"It's fine. I'll walk."

"I said I'm fuckin' driving you, Chanie."

"I'm supposed to meet Ginger."

"Well, tell her too bad. I want to talk to you, babe."

Babe!

Ginger messaged me while I was walking to Blue's truck: *Milos = neanderthal, barbaric, misogynist, pimp, opportunist, browbeater, intimidator, oppressor, pest, rascal, ruffian, tormentor, excrement, dung, manure ... LOL.*

I jumped in the truck and messaged her back: *Can't meet you this morning. See you at school.*

She texted: *Tuffy = tantalizing, Jeremy = scrumptious!!*

"Who the fuck are you messaging?" Blue stammered, coming down from a night of rum and opioids.

"I'm telling Ginger that I can't meet her."

"Your little friends are a distraction."

"No, they're not."

"I can't believe that's what you're wearing," Blue said.

"What the fuck? Are you Mr. Fashion now?"

"No! But Jesus Christ, Chanie. You're not going to work."

"I'm wearing leggings and a sweatshirt, Blue! Not exactly bootie shorts and heels."

"Wow! So sensitive! Poor little Chanie. Can't take the truth."

I looked out the window and ignored him.

"Chanie, you need to get more serious about our plan. Brenda and Milos are up my ass all the time. They said you need to bring in more cash or they'll take a higher cut."

"Are you *fucking kidding*?"

"I told them to lay off. That you're doing what you can. But Milos said that the deal's off with us. I no longer get to manage you. Brenda and Milos are taking over."

"No!" I slammed my fists on the dashboard.

"Holy fuck, girl! Simmer down. Almost made me jump through the roof."

"No way, Blue! This whole thing is messed up. I'm only supposed to be taking online calls, and that never happened. Instead, you drop me off by the roadside like a piece of garbage, and then that psycho Milos circles me all night like a vulture."

"Well, what am I supposed to do, Chanie? Tell them no?"

"Yes, Blue. Tell them no!"

"Well, it ain't that easy, girl. I had to lend my mom some of your cash and gave Brenda an I.O.U. of sorts. They need a quick couple grand out of you, so you're gonna have to skip a few days of school, if you know what I mean."

"No! I don't know what you mean. Call your mom and get the money back. That wasn't your money." My vision blurred, and my jaw quivered. "Get the money back, Blue! I can't do all things all the time. We're supposed to be in this together, but you're all robbing me of everything I earn."

"Don't be so fuckin' dramatic, Chanie! The old bird needed my help. Am I supposed to say no to my own mother!" He stared at me wide-eyed, holding his hands up.

"Am I supposed to be a hooker for the rest of my life?"

"Calm down. People are looking. The last thing we need is more people sniffin' around our business."

"Then maybe you should have let me walk to school like I'd planned."

"Don't get so cocky, girl. Me and Brenda got date-stamped videos of you drinking and, even better, working by the gates, slithering into some dirtbag's car. If I send that to your teachers, you'll be in jail with no future. No Nelson, no Sox, no nothing."

I jumped out of the truck and two-hand slammed the door. Ginger, Jeremy, and Tuffy waited by the stairs. I couldn't face them, especially Tuffy. I veered off and went behind the school, slid down the back wall, and pulled my knees to my chest. *Calming, smiling, present moment, perfect moment ... calming, smiling ...* I clenched my fists and stifled a scream. I had to get it together. I couldn't risk an intervention with Pastor Josh and Rie, especially after my fainting incident the day before.

The scent of Beach Coconut body spray drifted over me. Ginger plopped down, pried my fingers open, and wrapped them around a large coffee. "Chanie ..."

"Jesus Christ, Ginger! Don't lecture me right now." I hated the Blue version of me, short-tempered, snappy, and chronically lying, cheating, and scrambling to get by. She pushed her body against mine, leaned her head on my shoulder, and casually flipped through the pages of her thesaurus.

"Hey, Chanie."

"Oh God, what?"

"Blue equals fuckface!" Ginger cracked up and tapped my forehead with the thesaurus.

"Ginger, come on."

She snuggled closer and turned her phone sideways in front of us. "Chanie, you're gonna watch this with me."

"What now? More cat videos?"

"No! Just watch."

YouTube played its usual pre-video ads before loading a TED Talk video. The camera zoomed in on a beautiful dark-haired woman with olive skin and high cheekbones. She was tall and lean; she looked healthy and athletic. A silky red dress hung loosely over her lanky body, and she had a calm and reassuring energy, like a young Rie. This woman began to share her experience of domestic violence and how she'd nearly died at the hands of "the love of her life."

She was beautiful, educated, and came from a good family. She had gone to Harvard and had worked as a model. She shared how she didn't even realize she was being abused. And by the time she did, she didn't have the energy to care whether he killed her. She wasn't like me, the cliché runaway selling herself on the street, at the mercy of her big, bad boyfriend. She was the kind of woman every woman wanted to be. And yet, she was just like me. And when she said that when we leave our abuser, we are seventy times more likely to be murdered, I told Ginger to shut it off.

My life was absurd, like a low-budget movie. The hooker with a heart of gold and the mean, scary boyfriend. If I walked away from Blue, what would I be walking to? Jail, a criminal record, poverty, and prostitution? I'd have to leave my home, my new friends, and my potential. Sox and my life in Nelson. How would my story end? Was I a cliché on the road to becoming a statistic? Or would a real hero finally appear in my life and take me somewhere higher?

"GRADUATION IS IN FEWER than two months!" Mr. Lavoy said. "We're going to discuss everyone's post-graduation plans. Who wants to go first?" He looked around. "Ginger, let's start with you."

Ginger looked surprised, like she'd woken from a scary daydream. "Hmm. Let's see ... I'm planning to run away with my best buddy and live in the mountains. When we get there, I might apply to the Hairstylist Foundation Program at Selkirk College and maybe do yoga teacher training. I haven't decided yet."

"I'm gonna be a rap star and lay down freaky beats," Jeremy said, waving his hands in the air.

"That's realistic!" I snapped.

"Oh gee! The resident whore is now a career counsellor."

"Enough, Jeremy." Mr. Lavoy pointed at us.

Jeremy ignored him. "By the way, Chanie. I saw you kissin' your dad this morning when he dropped you off. Nasty!"

"Shut up, Jeremy!" I slammed my fists on my desk.

"I said enough!" Mr. Lavoy walked toward me. "Chanie, what are your plans?"

"I'm moving to Nelson, B.C., with my boyfriend and might waitress at a hotel or work as a chambermaid."

Mr. Lavoy looked like I'd flashed him. "I'm sorry, Chanie, but that seems to be a departure from what we've been working on together. What about the essay? And your student loan applications? Are there any post-secondary schools in Nelson?"

"That won't matter," I said.

"What do you mean that won't matter?" Mr. Lavoy replied.

"Blue says that I won't make it in the big schools. Says our program doesn't grade as hard as the real schools do. Basically, I'm fooling myself and will end up failing and owing the government a bunch of money for student loans, so I've decided not to bother applying."

Jeremy jumped up and spun around to face me. "Holy fuck, Chanie. He doesn't know shit. He's just trying to control you. Everybody knows he's beating the fuck out of you and you're too stunned to do anything about it!"

"Whatever, Jeremy," I snarled. "I don't want to rack up thousands of dollars in student loans just to flunk out and end up being a waitress. I figure I'll skip the debt and go straight to waitressing."

"Oh my God, you dumb bitch!" Jeremy strode toward me. "What the fuck is wrong with you?"

"Shut up, Jeremy! You're not my counsellor." I jumped up from my desk. "You're not even my friend, so shove your opinion up your ass!"

The class giggled. Ginger looked at me, tears welling in her eyes. Tuffy came and stood next to me.

Jeremy's spit flecked my face. "Your boyfriend is a monster, you stupid bitch! He's selling your ass to pay for his meth habit."

I lurched toward him, and we stood eye to eye. "Who the fuck are you to talk to me like that?" I screamed. "Your future is no better. Most likely jail, you son of a bitch!"

"Blue is no good! He doesn't need your help, just your money. Everyone can see it but you! How can you waste your life? You have a chance to be better, but you'd rather suck dick for your meth head boyfriend."

"You know *nothing*, Jeremy!" I shrieked. Tuffy stepped in front of me and tried to block Jeremy.

"Yeah! Well, I know this! The only way you're gonna leave

that piece of shit is in a fucking body bag, Chanie. We can all see it!"

"Shut up! You know nothing! He needs me. He needs me to help him. We'll take care of each other."

Jeremy slammed his fists down on my desk. "Oh my God! How can someone so smart be so fucking dumb?"

"Enough!" Mr. Lavoy pushed his way between the three of us. "Both of you, get out!"

I ran out of the room. Jeremy tried to run after me, but Tuffy stopped him. I ran all the way to the equipment room in the gym, where I took a Valium and sobbed into a dirty towel. I wished I could go home, but if I blew off another meeting with Rie, I'd have bigger problems. It was too much, all the teachers prying and poking at me, pushing *their* aspirations. Maybe my friends were a distraction. I texted Blue. And waited.

> Blue, I need to talk ...

> I need to see you. Bad day.

> You're right, Blue. Too many distractions. Need to focus on us!

> Can't wait to see you ... please come home tonight ... xoxo!

An hour later, I fidgeted in Rie's office, constantly glancing at my phone. Still no reply.

"How's the essay coming along?"

"It's not." My phone vibrated in my pocket.

"What's Mr. Lavoy teaching you on Friday nights?"

"A lot of grammar and punctuation." Another vibration from my phone.

"Nothing on the essay yet?" Rie looked distressed, as though it were her personal essay contest.

My phone buzzed again and again.

"No, Rie. Not yet. Why are you so interested in this essay?"

"Because this is an incredible opportunity that I think you have a shot at."

"I see."

"Can we talk a bit more about the letters to your parents?"

"I'm working on them. I'll have them the next time I see you," I said, amazed at how easily I lied about everything.

"Do you need to check your phone?"

"I probably should."

Get home now! 911

CHAPTER NINETEEN

I CALLED SIX TIMES, but Blue didn't answer. It had to be Sox. What else could warrant a 911 text? I should have saved him sooner and taken him to a safer home. I prayed it wasn't too late. My tiny, helpless kitten. How could I have left him there with those monsters?

The apartment was dark. The lights were off, the blinds were drawn, and there was tinfoil over one window. I dropped to my knees and reached behind the dresser. Sox's warm body melted into my hand, and he purred. "Thank God, little buddy." I pulled him out and rubbed him on my cheek. "I was so scared something bad happened to my little guy."

"Fuck the cat!" Blue snapped, slumped on the floor next to the bathroom door.

Sox jumped from my hands and scurried behind the dresser.

"Jesus Christ, Blue! You scared me. What happened to you?"

"Fucking Milos happened. That's what!"

I went over and kneeled next to him. His eyes were red, and it looked like a golf ball was trying to push out from behind his left eye. His nose slanted slightly to the right, and his bottom lip bulged.

"What do you mean, Milos?"

"The Serbian bastard came down here and strangled me," Blue said, pulling his collar down. I saw nothing but stubble and razor rash, but I nodded to keep him calm.

"And then he told me that you better get your ass to work so we can pay back the money I had to give my mom." He dropped his head and started sobbing. "I just wanted to help my mom. Is that such a bad thing?"

"It's okay, Blue." I stroked his head. "I'm here for you." I'd never see him cry. It made me nervous, like he was losing even more control of his emotions.

Blue slammed his fists into his temples. "I love you, babe. It's so hard watching you work all the time. I just love you so much, I can't control myself."

I grabbed his wrists to stop him from hurting himself. "That's why we have to save our money. So we can leave and start fresh somewhere else."

"I know, baby. I love you so much, Chanie. I'd die without you. You're the only one who understands me." He put his head down and wept some more.

"Yeah, it's been hard," I said, wondering why I felt so detached.

"I know. I'm sorry. I'm such a fuck-up. My mom is right. I'm nasty! I'm no good! Nobody wants me in their life. I should fuckin' overdose and be gone. Fuck everyone!"

"Baby, don't say that. I've seen the good in you."

"You're all I got, Jade — I mean, Chanie. I'll be a better man. I promise."

You're all I got, Jade!

I raised my voice slightly. "I'm going to kill Milos! And Brenda!"

"No, no, no, please, Chanie!" He squeezed my hand so hard I cried out. "Don't say a fucking word to them about this. I don't want to piss Milos off any more than he already is."

"He can't just come down here and beat you up."

"What do you mean, he can't? He just did." Blue banged his fist on the wall.

"I haven't even seen Brenda or Milos at all in the last couple of weeks."

Blue narrowed his eyes and clenched his fists. "I think they went to the mountains for a few days."

"Gross! Are they a couple or what? So weird," I said, trying to break the tension.

"Who knows? I think Brenda sucks his dick and gives him cash, so maybe. Who knows what goes on between couples? Please promise me you won't say a word!"

"But —"

"Jesus Christ, Chanie! Don't say a fucking word!"

"Okay, I promise. But promise me we stay committed to this plan and stop getting off track."

"I promise you. I love you, babe."

"What can I do to help you feel better, Blue?" I needed the moment to end. I wanted to open the blinds, get off the floor, and resume some type of normalcy.

"Why don't you go get some groceries, and I'll make us a nice meal, like we used to do."

An hour later, Blue grilled some burgers on a stolen barbeque he claimed was collateral. "Rich prick refused to pay for my work," Blue had said the day he'd brought it home. He smiled at me as he flipped burgers on the flaming grill, the brushed nickel lid gleaming in the sun. He seemed surprisingly upbeat for a guy who'd just been beat up. I didn't eat much.

I had no appetite after my shitty day. After dinner, I curled up under the blankets with Sox. Blue tossed me the iPad and made us toffee-flavoured coffee. He joined us under the covers and rested a hand on my stomach. He nestled his face into my neck and whispered, "This is what it'll be like in Nelson, babe. Lots of nights like this on our porch. No Brenda or Milos anymore, just us."

"I miss you, Blue. We aren't like we used to be."

He shoved his hands under my shirt. "Stress will do that."

"I don't want to feel like this anymore, I —"

"Shh." Blue slid my panties down and whispered, "I miss you, Chanie." He thrust himself into me.

I pulled every trick out of my bag. I moaned, groaned, and moved around beneath him. But nothing was working. I looked over Blue's shoulder and pictured Tuffy's velvet neck, his shoulders, face, and mouth. I squeezed my hand as though it were wrapped around his braid. I pretended Tuffy was inside me, in love with me. I invented an imaginary world where I had been perfect and untouched before him. *What would he feel like? The sweet scent of our sweat, our bodies blending, my legs wrapped around his body.*

Blue jerked and thrusted, and when he finally yelled, "Fuck yeah!" I mouthed Tuffy's name and licked my lips. I smiled at Tuffy, but Blue smiled back. I closed my eyes and curled my hand around Tuffy's braid. I held it all the way into a deep sleep.

"Chanie. Wake up!"

"What is it, Blue?"

"You gotta go to work."

"Oh my God, really?"

"Yeah, really. Did you dream we won the lottery or something?"

"No, but I thought maybe I could get some sleep."

"And you did. I let you get two hours."

Tears rolled down my cheek. Sox batted at my face with his paw, like he was sad that he'd have to hide behind the dresser all night instead of watching Netflix in bed with me. I sat up and rubbed my eyes.

"Come on, baby. If we push hard, we can get out of here in a few months." Blue rubbed my back a couple of times before giving me a light shove.

"I'm so tired, though." I couldn't focus. My eyes were heavy, my muscles even heavier.

"I know, love. But we're working toward a better life. On Sunday night we can count the money in the Nelson can and look at rental listings."

"Jesus Christ, Blue. I need to sleep sometime."

"I know. Just go to work for a couple of hours. I'll drive you downtown."

Less than thirty minutes later, I rode down the elevator with Blue.

"Smells like piss in here," he said.

"When doesn't it?"

I walked out the lobby doors as a cab rolled into the turn-around. The trunk popped open before it came to a full stop. The distinctive sound of Brenda's high-pitched, drunken voice pierced my ears. I turned around as she stumbled out of the back seat, Milos lumbering behind her like a clumsy Saint Bernard.

"Well, looky here," Brenda drawled, pointing up and down my body. "If it ain't Pretty Woman and Richard Fuckin' Gere. What happened to yer face, Blue?"

Milos pulled three suitcases out of the trunk and stood next to Brenda.

"Seems like a lot of luggage for a trip to Jasper," I said. "Where are the bodies?"

"Ha ha, hooker! Aren't you the funny one. I ain't in the mood for yer smart mouth. Me and Milos been on a flight for twenty-one hours, and we need to sleep. But you bet yer tight ass we's be havin a meetin' with ya in the next day or two. Seems we have some funds we need to talk about."

Been on a flight for twenty-one hours?

Blue grabbed my arm. "We need to get going, Brenda."

"Yeah, Blue. Get goin' and drop that little slut off and then come hear about our trip to Serbia. Them Serbs know how to show a gal a good time!"

"How the fuck can you afford a trip to Serbia?" I said.

"My spendin' ain't yer concern! We's did a trip to Belgrade. Checked out his hometown. Way nicer than this shit stain of a city."

Blue yanked me toward the truck.

"What did she mean, they went on a trip to Serbia? Didn't you and Milos have a little encounter earlier?"

"Oh, come on, Chanie. You know she's always talkin' shit. They probably just went to get their crap back from the pawn shop."

I kept quiet for the rest of the ride. Blue had *that look*, and I really couldn't handle getting a fist in the face on my way to work. I'd just shut up and bring home some cash. The faster the better.

"Take a cab home tonight, Chanie. I need to get some sleep," Blue said as he eased the truck to the curb.

"Really, Blue." I shook my head and opened the door.

"Wait a second." He reached under his seat. "Here's a mickey of Captain Morgan for you. My treat."

I'd taken two Tylenol 3s and drunk half the mickey by the time a white G37 pulled up to the curb. I hopped in. No chit-chat. No sizing up my trick. I just wanted to get it over with. My stomach growled as we passed A&W. I jokingly said, "Let's grab a Teen Burger," but the driver ignored me and stared straight ahead, fixated on the road as though driving through a snowstorm. Tense guy — too tense, really. Maybe he'd had a bad day — lost his job, wife, house. I didn't care. I'd had a lot of bad days.

He headed east on the Yellowhead Freeway, a common route to the industrial parks. Definitely not the place to be. Too many assaults, and quite a few murders. I usually made it a rule to stay within city limits because I'd had more than my share of long walks home from the outskirts of the city. I was scared. I felt like a trapped animal, invisible and at the mercy of the psycho at the wheel. I wanted out of the car, but we were headed toward the bridge at 140 kilometres per hour with Kid Rock's "Fuck U Blind" blaring from the speakers.

The bridge looked long, like an optical illusion of a never-ending tunnel. Big black pillars with huge ropes of cable lined the entire structure. Each pillar was emblazoned with graffiti painted by a wild street artist whose signature boasted bold strokes and brilliant colours. The white car roared as though racing for an invisible finish line. I took another swig of rum. We were moving so fast that the graffiti blurred like multi-coloured ribbons, the words unreadable amidst the blend of speed and colour.

"You gotta tell me you love me, okay?" the driver said, his

words frantic and choppy.

"Sorry?" I said, looking out the side window. "I didn't hear you."

"I said, you gotta say you love me, ya nasty slut!"

I turned toward him and snapped, "That'll cost extra, you fucking troll!"

He leaned over and screamed in my face, "You gotta pretend like you love me! Pretend you love me! You gotta say, I love you, Neil! I love you, Neil! I —"

"Watch the fucking road, Neil!"

MY HEAD POUNDED, AS though elastic bands were being snapped against my brain. Deflated airbags drooped from the steering wheel and dashboard. I looked around. Blood, glass, and car parts were scattered everywhere. The driver was dead, his face skinned and bloody, like raw meat left behind by an animal. I crawled out my broken window and fell to the pavement. I stared up at the pillar we'd hit. Big fat letters in neon pink said *Embrace Your Fire*. Tuffy was right. It was time for a fire.

Headlights glowed from the edge of the bridge, where only moments before Neil and I had argued. Just like that, in a few hundred feet, our lives had been changed forever. Maybe if I hadn't been such a bitch, his face wouldn't be hamburger and my mind wouldn't be filled with the eternal afterimage of his bloody head. I wouldn't be bleeding and broken and trying to escape a fatal car crash that I had caused.

I began running barefoot toward the end of the bridge. The last thing I needed was cops. I was high and drunk and battered from the crash. I'd never be able to explain that away. For a second, I considered running back to steal Neil's wallet so Blue wouldn't send me back out to work. As the headlights grew closer, my desperation took over, and I threw myself over the railing, where I tumbled into the ravine and landed a few feet from the river.

I rested on the riverbank. The moon and stars shone down on me, as though celebrating my survival. I didn't want to move. I didn't know if I'd die. I just knew, in that moment, that I'd have given anything to return to Mr. Lavoy's room, to see Ginger's smile and Tuffy's face, and even to hear Jeremy's smart mouth. I'd *try harder* — if I survived.

I smiled up at the moon and whispered, "Thank you for my life. Please don't let me die." I'd been spared so many times. I'd mixed booze and drugs, sliced my wrists, danced drunk atop the High Level Bridge, and played games with passing trains. And in all those moments *Some Thing* had saved me. And I owed that *Some Thing* something better.

I woke up to Blue's chatter. I could tell he was high. "The guy in the car was dead. I heard on the radio that the freak had tape and rope in the trunk. A couple of tarps, too. He's a suspect in the hooker killings, for sure! Chanie must have a horseshoe up her ass or something."

Some Thing ...

"What colour were the tarps?" I sat up too fast and puked on my lap. At first, I didn't know who was there or where I was. But then I saw Sox's tail poking out from behind the dresser. Blue, Brenda, and Milos were sitting on lawn chairs in my living room passing a bottle of Dom Pérignon back and forth.

Blue jumped up and walked over to me. "Holy fuck, Chanie! We didn't know how long you'd be out for. Man, we were shittin' bricks!"

"Was ya blowin' him while he was drivin', Jade? I got a bet with these two assholes that you was blowin' him when ya crashed." Brenda clinked the bottle against Milos's beer mug, and the two of them started laughing.

I pushed the dirty blanket away. "What happened to me?"

"Don't get up," Blue said, bundling up the blanket and reaching for the bottle. "You slept for two days. I woke you up a few times, but you just glared at me and went back to sleep."

My double vision caused my heart to race, so I closed my eyes. I saw Neil's face, the glass and the blood, the deep ravine, and the raging river. I started crying and wailed, "Oh my God! Oh my God! What a mess."

"Calm down, girl. It's just puke!" Blue raised the bottle as though saluting his puke comment.

"What about school?" I said. "And Ginger?"

"My mom called your school and told them you two crashed in her car. You have an excused absence as long as you have a note."

"Do I have a note, Blue?" *Maybe I'd been to the hospital? How did I get home?*

"Milos got you one. He's got a nurse friend."

Of course he does.

"How did I get home?"

"You called me," Milos piped up. "You remember, no?"

Hmm ...

Blue put the empty bottle on the dresser and scooped up his keys. "There's some eggs 'n shit in the fridge for you. We're goin' out."

I woke up at 2:23 a.m. with Sox snuggled under my chin. I wondered what day it was and how long I'd been incapacitated. I gently moved my fingers and toes, slowly waking my body like Annie Pema had taught us to do in yoga class. My bladder pulsed harder than my head. My muscles felt as though they'd been ripped apart and clumsily glued back together. Every part of me ached, as though I'd bruised from the inside out. I tiptoed around the apartment, my feet raw and tender, a few tiny cuts on my heels. I had to find my phone. Find a way out of the fog and back to reality. I had to reconnect to the time, date, Ginger … *Tuffy.*

I had seventy-six messages, mostly from Ginger:

> Jesus Christ, Chanie. I'm sick with worry. Where the fuck are you?

> Oh my God, girl! If I don't hear from you, I'm coming there with P.J. & RIE!

> Came by the apartment. Hate Blue's guts. Talked to you through the door. Call me!!

> P.J. & Rie told me it was an accident … I don't believe them.

> Goddammit, Chanie! Are you dead?

Pastor Josh had sent me a prayer, and Rie had sent me encouraging words asking me to call her as soon as I could. It felt good to be looked for. I didn't deserve it. I deserved to crash in that car and pay the proper karmic price for all my lies and deception. It was a wake-up call out of the lie I called my life.

Someday, I would tell everyone the truth about me. But I

wouldn't do it until I'd made something of myself. I remembered only bits and pieces of the crash: Neil's face, the giant pillar, the neon words *Embrace Your Fire*, the moon and the stars — something about duct tape and tarps, and yes, Milos carrying me up and out of the ditch. I remembered an undeniable gratitude for my life and a heartfelt commitment to try harder. But mostly I remembered the feeling of *Some Thing* being there with me.

I pressed my palms together, raised them to my chest, closed my eyes, and bowed my head. Deep inhales, long exhales, calm, slow, and easy. I let myself feel my body, feel the pain, the vibrations, the tightness in my chest. Feel my life happening in the moment. The sadness, the happiness, the fear. All of it. No rum. No codeine. No Valium. Just life. And then I began writing.

Dear Mom & Clayton:

I deserved to come of age without having my insides violated. That is the right of every little girl. Clayton, I could feel you coming for me long before you did, leering at me when my mom wasn't looking, slapping my ass, making fun of my body, and accusing me of giving blow jobs before I even knew what a blow job was. I didn't really understand what was going on. I just knew something was wrong, and that I never felt safe in my home. But now I've seen you in the hundreds of men who have paid to violate me. You turned me from teenager to tragedy because you wanted something from me that didn't belong to you. It belonged to me. Only me! And now it's been sold to so many ...

And Mom, I weighed ninety pounds the night they

raped me. I'd never even inserted a tampon. What do you think it felt like when those monsters tore into me? They ripped me apart. If you think that hurt, I can tell you this: The real pain was you believing his lies and tossing me out on the street like garbage. I hope you hear my father crying in your dreams because even though he's dead, he saw what you and Clayton did to me.

One day, when I'm strong enough, I'm coming for you. But right now, I'm busy reclaiming my life and taking back what is mine.

Chanie

And to my father:

I wish you could have stayed on Earth a little bit longer. I think we could have become good friends.

XOXO
Your daughter, Chanie

CHAPTER TWENTY

"WE'RE CONCERNED ABOUT YOU." Rie said.

"I understand," I replied.

"Can you tell us about the accident?"

"I'd rather not talk about it. Can we review my homework list, please?"

I wondered what Blue's mom had told them. Surely something dramatic and stupid. I knew the bridge had been closed the morning of the crash, but did Rie and P.J. know? I looked at the two of them leaning slightly toward me as though looking for hidden diamonds in my mouth.

P.J. set his teacup down. He swallowed hard and narrowed his eyes. "We need to know if you are safe in your home."

"Of course I'm safe!" I laughed and took a big swig of cold coffee.

P.J. and Rie sipped their tea in silence.

"I wrote the letter to my family," I said. "I have it in my bag."

"That's great, Chanie." Rie looked at P.J. "We can talk about that in a few minutes."

P.J. raised his voice slightly and put his hand on my forearm.

"I'm sorry, Chanie. We have to ask. Are you drinking or using drugs?"

I looked right at him and said, "No! I'm not using anything. I'm just tired."

He gently squeezed my forearm and took a deep breath. "Are you being abused in your home?"

I pulled my arm away. "Now that's just ridiculous. Can we please stop with the drama?"

"We're concerned." Rie intervened. "We've noticed your grades and attendance slipping. If there's something we can do to help, we need to know. But you have to understand you are accountable to us, and you made a commitment to this program in exchange for avoiding a jail sentence."

"I am trying! I am committed!"

"I'm sorry, Chanie," Rie said, her voice low but firm, clearly sick of my bullshit. "We have to make a note on your file saying we've discussed your attendance and missed assignments."

I bit my lower lip; the salty taste of blood flooded over my tongue, reminding me of the first time Blue had hit me. "What does that mean?"

"It means your attendance has to improve, and you can't have any more missed assignments."

"Okay, Rie. I get it!" I pushed my palms hard into my temples.

"Chanie, we're not trying to upset you," P.J. said.

"I said, I get it!"

I left the office, hating myself for snapping at Rie and P.J. The Blue version of me, an exhausted liar, a junkie street whore faking decency, wasting everybody's time. I carried my dark mood to English class, but I couldn't focus because of the guilt fogging up my head. Mr. Lavoy walked up and down the aisles reading a Rumi poem out loud, but all I could hear was Rie saying, "You made a commitment to this program." I'd made a commitment to nobody. Not even myself.

"Chanie. Chaannie," Mr. Lavoy called. "Earth to Chanie."

I looked up and raised my eyebrows.

"Would you care to answer my question?"

His question?

I shook my head and waved my hand as though shooing a fly.

Mr. Lavoy's face dropped. "See me after class."

My nostrils flared, and a chill coursed over me. It felt like a piece of plywood had been wedged through the back of my neck and across my shoulders. I didn't want to talk anymore. It was too risky. All of my lies teetered at the tip of a mountain, one slip away from an avalanche. I felt like I had to consult a flowchart and cue cards before every conversation. My lies crowded and bumped off one another like plastic bottles in a dirty river. I ran home that day to avoid Mr. Lavoy. It's not that I didn't care about the consequences; I just didn't know how to handle them.

Brenda intercepted me in the lobby when I walked into the building. "Get the hell away from me," I said, swerving around her.

"Ya can't talk to me like that, ya little slut. I'm sending Milos up!" She threw her juice bottle at me. It bounced off my shoulder and hit the floor. I kicked it back through the elevator doors, the overspray spattering the floor and walls.

I bolted from the elevator to hide in my suite but stopped dead in my tracks when I saw a lavender envelope in a checkered bag hanging from the doorknob. I wished I knew what delight felt like. That seemed like what a normal person might feel if they'd received an unexpected gift at their door. But I didn't have friends, aside from my school friends. And my neighbours didn't like me and referred to me as the *whore* on the ninth floor.

I took the gift from the door, went inside, and threw it on the bed. I needed rum, vodka, codeine — whatever. I found Blue's forbidden mickey of Smirnoff hidden in the freezer behind pizza boxes and an empty perogi bag. I yanked it out and took a long swig. "Don't touch my personal stash, Chanie," Blue had said when I'd gone for the bottle before. "I need it for when I'm stressed!"

I didn't care.

I'd earned the rights to that bottle and the proceeds in the Nelson can. I considered looking under the sink to check if he'd robbed me again, but what could I do about it, anyway? My day had already sucked enough.

Back in the living room, I found Sox surrounded by tissue paper, ribbons, and remnants of the gift bag, purring and kneading a mauve blanket with a yellow satin ribbon. It looked like a kid had thrown a birthday party on my bed. A couple of toy mice poked their heads out from the covers as though checking to see if the coast was clear. I snatched the lavender envelope off the bed and tore it open. The faint smell of lilacs floated up from a pale purple sheet that resembled the texture of Bible paper. Tiny violets and green leaves filled the page borders, and the script was perfect and graceful, like my grandmother's handwriting.

> Our dear young neighbour:
>
> A stranger's prayer can give you wings. It can also give you hope. Please know that we pray for you. When you are scared and lonely, we are right next door. Even if you don't come over, you can come

over in your heart. We see you, young lady. And you
matter!

We hope the blanket brings you comfort. God
loves you.

Esther and Dan

Ah! The church people in the suite next door. Nice people.
They cooked a lot of meals for dinner guests. Since they'd moved
in, the hallway smelled of soups and baking, a great improve-
ment from the usual stench of piss and cigarettes. One time,
they'd posted a notice about a food drive in the lobby. Brenda
tore it down, but I smoothed it out and reposted it. Dan and
Esther were Pastor Josh's kind of people. I wondered if they'd
ever met.

I shoved the tissue paper into an old grocery bag and rushed
it to the garbage chute. If Blue saw it, he'd freak out because
I'd drawn too much attention to us. I tucked the note into my
copy of Les Misérables and figured I'd tell him that Ginger had
stolen the blanket from Chapters. I ripped a page out of my
notebook. Compared to Esther's stylish stationery, it looked
like a note on a truck-stop napkin. I scrawled the note quickly,
terrified that Blue, Brenda, or Milos would come crashing in
and explode over the neighbours' having "noticed me."

> Thank you for the note and gift. So very kind! Please
> keep this between us and don't tell anyone else in the
> building. Thank you for your prayers.

I didn't sign my name because I didn't want to risk them saying it in front of Blue. He'd wonder how they knew it. Just
one more thing to piss him off. Another reason to explode and

slap me around. I tiptoed to Dan and Esther's door and slid the note underneath. I returned home, drank some more, and tidied up. A big, lumpy sadness bulged in my throat. The same kind of sadness that had touched me after my first story night at the shelter. The sweetness of people. It stung.

I wrapped myself in the purple blanket, crawled into bed, and let myself cry. I could feel Esther's motherly love as though it had been infused in the fabric. Sox nestled in and pushed his back into my stomach. He purred harder and harder, like he was sad there was only three pounds of him to comfort me. I gently rocked my body to sleep, imagining Dan and Esther praying for my wings, and then me — like a butterfly — flying away.

A loud bang woke me up. Sox leaped out of bed and shoved himself behind the dresser. It wasn't Blue. I heard Serbian slurs and drunken cackles outside my door. Brenda and Milos, drunk again, pounding on my door. My head ached, like sugar had slipped between the membranes in my brain and stuck everything together. I closed my eyes, but they banged even harder. I stayed still and wished I could make myself invisible. It got quiet for a while, long enough for me to fall back asleep. And then BAM! Like a gunshot, the door swung open and smashed into the wall behind it.

"Get out!" I screamed.

"Oh no, honey. We's talkin," Brenda said.

"Nope." I pulled the blankets up to my chest.

"Yep!" Milos said, grabbing my arm and yanking me off the bed.

"Looks like our little angel here fell off the wagon." Brenda slapped her knee and laughed. "I always knew ya would."

"Get out, you drunk whore!" I barked at Brenda, ducking

away from Milos. But he was fast and slapped me so hard that I tumbled against the dresser.

"Get some makeup on. You go work now," Milos said. "It's only nine o'clock, for God's sake. Who goes to bed at nine?"

"Where's Blue?" I said, rubbing my cheek.

"Fuck Blue," Milos said.

For the first time ever, I agreed with Milos.

Milos and Brenda dropped me off downtown. They parked around the corner, watching me like predators, waiting to take the money from my first trick. The only solace in my job existed in the moments between — between my home life, between school, and between tricks. That's where glimpses of nothingness snuck in. Those moments were the only places I could catch snippets of rest. But Brenda and Milos's presence invaded my *between* that night. I paced up and down, hypervigilant and anxious to get away from them. Even a moment in a john's car might give me a sliver of relief, as long as Milos didn't trail along behind us in his Lincoln. It would be hard to shake them. They had no cash and wanted to get high.

Esther and Dan must have prayed hard for me that night because he almost didn't see me. The shiny black car purred as it passed me, moving swiftly, as though trying to get home after a long day. I recognized the brake lights: BMW 435. The car revved as it backed up for almost an entire city block, jerking to a stop at my feet.

"My sweet Chanie! Where have you been?"

"Oh my God, Mr. Tanji!"

He flashed a wide smile and said, "I always knew I'd find my way back to you, my sweet girl. What is wrong with Brenda? Why did you change your number?"

"I didn't. They took my phone and gave me a different one a while back."

"I've called her a hundred times trying to find you. I think she blocked my number."

"That bitch!" I spun around looking for the black Lincoln. *Gone!*

"Well, get in before I lose you again." Mr. Tanji patted the seat. "Let's get you a chai and talk for a while."

I couldn't speak because I knew I'd start sobbing. I opened the door and hopped into the refuge of the BMW, grateful for the familiar dashboard and the scent of Mr. Tanji's cologne.

"Now wait a second here!" Brenda staggered up to his window. Milos lumbered a few feet behind her like a distracted dog. "Ya can't just come along and pick her up. We got a deal, Tanji."

"Oh please, Brenda. We've got nothing." Tanji shook his head.

"You need to pay up front tonight. Right, Milos!"

"Right! Pay up, buddy." Milos stuck his hand out.

"And then you'll both get lost?" Tanji gave me a crooked smile and reached for his wallet.

"How long ya takin' her for? She's got a quota, ya know."

"I'll take her for the entire night and have her back in the morning." Tanji nodded to me, as though it mattered whether I agreed with him or not.

"Ooh, yeah — that'll cost ya, big-time," Brenda said. She clucked her tongue and tapped her foot.

Mr. Tanji opened his wallet and counted out a pile of bills. "Here's $500. Good enough?"

Brenda snatched the cash from his hand.

He rolled his window up and drove away. "Oh my God, Chanie. Poor girl."

"What do you mean?"

"What's happening to you? You look terrible!"

My face flushed with shame, and I looked away. "Are you really keeping me all night?"

"I'd like to. Are you okay with that?"

"Depends on who and what I have to do, I suppose. I have to be at school in the morning."

"It's just you and me tonight." He reached over and held my hand all the way to the hotel.

I woke up the next morning in a king-sized bed at the Saw-ridge Inn. The only thing missing was Sox. Otherwise, everything was perfect. We'd spent the evening listening to the Chill Channel while munching on flatbreads, potato skins, nachos, and a dessert tray. He'd ordered us bottles of Perrier with lemon and lime wedges. He said, "We'll drink another time, sweet girl. Tonight, you tell me about your life. And don't leave out any details!" So I told him everything. And I cried *a lot*.

"Chanie, I'm not going to tell you that everything is going to be okay. You have lived enough of a life to know that those words are empty without action. But what I can tell you is that I will help you find your way."

I kept my eyes closed but raised my head to look at him. "How will anything ever be okay when I don't even know what I'm striving for? I think I want to be normal, but I don't even know what normal is!" I opened my eyes.

Mr. Tanji squinted and tilted his head slightly. "Chanie, what do you think normal is?"

I honestly didn't know.

And then he made me an offer.

In the morning, we ate eggs Florentine with fresh fruit. "Eat-ing meat doesn't sit well with my soul," he said as he peeled a grapefruit. I never wanted to leave. I could have hidden away forever in that room, but Mr. Tanji had to get to work, and I had to get to school. On our way out, I lingered by the hotel room door, teary-eyed and sniffling. He turned me toward him and squeezed both my hands. I looked into his electric eyes, and he said, "Think about my offer, Chanie."

Later that morning, I flipped through *Les Misérables* while we waited for Mr. Lavoy to show up for class. He poked his head in the door and told me to come out into the hallway. I figured it was because I was late *again*. I'd started hating my school life, mostly because of the fluorescent lights and prying eyes. The stress of living on top of the mountain of lies I'd created was making me paranoid. I was always waiting for the avalanche that would finally bury me and send me to jail.

I crossed my arms and pasted a concerned look on my face. Jeremy stood next to Mr. Lavoy, scowling at me. I ignored him. I had to, or I was afraid I might kill him.

Mr. Lavoy squinted at the two of us. "I'd make you two apologize, but that isn't going to do anything. Instead, I've decided that you will co-write a five-hundred-word essay on empathy and emotional intelligence. Hand it in by the end of the week."

"That's today!" I said, a wave of heat coursing through me.

"Yes, it is. Better clear your evening schedules."

Jeremy glared at me and walked into the classroom.

Mr. Lavoy scratched his chin and looked away for a second. "Chanie, I don't know what's happening in your life lately, but please fix it."

"I'm just having anxiety issues and can't sleep —"

"Cut it out, Chanie! You decide who and what you want to be. If you need help, there's a whole army of people here to help you. But if you want to drown, keep on doing what you're doing, and you'll get there soon enough."

"Mr. Lavoy, I —"

"You have one chance here. You can make or break your life. Write the essay and apply for loans or write your eulogy so one of us can read it at your funeral. You decide." He walked into the classroom and slammed the door.

I stood outside the closed door and wished for freedom. Real freedom, like Mr. Tanji had with his high-end job and education. "Think about my offer, Chanie," he'd said, his voice cool and even, the control of a polished politician.

"What do you mean, 'We'll hang out?'" I'd asked Mr. Tanji.

"Just like I said. We'll hang out once a week. I'll treat you to dinner, and then we'll talk about things. *Normal* things, as you like to call it."

"Normal things?"

"I can teach you about religion and politics. We can talk about current events. Things like how and why policy works and doesn't work. Finances, savings, investments. Real-world normal and boring." He paused and pointed one finger upward. "Boring, but essential!"

I giggled and shook my head. "Politics and finance?"

"We'll also talk about poetry and literature. History. Social issues. What do you think?"

"I think I'm a hooker, and all that stuff is way over my head!"

"It's not over your head. You just need a good tour guide, like me."

"So, you're saying you'll help me discover a world that isn't about drugs and blow jobs."

Mr. Tanji laughed. "Well, maybe a little bit about *metaphorical* blow jobs!"

I laughed with him, even though I didn't understand what he meant. But I had an idea that my world and the real world weren't so different.

I MET UP WITH Ginger and Jeremy after school.

"We better get to work, Jeremy," I said, tapping my foot, anxious to get home to Sox.

"Relax," Jeremy said, punching my shoulder. "It's your fucking fault we have to write this, anyways."

"Jesus Christ, Jeremy." Ginger shoved him. "Don't fucking touch her!"

"Jesus, Ginger! Do you have your period or something?" Jeremy said.

"Yes, asshat! I do."

"Well, chill the fuck out."

"Easy for you to say, dick. Have you ever had a period?"

"What do you think, genius?"

"Then shut the fuck up," Ginger said. She hugged me and gave Jeremy the finger. "Don't kill each other tonight. You're two of my favourite people."

"Man, I love that girl." Jeremy grinned as Ginger walked away.

"Do you want to work outside behind the school? It's still sunny," I said. Jeremy ignored me and played with his phone. I googled *empathy and emotional intelligence*. "It says empathy is the ability to put yourself into someone else's shoes."

"So basically, for me, that would mean I'd have to know what it's like to suck a whole lot of dick," he said, still looking at his phone.

"Jeremy, I have better places to be than here!"

He stopped texting and looked at me. "Like where you gonna

go? To get beat up some more by your dad? Oops! I mean boyfriend."

"Jesus, Jeremy! Why do you always have to be such a shit to me? You're dating my best friend. Why can't we make peace?"

"Okay, Chanie, you're right," Jeremy said, looking at the ground. "I had other plans for tonight, and now we have to write this fucking essay."

"Did you and Ginger have plans tonight?"

"No, I had dinner plans with my mom."

"Where were you going to eat?"

"What do you mean where were we going to eat? I was gonna grab a donair and eat at the cemetery."

I paused. "What do you mean?"

"It's the anniversary of her death. Five years today." He took a long pause and shuffled a couple of times. "I always go have dinner at her grave."

We sat in silence for a long while. His sadness moved me. It reminded me of how raw and broken I'd felt when my dad died. I reached over, stroked his arm, and said, "Hey, Jeremy. Let's go get a donair and write this essay with your mom."

"For real?"

"Of course," I said. My phone buzzed in my pocket. I ignored it and flicked the ringer off.

The cemetery sat between two busy city avenues, but the greenery made it feel as though we were hidden in a big forest. The trees towered above us, their huge branches holding hands with one another as though praying for all the souls resting beneath their protective canopy. The grass glowed electric green and lit up the earth like a fuzzy blanket. The sound of wind chimes danced gently in the breeze and complemented the beauty of the flowers and statues amidst the gravestones.

I followed Jeremy to his mom's grave. Giant magenta orchids stretched out of a copper vase, as though his mom was reaching out to welcome her grieving boy. Big, leafy greens poked up and out the sides of the vase, vibrant and healthy, like summer blossoms in full season. The arrangement shone like a floral celebration smiling up at the sun, so contrary to the sadness that lay directly beneath the stone on which they sat.

"I bought fake flowers at Dollarama," Jeremy said, almost as if he felt like he had to defend the artificial flowers on the grave. "I can't afford to buy fresh flowers every week."

"They're so vibrant," I replied, hoping to put him at ease.

"Ginger picked them last time."

"Very elegant," I said.

"You know, Ginger doesn't remember what happened to her." Jeremy's voice cracked. "She told me the cops picked her up when she was four years old, all bruised up and wandering around behind the York Hotel, clinging to a stuffed zebra. The hospital kept her for a few weeks before she went into foster homes."

"She told me her mom overdosed."

"She did. But the crackheads staying at the house might have messed her up. She doesn't remember a thing. Nobody knows what actually happened to her."

"Poor Ginger." I felt like I'd turned into a weepy puddle, the visual of tiny Ginger, alone, scared, and battered, wandering in a hotel parking lot dragging a stuffed toy in the dust.

"You know, she still has the stuffed zebra. She pulled it out one night when we got drunk together. I slept over there while Petey-D was out of town."

"That's so sad." I sniffled and wiped a tear from my cheek.

"What? The stuffed toy or that I slept over there?" Jeremy winked and flashed a cocky smile.

"Both," I said, and we laughed. "On another note, any idea what happened to Tuffy?"

"God knows. He won't talk to me about his life."

"He probably won't talk to me, either."

"You're probably the only one he'll talk to, Chanie." Jeremy looked down at his mom's stone.

"How about I go grab slushes for us and give you a few minutes alone with your mom?"

Jeremy nodded. "Okay. Root beer if they have it."

As I made my way to the north side of the graveyard, I read some of the names and dates on tombstones. So many sad stories: beloved mother, son, friend. What happened to people who were nobody's beloved? Did they waste away in the ground in an unmarked grave like they'd never existed at all? Was that where Perry went after they picked her body off the pavement from beneath the yellow tarp? Mr. Lavoy's words rang out in my head: "Write the essay and apply for loans or write your eulogy."

I shivered as though all the ghosts in the cemetery had just crawled into my pockets. Mr. Lavoy's words played over and over in my head. I got the slushes and almost sprinted back toward Jeremy, like he could chase the demons away. He didn't look like such a bad boy, kneeling over the grave with his hands held in prayer. He looked as small and scared as I was.

"You know, my mom was nice," Jeremy said, reaching for the slush in my hand.

"I'm sure she was," I said, pushing down the ghosts and Mr. Lavoy's warning in my head.

"When my baby brother died, she went off the rails. It wasn't her fault we had a shitty, used baby gate because my cheap-ass dad wouldn't spring for a new one. Fuckin' twenty bucks could have saved my brother's life."

"That's so sad." I began to cry *again*.

"I was eleven when it happened. My mom got so sad she didn't even brush her hair anymore. My dad blamed me for Mikey's death, like I'm the one who didn't buy a proper gate. He liked to slap me around. He always called me a piece-of-shit burden. Said that the wrong kid had died. That it should have been me."

"What a jerk! You were just a kid —"

"Anyways, my mom and I used to try and avoid my dad a lot. He was a drunk and a junkie. That was a no-brainer, but my mom would always make excuses for him."

"Where's your dad now?"

"He's over there." Jeremy pointed to the back of the cemetery. "I haven't talked about it — that night. Not even with Ginger."

"Maybe you need more time."

Jeremy's breath caught, and he looked at me. "I left the house one night to get away from the fighting. Smoked a bunch of weed at my buddy Steve's. Had a few beers too. I staggered home a few hours later. I could hear them screaming two blocks away. So I started running ... If only I'd stayed home that night." Big tears rolled from his eyes, and he slumped forward. He looked away, his face aged and tired, grief etched into his pupils like initials carved into an old tree trunk. We sat facing each other, cross-legged, like two kids playing patty-cake. I leaned toward him, and we pressed our foreheads together and cried for a long time. When we settled down, I placed my hand over his heart, and he took a couple of deep breaths before continuing his story.

"We had this Texas mickey. You know those great big bottles people fill up with spare change. We were saving for a trip to the mountains. When it was almost full, the son of a bitch made us pour it out on the floor to count it. I got so excited! My mom and I talked about all the wild animals we'd see in Jasper while we rolled the change together. But *instead*, he took the fucking money and went on a three-day bender."

"Jeremy —"

"I knew I wasn't strong enough to fight him. But when I came through the door, he was on top of my mom. He had his hands around her neck, and he kept bashing her head into the floor. I saw the mickey — grabbed it — and bashed his fucking head open!"

"I'm so sorry, Jeremy." We cried big sobs, the kind of sobs that can only come from violent childhoods, dead parents, and lost innocence.

Jeremy spoke between sobs. "I'm not sorry — Chanie — I'm not! The only thing I'm sorry about is that I didn't get there sooner to save my mom. But I'm even more sorry that fucker father of mine will never know it was me who killed him."

We sat quietly watching the sunset, our sobs fading away into rhythmic breathing. I held Jeremy's hands and breathed long, deep breaths. With each inhale, we peeled away the layers of pain he could no longer carry, and every exhale made space to plant the seeds of healing. Our energy felt like shy flowers in bloom, timid and afraid, but grateful to have finally found a safe place to grow.

When we got up to leave the cemetery, I looked up through the trees. Bronze streaks poked through the leaves, and the sun gently covered us in a golden light. I heard my dad's voice say, "No matter how dark it is, Chanie, always remember, the sun is making its way back to you." I lifted my face to the sky and whispered, "Thank you, Dad."

WE TITLED THE ESSAY, "The Magic of Transformed Hatred: The Magnificent Potential of the Most Powerful Human Emotion."

"Mr. Lavoy will be pleased," I said when we'd finally agreed on the last line.

"He will be. He's a smart guy. Seems he knew exactly what we needed." Jeremy smiled and nodded. "Let me walk you home."

When we got to the end of my alley, he hugged me long and hard. "Thanks for the talk, Chanie."

"I'm happy to be here for you," I said, honoured that he'd seen something safe enough in me to share the darkest parts of his life.

"You know what, Chanie?"

"What's up?"

"My mom had this look right before she died. Kind of grey. Empty. Like a picture of a war veteran in an old newspaper."

"That's so sad."

"You have that same look, Chanie."

CHAPTER TWENTY-ONE

"WHERE THE HELL WERE you?"

"Sorry, Blue. I had an after-school assignment."

Brenda clucked her tongue and nudged Milos. Milos nodded and walked over to Blue. The two huddled for a moment. There were garbled whispers, laughter, a loud click, and suddenly, Blue had a gun.

I froze in the doorway. For the first time in my life, I said a silent prayer to God.

"You and Blue is gonna chat now," Brenda said. "Come on, Milos. Let's give these two lovebirds some privacy."

I stepped aside so they could leave. Brenda stopped and smirked in my face. I squeezed my eyes shut and clenched my fists. Blue had a gun. I had nothing. Heat ran up my back and into my collarbone. I tried to stay calm, but all I could think of were the tombstones, the flowers, and the feeling I'd had in the cemetery.

My mom had this look right before she died …

"Get the fuck over there." Blue pointed toward the bed with the gun.

This was my life. Locked in my apartment with a gun-toting

meth head. The guy who claimed to love me and couldn't live without me. I closed my eyes and saw magenta orchids reaching for the sky, Jeremy's tears like big silicone drops, and Tuffy's crooked smile. I felt the vibes of Ginger's love squeezing me like a bulletproof vest. And then I saw my dad. And he was crying.

It happened fast. A high-pitched squeal blasted through my ears, like someone had blown a whistle in the centre of my skull. Then a hiss! Hot spatter pelted my cheek, and bright blue spots sprayed across my vision. I screamed for my dad and reached my arms toward him, but he wasn't there. It was Blue who caught me and threw me to the floor. I touched my head, sticky with blood, Blue's spit slowly oozing down my cheek. No bullet — yet.

"Where the fuck were you, you lying slut? I sent you a hundred fuckin' messages. Did ya think to respond?"

"My phone's dead!"

Blue grabbed my bag and pulled out my phone. "It says forty-eight percent battery!"

My body turned to liquid, and my muscles melted like plastic in a fire. He smashed the phone into my skull, threw it against the wall, and punched me in the left cheek. Sox jerked his tiny tail behind the dresser. I curled my body tight, but Blue grabbed my arm and dragged me across the floor. I felt repeated blows against my back and then my ribs. He clenched the back of my neck and pushed my face into the carpet. I whimpered and moaned, but he didn't stop.

I faded in and out of consciousness and dreamt I lay dead by a garbage bin, but instead of cops covering me with a yellow tarp, it was Rie and Mr. Lavoy. Pastor Josh kneeled over me in prayer, shaking his head and wringing his hands. I wanted to tell them I was sorry. Then I saw my dad kneeling on a grave. He wasn't crying anymore. He just looked tired, like he'd lost the biggest fight of his life.

I woke up to Blue pouring water on my face. He flipped me onto my stomach, pulled my pants down, and spit on his hand. He jammed his fingers inside me first, then penetrated me and came all over my back. A droning buzz dominated my senses, like a cable channel signing off at the end of the night. I closed my eyes and hoped I'd never open them again.

A while later, Blue poured more water on my face and yanked me upright. "Keep lying to me, you little slut, and see where it gets you," he yelled and then slammed my face down into the floor. "Running around with little boys in the graveyard. You really are a whore."

"We weren't doing anything wrong, Blue. It was homework!" I sobbed as I covered the back of my head with my hands.

"Spare me, Chanie. You better not be wasting your time writing that fucking essay we talked about."

I faded out again. This time I saw Jeremy sitting by my grave eating a donair. Dirty plastic flowers, faded and mud-spattered, were strewn about as though magpies had picked them out of the garbage. Jeremy scowled and said, "I told you so" and threw the foil wrapper on my tombstone before walking away. *Jeremy, please!* I called out in my dream, but I woke up to Milos's hand gripping the back of my neck. He pressed the gun to my temple and pulled the trigger. "Fuck around again and next time, gun loaded, yes. But not fast kill. Make you suffer for long time."

The weekend passed with a lot of rum and Tylenol 3. I stood under the stars downtown, my back against the wall, waiting for tricks. I didn't even bother bringing *Les Misérables* out with me.

I didn't give a fuck anymore. I did a threesome, an aggressive fireman, two drunk lawyers, and some really rough construction guys. My brain fuzzed, my ears rang, and everything happened in a haze. I thought about calling Mr. Tanji, but I couldn't face him because I wore the shame of my abusers. And it made me ugly.

I stood underneath the moon and shouted an apology to all the women I'd ever judged for not leaving the men who beat them. Like Perry. Poor dead Perry. We were all sisters now. And there were so many of us.

"I get it, sisters! I'm sorry now! They break us. They break us up inside!" I yelled, staggering back and forth on the sidewalk.

A white Dodge 1500 slowed and rolled the window down. "Shut up, you junkie slut!" the driver barked, spitting at my feet.

"I rest my case, cocksucker!" I stumbled against the building. "See that!" I yelled up to the moon. "It's guys like those!"

Something breaks.

And nobody understands what it feels like until they are broken.

CHAPTER TWENTY-TWO

I'D MET MY WEEKEND goal of not getting shot by my boy-friend. But Monday had come way too fast. Drugs, alcohol, too many men, and not enough sleep had exhausted me. I couldn't fake it anymore. Not even for another day. *Try harder.* How? They were killing me, beating me up, holding me hostage, and stalking my every move. *And the gun.*

Ginger stood at the coffee bar inside the Mac's using both hands to stir two extra-large coffees. She looked up through the window and mouthed *Holy fuck!* I pointed to the grass on the south side of the store and went to lie down. She came out a few minutes later and set the coffees on the grass.

"Oh, no more, Chanie! We are so done with this shit," Ginger said, brushing my hair back to look at my face.

I wrapped my hand around the hot cup. "I just have to get through the school week." One day at a time. That stupid motto finally made sense. One day. I could do one day.

"Jesus Christ, Chanie. You can barely even talk!" Ginger hung her head and started crying.

I held my breath to hold back the sobs swirling up from my belly. I couldn't let my tears awaken the bruises on my body.

They would sting and stab and remind me that I'd lost control of my life. Valium and alcohol had helped me get through the weekend, but I had no drugs left, and Blue refused to give me any more. I mentally recited the mantra: *calming, smiling, present moment, perfect moment.* Ginger held my hand, anchoring me to the earth. We chanted the mantra as we wept and wished for a miracle. When the sun dried our tears, we stood up, held hands, and walked to school. Because of Ginger, I could do one more day.

We decided to sit in the grass behind the school before class. Ginger hugged me close and said, "Chanie, he's gonna fucking kill you. I thought he might have because I texted you all weekend and didn't hear a peep from you."

"He took my phone. Oh my God! What did you say in your texts?"

"I just said I was looking for you. I thought the bastard might have taken your phone, so I was careful. But I did say a few nasty things about him in the earlier messages before I'd considered that he might have your phone."

I figured he'd already read all of my messages, so if they'd agitated him enough to kill me, he'd have done it over the weekend. I'd made a couple grand in three days, so I'd earned his good graces as of Sunday night. He'd even taken me to A&W for a Teen Burger as a *treat* for my hard work, but had invited Brenda and Milos along. I lost my appetite when they showed up. Blue ate my burger, and Brenda wolfed down all my fries. She tossed a fry at my face and said, "It's better she don't eat, anyways. Don't want her ass gettin' too big."

Ginger took out her foundation stick and went to work on my face. She texted Tuffy and Jeremy. They showed up a few minutes later with Egg McMuffins and hash browns. Tuffy gave me a bottle of water and told me to stay hydrated. He said it would help me heal faster. We sat in the grass by the school and ate McDonalds together. We looked like normal teenagers sitting in a circle, hanging out drinking coffee with textbooks open on our laps and backpacks filled with pencil cases and notebooks. Yet in our little circle in the sun, the imprints of rape, abuse, murder, and trauma made us different. We were stronger, more resilient, and ready to fight.

"Tell that fucker we're comin' for him," Tuffy said.

"They have guns," I said, massaging my temples. "Plus, they'll kill Sox."

"Then I guess I better make sure he doesn't see me coming," Tuffy said.

"He's so done!" Jeremy high-fived Tuffy.

"Let's get the cat out," Ginger said. "Then you have no reason to go back there."

My heart ached at the thought of Sox at the mercy of those psychos. "How the hell are we going to get Sox out?"

"All we have to do is wait until Blue goes out. You can sneak the cat down to one of us in the parking lot, and we'll get him somewhere safe," Ginger said.

"How do I account for the cat being gone?"

"Blame Brenda." Ginger shrugged. "Just act all distraught, like you don't know where he is. And when Blue gets all weird, just be like, 'She's a fuckin' liar. She took my cat!'"

"What about getting Chanie out?" Tuffy said.

"Yeah, Chanie. What about you?" Ginger cocked her head sideways. "Maybe Petey-D will let you stay with us?"

"Doubtful," I replied. "Plus, Blue, Brenda, and Milos will come for me. How will I signal you guys to come and get the cat? I don't have a phone anymore. And where's Sox going to end up?"

"Take my phone," Tuffy said. "I can get a burner phone later. But Sox might have to go to the Humane Society."

The thought of Sox in a shelter reminded me of the night I'd run away from home, terrified and vulnerable, crouched down by the door of a truck stop diner. I looked at Tuffy and said, "They'll find me if I stay in Edmonton. They have eyes and ears everywhere. Milos drives by me fifty times a night when I'm working."

"You can't leave Edmonton anyways," Tuffy said. "You have to stay here so you can graduate."

"There's only two months of school left," Jeremy said. "And fucking Poindexter here will graduate no problem *if* Blue doesn't kill her first."

"So really, all we have to do is keep the peace until we can all run away together. We can go to Nelson!" Ginger said excitedly.

"No, we'll have to go somewhere else," I said. "They might look for me there."

"How about we move down to the Waterton area?" Tuffy said. "We can get jobs in Lethbridge. There's a university there."

"Maybe," I said and lifted my face to the sun.

I WALKED HOME THAT day with one goal: saving Sox.

"How was school?" Blue asked.

Like you care ...

"Hey, Chanie. I asked you a question."

"It was fine."

"What's the problem today, girl? Did the cowboys get your little Pocahontas friend?"

I ignored him and closed the bathroom door. Sox sat on the floor licking his paws. I stepped into the shower and moved through my routine. Wash and shave everything, cover myself in baby oil, moisturize generously, and douse myself in body spray and perfume. Load up the makeup, tease my hair, and put on something slutty. I winced when I heard Brenda and Milos come in. I inhaled and exhaled to the mantra, trying to push away my anxiety. I quietly chanted to Sox, "It won't be long and we'll be gone. It won't be long ..."

I went into the kitchen hoping to find something to eat. I microwaved a packet of Mr. Noodles and ate an apple, my typical worknight staples, not enough to make me fat, but just enough to keep me from passing out.

"You know what?" Blue hissed over my shoulder as I stirred the broth packet into my soup. He pressed his body against my back.

"What now, Blue?" My guts twisted as I wriggled away from him.

"I found something today."

"What is it, Blue?"

"I found this piece of shit!" Blue slammed a rough draft of my essay on the counter. He stood in front of me, his eyes bulging, fists clenched. "I thought you weren't gonna waste our time on this shit, Chanie! How the fuck are we supposed to trust you if you're gonna be out runnin' around pissin' up trees that you can't never climb!"

"'Can't never climb,' Blue? Who talks like that?" I yanked my essay off the counter and tore it in half. "Fuck me for trying!"

"Jade! When you gonna learn, we got a business contract?" Brenda said, nodding at Milos. "The only thing we should be seein' from you is your ass out there makin' some cash. Know what I'm sayin'?"

"Calm down," I said, ducking out of the kitchen. My body was frail and broken. I knew I couldn't survive another beating, especially if all three of them attacked me. I looked at Blue, his stupid grin going nowhere but violent. My nerves blared like sirens, and my blood lit on fire.

"Milos and Blue gonna give you a little honour teachin' to-night, Chanie." Brenda nodded at them. "Realign yer loyalties."

Milos grunted, pulling his belt off as he stood up. Blue was lighting a smoke. I saw an opening and ran for the door, my body in overdrive, adrenaline making me blind and dumb to the consequences. I ran into the hallway with Milos close behind me swinging his belt buckle at my head. I tucked myself into a corner and screamed, "Back off, you fucking monster!"

"What the heck is going on here?" Dan stood in his door-way with Esther clutching his arm. "I just called the cops!"

"No need. No need," Brenda said. "I already called and got this all under control. Go on back inside."

"Are you okay, young lady?" Esther said.

"I said it's all good here. Management on scene. Now go on inside." Brenda waved them away with her hand.

"We are not going inside, *Brenda*, until she says she's okay!" Dan snapped, looking right at me.

I looked at everybody in the hallway. Blue, standing by our door, blowing smoke rings, completely unmoved by the drama unfolding in front of him. Brenda and Milos, inches from me, their chests heaving, faces red and fists clenched. Dan and Esther, remarkably calm in their doorway. It was like those moments people on TV talk about when they've been in a horrific acci-dent. How everything goes silent and feels like it's happen-ing in slow motion. It felt like that. Frozen in time. And then, the volume and speed of the moment came screeching back, and I bolted to the stairwell, yanked my high heels off, and ran down the stairs.

I raced down to the lobby, swinging from the handrails between floors. My chest felt raw, and my mouth was dry, but I ran for my life. I heard Milos yell at Blue to go get the truck. A forest fire raged in my chest, my vision tunnelled, and my legs felt like jelly, but I pushed hard. I had no phone, no money, just black platform shoes in my hand. I had nowhere to go and was too panicked to reason. I headed toward the police station because if Blue and Milos caught up to me, I'd run to the cops even though that would end my life as I knew it. *Please, Jesus, if you're real, please guide me now.*

And then I remembered.

I knew a place where they wouldn't find me. My throat burned, and tears streaked my face, but I pushed harder and kept going. I yanked on the side door. Locked! I ran around to the back door by the kitchen and caught it just as it was swinging shut. One tiny slip and the lock would latch, and I'd be at the mercy of Blue and Milos. I waited. And when it finally felt safe, I opened the door and tiptoed through the kitchen.

The gym felt like an abandoned warehouse: old, empty, and irrelevant. But for the forgotten people of the streets, it was home. They said, "Angels live here." That's exactly what I needed. Angels!

In the safety of the darkness, I fell to my knees and pushed my palms against the floor, as though trying to shove the truth of my life into the earth. Rage rumbled up through my throat, but when it reached the top it fizzled out like a damp firework. I flopped forward and whimpered as though Blue were right there beating me. Because violence lingers and keeps your body broken. Even when you're all alone, it doesn't leave the room with your abuser. It nests in your heart and eats at you so there's less and less of you left to fight, until there's nothing left at all.

I didn't move when I felt someone's hands on my back. It felt like the hands of Mother Nature had come to sift through the weeds of my pain to make space to plant flowers. Hands of kindness, harvesting my trauma for anything useful and throwing the scraps into a fire. Strong hands. Strength restrained. The adversary of cruelty.

"Stand up, Chanie. You have to stand up," Tuffy said, his voice raspy.

"I can't. I'm so broken." I squeezed my eyes tight.

"Nope."

I sat up and looked at him. His dark eyes, thousands of years old, generations of loss, pain, and violence, healed and weathered like a pearl.

"You've got to stand up, Chanie. If you don't, they win."

"I'm so tired. I don't even know how I could."

"My elders taught me that we can't let abuse live inside us. It's like leaving garbage on your floor. Maybe it was something useful once, but it rots if you don't throw it away."

"How does Blue beating me have a purpose?"

"Because your pain has been sent to be a teacher."

"It's because I'm a nasty whore. I've been a whore for years."

"No, that's not why. It's because you're special. It happened to you because you have the soul to endure it. You're destined to come out the other side. Then you can begin your path as a healer."

"I'm a whore, Tuffy. I'm filthy."

"The things you've done and the life you've lived are symptoms of trauma and inexperience. It's part of your path. Those things happened to your body, not your soul. Right now, they're just camping out on your spirit."

"But I *can't* do it anymore, Tuffy."

"Your pain doesn't have to reside in you. It's meant to be a passerby."

"It needs to go. It's killing me —"

"You have to help it leave. It's been the artist of your existence. You may not like the look of its work, but it created who you are. You owe it recognition, Chanie. Stand up! Put your shoulders back and take a deep breath. Come on, I'll hold your hand."

"What if I can't make it go away?"

"Remember the note I wrote you? About lighting your life on fire?"

I nodded.

"Then we light that fire."

I put my hand in his. He squeezed it. And his face, so strong, so stoic, gave me the strength to stand up and follow him.

He led me to the portable speaker and plugged in his phone. Wily Raines's haunting voice sang out, crisp and clear, like a private symphony. Tuffy leaned close and said, "Tell your pain you know it's real. Thank it for who it made you into and for all the lives you'll change because you survived it. Then move your body to help it leave. I'll hold you while you greet it and be here for you when it's gone."

I won't be the victim of a love song
I will only be the lonely

Walking through a dream
Towards your arms, your eyes, and your love
But it won't be you
Who I wake up to ...

I'd never danced with anybody before. That's not what men paid me to do. But in Tuffy's arms, I moved like water flows downstream when it knows it's headed toward an ocean. We drifted across the floor like feathers blowing in the wind. We were a muse for a love poem. A blend of a little bit of grace and a whole lot of edge, filing down our rough spots and sculpting something beautiful.

When I was twelve years old, I'd felt something that had made me believe I could draw stars in the sky with my fingertips and scoop the moon into my hands. And if I held the moon to my heart, I could light up the entire world. That was innocence. It's like it came to me and said, *This is how love should feel. Memorize this feeling because it's fleeting and easily stolen by the ways of the world.* That's the feeling I had when I first felt Tuffy. It was like he'd always flowed in me, our hearts meeting first, our lives meeting later. And when we danced, I felt the moon in my heart.

We slow danced for a while. Long enough for us to memorize the feeling of our bodies pressed against each other. When we lay down on the blue gym mats, I rested my head on his chest and listened to his heartbeat. He traced the lines on my hand with his fingertips. I pretended I'd never have to leave him and that all the bad would fade away. As long as Tuffy was holding me, everything would be okay.

Tuffy propped himself up. "Chanie, he'll kill you if you don't leave. You've got to try harder for something better."

"But that's what I'm doing."

"Yeah, but for who? They're stealing from you. What you think you have with Blue isn't love. It's the next best thing to the guys who pay you."

I thought I'd never regret Blue. Nobody else had ever spent time with me like he had. He'd made me dinners, we'd watched movies together, and sometimes we'd gone for drives. He'd even taken me to meet his mom. He'd planned a life in Nelson with me, like I was worthy of making a life with. For a while, I hadn't felt invisible or disposable. Nobody had ever made me feel that way, not even my mom. And Blue didn't pay me for sex. But I'd been paying him.

I couldn't see Blue through Blue. I could only see him through Tuffy. The contrast so stark; the clarity so painful. When Tuffy leaned toward me, I parted my lips and, like a craving finally fed, melted into him.

Fuck Blue. I owed him nothing.

CHAPTER TWENTY-THREE

I HAD TO GET Sox out. I'd reason with Blue. I'd pretend to be mad at the neighbours for "interferin' in our business." I'd plead for forgiveness and say that our future together was the only thing that was keeping me going. I'd even beg him to help me find a way to make things right with Brenda and Milos. I'd make him feel like he was in charge. That I *needed* him. I'd do whatever I could to buy time to find Sox a safe haven and get my things, especially my books. Then I'd figure out a hiding place until I graduated. And then I'd be gone.

I snuck up through the stairwell. Brenda was too weak to use the stairs, her body equally as sick as her mind. She claimed that she'd worked too hard her whole life and it had broken her down like an old workhorse. Alcohol, drugs, and a diet of french fries and gravy never came up in those conversations. Just how nothing was ever her fault and that the world would always "owe her somethin'."

The sweet scent of baked berries warmed the apartment hallway. Esther was baking again. The wonderful scent of a normal home filled with love. So odd and out of place in that rat-pit of a building. That was how my future home with Tuffy would smell, like fresh-baked berries and hope. There'd be no way it would resemble the rancid sights and smells of my apartment building: wallpaper peeling off the wall, plastic light fixtures aged the colour of bad cheddar disintegrating with every flicker, babies crying, garbage bags rotting in the stairwell, urine, grease, and dirty diapers. The building begged for a fire. It was ready to surrender its land to something better.

"Only two more months and we'll be free," Tuffy had said. But I felt like I was trying to swim to shore from a shipwreck with no land in sight, my muscles fraying, the water getting deathly cold. "Look to what you want, Chanie," Tuffy had whispered before kissing me goodnight, reluctant to send me home. I promised to text him every hour. I could still taste him on my lips and feel the heat of his body on mine.

When I opened the door, Blue was jerking off to porn on the bed with my iPad. Two spray-tanned blondes with gigantic boobs lay side by side with their legs spread. He looked right at me, smirked, and kept grunting and moaning and calling them sluts. If I hadn't been so driven to see Sox, I would have left again. If Blue thought I'd be shocked, he was wrong. I already knew what a piece of trash he was. It had just taken me a while to see it.

He didn't talk to me for close to two hours. He skulked around me and behind me. He even bumped up against me in the kitchen. I wanted to search for my purse and phone, but he wouldn't let me out of his sight. He stood in the doorway of the bathroom while I peed, and though staring right at me, pretended not to hear me when I asked where my backpack was.

I rolled with it and ignored him too. But just like the first whiff of winter, the air changed. The room became thick and congested, almost suffocating, as though we'd dropped from the ninth floor to six feet beneath the ground. Blue leaned against the dresser, pushing it closer to the wall against Sox. I had to do something, but what?

"Blue, please." I tried to reason with him as I watched Sox's tail quiver.

"What's the matter? Where's your fucking cat, Jade?" Blue began bucking his weight against the dresser.

"Blue! What the fuck!" I snapped.

Blue turned around and yanked the dresser away from the wall. Sox crouched down, terrified and frozen in place, unable to escape Blue's hand as it ripped him from the floor by his scruff.

"Get away from him!" I shrieked, lunging at Blue, grabbing his arm with both my hands. Sox squealed out a guttural meow as Blue threw him to the floor. The kitten scrambled into the kitchen and jumped inside the lower cabinet with the lopsided door.

"Fuck you and that nasty cat!" Blue slammed the dresser back against the wall.

"Blue, let's talk about things," I begged.

"What's there to talk about, Chanie? Your new boyfriend?"

"What's that supposed to mean?"

Blue snarled at me. And then he started singing:

I won't be the victim of a love song
I will only be the lonely
Walking through a dream
Towards your arms, your eyes, and your love
But it WON'T BE YOU
WHO I WAKE UP TO!

I'd never seen him look like he did in that moment. *How long had he been there in the gym?* His nostrils flared, his eyes bulged, and his upper lip twitched and curled like a snarling dog. He planted his feet in a wide stance, cracked his neck a couple of times, and then his knuckles, as though preparing to step into a boxing ring with a prize fighter. His jaw quivered, and his teeth clicked together. The light in his eyes went out, and I thought for sure he'd kill me.

"You don't laugh and smile like that with me, you dirty whore. I saw you all happy, dancing around like a fuckin' ten-year-old! Made me sick, Chanie! Fucking sick! Makes me want to punch your fuckin' teeth out!"

I couldn't move. I couldn't speak. I just stood there.

"You know what, Chanie?" Blue screamed, his spit spraying my face. "You know how we're gonna make this right?"

"No, Blue — I —"

"Little Pocahontas is gonna pay me for your services, slut! You ain't some free-for-all fuck doll for those little schoolboys. You belong to me. He owes me $250 and Brenda $350."

"Tuffy's not paying you," I said. "He's not a john. He's my friend. He owes you nothing."

Blue laughed. Great big exaggerated laughter. He looked so ugly to me with that ferret face I'd hated the first time I'd ever seen him. He looked so much older now, his looks decaying even faster than his soul. His eyes were dead, like dust. Like all the meth had eaten his insides. I looked straight at him and stood my ground, but my body quivered, and tears rolled down my face. Blue shook his head, clenched his fist, and knocked me out.

When I woke up, he told me the only reason he hadn't beaten me even worse was so I'd be able to go out and earn the money I owed them. "Protecting my investment," he'd said. "Can't afford to beat the shit out of you when we're so short on cash."

"Get your slut clothes on and get ready," Blue said. "We got you a little private party at a hotel tonight." He tossed a bottle of Tylenol 3 at me. "I mixed you up a little drink to take the edge off. These boys said they want a loose little party girl. I told them I got just the girl for them."

"Blue, please." I hated myself for begging.

"Hey! Maybe there'll be a little Indian boy for you. You seem to like them brown guys."

He walked over and handed me a rum. "Gotta run up and see Brenda for a minute. Don't do anything stupid, Chanie."

I nodded.

"Oh yeah! I got your phone with me. Your little Ginger friend sent you a bunch of smiley faces, whatever that means. Your fuckin' friends are gonna be the end of you."

I nodded again, grateful that Ginger had taken the time to invent a texting code. She'd send a smiley face and wait for me to respond with a predetermined emoji before sending more messages. This week's agreed emoji was the monkey with his hands over his face.

As soon as Blue closed the door, I moved fast. I filled two containers: one with cat food and one with water. I grabbed a baking pan and used my hands to scoop litter out of the cat pan. I tucked everything behind the laundry basket in the storage closet. Then I pulled Sox out of the cabinet and kissed his face. I told him to be a good boy, locked him in the closet, and promised I'd come back for him.

Blue walked in twenty minutes later. By then I'd had three rums. The pills and booze had calmed me, but my hatred for him boiled in my belly. Thankfully, my face wasn't bruised because he'd punched me in the side of the head. A strategic beating. It worked better that way anyway. Fewer questions at school, and I got to "keep my pretty face" for all the men who paid me.

When we got to the door, Blue shoved me away and looked out the peephole. "Fucking neighbours. Hang tight, Chanie. Them nosy church freaks are in the hallway. Looks like they're goin' out."

I heard Dan's low voice but couldn't make out the words. Esther laughed, and then the elevator doors banged open.

"Okay. They're gone. Glad they're moving the fuck out. After that little scene you caused, we don't need them hangin' around."

"How do you know they're moving?" I asked, hoping he was making it up.

"They gave Brenda notice after your little freak-out. Out by the end of the month."

Who would pray for me?

MY MOTEL CLIENTS LIKED to party and poured very big drinks. They tipped me a hundred bucks and paid for my cab ride home. I considered asking the cabbie if I could use his phone to call Tuffy, but the taste from the men at the motel still lingered in my mouth. I couldn't talk to Tuffy with a mouth full of shame.

The cabbie smiled and asked me if I was okay. I nodded and tipped him five bucks. I hid the hundred-dollar bill in the box of an abandoned truck in the parking lot. Screw Milos and his so-called accounter powers.

When I got home and tried my key in the door, it didn't work. I blinked hard to see if I had the right suite. My mind had been tricky lately, and I was high and drunk. I tried again, but no luck. I heard Blue walk up to the inside of the door, his text tones clicking away. He did strange things when he was high. Maybe he'd wrecked the lock somehow. I waited patiently for him to let me in, but he didn't. I tapped on the door. No answer! And then the elevator doors swung open, and Brenda and Milos stepped into the hall.

"Well, looky here!" Brenda said. "We got our little girl back, Milos."

"Brenda, back off. I just want to see Blue," I pleaded.

"Ya can't just cause problems like ya did and then come back here and not think there'd be hell to pay, *Jade!*"

"Brenda, please just let me go to bed. I'm tired."

"Too bad, bitch!" Brenda lurched toward me and yanked my head back with my hair.

Blue opened the suite door. "Get the fuck off her, Brenda."

"She ain't yer business, Blue."

"Yeah, Brenda, she is. Let her go."

Brenda shoved me toward Milos. He took a swing at me, but I twisted on my heel and turned away from him. He shoved me into the wall and slammed his fist into my back. I felt like I'd been stabbed, like a fireplace poker had been jammed into my flesh. I staggered between Blue and Brenda, hunched over and gagging. Milos tried to grab me again, but Blue stepped in front of him. "Fuck off, Milos. Let me deal with her."

"I just want to go inside," I begged Blue. I'd been begging Blue a lot.

"Look at her," Blue said. "You can't beat the fuck out of her and expect her to keep working. One of her shithead teachers is gonna call the cops."

I wanted to believe that Blue was trying to protect me because he cared, but I knew better. He needed money for drugs and his dealer. His only horse couldn't be out of the race.

"Why can't you get someone else to work for you, Brenda?" I snapped.

"Cuz you owe me big for givin' you a life, Jade. Plus, all them other little sluts turn into junkies and run off and die. Yer nice and clean, other than a bit of booze and codeine. That's why yer such a big moneymaker. It certainly ain't them little titties of yers." Brenda laughed and tried to grab my nipple. "Did ya tell her the new rules yet, Blue?"

Blue blew a smoke ring from his mouth. "You tell her."

"Hear this, Jade! We's all made a business decision to clip yer little wings. So we changed the lock on yer door."

I shook my head. I was in too much pain to focus. "What's that supposed to do?"

"Yer gonna need to give me the building key too, Jade." Brenda reached for my purse.

I yanked it away from her. "How the fuck am I supposed to get in here?"

"Yer gonna need to buzz me, Blue, or Milos. Then one of us will let ya in and come and unlock yer door for ya."

"That can't be legal, Brenda! It's my lease."

"Who ya gonna call, Jade? The cops? I'll tell them ya haven't paid yer rent and that I kicked ya out months ago."

"And then I go to jail, and you'll have to earn your own drug money."

Milos punched my ribs again, knocking the wind out of me. I dropped to my knees and hunched over.

"Back the fuck off, Milos." Blue pulled me up by my arm. "We don't need the fuckin' neighbours coming out here! Chanie, go inside."

I staggered inside and hunted for Sox. The storage room door was open. I limped over to the dresser and looked for him, but he wasn't there. I rummaged through the suite looking everywhere for him, but I couldn't find him. His dishes weren't on the floor, and his litter pan was empty and turned upside down. I ran to the door and swung it open.

"Where is he?" I screamed in Blue's face.

"Calm the fuck down before I slap you!" Blue shoved me away from him.

"Where the fuck is Sox?"

Brenda laughed at me, Milos joining in on cue. "Calm down, Jade. Me and Milos got him at my place till ya learn to respect us a bit more."

"I'll do whatever you need. Just bring my cat back to me."

"You gotta earn that privilege, Jade. We's also decided to fine ya on top of your regular earnings. We's gonna have a few drinks first and then come see ya later tonight when we decide what yer final punishment is."

"What the fuck do you people want from me?"

"I just told ya. We'll all have a talk and let ya know. In the meantime, Jade, get some rest, cuz yer gonna be workin' more than ya ever have. Yer gonna have yer fine to pay, yer regular earnings, and now I gotta feed that fuckin' cat of yers too. So food and shit and room and board."

I slammed the suite door and eased myself into bed. I tried to turn onto my side, but the spasms were too sharp. Blue came back in and walked over. He looked at me and shook his head.

"Jesus Christ, Chanie. What have we done?"

"Help me, Blue," I pleaded. He tried to reach for my hand, but I couldn't move.

"I can't take you to the hospital. What's wrong with you?"

"My back ..." I started to cry again.

Blue paced around the living room. "Let me call my mom. That old bird always has back problems."

I faded in and out while he chatted with his mom. A few minutes later, he stood over me, zipping up his coat. "Don't move, Chanie. I'll be right back."

I stayed still, repeating my mantra over and over, my breath finally slowing and easing me to sleep. When Blue's mom came in and sat on the bed, I woke up. My back spasmed, and I started to cry. She stroked my shoulder and shook her head at Blue. "What the hell did you do to her?"

"Fuck you, Mom. I didn't do anything to her. She had an accident."

"You're no better than your fucking father. Go to the Horton and get us some coffee. You owe us at least that much!"

"Whatever, Mom. She's fine."

"Go!"

Blue's mom stayed next to me and rubbed my back while I tried to sleep. "What the hell are they doing to you, Chanie?"

It hurt to talk, but I had to ask her to help me. "Can you please stop asking Blue for money? He takes it from me. It's making things much harder for me."

Donna looked as though I'd slapped her. "What are you talking about?"

"He said he keeps giving you money because you can't pay for rent and medication."

"I don't know what he's tellin' you, sweetheart, but that little rodent has never given me a dime. *That* little fucker owes me a pile of cash."

Blue walked in with coffee and muffins. His mom gave me two pills and then took two herself. "Take care of her, Blue. I'm comin' back in a few days to make sure she's okay." She patted my head gently and stood up.

"Mom left us some food," Blue said. "I'll heat you up some cabbage rolls and soup."

When had I last eaten?

I waited to sit up until Blue brought the food over. It smelled so good. He propped me up against the pillows and sat next to me while I ate. When I finished, he reheated my coffee in the microwave and brought me sparkling water to take more Tylenol 3.

"We gotta get you on your feet and get you back to work," Blue said. "Fucking Milos!"

Oh my God! I couldn't believe him, but I played the game. "I know, babe. I wish he hadn't hit me so hard. Now I'm getting behind, and we need some cash."

"Do you think you can work in the next couple of days? We're running through our cash like water. It's getting low."

"I'll sure try, babe." I didn't say a thing about the Nelson can because that dream, like my affection for Blue, was long gone.

"Stay in bed. Mom already talked to your school counsellor, so you can rest."

"Hey, Blue? Do you think you can help me with something?"

"Depends."

My eyes filled with tears. "Can you get Sox and bring him for a visit?"

"Get some sleep, Chanie."

A few hours later, Blue woke me up. Sox hung in his hand, limp like an old sport sock. "You can only have him for a couple of hours. I gotta go out for a bit."

Sox squatted on the bed, uncomfortable and dazed, his fur sticky, eyes black with terror. His tail looked like a sparkler, frayed and jagged. When I reached for him, he hissed and scurried under the duvet. He curled his body tight and quivered. I stroked his little back, aching to hear him purr, but he didn't. He just breathed short, raspy breaths. I lifted the blanket. He looked at me, his eyes flat, ears back, pleading for help. He was broken, like me. But we were still alive — for the time being. I reached for the pills on the bedside table and opened the cap. He couldn't suffer anymore.

I knew what I had to do.

CHAPTER TWENTY-FOUR

I PACKED *LES MISÉRABLES*, makeup, yoga pants, tank tops, undies, Tylenol 3, and a mickey of Captain Morgan. I searched everywhere for my grandma's rosary but couldn't find it. My phone was dead, and my iPad was gone. I took $700 from the Nelson can. I went into the storage room and took another $540 out of Blue's toolbox. I stuffed $500 into a dirty sandwich bag, wrapped Sox in the mauve blanket, and knocked on Dan and Esther's door. Esther took him and bundled him in her arms. I gulped back a sob and said, "He's a good boy, and he needs your help."

Esther squeezed my hand and pulled me close to her. "I work at Stingray Auto Body. Call me when you can." I nodded, picked my bag off the floor, and opened the stairwell door.

"God bless you," Dan whispered loudly. "We'll be praying for you."

I walked down the stairs slowly. The three Tylenol 3s I'd taken were kicking in and had numbed me slightly, but my ribs still jabbed when I moved too fast. I paused at the end of each flight of stairs and listened. Nothing but the usual sounds.

Sox was safe, and I was about to light my life on fire. But we'd both survived. And that was all that mattered.

When I reached the lobby, I stood behind the door and prayed. *Women are seventy times more likely to be killed in the two weeks after they leave their abuser.* They might kill me for leaving, but I knew that my death would be certain if I didn't.

An older couple stood in the lobby looking like they'd just come home from dinner. I nodded to them. They nodded back. I slipped out to the parking lot, took the hundred-dollar bill out of the abandoned truck, and made my way toward the road. My phone was dead. I couldn't call anyone, not even a cab. I strained my eyes looking down the street, hoping to see a taxi, but instead, the silver Audi came along and slowed down to turn into the parkade next door. I rushed over to his window.

"I'm sorry to startle you, but I need your help!"

His face contorted. "Get lost! I don't know you."

"Please!" I shrieked, horrified Blue or Milos would come back before I got away.

He rolled his eyes, but then unlocked the door. "Get in before anybody sees me talking to you. I don't want to get involved in your crazy life. What do you need?"

"I need a taxi."

"How about I drive you to wherever you're going and then we never talk again."

"I would be grateful," I said, and gave him directions to Ginger's.

I didn't know Ginger's buzzer code, so I waited outside until a young guy let me follow him inside. When I knocked on the door, I heard her run down the hallway. She swung the door open and said, "Thank God! I thought you were dead."

"I'm in trouble. Is Petey-D here?"

Ginger scanned the hallway. "Get the hell in here! No, he's not home yet."

"I stole Blue's cash. He's going to kill me — but I couldn't stay there. They hurt Sox."

"Oh my God, Chanie! Slow down." Ginger grabbed her purse and pulled out a bottle of Xanax.

"What am I going to do?" My head whirled from the codeine.

"What are *we* going to do? I'm not letting them kill you." Ginger's eyes blazed as though a flame had risen up inside her. "You know what we're gonna do?"

I raised my eyebrows.

"We're going to keep you safe. How much money did you get? Enough to get a place?"

"I stole $740. And I gave $500 to Dan and Esther when I handed Sox over."

"You didn't *steal* anything! That's your money. It's your ass out there on the street. It's not stealing. It's taking back what's yours."

It was my money. *And my life.* The painkillers had waned, and panic was beginning to overtake my adrenaline rush. I pictured Sox, cowering and terrified, to remind me that I'd done the right thing. Part of me thought I should run back before Blue discovered I'd left. Put the money back in the can and pretend everything was okay. Be patient and wait until I had a proper plan rather than acting on codeine and emotion.

"Oh my God, Ginger! What have I done?"

"Stop it! We're gonna find a way." She kept nodding as she reached for my hands.

"What should we do?" I couldn't think. The codeine, the

pain, the fear ...

"We have to find you a place to stay until we graduate. As soon as you're clear, you need to get on a Greyhound and go as far away as possible."

"What about in the meantime?"

"Let me talk to Petey-D. You might have to walk around naked for a few weeks, but it's better than what's happening to you now."

"True."

She grabbed her phone, her hands shaking. "I'm texting the boys."

Ginger led me down the hall. She ran a hot bath, lit a candle on the vanity, and closed the door. She sat on the floor next to the tub while I soaked. We ignored the bruises on my back, ribs, and arms. I wondered how I'd get Tylenol 3 and Valium without Blue. I'd been struggling on and off from withdrawal for weeks, but Blue always made sure I was fixed up for work.

"Where will I get my drugs from?" I crossed my arms over my ribs.

"You're gonna stop using drugs, Chanie."

"Milos and Brenda will come for me. They'll harass us at school. We won't be safe."

"Then we call the cops. They have to help us." She helped me out of the tub and handed me a pink towel.

"If the cops get involved, I get tossed in jail."

"Maybe jail would be safer."

I'd known girls who'd been to jail. It was a fate filled with beatings, bribes, and no place to go when they were released. "It's not. I thought the same thing as you. That they couldn't get to me behind bars."

"How can they?"

"Brenda and Milos know a lot of crazy bitches on the inside, and they could get one of them to hurt me. I don't want to die in prison. Plus, if I don't finish the program, I'll never have a clean record and will never get off the streets," I said, stepping into a mint-green tank top, slowly pulling it up.

Ginger tossed me a pair of fuzzy socks. "How do those losers have so much power?"

"Criminals run in tight circles. They all owe each other for something. All Brenda and Milos have to do is offer one of the inmates an eight-ball of coke and a place to stay when they're out, and those bitches will do anything."

"Jesus, Chanie."

"Plus, they'll wait for me to be released. I'll have no means of getting away. No money. No job. Nothing but a criminal record."

"We need to run away." Ginger handed me a bottle of hemp lotion.

Someone banged on the door. I gasped and grabbed Ginger's arm. My stomach turned, and I dry-heaved. Ginger helped me slide down the wall into a seated position. They knocked again.

"Shh, Chanie. It's probably Tuffy and Jeremy. Let me look through the peephole." She handed me her phone. "Dial 911 and be ready."

I took the phone, but my hands were shaking too much to dial. Ginger took it back, dialled the number, and placed it in my hand again. I sobbed a couple of times and held her arm for a moment. She put her finger to her lips to and tiptoed to the door, her muscles taut, ready for flight.

"It's Tuffy and Jeremy," she said, opening the door. Tuffy came straight over to me. He waved his hands and held his finger to his lips. His face was dark and strained, like he'd just seen an accident.

"There was a fat, sweaty European guy standing in the lobby, Chanie. He looked pissed. We waited out back until he drove away," Tuffy said.

Jeremy held Ginger while she cried. He reached over her shoulder and grabbed my hand. "We're all gonna get you through this, Chanie."

I'd never be safe from Milos. He was a predator, well-practised at stalking helpless girls and hunting them down when they tried to run. And they always ran. He'd probably followed me to Ginger's months before. Now he'd come for her, too. And it was all my fault. I leaned into Tuffy, wishing I could hide inside him. I didn't know what to do. All I knew was that for four tough kids, we were really scared.

"We can't stay here now," Ginger said. "He's already looking for us."

"I'll go," I said. "I can't drag you into this."

"Too bad, Chanie. We're sticking together," Jeremy said. "Stronger in numbers. It's us against the meth heads!"

I pulled Tuffy close to me. "What have I done?"

"Remember what I told you about fires, Chanie?" Tuffy kissed my neck.

"Yes. Total destruction. It's the only way."

Ginger stood up and waved us toward her bedroom door. "Let's light candles and hide in my bedroom until we know it's safe."

We went into the bedroom. Ginger's copy of *Les Misérables* lay in the centre of her bed. I moved it to the dresser. Her book felt different than mine, like it carried her energy and didn't like being touched by a stranger. She lit candles and a stick of frank-incense. The room felt sacred. Divine. We sat cross-legged in a circle on the bed, all four of us holding hands.

"Close your eyes and feel our connection," Ginger said, lightly squeezing my hand. "Let's breathe together."

The warm glow in the room streamed into my chest. Ginger called out the inhales and exhales until we flowed in sync. We gently gripped one another's hands. Breathing in, breathing out. I was in the forest again, the monochrome trees with icy leaves waving to me, the mandarin moon smiling down. I knew that place. I'd been there before. But this time, it was the four of us in the forest sitting in a circle holding hands. And when the copper owls came, they were bigger, stronger, and had massive wings big enough to protect all of us.

Ginger's voice sifted into the silence, soft and sweet, like pep-permint tea and honey. "Keeping your eyes closed, deepen your breath, and we'll come back nice and slow. Hold your peace inside and gently rock your body, slowly waking it back into the moment. And when you're ready, softly open your eyes."

I opened my eyes and saw my beautiful friends with their hearts wide open, the wisest parts of them ready to fight for me — to fight the fire I'd ignited. We felt like a mandala. All the colours of our history beautifully blended and woven together into a state of wholeness, interwoven like a dream-catcher, protected, ready, and strong.

"Let's all braid our hair like Tuffy's. Kind of like gang colours," Ginger said. "We'll keep our hair braided until Chanie's safe."

"What am I supposed to do with my hair?" Jeremy pulled on the five-inch length at the base of his neck.

"Hmm." Ginger looked around. "Cut off some of my hair to make him a braid."

"Take some of mine too," I said.

"How the hell are we going to attach it, Ginger?" Jeremy made a face.

"I'll braid it into your hair," Tuffy said.

We took turns cutting hair from one another. Tuffy created a multicoloured braid and wove it into Jeremy's hair.

"Go easy on my braid, Ginger. It's delicate," Jeremy said. "Don't be yankin' on it when I'm rockin' your world."

"Whatever." Ginger smiled, turning her back to me so I could braid her hair while Tuffy braided mine. "How do we get out of here without them following us?"

"I guess I should turn on my phone," I said. "It should be charged by now."

There was only one text: *Guess who just texted a dead girl ... xoxo – Blue.*

Jeremy grabbed the phone from me. "Fuck him! Fake him out. Ask him where he is and tell him you'll meet him. Then we can get the fuck out of here without him and his fat friend tailin' us."

Ginger nodded and took some more Xanax.

I texted Blue, my fingers shaking: *Blue ... I'm sorry, baby. I love you. Can we talk?*

We waited.

I tried again: *Blue, please. I love you. I need you. I'm scared!!*

We waited again.

Do you got all the cash, JADE!!!!

Yeah, babe. Are you at the apartment?

> Yep!! And you better be soon, or I'm coming for you.

> Where's Brenda and Milos?

> Right here waiting for you.

"Jeremy, call us a cab," Tuffy said. "Jeremy and I will take a quick look to make sure Milos is gone. Chanie, turn your phone off, and let's go!"

We chose the Sands Hotel on the north side. It was in the northeast part of the city, where Fort Road and Yellowhead Trail intersected, slightly north of the Coliseum and the Forum Inn, where I'd also spent a couple of nights during my career. I'd been to the Sands a few times with tricks but had been kicked out once because they'd had a girls' volleyball team check in at the exact same time I wandered into the lobby to buy a root beer from the pop machine. A burly female coach scoffed at me and said, "You should be ashamed of yourself." I scoffed back and said, "And you should go fuck yourself."

Two minutes later, the front desk called our room and told us to hit the road. My client, a hunchbacked old guy who hadn't combed his hair since his high school grad, asked me if I was proud of my conduct. I shook my head, like me sucking dick for money wasn't enough evidence of how I felt about my conduct. He couldn't have been too upset with me because he insisted I "finish what I started" in the back seat of his beige Camry out in the parking lot.

The Sands cost more than a motel, but it had a 24/7 front

desk clerk on duty. Added security. It made me feel better than relying on a flimsy motel door. The cabbie made us pay up front. I peeled $40 off my pile of bills and told him we were in a hurry. Jeremy rode up front with the driver, and I sat in the back between Tuffy and Ginger.

"Do owls symbolize anything special?" I said.

"Let me google it," Ginger replied. "Says here, 'The owl guides you to see beyond the veil of deception and illusion. It helps you see what's kept hidden.' It also says it represents wisdom, announces change, and, oh my God, Chanie! The traditional meaning of the owl spirit animal is the announcer of death!"

"Calm down." Tuffy chuckled. "It doesn't always mean death. It can mean a life change."

"Kind of like a forest fire." I smiled and snuggled closer to him.

"Yep! Very similar." Tuffy squeezed me tight.

I checked in at the front desk. I told him I needed two queen beds, just for Tuffy and me. I didn't want to risk being turned away if he thought the four of us would use the room to party. We looked like troublemakers. Me, standing there in an almost translucent tank top with no bra and a ratty bag, Tuffy wearing a white T-shirt that read *I Am Indian*, a parody of the *I Am Canadian* beer T-shirts.

"My sister and her boyfriend will be stopping in to visit this evening," I told the front desk clerk. He rolled his eyes and nodded.

"I only got one king. No room with two queen beds. Guess you'll have to sleep with your *sister*," he said with a stupid grin.

Later that night, the four of us snuggled in bed. Ginger lit up the room with a bunch of tealights and incense. I ordered pizza, nachos, and wings. We ate like starving soldiers fresh out of the trenches. We flipped through TV channels and argued about what to watch. Ginger shrieked when *Pretty Woman* came on the screen. She pointed at Richard Gere and said, "That's like the guy who drove Chanie to my place!"

I knew firsthand the immoral acts that hotel rooms were forced to witness. The cheating, lying, drugs, and suicides. I'd even known a girl who'd been murdered in that very hotel. She'd been stabbed and left in the bathtub. Her murderer had never been caught. He'd stolen her iPhone and, according to the hotel, the Bible from the bedside table. But that night, the room rested easy with no parties, prostitutes, or murders. Just four kids nestled into a king bed.

"You never told us what happened to you, Tuffy," Ginger whispered softly.

Tuffy stared up at the ceiling. "I come from somewhere nobody wants to talk about."

"We're in bed together, Tuffy — all four of us," Jeremy said. "And I'm not here for the sex."

Tuffy took a deep breath. He squeezed me closer to him. "I come from a place where my options were addiction, prison, or suicide. The houses are falling apart. There's no running water, no doctors. The schools are housed in portable class-rooms, and the teachers don't stick around. Barely anyone graduates."

"Sounds bad, buddy," Jeremy said. "How did you end up here with us?"

"Lots of gangs. They recruited my cousin. A few months later, he killed himself. Then my other cousin overdosed on fentanyl. He was young and left behind a couple of babies. I started getting high and drunk a lot, so my mom packed me up and sent me here to live with my aunt. She said I was 'too precious to die.' Anyways, I stole a bunch of stuff at Walmart to take home to my family. Got caught. They charged me, but I didn't get convicted right away."

"Oh my God, Chanie. He's a modern-day Jean Valjean, stealing for his family. Tuffy, you're so good." Ginger reached over me to rub Tuffy's shoulder.

"I got sent to another aunt right away and tried to go to school in another city for a while. A bunch of rich kids hated me. They called me wagon-burner, savage, Injun. They'd drum their chests and chant stupid slurs. Always tell me to go huff myself. So I beat them up. All of them. I got expelled. Then, when I went to court, the judge said that my crimes seemed to be escalating and we needed to 'nip it in the bud.' Told me to come to school here, and I'd get a fresh start."

"Who wouldn't beat them up?" Jeremy said. "Fucking white kids!"

"Jeremy, you're white too." Ginger chuckled and smacked his chest.

"Only my skin, you racist." Jeremy laughed.

Tuffy kept talking. "My aunt got pissed off at me. Told me I better get thicker skin because my skin colour won't ever change. She said our skin colour 'serves as a filter,' and that if people can't see past it, they don't deserve to get to know me."

"She's right," I said.

"Sure, she's right. But it still pisses me off," Tuffy replied.

"Who cares where we came from! We're like lotus flowers growing out of the mud," Ginger said.

Jeremy laughed. "What are you talking about, Ginger?"

"They're like water lilies. Flowers that symbolize rising from a place of darkness to a place of beauty and rebirth." Ginger smiled. "Just like us."

"Yeah, we're mud lilies," Tuffy said. "Let's get some sleep."

"Hey, Jeremy?" I said. "Can you see if the Bible's in the drawer next to you?"

"You need a little more help than a Bible," Jeremy said. "It's here. Do you need it?"

"Nope. I just wanted to know if it was here."

CHAPTER TWENTY-FIVE

THE MORNING SUN MARKED the beginning of the hunt. The light peeked through the curtain and swept a line over my face, waking me back into the reality of my life. I'd run away. I'd saved Sox and myself, but I'd dragged my three friends into danger. None of us would be safe now, not until we ran far away. The right thing to do was for me to go back and beg Blue to forgive me. That would buy safety for Ginger, Tuffy, and Jeremy. All I had to do was go home and hold on a little longer.

Tuffy squeezed me, as though he could feel me slipping away. Ginger stirred and pushed herself closer to Jeremy. We didn't want to move. We were warm, safe, and hidden away like little birds in a nest. We knew that the second I turned my phone on, our lives would change, so we gave ourselves some time to wake up and clear our heads. We needed to be ready for the inevitable threats and violence awaiting us on my phone.

"We need to pray now more than ever," Ginger said, waving us to all come close. We bundled together and held hands while Ginger read a Rumi prayer off her iPhone.

Jeremy took over and read the last few lines to end the prayer. He kissed Ginger's cheek, threw his lanky body on the bed, and said, "You're gonna have to read the messages sooner or later, Chanie. It's better we know what they're thinking."

I already knew what they were thinking. That I'd robbed them and abandoned my post as their slave.

Jeremy reached his hand toward me. "Hand me your phone."

I unplugged the phone from the charger and handed it to Jeremy. The four of us sat on the bed, quiet and uneasy, like we could feel Blue's meth-violent energy boiling over, coming for us, stopping at nothing. His life was garbage. Brenda's and Milos's too. They had nothing but their addictions and depravity. They had nothing to lose if they hurt me.

Jeremy scrolled through the messages with Tuffy next to him. My hands were shaking, and I didn't realize how tight I'd been clenching my jaw until Tuffy came over and tilted my face up to his for a kiss.

"It's all going to be okay, Chanie. You're not alone anymore." Tuffy put his arm over me and handed me the phone.

> Nobody's gonna want you when we get done working on your face!

> You're going to have to have a closed casket when we are done with you.

> I'm going to scatter your ashes by the wall where you worked downtown.

Ginger cried. Jeremy punched the wall. Tuffy texted Blue back.

> Chanie's not alone anymore!

Who's this? Her little Indian friend?

> Yeah! And I'm a bigger man than you!

We cowboys are comin' for you, Pocahontas ...

> Saddle up, Crack Head.

We embraced in a clumsy group hug before Ginger and I went into the bathroom to get ready for school. We crammed together in front of the tiny vanity, our closeness helping ease our anxiety.

Ginger looked at me in the mirror while she lined her eyes with emerald-green liner. "Did you take all the money from your place?"

"Everything I could find. Why?"

"I hoped there was more. Where are you going to stay now? Petey-D hates you, and Milos knows where I live. Should we talk to Rie?"

"God, no! It's just a couple of months. Plus, I can't stay anywhere long because Milos will find me. I've already put enough people in danger."

Ginger finished with the eyeliner and began sweeping her lashes with a squiggly mascara brush. "I'm staying with you.

Petey-D will have to do without my $500. That buys us about two weeks in a shitty motel."

"My rent money goes straight to the building owner. I authorized direct payment because I didn't want Brenda stealing my cash."

Ginger turned to look at me. "Is there any way you can change that?"

"Not without drawing a lot of attention to myself."

"How much do you have left after rent?"

"Maybe four hundred bucks."

"God help me for saying this, Chanie. But you may need to go out and work a few times." She turned back to the mirror and applied another coat of mascara.

"I can't do that to Tuffy."

Ginger smiled in the mirror.

We ordered bagels and muffins through room service. While we ate, we scratched out a two-month plan on the hotel stationery. We used the budget template from our Life Skills class to break down the numbers. Rooms ranged from $65 to $75 per night. We'd eat breakfast and lunch at school. If one of us worked the evening shift at the shelter, we'd bring home leftovers. The boys would eat dinner at their assigned homes. We could also contribute from our assistance cheques: Ginger, $1,100; Tuffy and Jeremy combined, $800; myself, $800. This bought us approximately forty to forty-eight nights, but didn't include phone bills, food, makeup, or other toiletries. We needed closer to sixty nights, plus start-up cash for our first month after graduation.

The shortfall didn't factor into our decision. Not then, anyway. The guys couldn't move in with us until school was finished. Petey-D wouldn't kick up a fuss about Ginger because his "no panties" rule wouldn't look so good if we called the cops. My apartment had been taken over by Blue, Brenda, and Milos — *and* their addictions. Tuffy said we'd figure it out. We'd have to get creative. Our Life Skills class hadn't prepared us for escaping a crackhead. I'd been resourceful since I was fourteen, but it had always involved the sale of my body. I had no other skills. We knew I could earn money fast, but nobody would say it out loud.

I didn't want to work because of Tuffy. I'd sold myself for years to pay for Brenda, booze, takeout food, and a shitty apartment. Two more months so that I could graduate and get out of the city seemed to justify the means. *But Tuffy ...*

"Let's get to class," Ginger said. "We'll talk about it later." We hugged each other, relieved to be going to class, doing something normal, something safe.

Mr. Lavoy walked up and down the aisles reading bits and pieces of Al Purdy's poetry. It sounded beautiful and tugged at my heart a bit. It even made me want to write a poem. But I needed ideas, not philosophy. Cash! Fast cash! I had enough money left over to get us to month-end *if* we ate most of our meals at the school. The old me could have knocked off a thousand bucks in a few nights. But the old me didn't have Tuffy. I wasn't for sale anymore.

I texted Ginger.

I have an idea!

What is it, Chanie? Tanji?

Not quite.

I approached Mr. Lavoy at his desk. "Can I please be excused a few minutes early today?" I smiled. "Need to call the doc. Kind of a girl thing going on." He nodded and waved toward the door.

The back steps of the school faced a park. I googled Diago Law Group. A picture of a white reception desk with stylish trim popped up. Flashy paintings splashed the walls and reflected off the windows onto the floor. A studious woman in a pencil skirt walked through the lobby with an open folder in her hands. Definitely not the office I remembered.

Three clicks later, there was *Derek!* smiling and leaning on a marble countertop, like a real guy's guy. The kind of guy you'd trust to drive your kids home from soccer practice. Not the guy who sodomizes teenage hookers on his boss's desk. No way! The website made it so easy: *Click Here to Meet Our Lawyers.* So I clicked again. Derek's real name was Donovan Winters, firm favourite for family law. And the lovely Chandra Williamson, firm favourite for youth and criminal justice, looking even more beautiful than she had in the picture I'd seen on her desk the night I'd *worked* in her office.

"Diago Law Group. How may I direct your call?" a sunny voice beamed.

"I need to talk to a lawyer, please."

"What area of law do you need?"

"Donovan Winters. Is he a criminal lawyer?"

"Yes. All of our lawyers practise criminal law."

"Do all of them work with youths?"

"They can. But that's Chandra Williamson's specialty. She's very nice."

"Perfect!" I said. "Can I please set up an appointment with her for a consult?"

"Of course." I heard her clicking away on the keyboard. "How's next Friday at noon?"

"That works for me!"

"Your name, please."

"Chanie Nyrider."

A few hours later, Ginger called in and made an appointment to meet with Donovan Winters the day before my appointment with Chandra. When I met with Rie that afternoon, I told her I wanted to talk to a lawyer about charging my stepdad. "Will you please come to the lawyer's office with me? I have an appointment next Friday at noon."

We changed motels three times in ten days. Blue and Brenda messaged incessantly. Milos didn't because he couldn't write proper English. Sometimes, I'd respond with a link to Narcotics Anonymous or the police website. I thought my phone might explode from the blows of their angry messages, but I'd just shut it off when it got to be too much. I focused on my studies and spent my nights watching TV with Ginger.

I slept fitfully on the nights Tuffy and Jeremy didn't stay with us. My death dreams were so vivid I could smell the pavement. I'd always see Perry's face, the yellow tarp, and my dead body on the ground. I often sat awake most of the night, too jumpy to sleep. Ginger gave me Xanax, which I took reluctantly because I felt like I had to stay vigilant. But it helped ease the intensity of the withdrawal from the Tylenol 3 and Valium. We kept our hair braided, we prayed together, and Ginger led yoga practices and meditations to help us stay centred. My body suffered, and I cried a lot. I slept when I could and never went anywhere alone, except with Mr. Tanji.

Mr. Tanji texted me.

We have a deal, Chanie.

It's not that simple, Mr. Tanji.

Yes, it is, Chanie. I'll see you at six.

When Mr. Tanji dropped me off after our session, he gave me some spending money. He told me to be mindful and not spend it on booze or weed. "Only food, medicine, and school supplies, sweet girl." I thanked him and put it in my boot so I'd have cab fare for my appointment with Donovan Winters.

The next afternoon, I lied to Mr. Lavoy and told him I had to leave for a doctor's appointment at 11:30. I figured all the praying we'd been doing had paid off because he said, "No problem. I hope everything is okay." Not even a mention of bringing a note to validate my absence. It seemed too good to be true, and it made me almost paranoid. I wasn't back in my chair a minute when Pastor Josh peeked his head in Mr. Lavoy's door and said, "Chanie, we need you in the office right away."

I acted cool, as though headed to the office to sign for a parcel I'd been waiting for. But I was terrified. Was it karma? Were all my lies finally floating and visible to my teachers? I had no idea why P.J. would have come for me. Maybe my mother had died? How would I feel about that? I sauntered toward the office door, contemplating whether I'd even go the funeral. Probably not. Clayton would be there, and I'd attack him and end up in jail. My mind was all over the place, but I knew for sure to keep an eye on the time. I couldn't miss my appointment with the lawyer. And then *her* nasty voice stopped me in my tracks.

"I'm like a street genius of sorts. Know what goes on in the minds of these little runaways. Could probably even be a counsellor here, if yer ever lookin'," Brenda said.

"Hmm," Rie replied. "Why are you here today?"

Yeah! Why? I stood outside the door.

"Well, ya see," Brenda said, "I've helped out a ton of these workin' gals. Wanna help little Chanie get clean, ya know. I'm like a mother to her. You could call me her street momma, I guess. Anyways, came to check up on 'er."

"Oh, holy fuck!" I said, walking into the office. "What the hell are you doing here?"

"Chanie! My girl! We's been worried sick about ya!" Brenda tried to hug me, but I shoved her away and stood next to Rie and P.J.

Rie cleared her throat. "Brenda says your rent is overdue and you haven't been living at your building."

"That's a lie because social services pays my rent directly. Call my worker." I smiled at Brenda.

"Hmm. Must be a misunderstandin' then, Chanie! Haven't got yer rent in months. Seen ya drinkin' quite a bit, though. Lots of late nights and slutty dresses!" Brenda smirked.

"Rie and P.J, this woman is no friend of mine. She needs to leave."

Brenda leaned toward me, pushed my hair away from my ear, and whispered, "You's gonna be dead soon, Jade. Just came to let ya know."

I slapped her hand off me and hissed, "I'm taking you with me, bitch!" and walked out of the office.

A few minutes later, Rie and P.J. came to Mr. Lavoy's class to check on me. I told them I was fine. Brenda was my crazy landlord with a huge drinking problem and mental illness. She was nothing to worry about.

Mr. Lavoy joined us in the hall. "If you're being harassed, I can call my cop buddy, Mitch. He can help you."

"No need, Mr. Lavoy. I really have to get to the doctor. Would you mind waiting for a cab with me?"

I texted Ginger when I got to the law office.

> Brenda showed up at the school!

> WTF!! Chanie! I wondered WTF P.J. wanted.

> We need to move out of our motel in the morning. At the lawyer. Chat when I get back.

> I'll tell the boys. Good luck, Chanie. Xoxoxoxooxo

"Ginger Slobodian." The receptionist smiled at me. "Mr. Winters is ready to see you now. Follow me." She walked me down the hall and pointed into his office, her shiny red nails long like eagle talons.

"Hello, Donovan Winters."

"Didn't I pay you to go away?" He recognized me right away. He rushed over and closed the office door.

"Nope! You paid to sodomize me and snort cocaine off my ass. And listen to you talk about yourself. A lot! And bitch about Chandra, enough details so when I meet with her tomorrow at noon, she'll know I'm not lying."

"What is this? Some kind of shakedown?" He laughed and

leaned back in his chair.

"I need your help. I'm in a bit of a predicament."

"How original. A hooker in trouble."

I gave him a quick rundown of my arrest record. I told him how, initially, I hadn't wanted to enrol in the Begin Again program but preferred it to jail. That I was grateful for another chance, but Blue, Brenda, and Milos were exploiting me. That they were very violent people who used meth and other drugs, so I'd run away. I just needed a little cash to get me through the few weeks I had left until graduation.

"Why the hell would you come to me?"

"Because when you drove me home that night, I saw a glimpse of humanity in you," I said, hoping he might soften his stance.

"That's funny." He laughed again and leaned forward with his hands cupped in front of him. "How much money do you need?"

"Maybe a couple grand. I promise to pay you back. I don't have anyone else to go to. Please!"

"You need to get out, young lady. The nerve of you, trying to extort money from me!"

"Young lady! Hmm. That's not really your style of language when you're dealing with women who don't agree with you. Let me see if I remember clearly. What did you call Chandra about a hundred times before you came all over her chair? Hmm. The c-word! I'm a hooker, and I don't even use that word. But you sure like it when you're playing edgy bad guy sodomizing a hooker."

"I could have you arrested right now Ms. ... Slobodian, is it?"

"Spare me, Derek — I mean, Donovan. Don't get all tough guy on me. I wrote your plate down when you drove me home," I lied. "Plus, lawyers aren't the only ones out there buying hookers — judges and cops, too. Lots of cops. I can find out where you live *and* who you're married to. I got nothing to lose, *Derek!*"

"Too bad you didn't come by after hours, dollface. Maybe you could have earned a few of those dollars you're looking for. I sure liked your tight little ass."

"Fuck you! You men take and take and take some more. You're never happy. You take from your wives, your kids, your colleagues. And when that's not good enough, you buy girls like me to feel big. And then you feel guilty. And yet, you do it all over again. I'm a hooker, not a hypocrite like you. At least with me what you see is what you get. No wedding rings and firm favourites, Derek! Oh, sorry — *Mr. Winters.*"

"Fuck you, smart mouth."

"Do something good so the next time you feel guilty after sodomizing some exploited teenager, you can ease your pain knowing that you helped one of us get off the street. Maybe ease the karma coming your way."

"Get the fuck out of my office!" Donovan said, hastily pointing to the door. "And never come back."

I stood up to leave. "My name is Chanie Nyrider. My appointment with Chandra is tomorrow at noon. Go ahead and check her calendar." I walked to his door. "And by the way, my school counsellor will be joining me tomorrow."

"Out!"

By the time I got into the cab outside, my phone had thirty-seven messages. A lot of hate texts from Brenda and Blue and a couple of nice ones from Tuffy and Ginger. I waited until the cab drove a few blocks away from the law office before calling.

"Diago Law. How may I direct your call?"

"Donovan Winters, please."

"He just stepped out. Would you like his voice mail?"

"Sure!"

I waited for the beep. "Hello, Donovan Winters. Thought I'd let you know I recorded our entire meeting on my iPhone. I didn't want to forget any of the advice you gave me today. Hope you don't mind! Thanks again. See you tomorrow."

The next day at 11:45 a.m., Rie and I walked into Diago Law. Mr. Winters stood at the front desk. "Ah, Ms. Nyrider. I've been waiting for you. Chandra Williamson asked me to stand in for her today. Please follow me into my office."

I nodded to Rie. "I'll be right back."

"You should consider getting a law degree, you little snake." His face was red, and he looked hungover.

"I didn't do this to be evil. I'm super desperate."

He handed me a cheque for $3,500. "Check the spelling of your name on this cheque."

"Can I please hug you?" I said, wiping tears from my face. "You just saved my life, Derek — sorry, Donovan."

"Do the right thing with this money, Chanie. I'll be pissed off if I ever see you working again."

"I'll pay you back."

"No! Just make sure you graduate."

I smiled at him and walked to the door.

"Oh yeah, Chanie."

"Yes, Mr. Winters."

"Get the fuck out of my office and never come back."

We both smiled and nodded.

THE FOUR OF US celebrated with Pizza Pops and cheap ice cream. Milos circled the school all week long, but we waited it out every day by working extra hours at the shelter and staying late to do homework. We had no place to be but at school and with each other. They couldn't watch us twenty-four hours a day, but they tried. When Blue and Milos started taking shifts, we got nervous. Sometimes, Blue would park on the street at the edge of the school grounds. Other times, Milos slowly circled the same way he used to stalk me at work. Brenda wandered in and around the field behind the school. The text messages never stopped.

We had four weeks left until graduation. I'd been feeling better. The drugs and alcohol were out of my system, and I didn't have to avoid feeling my life anymore. We tried to relax, despite being stalked. We laughed a lot more, slept better, and had healthy appetites. Part of me would miss being crammed into little motels, sharing clothes, and stealing food from the shelter. It was the closest thing to a family unit I'd ever known. We had great futures ahead. After our graduation, we'd be moving away together. I looked forward to the four of us living in a house, studying, cooking, and entertaining the friends we'd surely meet. Our lives were blessed because Ginger prayed for us and with us every day.

One Friday afternoon, I sat outside by the stairs waiting for Tuffy. The sun glowed, and the trees blossomed. I could smell the lilacs beginning to bloom. Students lounged in the grass by the school. Al sat under a tree reading aloud to Dingo. The sun smiled down on us, and we all smiled back. Except for Blue, high and raging, charging toward me.

I wasn't fast enough. He slammed me into the wall and started squeezing my throat. Voices screamed out. My vision blurred, and I struggled for breath.

"Kill 'im," someone yelled. "Fuckin' woman beater!"

Tuffy came out of nowhere, fast as a wildcat, and kicked Blue in the ribs. Blue cried out and released his grip on my neck. He curled into a tight ball, but Tuffy stayed on top of him and kicked him a few more times before grabbing him by the scruff and dragging him further away from me. Jeremy ran over and kicked Blue a couple of times, then bent down and punched him in the head. Tuffy kneeled over Blue and repeatedly hit him. Blue finally went limp and whimpered the same way I'd cried at the hands of him and Milos so many times before.

I saw Milos's huge frame lumbering in from behind the small crowd that was still cheering on Tuffy and Jeremy. Milos scowled and reached into his jacket. "Gun!" I tried to scream, but no sound came out. Tuffy and Jeremy ran toward Ginger and me.

"Cops! Cops! Cops!" Al yelled, jumping up and down. He ran toward the brawl and shoved Milos. "Cops coming!"

Milos pulled his hand out of his jacket and yanked Blue to his feet. They hurried to the car, but Milos stopped long enough to point trigger fingers at us. He flipped his hand back and pretended to shoot. Ginger yelled, "Fuck you, psycho!" and gave him the finger.

A couple of hours later, Blue messaged me:

Cowboys and Indians! Indian dies first –
then the rest of you!

I messaged back:

Tuffy dragged you around like a
cat toy! So: Indians 1, Cowboys 0!

We changed motels again. This time we moved to the outskirts of the city to the Royal Scot Motel. It was an old place with ratty rooms. It was close to Winterburn Road next to a used truck dealer. It sat on the north side of six lanes of highway where traffic never slowed to the 90-kilometre speed limit. A few other motels were peppered along each side of the highway, and a liquor store had recently opened in the motel just south of ours. Two tattered teddy bears tied to a light pole marked the spot where two pedestrians, probably staying at the Royal Scot, had been hit by a truck during a March blizzard. Apparently, they'd made a run to the new liquor store and never made it back. I wondered if we were staying in the same room that they'd been.

Our new spot was a longer commute, but well worth the peace of mind. Ginger said, "Let's not let those fucks ruin our weekend!" She opened her suitcase and placed tealights all over the room. "I'm going to plan dinner. We'll eat outside tonight at the picnic tables behind the motel."

I looked at my phone. "Tanji messaged me."

"Tell him you can't see him tonight, Chanie." Ginger shook her head. "All work and no play."

I texted Mr. Tanji.

> I got beat up at school today. Can we reschedule?

> A deal's a deal, Chanie. You accepted my offer.

> I'm so tired.

> I'll get us a Jacuzzi room and we'll have just a quick visit tonight, so you can get some rest.

THE JACUZZI SUITE CAME with a fruit basket, champagne, and two bottles of San Pellegrino. Mr. Tanji was in high spirits. He recited an upcoming speech he'd prepared about increasing support for domestic violence victims. My heart lifted higher with every word he spoke. His message was articulate, compassionate, and confident. He was the voice of the marginalized: the beaten, shamed, and forgotten souls on our city streets. Behind that black suit and shiny tie lay the heart of a warrior, a game changer. A leader. The kind of man who could change the world.

"Bravo!" I clapped my hands. "Amazing! You should run for mayor!"

Mr. Tanji laughed. "Call your special friend and tell him I'll send him an Uber. He can come spend the night here with you. I have to get going."

"Why are you leaving so early?"

"Dinner plans. Can't get out of it. But you and your friend have a fun night. Eat the fruit. Drink the champagne. And the room is on my credit card, so order room service at your whim."

"Why are you being so nice to me?"

"You've earned it, sweet girl. I love our weekly visits. I'll sure miss you when you graduate."

"I'll miss you too, Mr. Tanji."

TUFFY OPENED ME UP that night. His love felt like wild horses, powerful, beautiful, like a thousand desires running wild. He planted a forest inside me, its roots spawning and binding, fusing the salt in our souls. My senses pure, as though preserved in a vault. The bad memories fading, irrelevant and dull. Everything new. Sweet. Fresh. Perfect.

CHAPTER TWENTY-SIX

IT SEEMED LIKE WE'D *known and loved each other for our whole lives, Chanie. We are fated to be the best of friends. In life and death.*

Death …

That's all I thought of when Constable Mitch showed up with part of Ginger's braid in his hand. He said, "Found this downtown by the China Gates." *Where I used to work.*

Tuffy held me for three days. I screamed and cried and pleaded with God. I tore at the bedding until my fingertips bled, finally crying myself into silence. "There's no body, Chanie," Tuffy said. "We have to keep believing." I tried meditating to see if I could feel her energy, sense if she was alive. I'd see her face, her eyes, glowing — then murky — then gone.

Jeremy called us *leftovers*. Remnants. He tore his braid off. He said we should cut off our braids, too. He told us, "Ginger would have wanted us to pray." Tuffy agreed. We prayed together, holding hands in a circle. I struggled to connect and felt like I was failing Ginger because I couldn't feel God, faith, or anything but vengeance. So, a few hours later, when Jeremy burst into the room, his hair messy, skin pale and dewy, and said, "I think I killed Blue," I looked at him and thought, *I sure hope so.*

"What do you mean, you think you killed Blue?" Tuffy said.

"I went looking for Ginger at Chanie's old apartment," Jeremy said. "I jumped into the box of Blue's truck and waited a while. When Blue came out, I smacked him upside the head with a piece of lumber."

"Oh my God, Jeremy!" I said. "Did you guys get into a fight?"

Jeremy shook his head. "No fight. I knocked him out and left him on the ground."

A sharp knock on the door startled us. Cops? Blue? Milos? It didn't matter. All of it was ugly, and a bad fate seemed inevitable. It was like my life choices had opened the door to evil and my just deserts would find me, wherever I was.

"It's okay, kids. It's Mr. Lavoy. I'm alone."

Tuffy nodded and rubbed my shoulder. "It's okay. We should talk to him."

Mr. Lavoy brought us three bags of groceries and four stuffed bears. "These are for you guys. And the orange one is for Ginger when she comes home."

Mr. Lavoy pulled a chair up next to my bed. "Do you boys mind if I spend a few minutes with Chanie?"

I shook my head no. Tuffy said, "No problem." I pulled the covers up to my neck and turned my back to Mr. Lavoy. I kept my eyes closed and shrugged my shoulders close to my ears.

"Do you know how I started writing, Chanie?"

I ignored him.

"When my best friend of eighteen years committed suicide."

Dramatic. Just like my dad.

"He shot himself. We'd served on the police force for three years at the time."

"You were a cop?" I said, rolling onto my back to look at him.

"Yes. Me, Mitch, and Travis. Graduated high school together. We got sick of being bullied, so we applied to the police force."

"Travis is the guy who died?"

"Yes, Travis passed away. Anyway, Travis's mom begged me to write his eulogy. She said, 'Nobody else can capture his grace but you.' There's something about the word *grace* that moves me and inspires me to do better, Chanie. It makes me believe there's an invisible force behind me, helping me. Like maybe the word *grace* is really the name of an angel."

"What does this have to do with Ginger?"

"Here's the thing, Chanie. At first, I couldn't write a word. I was too angry. I tried to convince myself I hated him because it was easier to blame him than it was to accept the reality of his very deep suffering."

"But he chose to leave!" *Like my dad.*

"He chose to leave because he didn't know what else to do. Travis was in a lot of pain." His voice broke. "I know you won't believe what I'm about to say, but please listen anyway. There is magic in grief. Something mysterious and creative that's only available to us when we are broken wide open. Grief delivers us to a place of deep reflection and contemplation. It was in that place where I was able to find the words to pay tribute to my best friend's life. To honour him before his family and friends."

"Ginger's all alone now. What if she's dead?" I started crying.

"She has no one. She'll be buried in a field somewhere without a headstone."

"Why do you think that, Chanie?"

"Because I read something about potter's field in *Les Misérables*. That's how they buried Fantine."

"Let's look at your book." Mr. Lavoy picked up my copy from my bedside table. He flipped through the pages. "Here it is: 'We each have a mother, the earth. Fantine was given back to this mother ... So Fantine was buried in this free corner of the cemetery that is open to everyone and no one, where the poor are lost without a trace. Happily, God knows where the soul is.'"

I frowned at him. I was still on bad terms with God. I had only given Him a chance because of Ginger's faith. And He took Ginger from me.

"See, Chanie. *God* knows where her soul is. So, it doesn't matter because God has her in the palm of His hand."

"Do you actually believe in God?"

"Chanie ... I do."

"Why did you leave the police force?"

"Travis had some issues in his childhood. That's when Mitch and I'd seen the first signs of his depression. He'd had nobody but us. I mean, we tried to be there for him the best we could, but we were kids. We had limited life experience. It was during my deep mourning that I discovered my calling. I knew I wanted to help young kids, so I decided to get my Bachelor of Education and an English degree. Books and words have always spoken to my heart. They flow into me, and as I learned when I wrote the eulogy, they also flow out of me. Understanding and communication. I believe these are the antidotes to all evils."

"But you were a cop. That's a saving-the-world kind of job."

Mr. Lavoy laughed. "Yes, that's true. But by the time the cops show up, it's often ten years too late. Teachers at least get to try before the kid destroys their life."

"You've helped me, Mr. Lavoy."

"You can honour Ginger by writing a tribute to her, Chanie."

"I don't think I can."

"Yes, you can. This is brutal and heartbreaking, eviscerating, really. But don't let it take your life. You must keep moving forward. If I'd shrivelled up when Travis died, I wouldn't have become your teacher. You wouldn't have discovered *Les Misérables*, and you may not have discovered your talents, Chanie. I believe with the deepest conviction that we are always exactly where we're supposed to be."

I held one of the teddy bears to my chest and shook my head. "I can't do it. I can't! I can't! I can't!"

"You can." Mr. Lavoy grabbed both of my hands and squeezed tightly. "Everything is not as it seems, Chanie. You have to trust me."

I dropped my head and cried harder. Mr. Lavoy tapped my chin and said, "Look at me, Chanie." I looked at him. He looked strong and wise in the way that seasoned cops do. He gave me a firm nod and said, "Trust me."

When Tuffy came back, we showered together. He tucked me into bed and braided my hair. Jeremy sat on his bed holding the orange bear but joined us to hold hands and pray. Tuffy led the prayer while Jeremy and I cried, our emotions untethered, flailing in our grief. But Tuffy's stillness brought us back. He made us strong enough to get through the night. In his stillness, we finally rested into a sad state of calm.

"Tomorrow we have to go back to school," Tuffy said. "I'll be with you every step of the way, Chanie. *Do not* leave the school without the two of us."

I fell asleep between Tuffy and Jeremy. They watched TV late into the night while I dreamt of Ginger and me planting flowers in a graveyard.

We went to school in the morning, but I couldn't focus. Mr. Lavoy walked me down to the infirmary and told the nurse to keep an eye on me. I faded in and out of sleep, dreaming of Ginger every time I dozed. Rie stopped in to check on me, but I didn't feel like talking. Pastor Josh came and prayed for me. I pretended to be asleep.

Tuffy brought my phone to me at lunchtime. Blue was alive and texting threats, as usual. Mr. Tanji also messaged twice. *We have a deal, Chanie …*

"I can't see Tanji tonight!" I grabbed my phone.

> Sorry, Mr. Tanji … Can't do it.

> I know you're in pain, Chanie. We'll do something light tonight. To ease your pain.

"Tuffy, can you call him for me, please?"

"I'm sorry, Chanie. Just go see him. Jeremy and I need to do a couple of things. If you're with Tanji, I know you'll be safe."

"Oh my God, Tuffy!" I pounded my phone with my fingers and texted Mr. Tanji.

> Fine! Pick me up at 7!

CHAPTER TWENTY-SEVEN

I AM LIKE CONNIE riding in the back seat of Arnold Friend's car looking out the window at the world I could have lived in. Blue is holding a gun against my ribs, and Brenda is sweaty, blotchy, and grinding her teeth in the front seat with Milos, chanting, "We needs to fuckin' kill 'er! We needs to fuckin' kill 'er!"

An hour earlier, I'd pleaded, "Please, Mr. Tanji. I'm so tired. Would you mind? It will only take you a few minutes."

"Okay, Chanie. I'll go get you a latte. But when I get back, we get down to business."

"Fair enough."

I'd waited a few minutes to make sure he was gone and then slipped out the hotel lobby doors and hopped into a cab. Tuffy's words kept playing over and over in my head: *There's no body, Chanie ... We have to keep believing.* I told the driver to take me to my old apartment. Where else would they keep Ginger? He dropped me off in the back alley. I was careful. I checked the parking lot, the windows. Neither the Lincoln nor Blue's Chevy were in their spaces. I even walked down the back street to make sure they hadn't parked on the road. I thought it was safe. I'd only be a minute. I'd just tap on the suite door and check for Ginger.

While I waited by the back door for an opportunity to sneak inside, Milos pulled up. I turned to run, but Blue was too fast. He covered my mouth and dragged me into the back seat of the Lincoln.

"All I want is Ginger," I said.

Blue shoved a gun into my ribs. "Shut the fuck up," he said, jabbing me harder.

Brenda started chanting, "We needs to fuckin' kill 'er! We needs to fuckin' kill 'er!"

"All I want is Ginger," I repeated.

Blue mimicked me, and the three of them laughed. They were meth personified. Ugly, toxic, and deadly. Zombies with black hearts wasting away in the world.

"That Ginger sure is a tight little bird, eh, Milos!" Blue laughed and smacked the back of the seat. "Could make a ton of money off that ass."

I screamed and punched the roof of the car. "Fuck you!"

"Pull over, Milos," Brenda said. "Teach 'er a lesson."

Milos said, "We need quiet place. Out of city. My friend. He has place."

When the streetlights ended, Blue shoved the gun under my chin and wrapped his fist in the back of my hair.

Brenda turned to look at me. "Do ya got a favourite song, Chanie?"

"What the fuck?" I said.

"Yeah! She's got a favourite song!" Blue said. "Find that fuckin' Wily Raines song. You know, the one about bein' a cheatin' whore!" He squeezed my throat. "Isn't that what you and

Pocahontas were dancin' to that night? *Isn't it?*" He squeezed harder.

I nodded. *If I get my hands on that gun ...*

"Play the song for Chanie, Brenda. Kind of like a death row last meal, except a song."

"Yer so funny, Blue." Brenda cackled while she scrolled through a playlist.

Blue poked me again. "I hear this fuckin' song everywhere I go, Chanie. And every time, I gotta see you and Pocahontas dancin' around the gym!"

"Where's Ginger?" I shrieked.

"She's dead, Chanie. Fuckin' dead! Just like you!"

I felt my life leaving me. "Why, Blue? What is wrong with you people?" I started sobbing. *Was this really it?*

"Why ya cryin', sunshine?" Brenda said. "Here's yer little gay tune."

"Yeah!" Blue said. "Now I'm gonna change the memory of this song so when I hear it from now on, I won't remember you dancing with Pocahontas anymore. Instead, it'll be the tribute song of the last lesson I ever had to teach you, *Jade*. The song I played when I choked your last breath out of your slutty little body."

Wily Raines's voice took me back to that night in the gym, Tuffy's arms around me, us floating together as we danced. *I love you so much, Tuffy.*

"Do you love your song now, Chanie?" Blue hissed, his breath rancid, spit spraying over my face.

My upper lip curled, and I snapped, "You know what else I love, Blue?"

"What, Jade? Got some last words you'd like to share?"

"I loved watching Tuffy drop you to your knees like the pussy you are. I fucked him so hard that night while we laughed at you, Blue! Big man! Woman beater! Dragged around the parking lot like a shop rag. Curled up crying like a bitch!"

"Shut up, Chanie!" Blue barked.

"I'll die loving him, Blue. He'll come for you. And he'll kill you."

Blue shrieked like an animal being torn in two on a railway track.

And then everything went black.

I woke up in a Quonset naked on a workbench. My hands were bound, my legs tied. There were four guys: two Serbs, Blue, and another white guy. They raped me with something cold and hard. When I was awake, I panted and puked and screamed and cried. At first, I pleaded for my life; soon after, I begged for them to kill me. I faded in and out of consciousness. Blue's laughter. So much pain. Brenda's voice. Loud voices — yelling.

Riding in the trunk of a car.

Cold pavement. Shadows. And the yellow tarp.

I'm coming, Ginger …

CHAPTER TWENTY-EIGHT

WHAT WOULD I CHOOSE to remember about me?

Rape. Violence. Suicide.

Or grace.

I teetered between two worlds. One world touched by the sun, full of radiant beings, neon flowers, and trees one hundred feet tall. Magenta waterfalls, crystal mountains, periwinkle water, children and animals beaming with joy. Everything aglow. Whole and perfect. The other world, Tuffy's broken face, like a crumbled mountain, his stillness blown to pieces like the ruins of a war. Jeremy, heavily tranquilized, his eyes foggy and empty, like the windows of an abandoned home. Ginger — murdered. My body — destroyed. The fear of being hunted. The terror of remembering that I'd been caught.

In the first world, I stood very still at the edge of a field. I wanted to run and jump off the crystal mountain into the teal waters, pet the animals, and play with the children. My head was clear, and my body was vital and whole. But if I step-ped into the meadow, I knew I could never go back. I'd never see Tuffy, Mr. Lavoy, and Jeremy again. But it hurt too much to be alive anymore. I had too many bad memories, too many triggers, and too much karmic debt. I needed so much healing and had so little energy to do it. My life had become tired, tainted, and worn.

I took a step toward the grass.

A firm hand gripped my shoulder and stopped me.

Dad …

"I love you, Chanie." Those were his only words. He took a step back and swept one hand toward the earth and then raised his arms to salute the sun. A gigantic lotus sprouted up from the ground, the bud as big as the moon. The flower swirled and spun violet petals into the lavender sky, where they exploded and burst into thousands of tiny blossoms. The blooms rained down on me, fresh and sweet, and my body felt lighter than air. I threw my arms up and lifted my face to the sun. I twirled and danced beneath the velvety pink blossoms, and then Ginger was there, laughing and dancing next to me, holding my hand. We reached down and filled our hands with flowers and threw them high into the sky. "I missed you, Ginger," I cried.

And then a thud. Enormous pain. Grey. Cold. Dark.

"I missed you too, Chanie."

I opened my eyes.

Ginger was leaning on Jeremy next to my hospital bed. She was broken and sad, like Sox on the night that I'd saved him. We stared at each other, silent and grateful, and then we wept. Tuffy dusted my face with feathery kisses, sweet and gentle, like the pink blossoms that had fallen from the sky. Ginger took my hand, the way she had in the field full of flowers, and we all prayed together.

The nurse came in and smiled. "Welcome back. You gave us all a good scare."

"But I died," I said.

The nurse laughed, her face sweet and sympathetic. "You're okay, young lady. Keep calm. I'm going to get the doctor for you."

"No! I died! I saw the yellow tarp. They covered me with a tarp."

"Who covered you?"

"The police ... I think."

"Hmm, no. A great big man rode in on the ambulance with you. He'd wrapped you up in his yellow raincoat."

Foggy memories of the highway. Beaten and raped. In the trunk of a car and then on the pavement. The yellow ...

"Do the cops know what happened to me?"

"The doctor will see you soon."

"Who saved me?"

"He wouldn't leave a name. But he left you that little guy on the shelf."

Dingo!

When the police came to see me, I asked for Constable Mitch and Mr. Lavoy to be present. Ginger sat on the bed with me. Tuffy left the room while I talked about the details of the rape. I'd share it with him in private when we could grieve together.

A cop named Detective Filgate came to see me. He was kind of handsome, in a Richard Gere sort of way. He cleared his throat a lot and kept looking at Mr. Lavoy, as though asking him for permission to proceed. Mr. Lavoy gave him a crisp nod, and the detective pulled out his notepad.

"We were able to track your phone to a Quonset ten minutes out of the city. The place has been vacant for months. The owner abandoned it because of an illness. But there appears to have been some activity in the shop where they ..."

"Attacked me." I finished the sentence for him.

"Yes, I'm so sorry, Ms. Nyrider. This must be hard for you."

"It's okay, sir."

"Have you ever been there before?"

No! But I've been raped before.

"I haven't, sir."

"Well, by the time we got out there, you were gone. We couldn't find anyone. Anyway, we left fast because dispatch said you'd been brought into Emergency."

"They put me in the trunk of the car. I remember that. I also remember Milos choking me."

"Milos left the city," Detective Filgate said. "We've issued warrants."

"What about Blue and Brenda?"

"Blue is in the Remand Centre. Brenda — well, we just couldn't pin much on her. She was at home when you were brought in. Said she didn't know anything."

"She's lying."

"We know that."

"She was there with them. When they beat me up and raped me."

"Yeah, but the problem is that she's married to Blue. Technically, a spouse can't testify against her husband."

"What?!"

"Anyway, Blue's own mother won't bail him out, so I think he will be locked up for a bit. This would be a good time for you to get your belongings from your apartment and find a safe place to live."

"I'm moving to B.C. soon," I said. "I'm graduating in a couple of weeks. Moving away and starting over."

"That's a good idea, Ms. Nyrider. But you'll have to come back to testify. But don't worry about that right now. Rest up."

He gave my forearm a reassuring squeeze, nodded at Mr. Lavoy, and left.

The cops and the prosecutor didn't let me rest. The prosecutor said, "We have to build the case. Get the details while they're still fresh." *Fresh!* I told them to stop waking me up. I needed peace and quiet.

Rie and Pastor Josh tried to help. Rie said, "You need some privacy to process. Quiet time. You need to keep your eyes on healing." But everybody kept asking questions. Prying. Exposing every nerve. Keeping it *fresh!* I'd been raped, choked, and tossed into a garbage bin. I didn't want to talk about it anymore. Ever.

When Mr. Lavoy came to see me, I said, "I don't feel like talking today."

He said, "That's okay, Chanie. You just have to listen. Your essay was in the top five. I hope you've been preparing a speech."

Pastor Josh, Rie, and Mr. Lavoy brought our homework to the hospital. They spent every evening and weekend with Ginger and me, preparing us for our finals. Tuffy and Jeremy sat in on study sessions, and Allister offered to tutor us in his spare time. Everybody came together to make sure the four of us made it through. At first, I could only study for an hour at the longest, but my recovery came quickly, and I worked hard.

Mr. Tanji showed up on our scheduled nights. He said, "I can't miss our little visits, Chanie. Pretty soon you will move away, and I will miss you so much."

The hospital put Ginger and me in the same room. We felt safer together. The boys slept in chairs and on the edges of our mattresses because nobody knew where Milos was. None of us felt safe. Tuffy and Jeremy wanted to kill him. They said it was the only way to make sure he never hurt us again. Ginger said, "No more violence. Spend your energy on something better." But I wanted Milos dead.

"What happened to you, Ginger?" I'd been asking her every night, but she kept saying she needed time.

"Chanie, you don't want to know."

"Ginger, I do."

"Okay."

I went over and sat on her bed. She took a few breaths and folded her hands on her lap.

"The night you stayed with Tuffy at the Sawridge, Jeremy and I had a fight. He said our lives were a mess because of you."

"He's right."

"He's not, Chanie. You don't get it."

"I do get it! My mess almost got you killed."

"We are always exactly where we're supposed to be. No matter how good or how bad. Milos and Blue hurt me. You didn't do this to me, Chanie. They did!"

"Because of me."

"Because they're sick bastards. Not because of you. Anyways, Jeremy went to sit out behind the motel to cool off. I dozed off. Milos tapped so gently on the door, I just assumed it was Jeremy, so I opened the door."

"Oh my God!" I felt bile rise in my throat.

"Yep! Milos. Big man. Strong. In the back seat of the car before I could even scream for Jeremy."

"I'm so sorry." I started crying.

"Stop apologizing, Chanie. Or I won't talk about this with you anymore."

"But I feel —"

"It's bad enough I have to heal from what they did to me. And to you. So I can't be trying to take care of your guilt, too.

We need to be strong, for ourselves and for each other. I forgive any wrongdoings you *think* you may have caused me."

I couldn't speak. Ginger took my hands in hers. "They took me to your apartment, Chanie. Blue and Milos made me drink with them. I didn't want to, but it wasn't a suggestion."

"Fuckers!"

"Anyways, Brenda is a sick fuck, too. She watched them —"

"Oh no no no! No, Ginger!"

"Yes, Chanie."

"I'll fucking kill Blue!"

"Chanie, please. Please, please, please ..."

"I'm sorry, Ginger. I'm so sorry."

"Chanie! We're alive. We're going to end them. We're strong with Tuffy and Jeremy. The secret's out. The cops are on our side now. Mr. Lavoy and the other teachers."

"We need to end them, Ginger. Brenda too."

"That bitch ripped my mom's silver crucifix off my neck."

"Do you know where it might be?"

"It's in your apartment somewhere."

We had two weeks until graduation. Mr. Tanji paid for adjoining rooms at the Sawridge for the four of us. We studied, watched movies, and Ginger and I cried a lot. Tuffy's stillness returned, but a quiet rage festered behind his dark eyes. Jeremy too. He was grateful, but angry. Ginger implemented zero tolerance for talk of vengeance and told us that practising more mindful speech would help us heal. We maintained our composure. Grace ... *There's something about the word* grace *that moves me and inspires me to do better.*

"We *will* begin again," Ginger said. "Start fresh. New memories!"

"I will spend the rest of my life making the three of you happy," I said.

Constable Mitch showed up at the Sawridge a few days before grad. "Chanie and Ginger, I have some interesting news for you."

Fentanyl! I pictured the three meth heads dead in a pile on the floor of my old apartment.

"Milos's Lincoln was found smashed to bits off the railway tracks by Edson."

"What do you mean?" Ginger said.

"Looks like he got hit by a train. Maybe drunk? Maybe suicide? Who can tell?"

Some prayers do get answered.

Ginger and I fought hard, for our lives, for our love, and for Tuffy and Jeremy. I loved Tuffy more than I could ever have imagined loving anyone or anything, but I couldn't fully connect to him. Rie said it was normal, given the physical trauma of the rape. Ginger felt the same way with Jeremy. Tuffy and Jeremy said they'd wait forever if they had to. Because they'd wait forever, we'd make sure they didn't have to.

A couple of days before grad, I dropped Dingo off at the shelter for Al and went to the apartment to look for Ginger's necklace. I didn't consider Brenda a threat. Mitch had told me she'd been fired and had to move in with Blue's mother, and Blue was in custody at the Remand Centre. He'd also contacted the new landlord to get me a set of keys. A part of me wanted to see my old place, say goodbye, and put it to rest. I also wanted to find my grandmother's rosary and a dreamcatcher I'd never had the chance to hang.

I used the alley because I had to walk down that alley unafraid so I could put it behind me. I needed to change the memories and begin healing. The last time I'd been inside the building was the night that Esther and Dan had saved Sox for me. They'd visited me several times while I was in the hospital. Esther showed me pictures and videos of Sox. They prayed for me, and Esther held my hand and told me again how much I mattered to the world.

I stood in the lobby I'd stood in so many times before. The back door slammed and sent what felt like flames through my chest. Still jumpy. Scared. "It will take a long time for you to calm down," Rie had said. The trauma. It's the *trauma*. That's how everyone had come to define the last few weeks of my life: Traumatic.

The elevator bounced and squeaked and spit its doors open. I remembered the gift bag on the door with the blanket and the note. The love of total strangers who had told me that I mattered. Their gesture had given me wings. It had made me step up, save Sox, and then save myself.

I thought I heard a thud inside the suite but figured it was just a trauma response. I told myself that I was safe, that it was just a reaction from residual anxiety. The door creaked when I pushed it open. Fast-food bags littered the floor. Beer bottles, napkins, cigarette butts, and empty Tim Horton cups were scattered throughout the entire living space. The bed frame, barbeque, and TV that Blue had brought home were gone. My mattress lay on the floor, covered with stains that looked like coffee, or maybe blood. The Nelson can was in the centre of the room. I kicked my way through the garbage and bent over to pick it up.

I saw the barrel of the shotgun first.

And then Blue's feet.

I stood up and looked at him. His two front teeth were gone.

Beads of sweat glowed on the bridge of his nose, his skin was sallow, and his posture was crooked, like a crippled old man who'd lived a life of shame.

"Get the fuck in the bathroom!" He pointed to the door with the shotgun.

"I'm not doing this anymore, Blue. Please just let me go." I could hardly hear him over my pounding heart. The irony. I'd escaped and finally found my way out. And in an instant, Blue would take me out, and none of it would matter.

"Let you go, Chanie! What the fuck. Look what you've done to my life!"

"I won't testify. Just let me leave."

"No, Chanie. You don't get to *just leave!* You got all these people tendin' to your pain. What do I got?" he stuttered, his face wet with tears.

"You have a future too, Blue."

"In jail!"

"I just said I won't testify."

"You just don't get it, Jade — Chanie!"

"I don't get what?"

"I loved you. You were my girl. And look what you've gone and done."

"What *I've done* —"

"Yeah, what *you've done*! And that fuckin' Indian still owes me for your ass."

"Blue! *Please* put the gun down. We can talk."

"You ruined me, Chanie. Look what you've done."

"What have I done, Blue?"

"You've made it so I have to kill us both now."

I'd seen this guy on TV once who'd survived a plane crash. The plane crashed right into the side of a mountain and fell to the ground. "The fire was the issue," he'd said. "My lap was on fire, and I had to get the seatbelt off. So, it's like I just did what I had to do. *Something* took over and kept me calm. I got the belt off and walked away from the flames."

Some Thing ...

The interviewer had said, "I could never do that!"

The survivor had replied, "You'd be surprised what you can do when you don't got any other choice."

"Fuck you, Blue."

"Fuck me?" He pointed the barrel at me.

Something took over and kept me calm.

I shoved the barrel away from my face and yelled, "Yeah! Fuck you, Blue! Kill yourself and leave me out of it."

Blue crumpled forward, awkwardly holding the shotgun in one hand. "How can you say that to me?"

"How can I not? You beat me! You raped me! You sold me to other men! *AND YOU RAPED MY FRIEND!*"

Brenda kicked the door open. "What the fuck is goin' on here?"

I spun around. "Why are *you* here?"

"Why is *you* here, ya stupid bitch?" She slammed the door closed and strode toward me.

"Get the fuck away from me, Brenda!" I shoved her away as hard as I could.

"Blue! Are you gonna let 'er get away with that?"

I turned to look at Blue. He'd flopped down on the mattress, the barrel of the gun facing toward him, his body contorted and twisted, eyes bulging, mouth wide open, and toes splayed reaching toward the trigger. And then the loudest blast I'd ever heard.

Brenda fell to her knees, screaming, but I couldn't hear her. I couldn't hear anything. I only looked at Blue long enough to make sure he was dead. Not long enough to imprint the image of his crumpled body, the blood, and his brains blown everywhere. I needed to leave. As I turned my head, the glint of a silver crucifix flashed up from the floor. I scooped it up and slammed the door behind me.

CHAPTER TWENTY-NINE

"READ ME YOUR SPEECH, Chanie."

"Okay, Mr. Tanji. But only if you tell me why you did this for me."

"Because I had something to offer you."

"But I was a hooker."

"And I am a man who foolishly bought hookers. That doesn't mean we are disqualified from being better people or from living better lives."

"How can I thank you?"

"You can be great, my sweet girl. That's how."

Think about my offer, Chanie ...

I remembered that night. That was the night that Dan and Esther had left the note on my door telling me that they prayed for me. That *I* mattered. And then Mr. Tanji had found me pacing up and down the curb while Brenda and Milos stalked me from a few feet away. He'd held my hand while he drove us to the Sawridge. He'd listened to me talk and ignored the relentless beeping of his phone to ask me questions. Like I mattered. I'd told him everything that night: about my first rape, the arrest, school, the beatings, drugs and alcohol, the essay contest.

The essay contest! That's when he'd said, "Let me make you an offer, Chanie."

I'd accepted his offer. Since then, we'd met twenty-one times. He'd said, "Twenty-one is my lucky number." We had a routine: he'd pick me up, take me to the Sawridge, order dinner, and then we'd get to work. He brought the books that he said had changed his life: *The Bhagavad Gita, The Upanishads, The Dhammapada, The Tibetan Book of Living and Dying, The Way of the Bodhisattva.* He also brought books by his favourite authors: Eknath Easwaran, Pema Chodron, Thich Nhat Hanh, Sharon Salzberg, Chogyam Trungpa Rinpoche, and Jack Kornfield.

The books swelled with highlights, tape flags, and folded corners. He said, "These words and teachings are sacred. They deserve to be read mindfully." The pages showed the art of his soul through colours, notations, and symbols in the margins. "It's these markings that will tell you everything about the man I really am."

I'd read everything he'd told me to and made notes of my own. I'd asked him a thousand questions. He'd said, "You're lucky to be getting so much information so quickly, Chanie. Like SparkNotes."

"Let's call them Chai Notes," I'd said. "They're spicy like you!"

Mr. Tanji had laughed. He'd said, "My sweet girl. I will talk about our readings, show you great speakers, and tell you my greatest successes and failures before my audiences, but I will not read your essay or hear your speech until the night before. It has to be that way in order for it to truly be *your* accomplishment."

"Will it ever be ready?"

"Trust me, my sweet girl. All writing is eventually ready at some point. Maybe not for the writer, but for the reader. Trust the process."

"Why did you help me?" I held the cue cards in my hand. "Come on, Mr. Tanji. I'm not reading it until you tell me why."

"Chanie. I am a very rich man. But I haven't always been popular. I was often bullied as a kid. Anyway, I used to have a lot of self-esteem issues. Imagine a brown kid wearing a turban in junior high! I have a good job, but I made my money in stocks. Total luck. Didn't know what I was doing. I got really drunk one night and told my buddy to invest my whole inheritance. Big inheritance! It could have gone the other way. I am very lucky. When I hit it big, I did all the stupid things I thought rich men did. Drugs, hookers, trips to Vegas, always buying rounds."

I'd never seen weakness in him. He'd always seemed so powerful. On top of it. Like nothing could make him falter. Mr. Tanji commanded the room, whether on the news or navigating his rowdy friends through drunken nights.

He sighed and reached for a Pellegrino. "Do you remember the last time we were together before I found you again? Those two morons Amal and Amal were with me. And that silly Amal kept insisting on kissing you. You pleaded with me to make him stop, and I laughed at you and told you that I'd give you more money."

"I remember," I said. That was the first night I'd ever had sex with Blue and the night that Perry had died.

"You said, 'It's not about the money!' And I said, 'Of course it is.'"

"It's okay, Mr. Tanji."

"It's not okay, Chanie. When you looked at me, your face looked broken. That's when I realized you may have had higher expectations of me. The hurt on your face — it made me have higher expectations of myself."

"That's behind us now." I smiled, but his face looked dark and sad.

"Chanie, when I met you, you should have been playing with dolls, not selling your body on the street. I knew I couldn't save you then, but the essay gave me an opportunity to help you save yourself."

"I used to have a crush on you, Mr. Tanji. I used to imagine us slow dancing in a ballroom, like a prince and princess."

"What a sweet girl. I'm no prince, Chanie."

"You're my prince, Mr. Tanji."

"And you changed my life, sweet girl. I've never bought another round of drinks or a hooker since that night with the Amals."

"Come on ... Really?"

"Really, sweet girl. You never know how you affect someone's life. We can choose to be awakened by others or remain in a dull sleep. Chanie, you awakened me."

"I'm really going to miss you." I felt my nostrils flare as tears came to my eyes.

"Don't cry, Chanie. I'll never be very far. But, Chanie ..."

"Yes."

"Please call me Ali from now on. That's what my friends call me."

"Okay, Mr. Tan— Ali."

"Now, let me hear your speech!"

I took a few deep breaths but couldn't speak.

"Remember! Keep your eyes up. Let the audience see the life in you," Mr. Tanji prompted, his eyes alight, passionate, expectant, waiting.

He'd never lit up that way when I used to work for him. I'd done strip shows, lap dances, and sex shows. I'd been naked in front of him a hundred times or more. I'd played out fantasies and pretended to be a cheerleader, nurse, teacher, French maid, or whatever suited his fancy. I'd danced nude on top of pool tables at private parties and pole danced in his buddy's basements. But I'd never been intimidated until now because that had been Jade. Jade's body, not Chanie's. He was waiting for Chanie. *My* mind. *My* spirit.

"Remember, Chanie. Anyone can recite an essay. In order to touch your listeners' hearts, you must show them your truth."

"Okay, Mr. Tanji."

He smiled and sat back in his chair. "Any time, sweet girl."

I took a big drink of water and started reading from my cue cards. "Who told you that you have to be average? Mediocre? That you couldn't be what you wanted to be? You have to believe in yourself, no matter what challenges ..."

I rambled through the speech, making eye contact as often as possible. I waved my hands the way I'd seen Pastor Terence Travino do in his TV sermons. I paced back and forth. Dull. Flat. Regurgitated. Great content! No life, no vitality, no truth. The words were not my truth; they were bits and pieces of my notes and wishes.

It was 10:00 p.m., and I had twelve hours until I had to give my speech at City Hall. I had one person in the audience, and he looked bored. I dropped the cue cards to the floor and danced a little jig.

Mr. Tanji laughed. "Your speech is very sound, Chanie. But where is your heart?"

"Not on these cue cards."

"Well, we better get you a big chai latte, so you can get to work."

CHAPTER THIRTY

BIG DAY. SPEECHES AT City Hall at 10:00 a.m., graduation cere-
mony at 1:00 p.m. The four of us had made it. We'd survived. But
I couldn't stop crying. Fear. Nostalgia. Excitement. The reality
of leaving choked me. By the end of the day, I'd have to say
goodbye to the greatest treasures in my life: Mr. Lavoy, Rie,
Pastor Josh, and Mr. Tanji.

The first time I'd ever seen Mr. Lavoy, he'd been cradling a
copy of *Les Misérables* in his hands. He'd warmed the class
with his grey eyes and campfire smile, and then he'd quoted
nine simple words: "If no one loved, the sun would go out."
Those nine words had been the dawn of my darkness. The first
spark of the fire that had saved my life. And the flames had
been kept alive by my teachers, counsellors, and friends.

Where would I be without them?

How would I say goodbye?

I pulled the covers over my head. "Tuffy, I'm so scared." I
kissed his neck, tucked my face under his chin, and reached my
arm over his chest.

Tuffy pulled the covers off my face. "You worked on that
speech until two o'clock this morning."

"It's not just the speech —" A knock at the door startled me. I sat up.

"I'll get it, Chanie." Tuffy tousled my hair and kissed my tear-streaked cheeks. "Hold on, man," Tuffy called out as he wrapped himself in a fluffy white robe. I leaned over and kissed his pillow as he made his way to the door. He came back with a giant vase filled with wispy wildflowers, stargazer lilies, roses, daisies, baby's breath, and greens. A big shiny balloon tied with pink ribbon said *Celebrate!*

"What does the card say?" I said.

"It says, 'I think your dad would have wanted you to have these today! Ali.'"

"Wow, that's so sweet."

"There's another card." Tuffy handed me a pink envelope sealed with a gold sticker. I recognized Mr. Tanji's swirly writing: *Don't open this until you leave the city.*

I started crying again. I'd wept all through the night. "Tuffy, I can't stop crying."

"Chanie, I know you're sad. Don't look behind you. Look ahead. Look at what you've come through. It's going to be amazing. We'll get some dogs and horses. We'll camp in the mountains."

"I love you so much, Tuffy."

"I love you too, Chanie. So much that nothing can stop us!"

"How am I going to do this speech today? I'm a mess."

"You'll just do it like you've done everything else, with your shoulders back and my love in your heart."

Ginger and Jeremy met us in the lounge for the breakfast buffet. The Sawridge felt like a secret lodge in the mountains with its huge wooden beams, vaulted ceilings, rustic stone, and pine trees wrapped with violet lights. The walls were adorned with brilliant artwork and huge feathers in wooden frames. Big, beautiful dreamcatchers were mounted forty feet high with pink-and-yellow-tipped feathers that dangled beneath their webs. They hovered over us like protective angels. The server pointed to the biggest one and said, "That's the biggest dreamcatcher in North America!"

"What time is our bus to Kelowna?" Ginger said.

"It's at midnight," I said. "Should we stay awake all night?"

"Let's let the day take us where it may," Tuffy said. "We can sleep on the bus if we need to."

"How will we know where to go?" Ginger said.

"Mr. Tanji gave me the address and the keys to the apartment," I said.

"It seems like a miracle, doesn't it, Chanie?" Ginger started to cry.

"It *is* a miracle, Ginger." I smiled up at the dreamcatchers, their swirly, complex paths all flowing together in union. Perfect intersections, splendid patterns, dangling and waving gently like they were saying, *We brought you here to heal, but now it's safe to go.*

An hour later, I sat alone in a room at City Hall waiting to give my speech.

I wasn't ready.

Only hours before, I'd written a series of thoughts on the back of my original cue cards. At two in the morning, high on chai lattes and emotions, the words had sounded amazing. But I hadn't looked since. I couldn't.

"Anyone can recite an essay, Chanie." Mr. Tanji's words played in my head. "In order to touch their hearts, you must show them your truth."

"Ms. Nyrider. We're waiting."

"Okay." I took a deep breath and walked onto the stage.

My bohemian sundress flowed in the breeze, like the feathers of a dreamcatcher reminding me that everything was as it should be. Ginger waved a big sun hat in the air. She was so beautiful, her copper hair and blue eyes looked like the light of angels. We'd braided each other's hair that morning before we'd put on our matching dresses.

"Remember my dream, Chanie? The one about us gardening together in bohemian dresses and big, floppy sun hats?"

I'd taken her hands in mine and said, "'And you know, it seemed like we've known and loved each other for our whole lives, Chanie.'"

"It's what I pictured when Blue and Milos were hurting me. I closed my eyes and came back to us in the garden. It's how I survived."

"That's where I went too, Ginger. I looked for you."

"We are fated to be the best of friends. In life and death," we said in unison.

Life.

I took a deep breath and began my speech.

A MAN PULLED ME *out of a garbage bin. He saved my life. The newspaper titled the article "Prostitute Saved by Homeless Man." It should have read "Student Saved by Hero." The hero's name is Al, and my name is Chanie Nyrider. I am a graduate of the Begin Again program and will start my Bachelor of Arts degree at UBC in September.*

Last night, I recited my speech for my mentor. He said, "Your speech is very sound, Chanie. But where is your heart?" So I drank a couple of lattes and did what I've learned to do: Begin again and try harder. Speak and live my truth.

But what if I don't win?

Then I will embrace each day and keep trying. Winning or losing won't invalidate my love for literature. For learning. For growing and serving others. With or without the scholarship, I will do whatever it takes to live this life strong. Because I've come to learn that I matter. And that people see me.

If life gets hard, I'll try harder. And then even harder if I must.

I won't ever stop because ...

I believe.

I believe that angels surround us, and they wear the suits of homeless people, teachers, lawyers, and students. That magic exists in literature, art, and music. Look around. Who do you see?

A group of kids with braided hair.

Neighbours who see us when we don't see them.

People who fight for us when we can't fight for ourselves.

Those who come to know us rather than judge us.

And the people who commit their lives to rebuilding the lives of others.

So, if you don't want to try hard for yourself, do it for somebody else.

Be somebody's miracle. Because we are never so flawed that we cannot give.

There are incredibly cool people who suffer from mental illness.

And they deserve happiness.

And there are people weighed down with shame and regrets.

Those people still do amazing things.

There are people with addictions, and they find healing.

And go on to heal others.

Find yourself amongst your demons because there is gold in there.

Kindness will never fail you.

An open mind will never fail you.

Trying will never fail you.

Who do you want to be?

Who do you want to inspire?

Believe and push for your highest self.

Be someone's light.

Just keep trying.

And then try harder.

Because someone may be watching you and waiting for you to save their life.

CHAPTER THIRTY-ONE

THERE IS AN OWL that hangs out in my yard. At first, he scared me. I thought he'd eat Sox. But when he looks at me with his wise yellow eyes, I feel like we're old friends. The other morning, I smiled at him. He raised his face to the sun and then danced across a branch as though celebrating a new beginning.

Two weeks ago, I graduated with distinction from UBC. I completed my BA with a major in political science. Mr. Tanji — I still don't call him Ali — funded most of my education. I didn't win the essay contest, but I've never felt bad about losing because I got to speak my truth. I took a risk, and, while it didn't win me a prize, it won me a voice that I'd never heard before and haven't lost since. Besides, my story couldn't have been told in a few hundred words. It needed time and space. It needed courage and conviction and the fortitude to stay focused while that broken little girl I'd buried so long ago screamed and cried and fought her way out of the grave where I'd kept her hidden.

I used to be afraid to see her. I thought she'd be angry and full of hate. But when she finally rose, she came in quietly, like a gentle mist in the shadow of my reflection. I smiled at her pretty face. I welcomed that young girl who used to pose and play and mimic supermodels in the mirror. And as I embraced that part of me, I felt my wings rise and knew that beneath the dome of my battered wings, I'd be okay.

The dark memories. The sad truth of my youth. My one regret was never finding Al after he'd saved my life. We'd skipped the grad party to go look for him. We looked everywhere. The shelter. The street. Even the hospitals. But we couldn't find him, and we were getting dangerously close to missing our bus. "We'll come back for him, Chanie," Mr. Tanji had said, speeding toward the Greyhound station. "I'll watch for him."

Al passed away a few months after he saved my life. Mr. Lavoy called to tell us. He said that the shelter director, Bruce, had been with Al in his last moments and had kept Dingo for me. Dingo now sits on top of my first copy of *Les Misérables* in my living room. He watches over me like he did when I was in the hospital. Ginger and I planted flowers and a memorial tree in the yard, and we always include Al when we pray together.

I'm not completely healed, but I'm healing every day. I'm better. And every day, I try harder. I still dream of Blue from time to time. When I see him in my dreams, he never looks me in the eye. He waves to me to come closer, but I never do because I'm still afraid of him. With every dream, he is fading. Soon, he will fade away forever.

Last weekend, Mr. Lavoy called. "Chanie, you know what I'd really love?"

"What's that?"

"I'd love for you to speak to my class this year."

"What would you like me to talk about?"

"Tell them about your biggest life-changing moments."

What would I tell them? There were so many miracles I

couldn't see at the time they were happening. It's all so beautiful, this life. I don't remember all the bad because the magic keeps me awestruck now that I can see it from somewhere safe. It's like reaching a summit. That's when you can see all the splendour. Not so much when you're climbing because that's when you have to fight. But the miracles are always there, climbing next to you. They're dancing for you and waiting to dance with you.

ACKNOWLEDGEMENTS

I'd like to thank Angie Abdou for giving me a chance when others wouldn't. Also, Thomas Trofimuk, Marie Peiffer-Mitchell, and all the unseen heroes who have walked next to me on my life path. I'd especially like to extend my gratitude to Marc Côté, Sarah Jensen, Sarah Cooper, and the entire team at Cormorant Books.

And to Travis Jones. This book is for you. I miss you everyday, but I know that I am sheltered beneath your battered wings up there in the heavens.

Also, for those who come from a rough past for which you may feel you must apologize. May your life lessons have taught you to work hard, but most of all, to see miracles in the smallest of things. To be grateful, to be kind, and to understand and respect that everybody has a story and is a valued and worthy being. That eyes of judgement are no eyes at all.

We acknowledge the sacred land on which Cormorant Books operates. It has been a site of human activity for 15,000 years. This land is the territory of the Huron-Wendat and Petun First Nations, the Seneca, and most recently, the Mississaugas of the Credit River. The territory was the subject of the Dish With One Spoon Wampum Belt Covenant, an agreement between the Iroquois Confederacy and Confederacy of the Ojibway and allied nations to peaceably share and steward the resources around the Great Lakes. Today, the meeting place of Toronto is still home to many Indigenous people from across Turtle Island. We are grateful to have the opportunity to work in the community, on this territory.